King's Gambit

Book II of The CODM Prophecy

I0639821

Natasha E Scholey

ISBN 978 0 9873894 1 1

Gwydion Books
PO Box 391
Stirling
SA
5152
Australia

In loving memory of
Mr Keegan

Acknowledgements

I would like to say a big thank you Steve for your patience and support. Thanks to Michaela for your feedback. It was much appreciated.

Finally, many thanks to my Dad who never condescended!

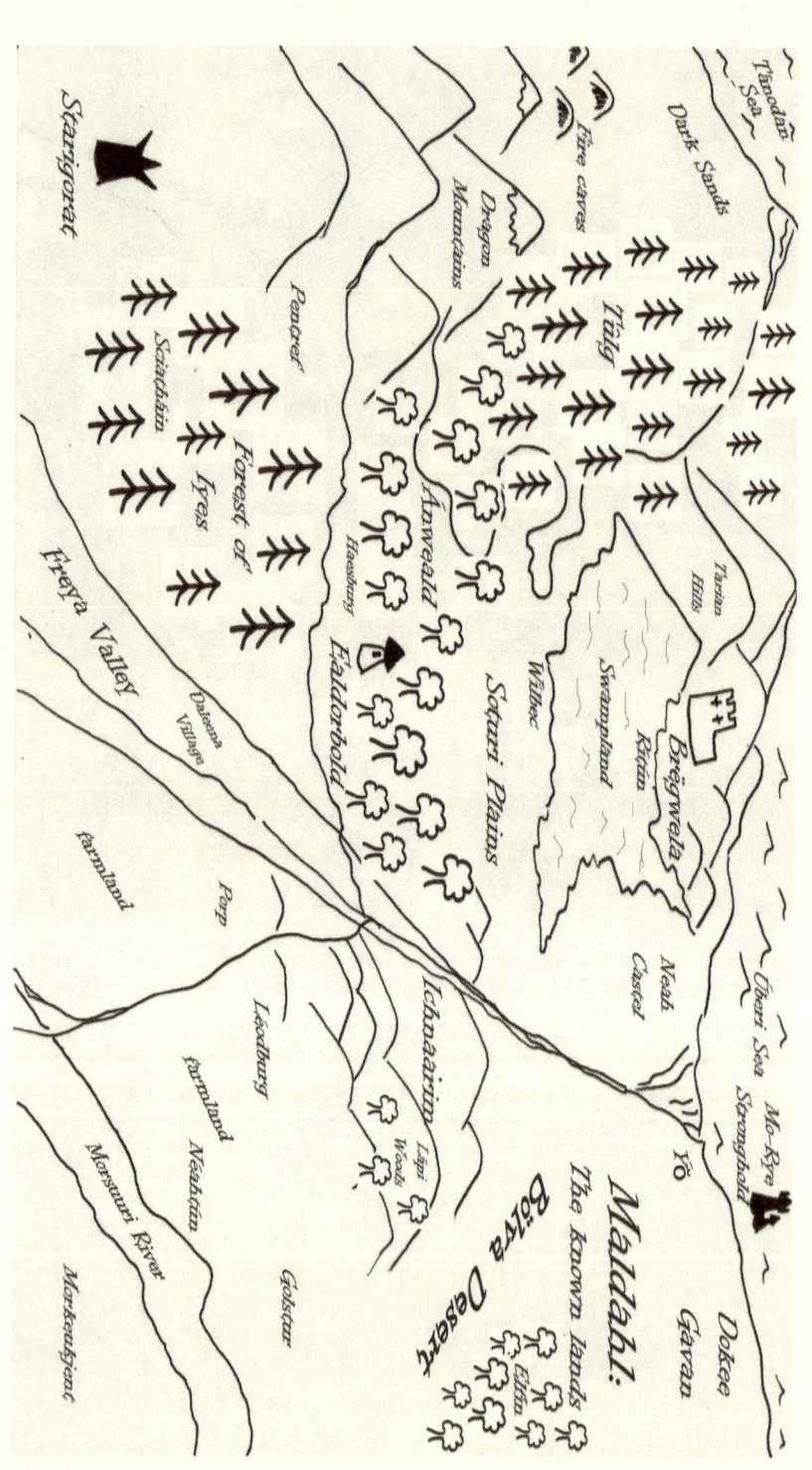

King's Gambit

'Tis all a chequer-board of Nights and Days
Where Destiny with men for pieces plays:
Hither and thither moves, and mates and slays,
And one by one back in the closet lays.

(The Rubaiyat of Omer Khayyam, rendered into English
verse by Edward Fitzgerald, 1st edition.)

Prologue

The sands of time rippled and swirled, as the Old Ones gathered about their latest creation. As gases compressed, planets were born and the sun smiled at her new companions. It was time for the Old Ones to bid farewell to the universe they had come to know. They drifted across the vastness of space, seeking a fresh canvas on which to begin their next work.

Mynogen, however, did not follow right away. He had become discontented with the making of planets and found that he yearned for more. As he passed between dimensions, he lingered for a moment—a moment in the existence of an Old One, but millenniums for those who would come much later. It was such a moment that would change existence thereafter, forever.

The Old Ones: beings of pure energy who possessed the power of creation. Yet, as powerful as they were, they remained content to make their huge spheres of rock and gas to surround a pretty sun or suns. Such baubles had become tedious to Mynogen; he no longer felt the beauty and balance of that which he had been a part in creating. Part of him wished to stop, to halt the forever wanderings of his kind and form something new. So it was, that his pause allowed him to ponder on that one point. He decided to create a new Mynogen, part of himself who would not be perpetually drifting.

How long he had existed, he knew not; he could not remember. As far as he knew, he had existed forever and would go on doing so, long after the universes that he had helped to shape returned to the void.

Removing mere particles of his being left him less than whole, but feeling more complete than he had ever been.

That piece, a fracture of self, he placed in the darkness, before leaving to join his brothers.

Over the eon that followed, the piece of Mynogen grew and adapted. From the non-corporal speck of an ancient creator came the first corporal life—a new god, Taiohāhn to some, the father god to others. In truth, He was to become many gods to many different people on different worlds, worlds separated only by a thin veil of reality.

Part One

One

Taiohãhn, master of the darkness beneath two worlds, lingered for thousands of years—alone. His realm was so vast that He wandered for centuries in the black wasteland, before discerning a boundary, a thin layer separating Him from the work of His father and the other Old Ones. Although unseeing, He could discern the heat of the sun from beyond His realm and craved its touch. It was then that the loneliness of His existence finally overwhelmed Him and He wept. As the tears fell, His realm was flooded with water, and He tore at the veil, feeling the rage and despair from years uncounted, left alone, abandoned by His creator.

Finally, after much effort and violence, the tiniest hole was punctured in the veil. The light of the sun pierced the darkness and it was beautiful—a single perfect shaft, both blinding and wondrous. In that instant, Taiohãhn envisaged what it was that He wanted, what He needed, for the first time—light and beauty. Feelings stirred within Him as He sought to harvest the light of the sun.

Removing part of His life force, as His father had done before Him, He sent it forth into the light and was at once startled by a flash as His inherited creation power worked its majick. Light filled a small space around Him and Taiohãhn, who had only ever known darkness, was struck blind. He wept once more, for having briefly known the light, He had to face forever in darkness.

'Why do you weep?'

The voice was in His head—no words actually spoken, but an intent that was instantly understood. Taiohãhn felt His body stir, as a feather-light touch reached His blinded eyes and returned His vision.

The beauty that met His new eyes was so dazzling at first, He almost longed for blindness again. Before Him was the being He had created from the light—a female part of himself, combined with the sun. The light giver—Anarkhane.

The goddess laughed and the sound warmed Him throughout the length of His form. She had healed Him—not only His eyes; She took away the lasting emptiness. She was a sun goddess, a healer, a being of light in the darkness of His kingdom, and She was beautiful. But His kingdom, She could not endure.

She rose into the darkness above, and smiling, slipped through the veil that surrounded His world. The light shone from Her and beneath her. Life began to form in the pool of Taiohãhn's tears; tall and green the trees grew—a forest surrounding the bubble of crystal light from whence Anarkhane was born.

It was then that Taiohãhn felt desire for the first time; Anarkhane was His and He wanted Her back. She, however, had no intention of living in His underworld forest and preferred Her sky kingdom of light.

When Taiohãhn was not exploring His forest, He would speak with Anarkhane, pleading with Her to return to Him. But the desire to create anew was in Her and She tried to populate the worlds occupying the space beneath Her sky kingdom—Earth and Maldahl, each one of them on two sides of the veil.

She shone down, offering light to the worlds below and the heat scorched the land. She did not possess the power of creation it seemed and realised it had been Taiohãhn's will that had created the trees in His domain; She had provided the light, but that was not enough for Her.

Taiohãhn, no longer had any inclination to create, His one desire having already been realised. Yet Anarkhane was saddened and could not be consoled. Taiohãhn sought desperately to amuse Her, to deflect Her from Her goal, but She continued to try and continued to fail. The more she failed, the greater Her sorrow. Her visits became less frequent and Taiohãhn spent countless years awaiting Her in His Chamber of Light—the only place in the Underworld that Anarkhane would enter, a part of Her realm that existed within His own, a beautiful chamber with walls of crystal and opal, which glowed still with the light of that first encounter.

Taiohãhn was angry. *Why is She so concerned with creating?* He thought. *Is not my company enough?* But Her relentless unhappiness finally brought Him to a decision. He would grant Her a gift. *If I give Her what She desires, then She will return to me.*

Two gifts He bestowed, the first of which was to make Her whole. She was a being of pure light and He granted her substance. Doing so left a crystalline deposit that He hid away; it was to be the second of His gifts. It was long in the making and much of His power and energy went into it. The beautiful crystal, green as His forest, He imbued with the power of creation—His power, inherited from His Father. He felt immensely weary on its completion, but cared not. It was what Anarkhane wanted and though it cost Him much of His power, He was happy to relinquish it in order to win Her love.

He waited in the chamber to present His gift and as if anticipating what awaited Her, She appeared. He had never seen Anarkhane look more beautiful than that instant; the moment creation was finally Hers to give. He provided the seed, now all that remained was for Her to plant it. She smiled a dazzling smile and embraced Him.

He felt a desire deeper than He had ever known erupt within Him and gripping Her firmly in His arms, He pressed against Her. The gem vibrated in Her grasp as it reacted to the proximity of both gods. She smiled demurely as His hands explored her flesh, investigating the soft contours of Her body. Her eyes closed as She began to work with Her stone. Her first attempts were small—tiny, simplistic organisms.

Taiohãhn's mouth found Hers and His lips pressed aggressively against them. She did not cry out, but breathed Him in, using Him to help Her make trees as beautiful as His forest surrounding. As they crashed to the floor, volcanoes erupted and seas boiled then foamed onto sandy shores. Taiohãhn's imagination ran wild and beasts with wings were created—huge monstrous animals that could breathe fire as hot as the flame within Him. He crushed Her beneath Him and the first fish formed legs and crawled onto land.

His fingers pressed and moulded into Her flesh and She returned the gesture whilst one hand still gripped Her stone. Each action created new life; each gasp formed a new sound on the worlds about them.

Taiohãhn bit into Her breast and felt tightness in the pit of His stomach. She created a giant serpent, which coiled around Her beautiful trees. He pushed against Her; His hand pinned her arm and the stone He had given Her, to the cold ground beneath them. Licking the blood from the bite He had inflicted, the first Vampire Ælves were born—creatures of passion with a lust for blood, created in His own image. Anarkhane saw them and wanted Her own creatures as beautiful—creatures that could dwell beneath the trees She had created and tend for the animals living there.

She yanked the stone away from His grasp, annoyed by His intrusion. His hand grasped Her by the throat, momentarily furious as He sat astride her opalescent form. He squeezed, and in His anger sent a huge ball of fire down onto Earth, blotting out the sun for years, destroying much of Anarkhane's work.

'NO!' She cried, Her eyes pleading with His.

He smiled, triumphant; His grip loosened and His hand traced the length of Her body. She trembled beneath His touch and the ground on their worlds shook; She began Her work again, Her breaths shorter, each exhale breathing new life.

Taiohãhn felt a burning sensation and flame spewed forth from His being and He pushed hard against Her again, burning a hole into Her flesh, into which He thrust His burning desire. She screamed and man was created—born in both pain and confusion.

Anarkhane fought against Taiohãhn, wanting the pain to stop. On both worlds, battles raged; tribes fought for territory and people began to worship, offering tributes to appease the gods of the Sun and the Underworld. Fires were burnt and sacrifices made.

Taiohãhn pulled away from Her, fighting to control the jet of flame. He saw the hole between Her legs and blew the flames, trying to extinguish the pain He had caused. Salamanders crawled forth from fiery caves, and as Taiohãhn thrust His tongue inside Her, beautiful mermaids sang. He worked His tongue in and out, savouring the sweet taste within Her. She was screaming again, but it was clear She was no longer in pain. Reaching down for where the flame had protruded from His body, She found the new appendage made flesh; She ran Her fingers up and down as predators closed in on their prey. Taiohãhn didn't know what He wanted more—for Her to continue in such a way or be inside Her again.

A sound distracted Him for a moment and the sensation below stopped abruptly. Anarkhane had dropped Her stone and as it clattered across the floor, She scrambled after it— less willing to be parted from it, than Him, it seemed. Anger rose in Him again and He climbed up behind Her, pushing into Her once more. Her cries were not of pain though and She willed Him on, moving against Him.

He gripped one of Her breasts and toyed below with His other hand, feeling His own muscular appendage as it rushed in and out of her—slick and hot, pulsating with pure pleasure.

Happy at last, He wanted to spend the rest of His existence inside Her, exploring Her. He thought about penetrating her in new places to increase their pleasure.

Perhaps if He had stopped to think, Taiohähn might have realised that His need was for them to be joined. He had lost a piece of Himself in Her making and He wanted it back, but there was no going back.

Anarkhane could feel the wetness between Her legs and felt it running down Her thighs. The sound of Him slapping into Her was putting Her off Her work. Where there had been pleasure, now a cold numbness began to spread. She wanted to go, to meet all the life She had worked so hard to create.

Taiohähn did not seem to notice Her sudden disinterest. He thrust harder than ever into the well inside Her, His member never tiring. Pushing Her head down toward the floor, He widened Her legs a little further with His knees and began to climb to a new sensation, approaching a climax that He felt would define His very existence. His new appendage felt so hard, that it ached and He could hear His own voice, as His breath became moans. He was so blinded by ecstasy that He delayed when Anarkhane dropped to the floor, sliding off His thrusting form and scrambling away from Him.

His eyes shot open and He cried out in sheer rage and frustration at Her rejection. She stood holding the gem before Her, weapon-like, Her eyes fierce and defiant.

'Come to me,' He ordered.

Anarkhane shook Her head in refusal and dissolved back into the Skyworld.

'Nooooo!' Taiohähn cried, making a grab for Her disappearing form. He rose to His feet, His erection as menacing as His demeanour. It was only then He perceived that a great part of Him was gone—lost to Him, and He would never be whole again.

Two

Anarkhane smiled as the fires were lit in Her honour. She loved Her people and they loved Her. She basked in their worship. Torches in hand, they circled widdershins about the hill. She appeared before them, the sun rising behind Her.

Gasps of delight sounded and torches were extinguished as the worshippers fell to their knees. She moved through the crowd, offering blessings and healing where required. Of all Her creations, the humans were Her favourite. The love they bestowed upon Her, fed Her being, ensuring that Her light would never go out.

Taiohãhn kept His distance, watching in envy the doting eyes upon Her. He too was worshipped, but not adored; although He had taken different guises on Earth, he preferred being simply Taiohãhn—Father god, King of the Underworld, Lord of the Animals.

He crouched in His loincloth—indicative of Celtic tribes. It had been a long time since He had appeared as Beli, Belenos or Bile. The people thought He was the husband to Dôn, or Anarkhane, as He preferred to call Her. They thought that He had children with Her. It was true they had created many offspring, but it was not through intimacy—She never allowed Him to do that to Her again.

He had tried to gain the adoration She had amassed, by making himself sun god in some places, but all attempts to gain Her love had failed. They had created new gods together, but in doing so He had only fractured himself further, as had She.

He rose and walked back into the forest. On Earth, Cernunnos was more familiar to Him than His other guises.

In that form, the people believed He mated with His goddess once a year. So great was their faith in the cycle, that He could almost feel the mythical copulation to mark the changing of the seasons.

As He crossed the veil back to His Underworld forest, He tore the antlers from His head. Leaves folded about Him, clothing him from head to foot in leather-like attire. He set the antlers on top of His throne and sat cross-legged, thoughtfully fingering the torc about his neck.

He was glad to be back. Earth was becoming increasingly distasteful to Him; so many pieces of Him, fighting for power—many facets of a whole, yet fractured. He preferred to lose himself in His own domain, His Forest of Forgetfulness. So others had named it, for it was said that the few who ventured there, forgot everything. Only the Vampire Ælves could resist the majick that He had placed there, and they still dare not venture beyond the path set for them.

It was the presence of the Moon Clans and that of His animals whose company He could occasionally abide, yet none were permitted admittance to His palace.

In the depths of the Forest of Tûlg, the annual festival of thanks had begun. The Vampire Ælves had fasted for weeks in Taiohãhn's honour. Now they awaited a sign to signify the feast to begin.

'As the moon rises,
On this most sacred night,
Hear us.
We meet at sacred yew,
And light the fires we burn in honour of thee.
The wizard's tree,
Gathered from the shade,
Bedwen by waterfall that have heard the footfall of many passers by,
We add dermen dar to feed our fire,

From marshy depths,
The battle witch of all woods,
To burn with greenest celynnen,
We burn in honour of thee,
With helygen from flowing stream,
We offer our life's blood in honour of thee.
Our blood within your cup,
Our grateful thanks for your bounty.
Shall we feed him to the flame or shall he join your clans most blessed?
Hear us.'

And Taiohãhn did hear ...

It had been so long since He had allowed their chosen to be sacrificed to the flames, but the sight of Anarkhane's adoring followers still filled His mind and He had no desire to offer a human immortality as one of His most beautiful creations.

He met Ravenwing at the eaves of the great forest and rode across the veil to Maldahl, to offer the Clans His answer.

'**Let him burn,**' Taiohãhn ordered.

Ravenwing stamped the ground impatiently and watched with disinterest as the Vampire Ælves obeyed without question and the man was thrust into the fire of many woods. Taiohãhn watched for a moment as one of Anarkhane's creations was consumed in the flames, before dismounting and going to greet them.

'You are most welcome here, Lord of the Trees,' one of the elders said. 'We are blessed by your presence and make you humble offering.' The Vampire Ælf was very tall and his face was like the marble of Taiohãhn's palace, perfect yet cold.

Taiohãhn accepted the chalice from the Clan leader and sat on the throne, which they had prepared for Him. The chair was beautifully carved, depicting his most beloved animals—wolf, stag and dragon. He ran a hand over the smoothness of its surface, knowing how long it must have taken to prepare.

Each year a new throne was placed before Him, as part of their thanks to Him. More often than not, He failed to attend, but still they crafted it and placed the blood upon it, to symbolise His presence there.

Taiohãhn stared down at the blood-filled cup for a moment. The wounds on their wrists from the twisted willow knife were already closed. Although He had created them that way, He found their lust for blood was not something He shared. Placing His right hand above the chalice, He closed His eyes, taking the blood back into Himself, feeling a small return of the power that He had imbued them with.

There was a whoop from the clans, signalling the beginning of their celebration. Men and women were brought forth and their blood ran as wine. No cries were heard, no screams of terror; all victims slept and remained unaware that their lives were draining away, feeding the thirsty clans of Vampire Ælves.

Once they had feasted, a lustful frenzy began. Taiohãhn turned away. He could not watch their lovemaking—not that night; not when the pain of seeing Anarkhane was so near. He turned back to the sacrifice, nothing more than a charred mess, its blackened empty eye sockets staring back at Him from the flames.

She will be furious when she discovers that I allowed this, He thought. But He did not care, besides, Anarkhane was far away, on Earth, enjoying the delights of the summer solstice. The thought of Her made Him burn with anger, and with one last glance to the bodies and orgy, He slipped silently away, Ravenwing escorting Him home again.

Three

'*T*aiohāhn!' Anarkhane yelled. The bubble of light within the Underworld was empty and She would not set foot beyond it, for fear of being trapped there. 'Taiohāhn!'

Taiohāhn stood outside the room; a smile spread slowly across His face. She *was* angry with Him and He was pleased. *Better to have some reaction from Her than none at all*, He thought.

'I know that you can hear me!' She cried. 'Why did you do it? You know when it's a sacrifice to you, it cannot return to me. He was mine!'

Taiohāhn stepped into the room, His eyes narrowing temporarily at the brightness.

'And you are mine,' He said, 'I made you. Without me, you would not exist; without me you would not have the power of creation.' His eyes glittered at the proximity of Her.

'I thought you care for me ... we created so much ...'

'And when will it end? I've divided myself so many times now, that I barely know myself any longer; Arianhrod, Nudd, Gwydion, the Dagda and all the others ... so many others, children of the nations to lead all aspects of their society. I did what you asked and I am tired of living up to your expectations of me, Anarkhane. I can no longer create and I will not divide myself further.

'They call those abominations our children ... *our children*? We never completed our joining. You led me to believe we would be together when all I did was tear myself further apart ... for you!'

Anarkhane frowned for a moment and took a step backward, as if not trusting Him to be too close to Her.

'I thought that it made you happy,' She protested. 'We've achieved so much. We are loved ...'

'You were always loved, Anarkhane, but you prefer the adoration of lower life forms to the love of your creator.'

He did not note Her reaction to His words. A bell rang throughout His palace indicating that He had a visitor. Such a visit was bound to be vitally important, as it was rare that any of His creations ventured so far into the Forest of Forgetfulness, and none would disturb Him at home without good reason. He did not move to the front door, choosing rather to speak to His visitor from His present location. He had much that He still wished to say to Anarkhane and knew that should He leave Her presence, She would flit off and He might not see Her again for years.

As His mind reached out, He saw a relatively young member of the Clan of the Hunter's Moon at His threshold.

'What is it you want?'

The Vampire Ælf appeared momentarily disconcerted, before he opened his mouth to speak. 'My Lord, we beseech you, hear us. Many of our kindred passed over to Earth after the feast and are now trapped. The gateways are closed to us. We do not know what is happening.'

'How many?' Taiohãhn asked, although He already knew the answer. It was commonplace for the Vampire Ælves to pass over after the feast and spend time with their families on the other side. Usually only one clan per year remained as it was breeding year for them. The only exceptions were any females who had chosen mates from another clan. Such a thing was rare, but not unheard of.

The young Vampire Ælf sounded panicked as he made his reply. 'Most of my clan, all of the Clans of Crescent and Blood Moon. I was left behind to mind two females who are with child.'

Taiohãhn's brow furrowed with concern. It was not the sort of news that He wished Anarkhane to hear and He realised that His chastisement of Her would have to wait.

'Excuse me,' He said to the goddess, and He disappeared.

He knew exactly why Maldahl was isolated. He had set up fail-safes thousands of years before, to prevent pollution of His beloved Maldahl. He knew that the only reason Earth was closed to the Moon Clans was if the gods He had created had tried to cross over. *But why now?* He wondered. *Why would they bother?*

Taiohãhn pushed His mind to the boundaries of His kingdom.

'Something is wrong,' He said sternly. 'I will investigate.'

The Vampire Ælf prostrated himself as Taiohãhn stormed back into His palace. He was surprised to see that Anarkhane had not left; rather, She had observed His reaction from His forelócian glæs—now His only route back to Earth. He felt apprehension for the first time as He made to cross over.

'Wait, I'm coming with you.' Anarkhane said.

Fear was in Her beautiful eyes, causing Taiohãhn to forget for a moment, His own concerns. His lips thinned into a line as He nodded in agreement to Her request and followed Her through the veil to the source of the disturbance.

Where they arrived was far from where they expected to be. They stood in darkness, a gentle drip of water falling from high above.

A woman stepped forward from the shadows. She was very like Anarkhane in appearance, except for her dark hair.

'Mother, grandfather!' she said. 'Most pleased are we to see you again. It has been so long.'

'Brighit?' Anarkhane stepped forward, embracing the one who had called Her mother.

Taiohãhn gritted His teeth in defiance of the titles used. 'What has happened here, Brighit?' He asked.

'We are lost, grandfather ... everything that you worked so hard to create ... all gone. There was a battle; many of us were destroyed. They landed at Beltane and we were certain we could defeat them, but oh ...' She collapsed in Anarkhane's arms, overwhelmed with grief.

Anarkhane stroked her head and kissed her softly. Taiohãhn's jaw clenched tighter still and He looked about Him. They appeared to be in a huge underground cavern. Stalactites clung to the ceiling and a stale smell hung in the cold air.

'It's nothing much at present, but in time we may come to call it home.'

'**Dagda**!' Taiohãhn exclaimed, approaching His son and clasping his arms tightly in greeting.

'We were betrayed, Bile,' Dagda said, 'betrayed by Eria, one of the new queens. She gave them a way to defeat us in return for the land being named after her ... betrayed over so trivial a thing. We fought and a pact was made, our land divided. We no longer reside above the ground, but below it.'

'**Where is she**?' Taiohãhn asked.

'Eria? I will have her brought before you.'

By now, many of the Tuatha de Danaan had gathered about their kin and voices were sounding—cries of indignation.

'Where were you?'

'Why did you forsake us?'

'We are gods; why could we not defeat them?'

Taiohãhn gazed from face to face, saddened by how many had lost their way. *I never should have made them,* He thought. *The more we created, the weaker they became. The loyalties of the people have divided just as my very being is divided.*

From amongst the crowd, Eria stepped forth. She opened her mouth as if to offer an explanation for her actions, but had not the chance; Taiohãhn, in the blink of an eye, unsheathed His sword and removed her traitorous head. Her dead, horrified eyes stared ahead, no longer seeing.

He held out His hand to Anarkhane.

'Come,' He said. We must leave this place.'

Anarkhane was tearful and clung tightly to Brighit.

'We cannot leave them,' She protested. 'We must take back what is ours.'

There was a murmur of agreement from the crowd.

'Ours?' spat Taiohãhn. 'We barely visit here ... Do you not see? It's too late for them. Change is already here; it's already begun—trade between nations, advances in tools and weapons. The people *welcome* these invaders with open arms. Our line is over; a new age is already dawning.'

'No! You cannot leave us,' Brighit whimpered.

'We do not belong here ... come.'

Anarkhane took one look at 'the children of the light', imprisoned in darkness, and she knew that She could not bear to be trapped there with them. She let go of Brighit and taking Taiohãhn's hand for the first time in over a thousand years, She turned away from the Tuatha de Danaan, parts of Herself, whom She loved.

As they stepped back into the Chamber of Light, Anarkhane wrenched Her hand free.

'We should not have left them!'

Taiohãhn sighed. 'They're finished,' He said. 'If we stayed, we were in danger of being trapped there as well; as their power recedes, so too will their hold on their followers. We are linked Anarkhane; without the faith of the people, our power wanes. We must remain strong. Keep your followers elsewhere, but forget the green country. It is lost to us now.'

'If I had not stayed so long here, then the invaders never would have won ... I could have stopped them.'

'Time passes differently here—that is just the way of things. Would you forsake your realm to live among the mortals? Are you really willing to sacrifice *that* much?'

Anarkhane sighed and sank to the floor. 'But it's not just our followers we have abandoned; it's our family—beings of our flesh, gods like us.'

'No, not like us; immortals perhaps, but gods? Their powers are not as great as ours, and it has become more diluted through their lineage. Our power is not inherited, but *given*. It is finite and has run its course in their final kings. You must let them go. It was foolish of us to believe that creating a family would make us stronger. Now we must hope that the other families we created, will prove durable enough to resist such tides of change.'

Anarkhane stood suddenly and grabbed Taiohãhn by the shoulders.

'But we could have stopped them!' She cried.

His eyes met Hers and He smiled sadly. 'You forget, *I* am of the Old Ones. I see more than you and I tell you, our time there is over. It is the time of men, and their advances will wipe away their sense of wonder in us … I have seen it and it cannot be changed.'

'You were never happy there. That is why you will not try,' Anarkhane snapped and disappeared.

Taiohãhn sighed deeply and ran His fingers through His hair. He could not get the face of Dagda out of His mind. He recalled how Anarkhane gave a piece of herself to Him to produce Dagda. The people now called it 'watering of the sacred tree'.

Dagda was the only one of them that I could stand. Have I really done the right thing? He considered.

Gazing into His forelócian glæs, He observed the invaders. The people from Iberia seem to complete Erin (as it was now called). It seemed to have progressed so much that the old gods were already being forgotten.

Perhaps not though, Taiohãhn thought. *The Tuatha de Danaan will gain an air of mystery as the 'hill people'. Dagda will look after them. Either way, I no longer have any influence on the matter.*

It was early morning by the time Taiohãhn entered the Forest of Tûlg. Many years had passed between His last encounter with the Vampire Ælves. He did not relish the task before Him. Although it was in His power to open their pathway to Earth again, He was disinclined to do so, unwilling to risk one of the Tuatha de Danaan crossing the boundary now that their divinity was waning. *Better that many races be separated forever, than to risk a challenge to my godhood on Maldahl,* He thought.

Addressing only the Clan of the Dark Moon elders on the matter, He embellished the truth to suit His ends. The clan bowed their heads solemnly, distraught, but too respectful of their Lord to contest His decision. They accepted that what He had done, He did for the good of Maldahl.

The Moon Clans stranded on Earth, received no such explanation and were left forever wondering what they might have done to displease Taiohãhn so.

* * * * *

Anarkhane became withdrawn from Her followers and took to standing on the coast of Ynys y Cedairn, looking out to sea toward the distant island, mourning the loss of Her family. A cold wind whipped Her hair and tears welled in her deep sapphire eyes.

The Dewydds were wary of Dôn's visitation on the cliff-tops of their home. The rain fell heavily, as if willed into existence by Her sorrow. She looked fierce and wild as She stared out across the sea. For weeks She had been there, unmoving and slightly weathered. She had not approached or spoken to them and they were at a loss to what such a sign might mean. Many feared it was a bad omen.

The Brethren began to gather from all over Albion; even as far as Gaul did they come. Fires were lit and they kept vigil day and night. The ovates gathered sacred oak and mistletoe to make offerings at Her well. Questions were asked and their fear began to grow …

'She is mourning … for what? For whom? What does this mean?

'I divine a troubled time for us. She mourns our passing.'

'You have seen our end then, brother?'

'Not Exactly … I saw ships, many ships on our beloved shores, invaders of great strength of arms, who threaten our way of life.'

Many Dewydds wound their way up the hill in solemn procession and gathered about Dôn.

'Blessed Mother, we need guidance. Who are these invaders? How shall we prevent their hold on our sacred way of life?'

They stood in silence, waiting for Her to reply. For many days hence, they beseeched Her, but Dôn stood rigid and silent, either unaware of their pleas or uncaring, they thought. However, She felt their homage and that in its turn brought Her a measure of warmth again until eventually, on the tenth day, She replied.

'The Milesians?' She said. 'Here? 'You are mistaken, Dewydd. They have their prize; you are quite safe. But let your bards sing of how greedy Breogán, spied from Brigantia, in tower tall, a land of emerald green. So desirous that he should possess this jewel, he set sail at once. The Tuatha kings—the fair ones, feared his intent and sent his body back to his people as warning of their folly.

Enraged were the people of Miled and set they forth, seeking revenge and to conquer. Many hardships on their journey did lie and great storm at Manannan's bidding, stole many lives.

'They landed at Beltane feast and swept ashore with vengeful hearts. But the Tuatha kings convinced them to respect three days of peace at their most sacred time. Wise Dagda—the goodly one, used the time granted to prepare for battle, but knew not that one of the queens had betrayed them all. And so it was, at the Battle of Tailtinn, the Tuatha de Danaan were defeated and the land was divided. Amergin it was, given the task, and now the Tuatha de Danaan are no more; they are the Aes Sidhe, driven underground from gods to myth ... but they must never be forgotten!'

She was trembling and pale causing the Dewydds to cast worried glances to one another. Unseeing their confusion, She leapt from the cliff into the sea below. The goddess of air and water at one with those elements, returned to Tir Fu Thinn.

'She said we are safe. It was Erin's conquerors you saw.'

Cathbu looked unsure. The Milesians heralded the close of the last age; the warriors he had seen in his awen, had swords of a new metal, strong and hard. They carried great standards, the like of which he had never seen. But he had no reason to suppose that Dôn would lie. He concluded therefore, that he must have been mistaken. Dôn had said they were safe and that was all that mattered. He concluded that his vision must have been linked with the birth of Erin, if that is what Dôn deemed it to be ...

As Anarkhane crashed into the sea, she let go of the Tuatha de Danaan, forever. The water cleansed Her being as She passed back into Her realm. She had lost all sense of time in Her grieving, not realising that so many centuries had passed since the new age had begun. Had She not let Her grief overwhelm Her, She may have paid heed to what Her Dewydd was trying to tell Her. Had She stayed a little longer, She may have seen the first of the Roman ships approaching; She may have been able to stop it. Instead, She retreated to Maldahl and spent years singing with Mermaids; she philosophised with Kappa and danced with the Elfín.

All the while, Taiohãhn kept His distance, yet forever watchful. He had not told Anarkhane of the Romans, of how over the years, a new religion was taking hold, slowly at first, almost imperceptible—even to Him, but mere glances to Maldahl to watch Anarkhane and years passed on Earth. The old gods were fading; those, whose traditions were too engrained in the lives and ritual of society to be extinguished, were embraced under the new faith … canonized.

No, He had not told Her—He dare not. So fragile She seemed, since separating from the Tuatha de Danaan. He could not bear to see Her broken. Instead, He went himself as emissary, but there were so many and as the faith grew, His own power began to dwindle. He was too late it seemed. It was time to call Anarkhane—She would never forgive Him if She were unable to at least say goodbye.

Four

'Who is He?' Anarkhane fumed.

'The One god? He's from the land of the Pharaohs, a god amongst the many who their slaves turned to, even as the king who elevated Him lay dying. His people returned to their many gods whom they had worshipped for thousands of years, but within the slave populace the idea of Him has grown and spread throughout the land, passing from tribe to tribe and even as the great nation dwindles, the idea of the One has grown, surpassing the people from whence the idea was born.

'He is like us in a way, different names, different peoples worship Him and yet He sprung from one single point, an idea, much as I did. The difference I fear, is that although He has many different names, He has never divided Himself, choosing to remain One and as such, He has only grown in strength and following, not depleted as we have.'

'He's nothing but an upstart!' Anarkhane complained.

'That may be so, but that upstart is more powerful than us combined. I tried to tell you how dividing ourselves was a dangerous undertaking. I warned you ...'

'But He must have been born of you to begin with,' Anarkhane reasoned.

'Unlikely. I have kept good track of my progeny and although I know of those in Greece and Egypt, even farther still across the world, this One is a stranger to me, the only familiarity being His seemingly similarity to the Old Ones. Either way, He is more whole that I can ever hope to be again. I foresee our downfall if we choose to make a stand. Perhaps we should return whilst we are still able. At least Maldahl remains unpolluted. There, we are Taiohãhn and

Anarkhane, nothing more. There we kept things simple and I am thankful that we did so.'

'Do we face our destruction?' Anarkhane asked, her brow creasing with worry.

'How can I be destroyed? I am an idea—an archetype of nature—as constant and everlasting as the seasons that I serve to represent.'

'You are a fool, Taiohãhn! Our power dwindles as the new religion grows. We've lost our foothold in the green country and the people of Earth begin to realise that the sun will rise without us; the harvest will come and go. Our offerings decline and in many places the followers of this Christ now call you Satan—their antichrist. I've just returned from one of my temples where they now call me crone, child eater.'

'No, not all,' Taiohãhn protested. 'Many rename you a saint. Your sacred wells are still honoured. We might find a way to adapt ...'

'We are gods! You are born of the Old Ones. Why *should* we adapt?'

'Would you have us fade out of all existence?'

'No,' Anarkhane snapped, 'I would have us fight! Let us take back what is ours.'

'Our Brethren have gone underground and we have divided ourselves too many times, seeking to gain control over too much. The Christ followers have a pure belief, an idea too powerful to be felled by our polluted form. We need to return to our realms; we need to draw in ourselves— become pure once more.'

'*Then* we fight?'

'No. If we cannot adapt then Earth is lost to us. We would be foolish to fight the Christ. Maldahl is ours; we must content ourselves with that. At least no other gods can interfere there; I have seen to that. Only one portal remains and I have entrusted it to Dagda. He will see that it is well guarded and none of them can use it. No immortal can ... we are the only exceptions. We are safe now, my love. We are safe.'

Taiohãhn moved to embrace Her, but drew away as She stared back, Her eyes hard — resolute, but what She was thinking was beyond Him. He had never seen Her that way. He had expected tears, anger, all of which He had hoped to provide comfort for ... but She was as stone, impenetrable. It was as She began to fade back to Her realm, that He noticed the gem, the creation implement He had made. She clutched it so tightly in Her hand that Her blood fell from the wound, its rich redness oddly contrasting against the green gem in Her grasp.

Taiohãhn sighed and walked back to His throne room, considering that She needed time to adjust.

Maldahl was a land born from passion, its changing landscape reflecting the breath of life and love — a gift from its gods. Anarkhane became determined to devote Herself to Her work there and spend Her time tinkering with creations, moulding and shaping each race, hoping to find contentment with the results.

The Ptee Tsa were furnished with stronger and more elegant wings and she taught them to sing like the birds; the Mo-rye's delicate sculptures pleased her eye and she showered them with gifts including the knowledge of working with metal, a skill that only Taiohãhn had given before.

In both anger and retaliation at Her audacity, Taiohãhn terrified the people of Maldahl with horrific nightmares, which spoke of a future of loss and darkness. Anarkhane, however, ignored His attempt to rile Her and continued Her prolonged stay among the people.

Taiohãhn grew impatient; the more time passed, the more He came to realise that She had found contentment and it was not with Him. It was then that a plan began to form in His mind. If She cared so much about the gem, then He would take it back from Her. He would remove a key portion of Her power and She would have to return to Him, if She ever wanted to create again.

Anarkhane was gathering flowers in the vast meadows of the northlands when He arrived. The people about Her ceased singing and prostrated themselves before their seldom seen Lord, causing the goddess to turn back to Her followers at the sudden silence.

'Taiohãhn?' She said, 'What brings you here?'

He smiled a slow smile and bowed in greeting. 'Why, to see you of course. It has been too long, Fair One. I have brought you a gift, in honour of this happy meeting.'

She let the flowers fall from her hands, Her eyes glittering at His words.

'A gift, my Lord?'

'Ai.'

Taiohãhn stared at the followers about her and they withdrew a distance, understanding His want for privacy. His eyes caught sight of the creation gem, as it hung from Her waist—an enormous green jewel that formed part of Her girdle. And so the people of Maldahl had come to see Her adornment as a symbol of fertility, as from it, they knew that new life would spring.

'First you must close your eyes,' Taiohãhn whispered, yet His voice carried loud and clear to Her hearing. He smiled as She obeyed without question.

She held out Her hands in eager anticipation and He seized the opportunity, binding Her wrists tightly. The majick He used was powerful enough to bind any mortal permanently, but Anarkhane was a god, and She was angry. Her eyes shot open, enraged, as She realised what was happening. She struggled against His binding; it was powerful, but still would not hold Her for long. He snatched at the jewel at Her waist. Long time it had been since He last grasped it. She screamed, incensed by His deception. The people around stood in fear—too scared to intervene. The gem felt different to how He remembered.

He held it aloft, trophy-like. 'I take back the stone, Anarkhane,' He said.

'You can't!' Anarkhane screamed. 'It was a gift.'

'Gift or no', your obsession ends now. You will take your rightful place at my side or you will wallow here in self-pity. Either way, your power to create ends here.'

'Noooo,' she screamed, as she tore free of restraint and grabbed for the gem.

Screams were heard from the crowd and the people scattered as a colossal storm erupted overhead. Anarkhane's tears mingled with falling rain and drowned the meadows about them. The gods grappled for mastery over the stone, causing chaos and panic across Maldahl. Even those who were not present felt the anger of their gods.

Over in the east, fireballs fell from the sky and scorched the earth. Bolts of lightning felled many trees. Powerful winds blew entire settlements away; waves rose into the sky and crashed into the land, causing devastation to the shore lands.

People all over Maldahl, sank to their knees, believing that the end had come, praying their world could be saved. But the gods heard no pleas, no prayers; they fought with a madness that shook the earth beneath their feet in terrifying crescendo.

Anarkhane attempted to raise an army in effort to rescue Her from Taiohāhn's wrath. And so the last creations of Anarkhane formed in the sludge about them—in the rising swamp water of their battleground; from Her very tears that had been shed, Her new children came into being. But their coming was too late.

Taiohāhn, in His last attempt to take the stone, tried to draw its power back into Himself. But it was too changed since its making. His mighty wrath fractured the gem, and it fell into pieces between them.

All was suddenly still—the calm after so great a storm. Anarkhane was pale and wide-eyed, trembling with disbelief. She opened Her mouth as if to speak, but Her words found no voice. She shook Her head, trying to deny the sight of broken shards at Her feet.

Taiohãhn felt a piece of the gem, still hot in His grasp. Opening His hand, He let it fall onto the sodden ground about them, among the writhing bodies of the last creations. Then the voices came like a wave across the land; angry voices, frightened and lost.

'What have I done?' Taiohãhn's voice echoed across the landscape in answer to His people's despair. 'We are lost.'

Anarkhane still shook Her head, Her eyes fixed on the broken shards. 'Can you not fix it?' She said at last.

'Our link to the people is severed, Anarkhane. We must return to our realms and quickly.' He bent down to gather the shards and disappeared from Maldahl.

Anarkhane followed. 'What do you mean, severed?' She asked, Her voice lost and fragile.

'Our power was locked up in the stone,' Taiohãhn explained, 'Without the power of creation, we are no longer true gods; Maldahl has lost its divine balance. The Old Ones will seek to restore stability and we must offer them that chance.'

'You ... you've doomed us all!' Anarkhane collapsed onto the floor of His Chamber of Light.

Taiohãhn set the shards aside and went to Her aid.

'All is not lost,' He urged. 'I will find a way to set matters to rights. I will speak to the Old Ones; I will make a deal with Mynogen. We will be restored; I promise you.'

Across the vastness of space, Mynogen heard his son's pleas. The Old Ones felt the loss of power on Maldahl and knew that harmony was no longer there. They began to drift back to the birthplace of Taiohãhn, to undo what had been done. It would take a long time for them to travel so far, time that Taiohãhn planned to use wisely. Mynogen made it clear that they were only interested in balance and order. If Taiohãhn could find a way to restore that, then Maldahl would not be destroyed.

Both Taiohãhn's and Anarkhane's power was bound to the stone. That could not be undone and neither could remake the stone, having severed their connection to it. Mynogen explained that an old majick would reunite the stone—the two most powerful majicks on Maldahl could bring it together once more. But there must be a sacrifice—a willing sacrifice at the time of reunification. Once He had possession of the gem again, He would be able to rule, but it must be equal. Anarkhane had to agree to rule by His side—light and dark, balance and harmony.

A plan began to form in His mind. It was long in the making. He began to forge a sword to house the largest of the broken shards—a magnificent weapon made from His own metal, light and strong. Other objects He made—a crown, a ring, and a pendant, but one stone He set in the Chamber of Light, placing it on a plinth to remind Him always of what must be achieved.

He called forth Anarkhane to Him, for without Her agreement, His plan would fail.

'We will choose two champions, powerful enough to rule Maldahl and appease the Old Ones, whilst seeking to reunite the gem of creation.'

'But how can we be sure that they will give up the power once we have bestowed it?' Anarkhane huffed.

Taiohãhn smiled. 'We still have influence over Maldahl. Let us create a prophecy that, once embedded, the champions will fight to fulfil. It will be so implanted in the culture and history of the people, that none will seek to question it. Mynogen agreed to use the nightmares I sent to the people, to help us achieve this. They all spoke of the ending of the world; we can use the same dreams to give the people hope and direction.'

Anarkhane frowned. She had been annoyed that He sent Her people such night visions, and was reluctant to allow Him to do so again; She was reluctant to His entire plan. She did not want to rule by His side, but neither did She wish to be forever trapped in Her kingdom, until She faded out of existence.

'I will take one and teach the art of war and battle,' Taiohãhn continued. 'You will teach healing and majick to the other. We must be equal in this. Is it agreed?'

'Yes,' She sighed. 'But which one will be the sacrifice? How will we make them willing?'

'It matters not. Both will be of equal power. Either death will do. Now I will speak to Mynogen again and see if I can halt their coming here.'

Anarkhane gave a half smile. She looked so pale—a mere shadow of Her former glory.

Try as He might, Taiohãhn was unable to halt the journey of the Old Ones; no matter how much He pleaded, Mynogen explained that it was necessary. The plan had been agreed, but for one detail. The Old Ones insisted that they would remain to oversee and would train one of the champions, leaving the gods of Maldahl to train the other between them.

And so it was, that Taiohãhn sent three gems across the veil to Maldahl. He spoke to wizards and wise men in dreams; the prophecy was born and began to weave itself as a thread of light into the dark times of Maldahl's godless present.

The Elders of the Clan of the Dark Moon wrote a book at His bidding—the CODM prophecy. Only in this, did He mention the defeat of one of the champions. He had to cause the death of one and somehow make them willing to die for their cause. What better way than to die in defence of their land—to die to save Maldahl.

Exzalander would be His champion's name, a name of power with taboo majick attached. He created the name with deep spell working, so that only His chosen could be called thus. All others would be struck dead for their affront to Him and His prophecy. So could His chosen always be known to others.

He knew the exact moment the Old Ones were due to arrive; timing was crucial. Anarkhane would bless the chosen king and queen with child and He would do the rest. Now all there was to do was wait—wait for the prophecy to become part of history.

Part Two

Six

'*N* said no, my husband!'

'But my love ...'

'What part of no do you not understand, Tuâth?' The queen flounced from the king's bedchamber, slamming the door behind her.

Tuâth sighed. He could understand her reasons; he had heard the stories, but he had been chosen. Taiohãhn had visited so often in his dreams, that he was no longer surprised. He was fearful for the dark times ahead, but willing to do as he was bid. His wife, however, was going to take a little more convincing.

Queen Shénnin stormed across her chamber and seated herself at her dressing table. Her lady-in-waiting gently brushed her hair, in effort to soothe her.

'What is he thinking, Clarissa?' Shénnin said. 'He is crazed, I am sure of it.' She clutched her belly suddenly and cried out in pain.

'My queen, what ails thee?'

Another pain ensued, sharp and insistent in her swollen womb. 'My baby,' Shénnin screamed.

Clarissa assisted her into bed as the wizard was sent for. Tuâth was not admitted until after the babe was heard crying.

'I have born you a daughter, Milord,' Shénnin said, offering an exhausted smile.

'Ai wife, that I already knew.'

The queen frowned as she recalled Tuâth's so-called reason for knowing and at last she passed out from pain and exhaustion.

'Would you like to hold her, Your Majesty?' Clarissa asked.

Tuâth beamed and nodded, receiving into his arms his little girl, her red hair still wet on her head, her eyes closed, completely unaware of her importance.

'So tiny ...' Tuâth breathed.

'Ai, and so beautiful, Your Majesty. If we still had gods, I'd say you'd been blessed.'

A frown came to Tuâth's face. *Little does the wench know,* he thought. *There are still gods and I hold in my arms, their champion.*

'Take her from me,' Tuâth ordered. 'Come Ardahl, I would speak with you.'

The girl bobbed a curtsey and obeyed her king, a little confused as he swept from the room, the wizard at his heels.

The young king followed Ardahl as he led him deep into the catacombs of the palace, along winding paths that seemed to shift and change—majick Ardahl used to maintain his privacy. The king stuck close behind him, having no desire to be lost in the darkness. The door creaked open in front of the old wizard, and they stepped into the tower.

'Here we may talk freely, Your Majesty,' Ardahl said, 'away from the prying ears of the court.'

King Tuâth walked into the tower and over to the window, staring down at the castle below him.

'It always amazes me how you achieve such a feat, Ardahl,' he mused.

'Tis trickery, nothing more,' the wizard laughed. 'But come, you did not request to meet with me here merely to flatter me. There was a tone of urgency. What did you wish to discuss that you could not risk being overheard?'

'Yes, to the point as always, Ardahl; I am grateful for that. It is about my daughter and the name you are to give her at the ceremony.'

'Is that all?' Ardahl chuckled. 'You spoke as if some catastrophe was to befall you. Well, do tell me, Your Majesty, if it truly cannot wait until the Ceremony of Naming.'

'I have been having dreams, Ardahl—visitations if you like.'

The old wizard took some meat from an abandoned plate and handed it to his vulture, which bobbed its head in thanks.

'Visitations you say? By whom or what? Why have you not spoken before? Does someone intend you harm?'

Tuâth sat in the old man's chair, his fingers running across the velvet, balding in places.

'Too many question at once,' he said. 'I will tell you, but calm yourself, my friend. It was Taiohãhn who spoke to me.'

'Taiohãhn? Are you certain?'

The king nodded solemnly. 'As sure as any man can be, Ardahl. The prophecy will come to pass and my daughter is to be Taiohãhn's champion.'

Ardahl's mouth fell open and he leaned back onto his desk as if to stop himself from falling. 'Are you certain, my Lord King? It could be an evil sprite sent to threaten the new babe.'

'I am certain, Ardahl; deep within me I know it to be true. I knew the moment I set eyes upon Him, for we are all part of the Father God and I felt humbled and well ... saddened, as if I realised a part of me that had been missing and could not be returned.'

Ardahl approached the king and pressed the heel of his hand to the sovereign's forehead. Closing his eyes, he spoke words in a tongue alien to Tuâth. His eyes opened suddenly and he gasped.

'Tis true, My Lord King. Tis true ... I am indeed to give her that forbidden name. The darkness is coming and your child is the light. Praise be.'

'Indeed, we are most blessed. Now that you know and believe, perhaps you could find a way to convince the queen. She'll hear none of it.'

The king rose from the chair and Beaky squawked at the sudden movement. Ardahl the wizard bowed low, barely able to disguise his growing excitement.

'I will see you back to the palace, My Lord King.'

On arriving back, Tuâth found that his queen was awake and cradling the newborn babe in her arms. She looked up at her husband and smiled, until the seriousness of his countenance brought a scowl to her face.

It is a difficult task, he thought. *But in the end, she will have no choice. It is up to Ardahl now, to make her realise that.*

* * * * *

People gathered from all corners of the known lands for the Ceremony of Naming. King Kryepast had travelled from the kingdom of Starigorat, Southwest of the southern borders of Shénnin's lands. He brought his entire entourage, including his own infant son, to bear witness to the naming of the new princess. The crowds cheered as the foreign king waved to Shénnin's people. He kissed the queen chastely on the cheek and did the same to his friend, King Tuâth.

Representatives from the Forest of Tûlg and Elfín were also in attendance, along with many other races—happy faces enjoying the spectacle. The air was filled with cheers and song; flower petals seemed to rain from above, as children deemed too small to attend, leaned dangerously out of windows to decorate the people and streets below. Bursts of fire shot into the air and were quickly extinguished by fire-eaters' mouths, to the squeals of delight of all those within sight. There were jugglers and acrobats, all manner of performers, hoping to take advantage of the large audience to increase the content of their purse or perhaps gain a patron. Smells of sweet pastries and sugar treats wafted through the air from the many stalls, which lined the side of the road, hoping to tempt the masses who had gathered into parting with their money. There were peddlers selling flags and streamers, badly sewn and cheaply made, but purchased nevertheless, another way for the day to aid in the happiness of others, especially those hoping to make a quick coin.

The thirteen wizards of the Order of Vivianne, gathered in the Main Hall, their ceremonial robes glinting in the candlelight. Ardahl was at their head, though not of their order. They were an ancient society, formed by Queen Shénnin's grandmother. The wizards themselves had not changed since their initiation those many years ago, and although Queen Vivianne was dead and gone, her wizards remained, to teach the people of their history and guide the subsequent kings and queens in past mistakes and possible futures.

Ardahl was not of the order, and although looked older was in fact younger than all of them. He had grown up in the north kingdom and befriended Tuâth when the king was still a boy, so it was natural when the king went to live with Shénnin, he brought his friend and advisor with him. Although the Order of Vivianne had been welcoming of another wizard, their oaths forbade them from revealing their secrets to any. It had meant that they rarely worked together or consulted. As a result, Ardahl became less of an official advisor and more of a trusted friend; it suited him just fine. But on official occasions, they were all seen and perceived to work together and many people ignorantly believed him to be head of the order.

Ardahl raised his arms in reverend greeting. 'Welcome all,' he said. 'We are here to bear witness to the naming of this child. The young princess born to our beloved sovereigns, Shénnin and Tuâth.'

There was a murmur and applause from the hall, which spread outwards across the crowds. Ardahl waited patiently for silence before continuing.

'A child who will take over from her father, the High King and so rule over all middle and north kingdoms as well as here in the south. Happy are we at the union of High King and Queen of the south, and we rejoice at the blessing that they share with us all, an heir who will further reinforce the bond between the kingdoms, offering strength and prosperity to all her people.

'A name for our future sovereign is no small undertaking, for as we all know, a name defines us, helping to shape our very future. A name once given cannot be taken away. From the poorest man to the king himself, a name is a possession that remains ours for all our life and lives on after that life has left us.

'In selecting a name for the princess, our king was not alone. For a future of such importance, it seems only fitting that the gods themselves had a hand in the choice.'

As Ardahl stared out at the crowd, it was clear to him that the people had not taken his words literally. They smiled back, assuming Ardahl had meant that the gods were turned to for guidance in important matters—a quaint custom, still practised by a few, despite the fact that the gods were long gone.

He realised that he was pausing too long; the crowd was getting restless, eager for him to finish so that the celebrating could really begin. He swallowed hard, wanting his task to be over and yet reluctant to be the one who revealed the truth. Clearing his throat, he spoke again.

'Hear ye this, that from henceforth, this child shall be known as ...' he paused, suddenly concerned at the name he was about to speak. 'She shall be known as Exzalander.'

There was a gasp and the whispers began; they spread throughout the hall, to the courtyard and beyond. In mere moments, there was excited chatter, which could not be silenced. Those nearest the child gazed on in horror, waiting for her to die. When she did not, more whispers, more shouts, some of indignation.

'What is the meaning of this, Tuâth? This is an outrage!' boomed King Kryepast over the crowd.

His son began to cry at the sound of his father's anger and his wife fought to calm him. Shénnin took back her child, who also shed tears at the surrounding commotion.

'Silence,' Tuâth called over the din. 'I said SILENCE!' His command was enough to stop the crowd's tongues. 'I did not choose the name for my daughter,' he said. ' It was Taiohãhn who had that honour.'

There was another gasp from the congregation and Kryepast took his seat, shaking his head in disbelief.

'It was foretold that Exzalander would walk among us … well, that time is now. The prophecy is coming to pass at last; rejoice, for balance will be restored to our world and our gods will return to us. Taiohãhn's chosen is here!'

Some of the crowd knelt before the king and wept tears of joy at the thought of their absent gods—gods who had been separated from them for many lifetimes. There were those in the congregation, however, who could not get away fast enough. The orderly crowd beyond the palace, scattered in fear and confusion, many not understanding what had occurred, but the panic hit them like a wave, the tale growing taller the further it spread amongst them.

The day was a disaster. Those who looked back on it having parted with coin, or been relieved of it, said that it was a bad omen.

The Feast of Naming was less attended than anticipated; many of the guests left without a word to their host. For those who remained, there was animated discussion about what had occurred that afternoon.

Shénnin retired early, taking Exzalander with her. She felt utterly exhausted. The fear for her baby's life had been eating away at her for weeks. As Ardahl had spoken the name, she felt affeared that she would faint. The noise, the crowds and the questions were too much for her. She was relieved

Exzalander lived, but beyond that, she was too tired to think about anything else. She placed the baby into the cradle by her bed, and sank back onto silky softness, falling at once into a deep slumber.

Tuâth remained long after most had departed or retired. He held counsel with King Kryepast, relating the visitations and words of Taiohãhn, in effort to make him understand. Kryepast, after several hours and many goblets of fire wine, conceded that Tuâth could call his child what he will, but he refused to believe the prophecy, calling it merely superstition, but agreed to consult the prophecy—if only to prove Tuâth wrong. By the end of the evening, both men were friends again at least.

Many days passed and as the child showed no signs of dying, all was at peace once more. Life continued as normal for the most part. The order of Vivianne spent many weeks in closed counsel, consulting old documents and lore. It was such reclusive behaviour that started the first whispers amongst people who were already on edge.

'They're up to somethin', you mark my words!'

'Why all the secrets? If it's for the benefit of all, why hide behind closed doors?'

The Order of Vivianne had always been respected for having the people's interests at heart, yet since the shock of such tidings many blamed the Order, unaware that the wizards themselves had been ignorant of the news.

Exzalander grew into a beautiful little girl, who was caring and loving to all. The people adored her, whereas over the years, the Order of Vivianne attracted nothing but suspicion. They became more secretive and took to visiting dark places. Rumours began, saying the wizards attempted to force such a great destiny upon the child, and they tried to manipulate the future for the people of Maldahl. The once respected wizard community gained a reputation for mystery and manipulation.

Queen Shénnin heard the rumours among her people and was concerned. Exzalander loved Ardahl as much as her own parents. No matter how much the queen discouraged it, Exzalander would not leave the old wizard alone. The fact that it should have been impossible for her to reach the tower did not deter her either. Shénnin entreated her husband to move them to his castle in the north, but he would hear none of it and Exzalander continued to make daily visits to Ardahl's tower, learning all that she could from the wizard, preferring his lessons to that of any court tutor.

As the people's distrust for the wizards grew, Tuâth felt obliged to choose a way to better represent his people. He appointed a council to take over the responsibilities held by the Order of Vivianne. The wizards gathered to meet the Council and it was at that first meeting where politician and wizard sat as equals. It was at that meeting when the wizards became even more unpopular, introducing Tuâth to the contents of the CODM prophecy. Tuâth was aware of his daughter's importance, how she was expected to lead Maldahl away from darkness, but never before that day, had he questioned what that meant.

All of Maldahl felt keenly the loss of their gods, and were often afflicted by a sense that their life served no purpose. Tuâth had rejoiced at the thought of the world finding a path once more, filling the emptiness ... but still, a sense of loss was not darkness. It was only when the CODM prophecy was revealed to him in full, did the king realise that he was not going to be around to see his little girl grow to greatness.

He sat calmly staring ahead as his death was foretold, his knuckles white from gripping the throne, the only indication of his inner anguish. He had expected his child to be a spiritual leader, bringing the people back to the gods, not to have to fight — to kill. He felt sick. Exzalander's love for a man would signal the darkness to come.

Death will follow ... so many deaths, Tuâth thought. *How can this be? Why was I never told such a thing before now? Could the prophecy be wrong?*

The ancient Vampire Ælf explained to all there, her people's close connection with the god, Taiohãhn. It was destiny.

Tuâth remained with the counsellors well into the night, long after the representative from Tûlg had gone and the wizards had been dismissed. Indeed, the king remained in counsel for many days, leaving but rarely, for a brief visit to his wife and daughter. The wizards were not permitted access to the king during that time.

He was angry, feeling somehow that he was being manipulated. The counsellors, rather than alleviate such fears, fed them ...

'How can we trust a Vampire Ælf? They eat people.'

'Too long have their kind been permitted their vile practice.'

'Those who predict such evils must be evil themselves ...'

Tuâth began to believe that the killers plotted against him, that they would bring an end to his reign. He had no desire for his child to suffer and began to think of ways he might avert the prophecy foretold. The counsellors, seeing a chance to rise in power, were only too eager to assist.

Seven

The captain of the guard swung his youngest son in the air, much to Caitul's delight.

'Again father, again.'

Thomn smiled down at him. Caitul looked more like his mother than himself. His inquisitive eyes stared up with wonder at his father.

'Perhaps later, little one; the king expects me and I am already late.'

Caitul bowed his head and stuck out his bottom lip

Yes, definitely more like his mother, Thomn mused.

'Come Caitul, let your father be. He has his duties and you have chores, young man!' Elsbeth pushed him good-naturedly toward the house.

'Oh mother,' Caitul complained.

Thomn took a good look at his wife—her pale eyes, soft warm lips and curvaceous form, and found he was suddenly unable to move.

'Thomn? You're late remember …'

'Oh … yes. Yes, my love.' He swept his wife into his arms and kissed her warmly.

'Be off with you,' she laughed, holding him at arm's length.

'Very well, wife, but I *shall* continue this later.'

She smiled suggestively at him and he felt a stirring in his groin; sighing, he tore himself away from sweeter things. It was a pleasant day, the sort of day he liked to walk to the palace, but he was running late, so horseback it was. The ride was not far but he felt every second keenly of it. Although it was supposed to be his day off from responsibility, the king had summoned him and it was his duty to answer such summons. Still, he could hardly help feeling a little inconvenienced. *It has been weeks since I last spoke to or even saw King Tuâth and now such urgency—on my day off,* he thought. *Well there is nothing else for it.*

He dismounted and handed the reins to the stable boy with a nod of thanks then strode off toward the counsel chambers.

'The Captain of the Guard, Your Majesty.'

Thomn adjusted his livery, aware of his king's tendency to notice such things as untidy appearance in his subjects.

'Thomn!' the king said, in greeting. He remained seated and his smile did not extend to his eyes.

The salutation seemed warm enough, but something was not quite right. Thomn felt the keen stare from every counsellor present as he crossed the chamber to pay homage to his liege.

Yes, something is definitely amiss, he thought. He knelt before King Tuâth and greeted him solemnly.

'Rise Thomn, our most trusted friend in these dark times …'

Thomn got slowly to his feet. *Dark times?* he thought. *It is sunny and pleasant outside and the warmth of my wife's body did not seem so dark.* 'Milord?'

'News has reached us of a threat to kill our person,' Tuâth said. 'A plot to overthrow the monarchy and plunge much of Maldahl into chaos.'

Thomn glanced about; all eyes were fixed on him, unblinking.

'Is it Kryepast?' he asked. 'Does he strike against you, Lord King?'

'No,' Tuâth hissed, as if he had expected Thomn to instantly know to what he had been referring to. 'The Vampire Ælves it is who seek our downfall.'

Thomn let out a single laugh, sudden relief washing over him. 'Who has been filling your head with such nonsense?' he said. 'The Clan of the Dark Moon have no care for Your Majesty's throne.'

A counsellor spoke from the dimness of the chamber. The man's voice was hard and cold, filling the captain with dread. Already there had been those that had spoken out against the Council, only to find themselves in the stocks … or worse. Thomn had a reputation and family who depended on him.

'All I am saying,' he proceeded carefully, 'is that there is no evidence to suggest such a thing. They have never shown an interest in anything we do before.'

'Exactly!' Tuâth said. 'They care not for our laws or way of life. We are nothing more than food to them. Besides, there *is* evidence; it is written down and kept in their village—a book of prophecy. I want you to retrieve it for me, Thomn.'

'You want me to take a book from them?'

'Yes … and I want you to exterminate all that you find there. Concentrate on the females. If vermin cannot mate, they cannot spread. We must eliminate this threat, and quickly. Can we trust you, Thomn, to do your duty?'

Thomn stiffened, standing tall. 'Of course, Your Majesty,' he replied.

'And Thomn.'

'Yes, Your Majesty?'

'Never seek to question us again. Is that understood?'

Thomn bowed low, a cold fear creeping down the length of every limb.

'Yes, Your Majesty.'

'Good. You may go. Ready your men and perform your duty. Return to us our champion.' Tuâth smiled. There was no warmth there, only desperation and fear, a paranoia that had been fed by the power hungry counsellors who sat there, in the dark—watching and waiting.

Thomn bowed once more and left swiftly. *What is to be done?* he thought. *To question the king's orders, is to be put to death—my family shamed forever.* Yet, in his heart, he was unsure he could commit to such a terrible deed. He reached out and gripped the stone wall to steady himself, as a wave of dizziness and nausea ensued.

'They are not human, Thomn. When you look into the eyes of a Vampire Ælf, you are looking into the eyes of a killer—a murderer who has gone unpunished for its crimes many times over. Remember that.'

The counsellor, who had followed him from the chamber, gripped his shoulder as if to comfort him. It was none; there was no comfort in the world for him now. He met the gaze of the young man before him. It was clear that *he* at least, believed what he was saying.

Thomn nodded, but unable to voice a response, walked away.

How can a day that started so perfectly, come to this? He recalled the king's look of anger as he questioned his duty and his resolve stiffened. *Like it or not, I have been issued an order from my king, an order that was given for the benefit of all Tuâth's people. I have taken an oath to obey and it is not my place to question it.*

Captain Thomn gathered the guard and bid them arm themselves. It was not until they were well away from the palace grounds, that he revealed their orders.

Elsbeth clung tightly to Caitul.

'Where is father?' the boy complained, 'Why did he not return?'

She stroked his hair from his eyes and kissed him gently on the brow.

'He has been given a mission from the king. I am afraid the king's orders must take priority over your story tonight, Caitul.'

'I don't see why,' Caitul replied, with a pout.

'Because he is the king and your father has taken a sacred oath to obey him. Perhaps you are yet too young to understand such things.'

'No mother, I am ten ... I am almost old already!' the boy argued.

Elsbeth laughed and ruffled his hair.

'Ai, perhaps you are at that,' she said. 'Now off to bed with you!'

Stubbornness forgotten, Caitul clambered into bed with thoughts of quests and great deeds filling his head. 'Will I ever make an oath, mother?'

Her eyes darkened for a moment, but Caitul failed to notice. Her first-born as well as her husband, were in the service of the king and now her little one was so eager to swear his life away too.

She smiled gently. 'Perhaps you will,' she replied. 'Maybe you'll find another path to tread.'

Caitul lay back and his mother kissed him goodnight.

'On no mother, I want to be a great man, like father.' He yawned, and whatever Elsbeth said in return, he did not hear, for he slept, dreaming of honour and glory.

Thomn marched the men well into the night, before stopping to take rest, anxious that he could get the task completed quickly so that he might forget it and move on. The men knew better than to grumble around the captain. They both trusted and loved him, knowing he would not march them so long without good reason.

'Well met, Thomn,' came a voice from the darkness.

'Who goes there?'

Thomn's hand reached for his sword, but lowered as he saw the old wizard step into the firelight.

'Ardahl! What are you doing here? You shouldn't sneak up on me like that!'

'I do not sneak, Thomn.'

The old man sat by the fire, warming his hands. He looked much older than when Thomn had seen him last, and deeply troubled.

Ardahl nodded, as if answering a question that had not been voiced. 'A sad business,' he said.

Thomn stiffened. 'Why are you here, wizard?'

Ardahl stared at Thomn and the captain did not like it. It was as though he looked directly into his soul.

'Why do you think?' Ardahl said. 'I have my orders too. Or did you think you could escape the clan's majick alone?'

Thomn bowed his head. 'In truth, I had not thought about it. Why did you not leave with us this afternoon?'

'Ah, you know how much I delight in the company of others,' he said, with a smile.

'Why is the king doing this?'

Ardahl glanced about him, as if he feared who might be listening. 'There are those who whisper both truths and poison in the king's ear. He is so fearful of his own death that he no longer has the wits to discern one from the other. But in this matter, perhaps he is right, Thomn. These predators have long gone unhindered. It was once when we sent them our criminals, but their numbers grow and more disappear ... innocents. They must be checked. That book must also be gained and the clan elder would never relinquish it willingly, therefore we must take it.'

Thomn nodded, feeling more able to perform the task ahead. He did not trust wizards in general, but Ardahl had always been more straightforward than most.

'But what of these counsellors? Many are concerned about the power they hold.'

'I blame myself,' Ardahl said. 'The king is a busy man. There is simply not enough time for him to perform his duties alone. Had I not been so dedicated to my experiments, I could have prevented it. I always advised and assisted in the past, but now ...'

'Yes?'

'Tuâth has limited my office. No wizard can advise the king. These counsellors breed mistrust of our kind. I was blinded by my work and did not see until it was too late. Now someone other than I must try to curb their power, or it could well be that Exzalander will have no throne to inherit.'

'Do you really think it will come to that, Ardahl?'

'I would say not, if it were not for my apprentice; he dream-paints and some of the things he has shown me of late … well, they are best left unspoken.

'I notice that you are not eating that sausage there. I do hope that you were not planning on letting it go to waste.'

Thomn smiled and broke half the sausage, handing it to the wizard along with some bread.

At dawn upon the fifth day from Ealdorbold, the soldiers approached the outskirts of the Vampire Ælves' dwelling place. The light greeted the sky beyond, but could not be seen beneath the trees; it was forever night in the Forest of Tûlg. The first the clan knew of the attack, was the blinding light Ardahl unleashed upon them.

Soldiers poured in from all directions, hewing all who stood before them. No heed was paid to pleas for mercy. The clan, still half-blinded, began to scatter. Some stood and fought back, but their sleep spells simply rebounded from their targets as Ardahl's majick did its work. Ardahl had completed his task well, and he watched as the troops carved a bloody mess toward the elder's cave.

The screams tore through Thomn, and he kept having to remind himself that they were not women. A particularly striking Ælf bared her fangs with a hiss and it was all he needed to complete his work. After such a display, it was easier, for he imagined one of his children or his beloved Elsbeth in their clutches, and he removed the thing's head. Felling all before him, a vicious smile was on his lips and he wore their blood like war paint. His battle lust infected the men under his command and in all too short a time, no Vampire Ælf was left intact. All were dead, dismembered, their beautiful eyes betraying the horror of all they had witnessed in their final moments.

The cave of the elder was not as Thomn had expected. The walls glowed faintly, piercing the darkness before him. It was not foul and loathsome, but beautiful—enticing even.

'Where are the men?' Thomn shrieked at the old woman.

She hissed at his intrusion, staring defiantly back at him and although death was so near, she did not tremble.

'They are not here,' she spat. 'That much is clear, or you would not have so easy a victory. I name you Thomn-the-Cleaverhand, murderer of my people. You will live to rue this day. May each life that you took, weigh as years upon you; may your guilt burden you to early death; may you ...'

Whatever curse she wished to add, was silenced as Thomn's sword, heavy with the blood of so many, pierced through her breast and she spoke no more. Thomn's hands began to tremble and he fought back a sense of panic that waxed within him. Pushing the lifeless body from his blade, he wondered if the taint would ever be cleansed. He tried to think of the fangs and the murder in their eyes, but he was faltering. Approaching the altar, he gazed upon his prize, bathed in moonlight streaming in from a hole above. He grabbed it swiftly and left.

'Do you have it?' Ardahl asked.

Thomn held out the book to the wizard, not caring how much his hands shook.

'Thomn-the-Cleaverhand she called me ...'

Ardahl grasped the book, steadying Thomn as he did so. 'Yes, this is it,' he said. 'You have done your duty well, Thomn; take comfort in that. It is over now and darkness may yet be averted.'

Thomn released the book and staggered away from the wizard.

'No,' he whispered, 'the darkness has begun, here, now. This is it and it will never be light again.' He collapsed to his knees, the truth of what he had done, overcoming him at last.

Caitul awoke in a sweat, calling out to his father. Elsbeth went to her son's side and found him trembling, a fever upon him.

'Father! He's lost to us, mother ... lost to us.'

Elsbeth cradled her son in her arms, but no words could comfort him. He burned and shivered, his face ghostly. She kissed him swiftly and then, wrapping her cloak about her, she fled the house in search of a healer. Many hours passed before she returned and ran to his bedside, fearful for what she would find.

The wizard, Fahl, knelt beside Caitul, checking his head then listening to his heart.

'Fahl, tell me, is he ... will he ...'

'No Elsbeth.' Fahl smiled. 'Looks worse than it is.'

She took the wizard's hands and kissed them.

'Thank-you, oh thank-you.'

Fahl touched the woman's head, before turning to his bag of medicines. He began to mix a tonic for the captain's son. All the while, Caitul whispered for his father to return.

'Oh Lord Fahl, you don't think my Thomn ...'

Fahl's expression was unmoving as he handed Caitul the tonic.

'Your husband lives, Elsbeth.'

She knew she should be relieved, but there was something in the man's eyes that filled her with dread.

'I am to follow him,' Caitul whispered.

Fahl packed away his bottles, smiling at the boy's words and looking deep within him. He snapped his bag shut suddenly.

'No young Caitul; you will be a great knight methinks.'

Elsbeth smiled at the man's words and the reaction of her son, offering to see Fahl to the door.

'I cannot thank you enough,' she said.

Fahl reached out and touched the young woman's cheek. Her eyes met his and she was suddenly troubled. There was sorrow there and she knew somehow that he was saying farewell to her. Before she could question him, he stepped through the door and was gone. A sadness filled her being; it felt as though the world had just changed a little and not for the better.

Eight

News travelled before the company of the great deed performed and the name used as curse to the captain, was shouted to honour him.

Fahl hurried to meet his brethren, eager to share what he had seen in Caitul's mind as he had tended him. Taal closed the great door behind him, concerned that prying ears might report back to the Council.

'There has been an atrocity committed, friends,' Fahl said, shaking his head, 'one that is being celebrated in the streets.'

'We know. Brother Elsta saw it. It was murder plain and simple. No glorious battles as the tales are telling. It was the planned annihilation of an entire race.'

The Order of Vivienne gathered closer still, as if the very walls about them were an enemy,

'How could Tuâth have sanctioned such an evil?'

'He no longer sees the truth. We are in great danger. This was but the first step I fear. We must flee before Tuâth's vipers decide to bring such 'justice' closer to home.'

Zahin paced toward the window and stared down at the streets below—his home. 'You don't really think they plot against us?'

'Do not be so naïve, Zahin. I think they have sought our removal from the beginning. If we stay, death will follow.'

Elbrus laughed harshly. 'Do you honestly think that they are powerful enough to be a threat to us?'

Fahl put his face in his hands, shaking his head. 'Do you not see?' he asked, 'a fight is what they want. If we kill any guards, even in self defence, that is somebody's husband or father … the people will not stand by us; they will say the Council was right all along.'

'Not all surely,' Elsta said.

'No, perhaps not, but would you really want the responsibility of the fate of those who might support us? Our time here is over. We must find a place of safety where we can prepare for Exzalander's rule.'

'I think we are exaggerating here, Fahl.'

Fahl stood and joined Zahin at the window.

'People are celebrating the death of majick users,' he said. 'They dance and sing. Do you really believe they would not do the same at our demise?'

'We are not killers!' Taal protested.

'It is not *that* which the people despised,' offered Fahl. 'It is the majick they feared. We've been so blinded by our duty that we abandoned the people long ago. Believe me when I say, it is time to leave.'

'What of Ardahl?'

'What of him?' snorted Uele. 'Who do you think protected the soldiers as they slaughtered Taiohãhn's children? He is not one of us and we need to put as much distance between ourselves and him as we possibly can.'

The wizards joined tightly in a circle of power and gripped each other by the arm. As they broke away, the door to the chamber was flung open; High Counsellor Danah walked in, followed by Sohãhn and Briam.

'What's this my lords? A secret meeting?' he said. 'You should be careful; people might think that you're up to something.' He smiled, glancing to Briam, as if to affirm his words.

Fahl closed in on the head of the Council and fixed his eyes upon him—unspeaking. The Counsellors smile faded and he began to shift uncomfortably under the wizards' gaze. Then one by one, as if following some command given by thought alone, the wizards left the room and walked in single file along the corridor, down the stairs. They made their way past the Great Hall and out into the courtyard.

By the time the wizards reached the wall, many servants had noticed and a few chose to follow the procession. The Order of Vivianne passed through the main gate; they took no possessions, they took no leave from their king, believing he deserved no explanation at their parting. Many had gathered, but did not understand the gravity of what was happening. The Counsellors sent a message to the king, but all was done too late. The Order of Vivianne passed from the present and were never seen by any living in those lands again.

Many claimed they were pleased at the wizards' departure, saying the less meddling in majicks, the better. But in the heart of all, they knew that a power ancient and venerable had abandoned them and they all felt the more lost for it.

Tuâth set foot outdoors for the first time in months. The sun passed behind a cloud and yet the king still squinted in the light of day. His people bowed before him and he realised suddenly how completely disconnected from them he felt.

'Father!' squealed the young princess, and jumped into the king's arms.

'Well hello little one. How nice to see you.' Tuâth attempted a smile and caught Shénnin's gaze; her eyes held his for a moment—hard and unforgiving.

'Father, is something the matter?' Exzalander asked.

'No little one,' he answered too quickly. He had long ceased to call her Exzalander; it was as though he had changed his mind about the prophecy and wanted to do everything in his power to avert it. He squeezed her tighter still until she struggled against him, the sound of approaching horses drawing her attention away.

The company had returned.

'Horses!' the young princess squealed. She ran to greet the host and Thomn dismounted next to her.

'Greetings Captain Thomn,' she said demurely.

His face was grey and older than Exzalander remembered it. His smiles were all spent and it made her frown. She beckoned him with her finger and he fell to his knees before the girl, her green eyes shining. Reaching out, she touched the corner of his mouth, as if she could will happiness back to him. Thomn's eyes were bloodshot and his lip trembled as if he would cry.

'Exzalander! Come!' demanded Shénnin. Her voice had such a state of urgency about it that Exzalander obeyed at once.

She took her mother's hand and was half dragged back toward the palace. Exzalander glanced back over her shoulder and saw Thomn staring after her. She gave a smile and a little wave, but he did not return the gesture.

Tuâth stepped up, seeming to ignore what had just happened. 'Thomn, glad are we at your return,' he said. 'Your campaign was a success we hear. You have done us great service and your loyalty will not go unrewarded. I hereby make you Lord of Haesburg and it is a title well deserved.'

Tuâth's hand touched the captain's shoulder, in a manner of friendship. Thomn hated him at that moment. As the household shouted his cursed nickname, his jaw clenched and he looked at the floor, afraid that he might do something he could regret.

As if sensing his dangerous mood, the king stepped away from his captain and addressed the rest of the men.

'Welcome all, drink your fill; celebrate and be at your ease tonight. You have done well and have the gratitude of your king.'

The guard cheered and dispersed, heading towards the barracks. Ardahl arrived and bowed low.

'Do you have it?' Tuâth asked, trying not to allow his sense of urgency to show.

Ardahl smiled and nodded.

'Good. Follow me.'

Tuâth brushed past Thomn-the-Cleaverhand, as if he was no longer there. It was a long while before the captain dare raise his head and get to his feet, so powerful was his rage.

Elsbeth kept Caitul to his bed, despite the fact that he appeared to be better. She was concerned about the things being said in the streets and did not want Caitul to hear. She was pacing by the time her husband returned. Running to him, she clung tightly to his chest. When he did not return her embrace, she stepped back.

'Thomn, is it true?'

Thomn pushed past his wife and removed his weapon belt. As he placed it on the side, Elsbeth grabbed his hand.

'Thomn? Husband? Why will you not speak?'

He collapsed into his chair and burying his head in his hands, he wept. Elsbeth gently stroked his hair, too scared to ask again what ailed her beloved.

In the throne room, Ardahl presented the king with his prize.

'Why will it not open?' Tuâth asked.

Ardahl shrugged. 'I know not, Your Majesty. It is protected by majicks of which I am unfamiliar. I will begin trying to unlock it at once, if that is your wish.'

'No. It is to be placed in my study. I do not want anyone to consult it.'

Ardahl bowed low. 'As you wish.'

'Was there much resistance?' Tuâth asked, as if his orders had been quite different to those that had been carried out.

Ardahl paused.

'What is it, Ardahl? Tell me.'

'The males were not there. The captain and his men butchered every woman present.'

To Ardahl's surprise, Tuâth smiled.

'Excellent ... excellent. Kill all the females in a nest of rats and the males will die out eventually. All is well. You may go, Ardahl.'

Exzalander's hand had begun to pain her, from where her mother gripped too tightly, but she was too wary of Shénnin's mood to risk breaking free. It was not until she was within the queen's own chamber, did Shénnin release her.

Exzalander usually enjoyed being there; her mother had many beautiful things and never minded Exzalander playing with them. But today was different; there was an air of tension and it seemed to be affecting everyone.

She sat on the edge of her mother's bed and her lip wobbled. Shénnin was too preoccupied to notice. Her lady-in-waiting was swift on Shénnin's heels and entered, asking if the queen required anything.

'No thank you, Clarissa, you may leave me.'

'Yes Your Majesty,' Clarissa said, bobbing a curtsey, and her eyes fell upon the young princess.

The queen noticed the maid's delay in leaving and her eyes followed Clarissa's gaze. She waved the woman away and her demeanour softened.

'How now Exzalander? What's this? Do I find you weeping?'

Exzalander sniffed stubbornly, sticking out her bottom lip in defiance. 'No mother,' she said.

Shénnin sat beside her, holding her close.

'How would you like to go away with me, Exzalander? We can visit some beautiful places and meet new people. Does that sound nice?'

Exzalander swiftly wiped all traces of tears from her face. 'Maybe ... can Ardahl come too?

Shénnin's eyes closed and her brow creased into a frown. 'No my dear one. Ardahl is far too busy for such journeys.'

The young princess swung her feet and crinkled her nose as she deliberated, making her mother smile.

'I suppose ... as long as we were not too long. Ardahl needs me,' she said, trying to sound grown up. 'His new apprentice is hopeless!'

Shénnin laughed at her daughter's attempt to sound like the wizard. Hugging her tightly, she kissed her brow. The princess, feeling the tension had lifted, was quite happy in her mother's arms for a while.

Her boredom was just beginning to set in when Shénnin called Clarissa back to her and told her to watch the princess, ensuring that she did not visit Ardahl.

'I must speak with the king on a matter of some urgency,' Shénnin concluded. She swept from the chamber before Clarissa had even finished her curtsey.

Exzalander jumped from the bed and bounded over to the young maid, throwing herself into her arms.

'Hey you,' Clarissa said, with a smile. 'So what would you like to do?'

'Hide and find!'

'Very well.'

'Yay!'

Clarissa placed the girl down and covered her eyes whilst Exzalander dashed from the room in search of a suitable hiding place.

Tuâth placed the ancient book on a stand in his private study. Despite the Council's protestations that the prophecy had been averted, a seed of doubt began to grow within him.

The wizards, some of his oldest allies, had left him, and his decision to attack the Clan of the Dark Moon seemed not so sensible as it had. He recalled the ashen face of his trusted servant, as the horrors reflected back in his eyes to the one who had ordered their doing. He inwardly questioned why he was suddenly so concerned, concluding that it might be the proximity of the book.

'An evil looking thing to be sure,' he murmured, and left the study, his mind a whirl of dark thoughts.

'My lord, I would speak with you.' Shénnin's eyes were hard and issued silent warning.

'Shénnin, you look truly beautiful today,' he flattered. 'I feel as though I have not seen you in so long.'

'It has been a while, my husband.'

Tuâth offered his arm and they walked off toward the gardens.

'I am leaving, Tuâth and I am taking Exzalander with me.'

The king glanced about him uneasily, fearful that one of the household might have heard.

'You are queen, Shénnin. Your place is with me. Come now, what has brought this on? Do you no longer love me?'

He took the Queen's hands in his own, offering them a gentle squeeze, as if to coax a favourable reply.

'I no longer know thee, Milord,' Shénnin replied.

She pulled her hands away and left her husband standing momentarily still in his position, as she seated herself by the fountain. Motionless, he stood, like some ridiculous statue before his sense returned and redness filled his cheeks as his anger began to grow.

'I am not sure that I comprehend your meaning, Shénnin,' he said. 'I know that I have been a little preoccupied of late, but I have been engaged by some very important matters of state ...'

Shénnin's eyes were all daggers as she interrupted him.

'I know what it is you ordered, husband. Do you really think I want our child exposed to that?' she said. 'I also know the wizards have left us. The Order of Vivianne has served my family for over a hundred years and now they are gone. Two powerful allies lost in a matter of days. Your obsession with our child's future is driving you to madness.'

'Speak no more, you know not what you say ...'

Shénnin held his face firmly in her hands, locking her eyes on his. He stared into them, wondering how he had come to forget how beautiful she was.

'I say I must speak, husband, for if not me, then who? Nobody else would dare. I cannot say what our future holds, but if it truly is preordained, then everything you have done will not save us in the end. All you have done is estranged our house from powerful friends who may have aided us. You are seeing enemies everywhere and yet you allow our child to while her days away with one of the most powerful wizards we have ever known ... I do not want Exzalander to play with a man who was responsible for murdering women. I am taking her and we are going to Brëgwela. Instead of wasting away worrying, I would like you to join us. I want us to be a family again, Tuâth. I love the man who I married and I want him to return to us.'

As she moved to take her hands from his face, he took them in his own once more and gently stroked her smooth skin beneath his. Without warning, he leaned forward, planting his lips upon her own, firm yet loving. She returned his kiss with a longing that she had not been aware that was lingering within her.

'I've been a fool,' he whispered in her ear, leaving her tingling. 'I will come with you. I have the Council to take care of matters here.'

'That is well, my Lord King and dearest husband.'

Tuâth smiled at her. It hurt to do so and he realised it must have been quite some time since he had allowed himself such a luxury as smiling.

'Ready yourself then. I will give us two days in preparation.'

'Two days, to prepare an entire entourage?'

Tuâth laughed. 'Ai, it will suffice.' But as soon as the laughter shone in his face, it faded once more; his brow tightened and fear was in his eyes.

'What is't Milord?' Shénnin asked.

'I know not. I just had the strangest feeling ... where is Exzalander?'

'She is with my lady-in-waiting.'

'Are you sure?' he said, gripping Shénnin a little too tightly.

'Yes.'

'I left my study open,' he said, as if that explained his odd behaviour. 'I must lock it. Begin your preparations, Shénnin.' With that he began to return to the palace—a gentle jog at first that soon broke into a run.

Shénnin stared after him, a sense of hope building within her.

The room smelt musty. Exzalander traced her tiny fingers across several of the dust-covered volumes, ignoring the smell in the air, searching for something interesting to read in order to pass the time. She walked toward the back section of the study, being careful to keep her footsteps light, so as to escape discovery. A strange looking book sat on a pedestal to the corner of the room; its odd black cover had the appearance of carved ebony.

She paused for a moment, her delicate hand hovering above the work, fearful to touch it and yet unable to resist. The weird carvings seemed to shift as her fingers made contact, and she continued to fondle the book, intrigued by its magical quality.

Footsteps sounded in the hallway and she heard quite clearly, Clarissa calling her name. Fearfully, she watched the door, expecting discovery. However, the footsteps receded; obviously the lady-in-waiting did not consider that she might be brave or fool enough to incur the King's wrath by being found in his private study, but Exzalander was not afraid of the King. Her father had never raised his voice to her, let alone his hand, so there was no possible punishment that she feared from him.

Once the danger had departed, Exzalander turned her attention back to the book. She leaned over it, peering at its peculiar design. It looked like a palace surrounded by trees, gently bending in a wind. Her eager hand reached out to touch it once more, when she noticed the stains; red marks that were darkening by the second, like ageing blood. Aware that the only thing she had touched had been the book, she rubbed her index finger curiously along the edge of the cover, unwilling to disturb the odd design again. Fresh liquid oozed onto her skin and she gasped, certain that it *was* blood. Fear crept upon her and she backed away, wishing that she had never dared to touch it, regretting that she ever came into a place where nobody would think to look for her.

To her astonishment and fright, the book flicked open, its pages fluttering wildly, whispering her name. She cowered on the ground, unable to move or utter a sound as the book illuminated from within. Fragmented images leapt from the pages, and Exzalander watched in wonder, as great battles ensued and mighty warriors stood together, their capes blowing proudly in the wind. She saw a waterfall; one figure bent over another as if willing him back to life.

Shifting forward, she no longer feared the sights before her. She stood once more before the book, as the figure of a woman on a hill materialised, wearing a long red dress and a dark cloak, which seemed to change colours as the sunrays glinted off it; at her waist hung a belt, which carried an array of weapons. As the woman unsheathed her sword and held it high, the morning sun breathed light on her form, and her sword shone with a blinding radiance, which swallowed up the image until only the sword remained.

Exzalander reached out, compelled and unable to stop herself. Her hands gripped the hilt and the golden light filled her being, bathing her in its brilliance. She stood rooted, staring, unable to breathe or even blink for fear that the darkness would come and she would never know such beauty again. In the pommel, the green stone began to liquefy and strands of the strange fluid reached out to form yet another link to her.

A shock ran through her body, the sensation no longer pleasant, causing her to panic. Unable to remove her grasp from the phantom sword, she backed away, hoping to disrupt the image. However, the sword began to gain substance rather than lose it and she felt it solidify in her hand. The pain increased and the light grew brighter; the liquid gem held open her mouth and eyes, several tendrils entering her orifice, holding tight her vocal cords, clinging and crawling, until they wound tightly about her heart.

Tears streamed from her open eyes and she wished the nightmare to end, that her Daddy would hold her and tell her it was all right; it was just a bad dream. The buzzing sound grew so loud in her head that she thought her teeth would shatter. Her body shook with the pressure, but she was not permitted to fall.

'Prepare yourself, Exzalander; the pain is yet to come.'

She felt a searing heat, which seemed to strip her very flesh and leave her bones exposed to such extreme cold that they split and cracked.

In her a mind, she heard a scream, the sound she would have made had she been able. She could not tell if the pain had lessened or whether her body had adjusted to the torture by numbing her senses. The green gem seemed whole once again, and the light began to dim. The scream she had envisioned in her mind found its voice, just seconds before she lost consciousness.

Tuâth scolded the princess, until she told him what had occurred. Before she could finish her story, he swept her up in his arms, holding her tightly. Removing her from the room, he locked the door behind them. All the while, Exzalander continued to tremble in his arms and her pallid face buried into his shoulder.

Clarissa turned the corner, and spying the king with her young charge exiting his private study, she fell to her knees.

'Forgive me, Your Majesty,' she said. 'We were playing a game and she got away from me.'

Exzalander gripped her father even tighter and he rubbed her back.

'It's all right; I will take her,' Tuâth said. 'No harm done. The queen is in the gardens. She wishes to speak to you on a matter of some import.'

'Yes Your Majesty.' Clarissa waited until the king turned away before getting to her feet and rushing back to the palace gardens.

King Tuâth sent for Ardahl. Despite his new mistrust of majick, the wizard was the person he depended on when it came to his family's safety. He would be sorry to have to leave him, but knew it was one of the reasons that Shénnin was so determined to go.

Ardahl felt Exzalander's brow and checked her pulse.

'I found her on the floor,' Tuâth explained. 'She had touched the book.'

'Was it open?'

'It was not when I found her, but she said that it opened on its own, when she looked at it. Will she be all right, Ardahl?'

The wizard gave a reassuring smile. 'Yes, there is nothing to fear; she has had a fright, that is all. Give her a little rest and she will forget all about it.'

Exzalander's eyes opened and she saw her friend standing over her.

'Ardahl,' she said. 'May I visit you, when we go away?'

Tuâth's head snapped up from his brooding. 'How can she possibly know that?'

Ardahl's eyes went from his young charge to his king.

'You are going somewhere, Your Majesty?' he asked.

'Yes, but it was only just decided. We have told nobody … I believe she already possesses gifts. I think she called to me for help, Ardahl. I thought I heard her—in my mind. It's why I returned to my study.'

'Yes, well I've seen her do a great many spectacular things for her age,' Ardahl affirmed. 'Things that should not be possible for a female of our race … Do you really have to leave, Milord?'

Tuâth reached out and the two friends clasped hands tightly.

'I am afraid so. I have made many mistakes of late and I must bring my family back together again. I must put the needs of my kingdom and my people, above those of myself.'

'But your people are *here* … you will be abandoning them.'

'My people lie across much of Maldahl, as well you know. It need not be forever. I should have spent some time at Brëgwela before now anyhow. It is what is expected.'

'I will miss you, sire.'

'And I you, old friend.'

Exzalander sat up. 'I don't want to go if I'm not allowed to visit Ardahl,' she said stubbornly.

'Ah, somebody's feeling better I see.'

Ardahl beamed at her and she wrinkled her nose. Tuâth and Ardahl sat either side of her on the bed.

'It's not as if you're never going to see him again, little one,' coaxed the king. 'Of course we can arrange for you to visit, if that is your wish.'

Exzalander clambered to her knees, threw her arms about her father and kissed him, appeased by his words. Ardahl smiled wryly, understanding Tuâth's reason for lying to the child.

In all, it was two months, not two days, before they were ready to leave. The royal entourage was not as large as would have been expected and there were those who had given many years of service who remained behind.

Thomn-the-Cleaverhand was not at all surprised to hear that he would not accompany the king to his ancestral home. The king had explained that since he had been gifted title and land, that they needed to be maintained. Thomn had not wanted title or gifts for what he had done and he knew the real reason for his not attending the king at Brëgwela was that he had become so withdrawn; his daily duties had barely concerned him of late. He was to remain on duty at Ealdorbold. His oldest son, Theyl, was to take his place at Brëgwela, and his mother could not have been less proud.

'How can you think of leaving at a time like this?' she ranted. 'Your father is a broken man. If he's to recover, he will need all of us to aid him.

Elsbeth held her son by the arm, and he gazed down into his mother's concerned eyes, trying to smile.

'Father is pleased for me, mother. Can you not find it in your heart to be happy too?'

She winced at the mention of her husband and let go of her son. Walking over to the fire, she removed the boiling pot from the coals. Keeping her back to Theyl, she began to chop vegetables on an old, worn out board.

'He's not your father anymore, don't you see, Theyl? He's a shell, just an empty shell. He needs your help.'

Theyl approached his mother and stopped her chopping with a firm hand. She wheeled around, and burying her head in his chest, she wept. She had been holding so much in, trying to be strong and pretend everything was normal for the sake of Thomn, but it felt that a large piece of her had died along with Thomn's good spirits.

Theyl held his mother close, trying to console her. She pushed him away and wiped her eyes, smiling for his sake.

'Don't mind me,' she said. 'I'm being silly. Tears will solve nothing; I know that well enough. But you ... he'll listen to you.'

Theyl raised his eyebrows and shook his head. 'What could I say, mother, that would ease his guilt? It is a burden that will lessen on its own, in its own time. Besides, the king himself orders me; I have no choice in this matter. I *must* go.'

She continued to smile at him, blinking back the remainder of her tears. It would not do to leave his last image of her, a grief-stricken one.

'Be careful, my son. I will miss you.'

'And I, you.'

One final embrace and Theyl was gone. He made his way to the head of the retinue, having been granted the honour to set them off. Neither Thomn nor Elsbeth went to bid them a final farewell. Caitul however, watched from the woods, following for some way, keeping to the shadows of the trees. He saw his older brother in the shiny new mail and he wished above all else to take Theyl's place.

It was past nightfall before Caitul returned home. He had fully expected a scolding, but Elsbeth sat alone at the table, staring beyond the uneaten dinners. She barely acknowledged him as he greeted her, and he could not push back the pang of loneliness he felt. Despite his many protestations of how grown up he was, all he wanted at that moment was to see her smile as she gathered him up in her arms. But there was no embrace—no warmth; his father's guilt and his mother's all consuming concern for her husband was the only company to be expected now.

Part Three

Nine

Another flash of light was seen from Ardahl's tower as his experiment exploded. Beaky squawked and flapped his wings, as if to fan out the flames.

'Oh dragonsfart!' Ardahl cried, adjusting his spectacles. 'Here boy, what are you waiting for? Put that fire out!'

The old wizard passed his young apprentice a bucket, shooing him toward the accident. The flames were spreading and the smoke made his lungs tighten. Gailon accepted the bucket with a frown—clearly confused.

'But it's empty, Master,' he said.

'Yes empty, boy, like your head! What must you do?'

Gailon smiled with sudden realisation, and muttered a water spell. However, the bucket did not fill, instead, a heavy rain began to fall inside the room. Gailon's eyes filled with fear, as scrolls, utensils and books all soaked up the water. The flames died down, yet he felt that would be little consolation if his master decided to beat him for the damage he had caused.

Ardahl raised his arms and without a word, the rainwater gathered in a single sheet and emptied into the bucket in Gailon's arms, much to his relief.

'Not bad boy, not bad at all,' Ardahl said. 'You're learning. You need to focus, though. No use in panicking in a crisis. That's when mistakes happen … and believe me, boy, a wizard's mistake rarely does anyone any good!'

The bucket felt heavy in Gailon's arms, and he set it down on the, now dry yet slightly scorched, workbench. He felt himself smiling at his master's compliment.

'Now make yourself useful and set some of that water in a cup,' Ardahl ordered. 'We're about to have company.'

'Company? No-one but I knows the way up here anymore.'

'Don't question me, boy ... ah here we are.'

Gailon picked up the cup and almost dropped it again, as a woman appeared from nowhere.

'Your Highness, what a pleasant surprise,' Ardahl said, bowing low. 'It has been too long.'

As he returned to standing, Gailon observed the grin on the wizard's face. It made him look so different. The apprentice had never seen his master smile like that before.

The woman turned to face them both and it seemed to Gailon that her smile filled the dusty old room with sunshine.

'Ardahl, it's so good to see you,' she said.

Running to the wizard's arms, they embraced as old friends. Gailon still stood with an empty cup, gawping at the vision before him. He had not seen the princess since the day she had left and he had been so young that the memory was a dim one. The many years, which had passed since, had truly been kind to Exzalander; she was beautiful. Her smooth, white skin, brilliantly contrasted against her shimmering red hair that hung loose down her back, not braided, as was the fashion at Ealdorbold.

'What are you staring at, boy?' Ardahl growled. 'Get the girl a drink won't ye!'

Gailon found his mouth was hanging open and immediately closed it.

'Ardahl, may I sleep?' Exzalander yawned. 'I am so tired. It still exhausts me to travel thus.'

Still? Gailon thought. *So she has done this before.* He filled the cup with water and held it toward the princess, unblinking in case he lost sight of the beauteous vision before him.

Ardahl noticed his apprentice's fixation and raised a solitary eyebrow of disapproval.

'Come, rest,' he said. 'We will speak later, when you are refreshed.'

She walked over to the bed. 'My thanks to you, Ardahl,' she said.

'Drink?' offered Gailon.

He thrust the water-filled cup under Exzalander's nose. Several drops sloshed in her face and he opened his mouth to apologise, but his throat felt dry and he could not form the words. Her green eyes shone back at him, as if noticing him for the first time,

'Thank you,' she said. Receiving the cup from his hands, it fell from her grasp, crashing to the floor and her eyes closed involuntarily.

Ardahl gently lowered her to the bed and covered her sleeping form with a blanket.

'Clean that up!' he barked at Gailon, who remained unmoving.

'But it's … that's …'

Ardahl stood up and gave a hard stare at his apprentice. 'It's Princess Exzalander, boy. What is wrong with your tongue today? Ordinarily, I have to fight to shut you up.'

'But she just appeared … she's not supposed to here … is she?'

'No of course not! Which is why, young Gailon, that you will say nothing of this to *anyone*; do I make myself clear?'

Gailon ducked his head in acknowledgement and found himself staring back to Exzalander's sleeping form.

'Why did she fall asleep like that, Master?'

Ardahl, seeing his apprentice was too distracted, cleaned the mess up himself.

'She fell asleep, because such majick as she used to get here, is extremely draining. Very few wizards in our history have ever been able to do such a thing, and of those few, even fewer lived to try it a second time.'

Gailon's eyes widened. 'Can you do this majick, Master Ardahl?' he asked.

Ardahl found himself smiling again. 'Yes, I have done it once ... but it nearly killed me. Instead, I experiment with bending reality itself—finding ways to link one place to another, rather than actually moving ones self. Do you wish me to show you?'

'Truly?'

'Yes, but only after Exzalander has returned home. For now, she is our welcome guest. Fetch her some food, BUT no mention of whom it is for, understand? If I hear even a whisper of her presence here being known, then you'll finish this apprenticeship scrubbing out chamber pots!'

Gailon stiffened, knowing the wizard too well to suppose his threat to be an empty one.

'Of course not, Master; I would not dream of it.'

Ardahl nodded, satisfied with Gailon's honesty, or at least, fear of reprisal. He waved the apprentice away, smiling to himself. He normally had more warning of her visits. It gave him the opportunity to dismiss Gailon for a while, making the apprentice the most envied of the household, as nobody else was afforded holidays.

The signing up of new recruits had been brought forward due to a royal visit from Starigorat. Caitul donned his leather jerkin and looked back at the bed where an old sword lay. It was a plain weapon, but perfectly balanced; it was shorter than was the present fashion, however, it was not fashionable young men who were being tested—but capable ones.

He picked up his grandfather's sword and placed it reverently into its scabbard. Hearing voices from the room beyond, he sighed; *so many years have passed where my parents have scarcely noticed me and now they want a say in my future,* he thought.

He took a look at himself in the mirror. He was tall, much taller than his father, taller even than his older brother, Theyl. It was his height that made him look gangly when he was younger, but since he had started daily training, he had begun to fill out. He placed his hand to the hilt of his sword and smiled. As his reflection smiled back, he realised that he barely knew the young man before him. No trace of the happy child he had once been remained; too much pain and loneliness had been his lot. He was nothing more than an empty vessel, yet not content to remain empty; he longed to be filled.

Caitul clenched his jaw and brushed the hair out of his eyes. He felt suddenly nervous about what he was about to do. He had wanted such a thing for so long, yet now his dreams were in his grasp, he felt unsure. Closing his eyes, he held his breath, waiting for the fear and uncertainty to pass. Pacing across the room, he opened the door; ready at last to face his angry parents.

They had stopped shouting; Elsbeth sat, her head in her hands; Thomn stood by the fireplace, staring at flames that were not there.

Thomn spoke, without looking up. 'You're not doing this, Caitul,' he said.

Caitul breathed slowly, trying to remain calm, telling himself that he was supposed to be a man now, and should act like one. 'Father, this is what you always wanted for me. I am surprised that you would allow mother to influence you so …'

Both sets of eyes shot up and glared in Caitul's direction. He felt a sharp feeling of satisfaction at their reaction.

'Your mother is right, Caitul. I will not allow you swear allegiance to a murderer. There is no discussion to be had on this matter …'

'Murderer? What are you talking about? Oh never mind, I know. How can I not when the blood you shed, stained my very existence for so long? It was *your* hand that killed those women, father!'

'On *his* orders!' Thomn snapped. 'When you make an oath, you have no choice. I will not let you be so ruled by a madman, Caitul; that is final.'

'Your words are akin to treason, father. Like it or not, I *will* join the guard.'

Thomn saw a glimpse of the little boy he used to swing around in his arms. He laughed, but it was an empty sound, made by one who had heard laughter, but forgotten how to do it. Elsbeth looked at him, her tired eyes lost in despair.

'Then you'll have to wait another year, Caitul,' he said. 'You forget you are but eighteen and are not of age until next week. Had they not moved the trials forward, you would have been able to try out without my consent; as it stands though, you need my permission and I will not give it.'

Caitul's face faltered and he looked from his father to his mother, then stormed from the house, knowing there was nothing else he could say. He headed for the trials.

'They must let me join—they must,' he hissed under his breath, but his hope and confidence were failing.

As Thomn had warned, Counsellor Faran would not even let him try. He had all records before him, and without permission from the captain, Caitul would not be able to join the guard until the following year. All the pleading about technicalities made no difference.

Caitul hissed his annoyance and stormed away, straight from the grounds, beyond Haesburg, onward into the forest. The sun passed overhead and still he walked on. He cared not where he was headed, as long as he could be away from the madness that was his life.

Eventually he sat, his back to a great tree, as old as the forest itself. He was deep in Ánweald and all about was shady and cool. Unclipping his scabbard from his belt, he unsheathed his weapon, considering its previous owner; he had never met his grandfather, but by all accounts the man was known to be worthy, both honourable and loved. *Still, accounts are not always to be trusted*, he mused.

He began to dream of leaving home. *I could go where I am not known as the son of the great Thomn-the-Cleaverhand, start anew ... but what could I do? A sword for hire?* He felt suddenly chilled and looked about him. It was not a part of the forest that he was familiar with. He shivered and fixed his sword back in its place. The hairs on the back of his neck were on end and he was on his feet in an instant.

A cold fear struck like a hundred hungry knives. Tûlg bordered the far side of Ánweald. Those who were left had been known, on occasion, to risk hunting out so far. If they were to discover who he was ...

His eyes searched the shade beneath the trees—expectant. *Something is amiss*, he thought. *I have to calm my feelings. Fear is not a friend in a crisis. Fear is unworthy of a warrior.* That was something his father had taught him long ago, back when life was simpler. He held up his sword and stood unmoving, listening for the cause of his fear, waiting for it to reveal itself.

He did not wait long.

A man dashed out of the trees to his right, nearly running headlong into Caitul. He had both dagger and sword drawn and grinned viciously at the captain's son.

'You'll not take me without a fight!' the man spat.

He was almost a foot shorter than Caitul, with much darker colouring; Caitul had not seen anyone of the household with hair as dark. The man's style of dress bore similarities to that of the court of Shénnin, and yet it had a foreign look to it. The richness of the cloth left Caitul in no doubt that the man was a noble. Caitul held up his sword hand, but remained ready to defend himself if necessary.

'I mean you no harm,' he said evenly.

'Fiend! You think you can trick me with your honeyed tongue. Your spells have no affect on my people. Prepare to die.'

Caitul's head was spinning. *The man is a foreigner that much is clear, but his words make little sense ... unless he thinks that I am the one pursuing him.*

The man twisted, using both sword and dagger in a manner Caitul was unfamiliar with. The stranger was a blur of motion and Caitul barely blocked the attack in time.

'I am not your enemy,' Caitul protested, as he pushed the stranger away from him.

'You lie! I will not be taken for sport, foul thing.' He attacked again.

Caitul fought well. It was true that had he been of age then he would have been recruited without question, for his skill with a blade was remarkable. Still, here was a sword arm he was unfamiliar with and it took all his skill to adapt to the fighter's unusual style and pace. The man used his feet as well as his weapons and Caitul found he was enjoying himself; all frustration gone, he was doing what he loved and his opponent was most worthy of him. However, he could not fight forever; he knew that whatever the foreigner had been running from could not have been far behind. As if by decision alone, he ended the fight. A punch through the man's defence knocked him onto his back, causing him to drop his sword.

Cursing, the stranger reached for his fallen weapon, but Caitul held his own sword to the man's throat for a moment to prevent him, before holding out his hand. The man scowled and slashed with his knife. Caitul disarmed him with ease.

'I told you I am not your enemy. Why were you running?'

'You know why!' the man spat. 'Stop toying with me and let us finish this.'

Caitul sat on a fallen tree, resting his sword across his knees. 'I will fight no more,' he said.

The stranger backed away and bent to retrieve his sword, not taking his eyes from his opponent for one instant. The sword, however, was not where he had dropped it. The man glanced briefly about him, realising it was nowhere to be seen.

'What trickery is this?' he spat.

Caitul's smile fell from his face and he sat in frozen fear, realising that whilst they had been fighting each other, another had been stealthy enough to remove the stranger's weapon, without being seen or heard. He searched the shadows and jumped to his feet as the pair of cold eyes blinked back at him. The stranger followed Caitul's gaze and saw at last who had actually been pursuing him.

Had he not been so afraid, he might have felt foolish for mistaking Caitul for the thing before him. The only thing the creature shared with Caitul was his great height. Its pale eyes shined and its silver hair was like moonlight in a sky of darkness. It was a thing both terrible and beautiful, appearing more art than life.

A Vampire Ælf.

And he had watched their entire encounter. The Vampire Ælf laughed as it played with the stolen sword, and it was a sound that sent shivers down the length of Caitul's spine.

'How very amusing this has been, but now I am hungry,' the Ælf said. '*You* may avert my spells, but this boy cannot. Do not worry, boy, for your worries are over. Soon you shall sleep and dream the most pleasant of dreams.'

Caitul froze with fear. The Vampire Ælf meant to put him to sleep—to kill him by draining his blood.

'NO WAIT!' he cried. 'You will not want to eat me when I tell you that which you do not know.'

The Vampire Ælf raised an eyebrow, assuming it was some trick. He noticed the other human crawling to retrieve his dagger, but felt amusement rather than a genuine threat.

'You will wish to fight me to the death when you learn the truth,' continued Caitul.

'And what truth is that, human?'

'Who my father is.'

'Why should I care? You are but a meal to me, boy.'

'Thomn-the-Cleaverhand! I am his son!'

The hiss that ensued was the only warning Caitul had before the Ælf leapt at him. No human could leap like that, but Caitul was ready. Many times had soldiers at the palace described the night of the slaughter, so he knew all about how the creatures fought. He moved swiftly and was behind the Vampire Ælf as it landed, thrusting with his blade.

Dark blood flowed forth, but the being yet stood. It fought Caitul with a blind hatred burning in his eyes. Such a look Caitul had never experienced before; it was as though he was being peeled open, layer by layer, to reveal his very soul within. Blind hatred may have given the Vampire Ælf incentive, but it had made him careless. In his fury, he had forgotten all about his original quarry. Having reclaimed his dagger, the man joined the fight.

The two fierce warriors fought against one enraged and injured Vampire Ælf. It was a hard battle, but both warriors adapted quickly to the style of the other and so synchronised their attack to full advantage.

In the end, the battle was won by the original injury. It was a mortal wound; the Vampire Ælf had been too driven by his wrath to realise. He fell to his knees and collapsed to the ground issuing a final curse to Thomn and all his kindred. Caitul decapitated him and at that moment, he held no pity for his father; he had seen their true nature and could only find relief that the thing was dead.

The stranger bent down to retrieve his sword from the fallen Vampire Ælf and collapsed. Caitul turned him over, noticing a gash across the man's left shoulder from which he was losing a lot of blood.

'You fought well, son of Thomn,' he rasped. 'I shall see you well rewarded.'

'Thank me later. For now, let's get you some help before you bleed to death.'

He assisted the stranger to his feet and they hobbled toward Ealdorbold, Caitul supporting the man part of the way and carrying him the rest.

Abuzz with activity, the courtyard was not as Caitul had left it. There were horses, carts, lots of people, many of whom he did not recognise. It appeared that the visitors from Starigorat had arrived earlier than expected.

'Caitul!' called Thomn, pacing over, his full ceremonial uniform looking as though it had seen better days.

'Father, this man has been wounded.' He panted. 'I need Ardahl.'

Thomn signalled to some of the servants to relieve his son's burden.

'I'm afraid Ardahl won't concern himself with healing, but I'll see the man's taken care of.'

As the servants carried the stranger, Caitul took his hand.

'You're safe now, my friend,' he said.

The man's eyes opened and he tried to smile back. 'You have my thanks, son of Thomn.'

Caitul cringed, knowing that his father was in earshot.

'It's Caitul,' he said.

'Ah … thanks to you, Caitul. I am …' but he passed out before he could introduce himself.

Thomn, being curious, took a closer look and quickly signalled another servant.

'Send for Ardahl, *immediately*!' he ordered. 'And tell him that I don't give a kelpie's arse how busy he is!'

Caitul frowned and paced after him as the man was carried inside.

'But father, I thought you said Ardahl would not heal him.'

'Yes, but that was before I knew who *he* is.'

Caitul shrugged.

'He is the son of King Kryepast. The man you have rescued, is the Lord Katahl!'

Ten

'Gailon! Don't you ever knock?' Ardahl dropped his flask and the purple contents spilled out, burning into the table. 'I told you that I was not to be disturbed—for any reason. What part of my orders did you fail to understand?'

'I'm sorry, Master, but Prince Katahl has been seriously wounded. He's housed in the Princess's old chambers. Your presence has been requested.'

Ardahl sighed, not seeming the least bit concerned for anything other than the disturbance.

'He's not a prince,' the wizard grumbled. 'Kings of Starigorat are chosen by the people … I suppose I should go to him, if I must. After all, Tuâth will not be happy if I let the son of his best friend perish. Bring my medicine chest, boy. I shall see you there.'

The wizard stood outside the room, staring at what, at first glance, appeared to be a mirror, but it was much more than that; with the device, Ardahl was able to travel instantly to the places that he had managed to connect it. One such place was near the princess's quarters. He had created the doorway as a way for Exzalander to sneak back to her room, without anyone knowing she was in the tower; it never quite worked out that way, though.

'Don't tarry boy!' he called, as he stepped through and was gone.

Gailon dashed about the room, searching for the case, but saw no sign of it. So long had it been since his master had last made use of it, he wondered if the old wizard had not just disposed of it and had now forgotten. Whatever the reason, it was no longer there, and the sooner he let Ardahl know, the better, the apprentice figured.

'I am here, let me through.' Ardahl pushed though the multitude of servants and made his way to his new patient.

The King of Starigorat, sat at his son's bedside, much paler than Ardahl remembered. Ardahl nodded a greeting to the king and inspected Katahl's wound. He had been stripped and washed, but the gash was still bleeding.

'It does not appear too deep, King Kryepast,' Ardahl said. 'I will attempt to close the wound, if I may.'

'By all means, anything you need.'

'I require only peace.'

Under normal circumstances, the King would have had a man beaten for daring to speak to him in such a manner, but they were not in usual circumstances and Kryepast valued his son's life far more than his own pride.

'Very well, I will leave the servants outside the door, should you require them.'

'My thanks, King Kryepast.'

Closing his eyes, Ardahl placed his hands over the wound and began to work. His major worry was that the young Lord would bleed to death before he could seal it. Cell by cell, he repaired the damage; all the while Katahl grew paler as his life's blood continued to seep away.

The door crashed open and Gailon dashed in, instantly regretting it as he saw his master's face at the interruption.

'Forgive me, Master Ardahl; I could not find it.'

The wizard sighed in exasperation. 'Never mind. I need hydra skin and quickly. It's on the top shelf of the middle bookcase.'

Gailon ran from the room and sprinted off toward the catacombs, determined not to disappoint his master again.

'Oh and I need … oh blast it. Hey girl come here!' Ardahl called to the servant, who was closing the door the apprentice had left open. 'I need you to put pressure on this wound.'

The girl looked terrified as she approached and Ardahl's manner did nothing to put her at ease.

'Put your hand here and press,' he ordered.

The girl winced at the feel of blood on her hand.

'That's it. Now stay like that until I return ... unless you want him to die,' Ardahl finished cruelly. Dashing after his apprentice, he left the terrified servant in charge of the young lord's life.

Gailon was a quick runner and it did not take him long to reach the tower again. He dashed in, giving Beaky a fright. The hydra skin was exactly where Ardahl had said it would be and he gripped the jar triumphantly.

As he made ready to dash back, he noticed Exzalander still sleeping. If anything, she looked even more beautiful than she had before. He drew closer, transfixed by her slumbering form. The food he had brought her, still sat on the small table at her side.

Gailon carefully set the jar down. Reaching out, he stroked back a piece of hair that lay across her face and smiled. The stories his mother had told him of old seemed to have come to life. All he had to do was kiss her, and she would awake ... no more sleep of enchantment. He grinned and bending over her, he touched his eager lips to hers and held them there.

Whatever he imagined would happen, did not include a very angry wizard dragging him away by the ear and beating him about the head.

'I'll deal with you later,' Ardahl fumed. 'OUT!'

Gailon ran as if his life depended on it, indeed he believed that it did. If he lingered, he might have seen the man smile, then giggle and finally guffaw at the boy's audacity.

Gailon was so terrified of his master that he decided it would be death to return. He kept out of the way, hoping that he would be sent for, but hoping in vain.

Ardahl was quite content with Exzalander's company and she was more than capable of assisting him in Gailon's absence. Assisting though, was not as much fun as she remembered and consisted mostly of making tonics to be given to Ardahl's new patient. When Ardahl was requested to take up temporary residence in Katahl's chamber, Exzalander grew even more bored. Tired of being alone in the tower, she threw a cloak about herself and went in search of her friend.

She felt a jolt as she reached her old room ... *so many happy memories.* Quietly, she opened the door and stepped in. The room smelt stale, neglected and there was another aroma, an unpleasant odour of decay that made her stomach turn.

'Ardahl?' she whispered. 'Are you here?'

There was no answer other than a slight cough from her old bed. She approached cautiously, observing the man who had demanded her friend's attention. *He is ill, to be sure,* she thought. His pale skin seemed to hang on his bones and his blue, black hair hung lank at his shoulders. The wound was closed, but there was a colour to it that was all wrong. It was infected inside—the smell in the room, from where Ardahl had attempted to drain it.

'Ardahl is speaking with my father,' Katahl rasped, and then began to cough again.

Exzalander dashed to his side and held a cup of water to his pallid lips.

He drank gratefully. 'Thank you,' he said. He was barely audible and sank back into the sweat-soaked pillows.

Exzalander found herself suddenly furious at that moment, wondering how the man had been allowed to get into such a state. She dipped a towel in the bowl of water at his bedside and dabbed his forehead. She could feel the relief the action brought him. The door opened behind her and she turned suddenly, expecting to see Ardahl. However, it was one of the serving girls with food for the patient.

'Oh forgive me,' said the girl. 'I came to feed him.'

'Leave it with me,' came Exzalander's stern reply. 'Fetch me clean water for washing and clean linen, at once!'

The girl stood, unmoving. 'I'm sorry maam, but I take instructions from Ardahl and he has not ordered such a thing.'

Exzalander removed her hood; the slow realisation entered the girl's eyes, and she curtseyed low.

'Forgive me Your …'

'Shhh,' Exzalander cut in. 'No-one is to be told of my presence here. Am I understood?'

'Yes Your H … maam.'

'Good. Now give me that soup and kindly follow my instructions.'

The girl ran from the room as if there was a fire at her heels. Exzalander closed the door with her foot then made her way back to the fitful patient. Despite his ill state, it was plain to see how handsome the young man was. She blew the soup on the spoon and held it to his lips.

'Eat,' she urged.

The man stirred once more. 'Not … hungry,' he replied and rolled his head toward her. His eyes seemed to brighten just a little as he saw her for the first time and he struggled to keep them open, lest his vision prove to be mere dream, destined to disappear into the ether.

'Please, you must eat,' Exzalander urged.

He smiled at her then, a weak smile, but a smile nonetheless. He opened his mouth, determined to obey the apparition beside him, in everything.

On the servant's return, Katahl had eaten all that he was able and was enjoying having his head bathed once more.

'I've brought what you asked for, maam.'

Two servants entered, one of who would not look at Exzalander and had obviously been suitably threatened by the other.

'Excellent. Now help me get him into that chair. I will wash him whilst you put clean linen on the bed.'

The women did not curtsey, as if too afraid to, but obeyed Exzalander's order, without question. Katahl did not weigh as much as he should, due to his sickness; it made it easier to lift him. His cries of pain stabbed Exzalander as surely as if the pain had been her own.

'I am sorry,' she soothed. 'I am trying to help as best I am able.'

The chair was large enough for two and the patient fitted into it easily. The water was placed at Exzalander's feet and she began to cleanse him. Katahl reached out and without warning, he touched her face. She felt warmth rise to her cheeks; no man was permitted to touch her in such a way, but she was loath to prevent him. It was a pleasant feeling, not just where he touched, but the sensation travelled through her body, to the pit of her stomach. She tried to smile, but could not. Propriety got the better of her at last and gently removing his hand, she continued in her task.

As the girls finished making the bed, they all lifted the patient once more to place him back. This time, however, he did not cry out.

Ardahl entered the room. He noticed the sheets on the floor and the young lord being carried back to bed by three disobedient girls who would know his wrath.

'What is going on here?' he demanded.

One turned, her green eyes daring to glare back at his, and then realisation struck. Katahl observed the wizard's reaction and stared back to Exzalander. Her river of red hair hanging past her waist was all he could see.

'Leave us!' Ardahl barked.

The two girls obeyed, one with a worried glance to their future queen.

'What are you doing here?' he asked.

The princess sat and gently coaxed Katahl's head back, so that she could cool it down once more.

'I came to say goodbye and found your patient in want of much care. Therefore I have decided to assist you … Milord,' she finished carefully, hoping that he would take the hint.

Ardahl understood well that she had not revealed her identity to Katahl; he grimaced at the futility of it. She was clearly unaware of who it was lying in the bed.

'Yes of course you may,' he agreed. You are most welcome. May I speak with you a moment?'

'No!' came Katahl's panicked voice and he grabbed for her hand. 'I would like her to remain with me.'

The feeling was there again, like butterflies fluttering inside her. She breathed hard to regain control and realised too late what Ardahl's answer to such an order was. He muttered a sleep spell and Katahl's eyes closed tight.

'Ardahl,' Exzalander snapped, 'you should not have done that!'

'And you should not interfere, Your Highness. I think perhaps it is time for you to return home. King Kryepast is to journey north tomorrow and you need to be there and awake by the time he arrives—or it's my head!'

'But I can help him, Ardahl. I have an idea. Please assist me in this and then I promise, I *will* leave.'

Ardahl stared hard at her face for a moment and then sighed, utterly incapable of being angry with her for long.

'Let me hear your idea,' he surrendered.

Exzalander beamed and signalled for him to come closer.

'The poison inside—if we remove it, then he will get better?'

'Yes,' Ardahl said, with a frown. 'I keep draining the infection, but I can never get it all; I fear it is spreading.'

'If we made an incision, the poison could be moved by majick,' suggested the princess. 'You taught me how to move objects with my mind … well, why can I not move the product of infection through an incision? Once it is taken from the body, I could move your treatment into the heart of the wound to aid his healing,' she finished eagerly.

Ardahl laughed. 'So simple ... why did I not think of that? I was so caught up in healing remedies and I forgot about my more basic majick skills. Let us try it then, but I think it wise that I perform the task. Do you wish to make the incision?'

The princess stared distastefully from the wound to the knife he produced and she backed away.

'Oh Ardahl ... I don't think I can.'

The old wizard smiled at her reaction, wondering how much her father had told her of her destiny. *The future warrior of Taiohāhn—squeamish at the thought of a small cut,* he thought.

'How about you hold the bowl and close your eyes. I will do the rest.'

She readily agreed and at once, screwed her eyes shut. She knew the moment Ardahl had used the dagger, as the smell that invaded her nostrils threatened to make her faint or vomit—or both. It seemed an age sitting there, gripping the bowl whilst the wizard worked. She was tempted to take a look at his progress, yet could not summon the will, fearful that she would lose all control over her faculties. She felt a towel over her hands and the smell retreated a little.

'It is done,' said the wizard at last.

Exzalander cautiously opened her eyes and placed the pus-filled bowl at the bedside, cringing. Already the patient had a little more colour in his cheeks, and the wound was almost invisible.

'It worked?' she asked.

'I believe so. Although I won't know for certain for a while, but you promised you would go.'

Exzalander stroked the patient's hair and boldly kissed him on the forehead, before turning her attention to Ardahl and giving him a bear hug.

'Farewell Ardahl, I hope to see you soon. Perhaps next time we might actually have some fun.'

Ardahl smiled. 'We can only hope, Your Highness,' he said, and bowed low.

When he stood once more, she had disappeared. He felt a sense of both sadness and relief as she left him.

'Until next time,' he whispered.

By the evening, Katahl was awake and asking for Ardahl. To his pleasant surprise, he found Caitul had accompanied the wizard to enquire after his health.

'Caitul! How wonderful to see you. I have not had a chance to thank you for all you did.'

'No thanks are necessary,' Caitul said, bowing.

Katahl beamed at Caitul's reverence; none of Shénnin's household ever bowed to him. Such a bow was a statement of loyalty and by doing so Caitul was showing how much Katahl meant to him. Katahl signalled for his new friend to come forward.

'I have never seen a fighter like you,' he said. 'Are you in the Guard?'

Caitul clenched his jaw. He breathed and thought carefully how to answer. He did not wish to upset his new friend by informing him that it was his family's arrival that had ruined his life.

'No ... I hope to be though,' he said.

Katahl slapped him on the shoulder, wincing as the tenderness of his wound got the better of him.

'Bah,' he said, 'you are made for greater things than that. Your skills will be put to better use in *my* house. I ask you to become First Knight. At present my guards are of my father's choosing, but I am just come of age and have already been chosen his successor. It is therefore my responsibility to choose my own knights. You have proven yourself most worthy, my friend and I would have no-one else.'

Caitul felt suddenly torn between his own ambition and his creeping doubts.

'What say you, Caitul? Will you accept this honour?'

'It is indeed an honour,' Caitul agreed. 'But I am sure that there are others more worthy than I. You would do better to choose someone from your own house surely. They will know your culture and ways. I alas, am ignorant of such things.'

Katahl stared hard at Caitul, as if trying to fathom him out, and then he laughed.

'Mere trifles, my friend. I choose he who is most fit to serve me, and that man is you. Nothing short of you breaking an oath to another, would change my mind. As you have already, by your own admission, claimed you have made no oath, then I am determined my First Knight shall be you.'

Caitul suddenly beamed and stood up tall. 'Then I'm your man, Milord.'

'That is well. I will send word to my father. You will accompany him to Brëgwela and on your journey my other chosen will begin your instruction.'

'And you, Milord?'

Katahl gave a slow smile, which hid more than he said. 'I will remain here. I am not yet well enough to travel.'

'Forgive me, Milord, I was led to believe you were mending.'

'Tis true, but I need more rest. I will see you on your return and you can tell me all that occurred. Perhaps you will catch a glimpse of the Princess Exzalander. I hear that she is quite a beauty.'

Ardahl winced and found himself glad that Katahl was not to accompany his father. '*Disaster may yet be averted*,' he thought.

Caitul bowed low and left the young lord to rest.

'Now Ardahl,' Katahl said excitedly, 'you must tell me who she is.'

Ardahl swallowed hard as he approached the bed, hoping he had misread the look in the young lord's eyes.

'Who, Lord Katahl?'

'The girl of course; I *must* see her again.'

Ardahl opened his mouth to reply, and then closed it, unsure how to answer. *The truth is bound to get out eventually,* he considered. *Yet I can at least prolong the inevitable by lying, yet lying to a noble (albeit a foreign noble) is not something I relish doing. Although, if King Tuâth discovers that his daughter has been visiting me without permission and in such a way ... not to mention whose bed she had slept in ...*

'Well wizard? Tell me,' Katahl insisted.

The wizard Ardahl was so relieved when King Kryepast arrived that he almost kissed him. He nodded to the two men and made a hasty exit. Now that Katahl was better, he would not need to attend him.

My orders come directly from the king, he thought. *I only saved the boy, as I knew that Tuâth himself would have ordered it done. I'm safe ... for the moment.*

Eleven

Having been informed of his son's decision, Kryepast approached the Council regarding Caitul. He knew there was nothing they could legally do to prevent his acceptance of position, but requesting his release was a sign of respect to his host.

'Caitul ... ah yes,' High Counsellor Danah said. 'His father is captain of our guard and Lord of Haesburg. He is a worthy man who has done this kingdom great service in his time. You have good leave to accept his son into your service. We wish him well. And may Your Majesty have a safe trip to our beloved king and queen.'

'My thanks to you, Danah. I leave my most treasured possession in your keeping until our return.'

'We are honoured to care for him and will treat him as a prince of our house, I can assure you.'

Elsbeth stood staring at her son, his shiny black armour, reflecting her shocked expression. Caitul had expected her words of scorn not the tight embrace, which followed. He wished suddenly that the metal skin did not obstruct the warmth of that embrace; so long it had been, it was but a distant, yet pleasant memory.

'I am so proud of you, my son,' she said. 'Long have I waited for this day.'

Caitul stepped back from his mother, confusion darkening his features.

'I have known that you would become a knight and serve another, for I was told,' she said. 'The wizard Fahl attended you long ago and he looked into your future. I did not tell you of it again, as you had seemed to forget. The wizards had become so unpopular and were officially banished so I thought it best not to refresh your memory.'

Caitul ruffled his hair, as he always did when thoughtful. 'It came to my mind as you spoke of it,' he said. 'Like a dream long lost. So are you truly happy for me, mother?'

Elsbeth took his hands in hers and kissed them.

'I am sorry that we were not as happy as we should have been, my son, but I never stopped loving you.'

Caitul felt suddenly torn in two. He had become so accustomed to the coldness of his mother, that he had weathered himself against it, but now, wrapped in the warmth of her embrace once more, it was as though the walls he had built to protect himself, simply melted away. He was a boy again, basking in his mother's love.'

'I shall miss you, mother,' he said at last, trying to steady his rising emotion.

'Oh my son,' she cried, and the tears were of both happiness and regret. 'You must say goodbye to your father, Caitul. Don't leave without making peace with him, please.'

Caitul squeezed her, reassuring her that he would. He had few possessions to pack, but his grandfather's sword, he wrapped and stored away with great reverence. Taking one last look back at his room, he went in search of his father.

As soon as Katahl was well enough, he began his hunt for the girl who had cared for him. Nobody had provided him with any answers and Ardahl could not be contacted. He realised that if he ever hoped to find her, then he would have to do so himself. But all the servants he spoke to, said they knew nothing and that it was Ardahl alone who had cured him.

He sighed in frustration as he left the servant's quarters and headed out into the palace gardens. Taking a deep breath of air, he felt instantly refreshed, for too long had he been indoors. He sat by the fountain and ran his hand through the water, playing back in his mind all that he could remember of the girl. It dawned on him then, the way in which she had spoken to Ardahl had not been the manner of a servant at all. He searched hard in his memory for the clothes the girl had worn, but all he could recall was her cloak, that and her eyes, as they bore into his very soul.

He shook himself suddenly, trying to divert his feelings back to facts, which might assist in locating her. *She had been coming to say goodbye*, he thought. *She was well acquainted with the wizard and he was certainly not her superior. Her accent was a little strange — more than a hint of northern to it, so she might be from Wilbec or possibly Brëgwela. The wizard seemed to be uncomfortable for her to be seen with him.*

Perhaps she is an illegitimate daughter ... an old mistake or ... his lover? No, she could not be ...'

'Milord?'

Katahl blinked and saw a young serving boy before him.

'Milord, I was sent to look for you and inform you that you should be resting.'

'I am done resting,' Katahl replied, with a frustrated sigh. 'I want to speak with the wizard.' He stood suddenly and glared up at Ardahl's Tower, as if he would scale it if necessary.

'Forgive me, Lord Katahl, but there is no way that we can reach him. His apprentice has not been seen in over a week now and he is the only one here who knows the way up to the tower. Everyone has been made aware of your request and should Ardahl or Gailon show themselves, then they will be told to meet with you. Until then, there is nothing that can be done, but be patient.

'Many amusements have been arranged for your pleasure and your father informed us of your favourite dishes so you can feel more at home here. If there is ought else you would like, then I'm sure that I can arrange it.'

A smile began to spread from ear to ear and Katahl looked back to the eager young boy.

'Yes,' he said. 'I would like to see all of the servants who attended me whilst I was sick. I will be in the Council Chamber and I expect them to attend me there within the hour. *That* is what I want.'

The boy nodded and ran back toward the palace.

'I *will* find her,' Katahl said. He felt as though the sun had come out from behind the clouds at last.

Caitul was enjoying life on the road more than he thought possible. He had become acquainted with the other knights and was quickly learning the rules and etiquette required to be a member of Kryepast's household. They were not all that different to those of Tuâth's guard—a little more pomp and ritual perhaps.

He sat by the fire with fellow knight, Nimrïn and rubbed his arms. Nimrïn smiled, passing him a piece of bread.

'Just got to get used to this new sword,' explained Caitul. 'It's bigger than what I'm used to that's all.'

His companion laughed; it was a good-natured laugh that lit up his entire face, accentuating the lines around his brown eyes. 'Well, you have the height to pull it off,' he said. 'Keep practising and you'll soon have the muscle to match.'

Caitul lay back and watched his companions as they ate and sharpened their weapons, as well as their wit. Nimrïn was his favourite companion; he was the warmest and had a mischievous sense of humour. The other knights teased Nimrïn because of his insistence on growing his hair long, which he wore in a ponytail that hung past his shoulder blades. He was tall, though not quite the height of Caitul, and he was stockier. Dahal was the most severe of the knights; he rarely smiled and seemed to fix his face into a permanent frown. He was the shortest of them, his hair closely shaven in the manner of the Ptee Tsa with whom he had lived for many years as escort to Starigorat's ambassador. Nimrïn joked that Dahal had still got feathers up his ass, which is why he was so humourless.

Finally, there was Aarnon, who was good-natured and softly spoken. He seemed to have received the most schooling and only really spoke when he felt there was something worth saying. He had dark hair, as did the majority of his people, but his was flecked with red, which was unusual and indicated a person of majick ability or potential. Wizardry being frowned upon (and outlawed in several places) meant that Aarnon was not sent to be apprentice. His mother had attempted to colour his hair so that he was not discovered and sent him for combat training at the fortress instead. It had been Katahl who had discovered Aarnon's secret when they sparred in the rain. As the water washed the colour from his hair, the other men backed away, all but Katahl who was not as superstitious as others. Aarnon had been devoted to Katahl ever since.

Caitul smiled. He was lucky to have such companions, lucky to be so welcomed. He began to feel that his life, which had been on hold for so many years, had finally begun again.

Lord Katahl sat in the Council Chamber and spoke with Counsellor Sohãhn, until the servants arrived.

'Now Sohãhn, perhaps you might assist me in a mystery. These two women assisted Ardahl in curing me. Is that not so?'

The women nodded timidly. They had never been in the Council Chamber before; servants knew that it was better to remain unnoticed by counsellors.

'Excellent,' Katahl said, with a smile. He beckoned them forward. 'Now tell me, who was the other woman who was there the day my fever broke?'

One woman glanced nervously to the other, but that other seemed confused.

'There was no other, Lord Katahl,' she said. 'Ardahl does not like a lot of people around him, so only *we* were chosen and we worked in shifts.'

Katahl stared hard at the woman who had kept silent. She still stole nervous glances to the other girl, but for the most part, she stared at the flagstone floor.

'You were together *that* day. I remember it. You helped me to the chair and changed my bed linen.'

'Forgive me, Milord,' stuttered the girl. 'I have no wish to contradict you, but you were very ill; you could have imagined it.'

Katahl clenched his jaw in frustration and turned to Counsellor Sohãhn.

'I did not imagine it, Sohãhn. These two and one other were in my room that day.' Turning back to the servants, he tried to soften his manner. 'You are not in any trouble. I just want to know about the third person, then you are free to go—with my thanks,' he finished, jingling his purse as a means of encouragement.

But still the woman remained adamant that she had tended to the lord alone. Counsellor Sohãhn approached them, holding the eyes of the girl who had spoken, as if discerning the truth to her words. Without warning, he grabbed the other girl, holding her face in his hand, squeezing until she whimpered with pain.

'And you? Why do you stay silent? Answer Lord Katahl's questions, or face punishment. I am sure that I could think of something suitably amusing for you, something that could last days if necessary.'

Her eyes widened in terror, spilling hot tears down her reddened cheeks. Katahl made a move to intercede, but stopped as the girl began to speak.

'We *did* tend the Lord Katahl together,' she stuttered.

'And was there another?' Sohãhn barked.

'Yes,' the girl sniffed. 'But I don't know who it was. I was ordered to keep my head down and not look at the woman if I wanted to keep my position. I was scared and did as I was bid. I have a sick mother to feed. I can't afford to lose my ...'

The girl gave way to tears and Katahl rested a hand on the counsellor's shoulder to draw him away from her. Sohãhn let the girl go, yet continued to glare as Katahl guided the weeping girl to a chair, pouring her a goblet of wine to calm her. He turned his attention back to the first girl, who was staring confused at her friend.

'What say you now?' he asked.

'It's not true ... least ways if Molly did attend you with someone else, then it wasn't me. I swear it.'

Both men turned to Molly, whose tears had slowed and the wine did its work.

'But it was *you* who ordered me,' she said. 'Why don't you tell them what they want to know? Please Hettle.'

Counsellor Sohãhn approached the fire and held a taper to the flames. He crossed back to where Hettle stood, confused and expectant. Passing the light before her eyes, he watched the reaction closely.

'What is it, Sohãhn?' Katahl asked.

The Counsellor blew out the flame and sucked in his cheeks as if suddenly angry, but not wanting to show as much.

'Wizardry ... she tells the truth as she recalls it. Ardahl must have put a spell on her.'

'Can we remove it?'

Sohãhn raised his eyebrows at Katahl, as if surprised by the man's ignorance.

'Only Ardahl can do that,' he said.

Katahl turned back to Molly, who had finished her wine and appeared to sway slightly.

'When did you last see Ardahl?' he asked.

'He arrived just as we put you back into bed and sent us from the room. He was very angry.'

'And that was the last time?'

'Yes. I was not meant to be working that day and had been granted some time to nurse my mother. I have not been in the palace grounds.'

Katahl smiled reassuringly, pressing a silver coin into the girl's hand.

'I hope that your mother gets better soon, Molly,' he said.

He rewarded Hettle in kind and dismissed them with thanks, all under the disdainful eye of Counsellor Sohãhn, who did not like the young lord's way of dealing with troublesome servants.

'Why all the secrecy?' Katahl asked. 'How can I possibly find her now?'

'Forgive me for asking, Lord Katahl, but why is it so important that you do so?' He poured them both a goblet of wine, and yet drank none of his own.

'You will excuse me if I refrain from answering. It is not a question with which I am comfortable at present.'

The counsellor smiled knowingly, as if guessing the answer without Katahl having spoken the words.

'Describe her to me, Lord Katahl. If, as you believe, she is not a servant, it could be that I am acquainted with this woman. Perhaps I can assist. Is there anything in particular that you recall about her?'

Katahl took a deep draught of wine and grinned at the counsellor.

'She was beautiful,' he said. 'She had eyes as green as the grass in spring and her voice was soft, yet authoritative at the same time. Her hair ... well I have never seen anything like it; it was pure red and shone like the evening sun.'

Had Katahl not been gazing dreamily into his cup, he might have noticed the colour drain from Sohãhn's face; he might have seen the look of realisation in the man's eyes. But all he saw was his own reflection in the deep burgundy contents of the goblet.

'Red you say?' Sohãhn said, his voice revealing nothing. 'That is interesting. Such hair colour is indicative of wizard skill. Perhaps Ardahl has been training this person. If so, it is no wonder that he wishes it to remain a secret. Such an act would be considered treason and would so mean his death. I will order an investigation, Milord. Trust me, if I find out who your mystery girl is, you will be the first to know.'

'Thank you my friend.' Katahl beamed, and raised his goblet.

In Sohãhn's mind, he was already plotting the removal of Ardahl, either for treason or for, as he well knew, harbouring and training the princess herself. Sohãhn smiled back at the lord and this time, he took a drink, feeling the need to celebrate.

Twelve

Beth was a good liar, the best in her opinion, for she knew how to lie to a king. She had done so successfully for many years and her skill with dishonesty only improved with practice. She took great pride in the trust her mistress placed upon her and she was well rewarded for her work. For the most part, Beth was a mediocre lady's maid, but there were occasionally times when other skills were required. It was on the latter that she was tested and so appointed.

Beth was servant to the royal house of Tuâth and Shénnin; her mistress was none other than the heir to the throne, Princess Exzalander. It was a great honour and responsibility and Beth enjoyed her work. She had it easier than most, as Exzalander was more independent than expected of a person of rank; the princess valued her privacy too, so there were often times when Beth had free time. She used such occasions well and studied hard. The past week had been most enjoyable. She had practised handwriting and read two books. Exzalander had given her use of paints and canvas too. She made the odd appearance to collect food for the princess and lie about Exzalander's whereabouts and commitments.

She enjoyed sitting alone in the royal chamber, eating Exzalander's meals. The royal chef was a master at his craft and when Beth passed on Exzalander's praise, it was really coming from her.

Beth plumped up the pillows on Exzalander's bed and lit the fire. Expecting Exzalander's arrival from one her "trips" had become a sense with her. Sure enough, no sooner was the fire blazing, that Exzalander returned, right in the spot from whence she had disappeared.

'Welcome back, Your Highness,' Beth said, with a deep curtsey.

Exzalander stumbled and Beth ran forward to assist her.

'My thanks,' the princess said. 'Any problems?'

Beth removed Exzalander's cloak and unclasped her dress, all the while guiding her over to the bed, as she knew what was to follow.

'Nothing I could not handle. The king did want to speak to you earlier—something about a royal visit. I told him that you were sick and did not want to be disturbed.'

'What would I do without you, Beth?' The princess yawned, as her dress fell to the floor and she slipped into bed.

Beth drew up the covers and smiled down at her mistress as she fell asleep.

Captain Theyl turned out the guard in preparation for King Kryepast's visit. He was pleased to see all uniforms clean and shiny.

King Tuâth inspected the eager guards with a nod of approval.

'I expect that you are looking forward to this visit, Theyl,' he said. 'Kryepast's people are bound to bring you a letter from home.'

Theyl tried to smile at the king. Although Tuâth had made every effort to befriend him, he remained wary. The memory of his father still haunted his thoughts. He did not ever want to feel betrayed as his father had and if he was never a friend to the king, then he was just a soldier following orders, should some heinous command be issued.

'Yes, they may,' Theyl replied, 'though my parents seldom write.'

He saw a shadow pass over Tuâth's face for the briefest of moments and then was gone. The king nodded and walked away. Theyl found that he could not be sorry for making the man remember what had been done to his family.

Queen Shénnin walked out to meet her husband. She had arrayed herself in deepest purple in honour of their expected guests, for purple was a favourite in Starigorat.

'I have sent for Exzalander,' she said, 'but her maid insists that she is too unwell to leave her bed. It has been three days now and I am worried. Every time I visit her, she is in deep sleep and I am unable to rouse her. Do you think that we should send for Ardahl?'

Tuâth frowned. 'It will be days before the message reaches him and days more before he will arrive. If she is not in pain or distress, then I say no; leave it for our healer here.'

'It seems likely that she may sleep through Kryepast's visit. How is that going to look?'

Tuâth leaned forward and kissed his wife on the cheek.

'She cannot help being ill, my love.'

Shénnin pursed her lips. 'I know ... I just wish I knew what was wrong with her,' she said, taking her husband's arm.

'Well whatever it is, I am sure that bed rest is the best thing for her.'

Bugles sounded suddenly, as the king of Starigorat was sighted in the distance. Envoys were sent to greet them and lead them to the castle.

The king and queen beamed at their old friend's approach and Captain Theyl stood the castle guards to attention as the procession rode in. There, among the knights, was a face so similar to his brother that he felt his heart jolt. It had been many years since they had last seen each other, but still he thought the man looked like Caitul. The knight noticed Theyl as well and he smiled, giving a wave in greeting. There was no doubt—no mistaking that smile.

'It cannot be,' Theyl whispered, as he stared back.

Tuâth came forward and hugged his friend in welcome. Compliments were exchanged and then began the questions.

'What a pity your son could not attend,' Tuâth said, 'I had so hoped to meet him again. He must be a grown man by now.'

King Kryepast nodded as he was guided across the courtyard.

'Pity indeed. He set off with us, but insisted on hunting alone in your woods. He was injured and is still being cared for at Queen Shénnin's Palace.'

''Tis most grievous news,' Shénnin affirmed.

'Oh, do not concern yourself. Ardahl worked miracles on him, and your boy here, saved his life.'

'Our boy?' Tuâth asked quizzically.

'He is the son of Thomn-the-Cleaverhand and now First Knight to my son and right pleased we are to receive him into our house.'

Theyl, who stood nearby, could scarcely trust his ears — *my brother: a knight.*

Tuâth smiled to Caitul and beckoned him forward.

'You make us proud, Caitul. I expect you would like to speak with your brother. Your Majesty, I am sure that you would not mind Caitul being released from his duties for a time, so that they can reunite.'

'Of course not, Tuâth. Caitul go, be with your brother. We will send for you if we have need of you.'

Caitul bowed in the manner of the knights of Starigorat. It was a short bow with a hand to the heart in symbol of loyalty. He walked over to his brother, who continued to stand to attention, until Tuâth dismissed him.

As the royal party entered the castle in search of refreshment, the two brothers, long parted, embraced one another and laughed at the strange meeting.

Beth stared down from a window high above and smiled at the pretty colours of the procession. She would have liked to attend, but as the princess was still abed, Beth's place was at her side. She sighed as all the beautiful dresses and splendour moved from sight, and her eyes fell upon the handsome Theyl, as he walked off with a knight of Starigorat.

The soldiers cleared and all returned to normal. Beth went back to her book. Several hours passed before a knock came at the door and she moved to answer it. It was Clarissa, come to enquire after the princess again.

'She is still sleeping,' Beth said. 'If there is any change, then I will send word.'

Clarissa nodded her head stiffly and glanced to the unconscious Exzalander, tucked up in bed. Clarissa did not much care for Beth and made little effort to hide the fact. She found the girl over confident with an air about her, as if she was somehow better than other servants. She made her way along the corridors and descended the great stone stairs. Even from that distance, she could hear the celebration coming from the Great Hall. She did not relish having to give her mistress the news.

The room was all smiles and the wine flowed freely as she entered. The three royals were deep in conversation; Tuâth held his wife's hand, kissing it at some remark from his friend. Clarissa bent, whispering in Shénnin's ear and saw the answering frown as she stood tall and took her place behind the queen's throne.

'So Shénnin, I see your lady returns,' King Kryepast said. 'Where then is your daughter? Not shy I hope. Has she heard how all the knights are eager to make her acquaintance and put her dance skills to the test?'

Shénnin felt her husband tense. He kept his countenance, all but a vein protruding from his forehead. She knew only too well, the cause of his concern. He was not being an overprotective father, nor was he refusing to see that his daughter was no longer a little girl. No, Tuâth was haunted by the prophecy of old and although it had been many years since he had allowed it to hang as a dark cloud over their lives, occasionally something would remind him and he fought to hold to their present happiness so that he did not once more, fall into despair.

Shénnin reassuringly squeezed her husband's hand.

'I am afraid Exzalander will have to disappoint the young men who accompany you,' she said. 'She has been unwell and keeps to her bed. I had hoped that there may have been some improvement, but alas, she is still not well enough to join the company.'

'I am sorry indeed to hear that,' Kryepast said. 'Both our children abed … you would think the young would be made of sterner stuff; still, we can be merry and pretend that we are still young, as our children are not here to chide us,' he laughed.

Tuâth raised his goblet and drank to that happy thought.

Caitul introduced Theyl to his fellow knights and they wiled the night away, reminiscing about frivolous and trivial things from their childhood. Caitul, who was unaccustomed to alcohol, eventually sagged forward and was carried from the hall to Theyl's abode, where the captain found Beth waiting for him.

'Who is he?' she asked, with a breathy voice.

'My brother. Help me to bed with him will you.'

She obeyed at once and assisted Theyl carry him indoors where they proceeded to strip him of his footwear and outer garments and lay him into bed.

'Where will you sleep now, Captain?' the girl asked suggestively, flashing Theyl her most seductive smile.

Theyl gave a crooked grin in return and shook his head. 'My brother …'

'Is asleep and will not wake easily,' she cut in, taking his hand and pulling him toward her.

He stared down at her beautiful dark eyes and his gaze slid further still, to her ample bosom.

'Beth, we've talked about this,' he said. 'I'm too old for you.'

She pressed against him and he felt a stirring in his groin, which he fought to keep at bay.

'You would not refuse me, Captain?' she breathed, as she put her arms about him. 'That is most ungallant of you.'

He was losing control and the wine he had consumed, only made his defeat more certain. He breathed hard as she rubbed against him.

'Damn it woman … should you not be tending the princess? I thought that she was ill.'

Beth stood up on tiptoes and stopped his mouth with her parted lips. It was more than Theyl could bear and he returned her kiss whilst tearing at her bodice. All thoughts of the presence of his brother had gone from his mind, as he grappled her to the floor.

Exzalander awoke, both hungry and eager that she must not upset her parents by her continued absence. After Beth helped her into her white and purple gown, she was dismissed, leaving Exzalander to make her own way to the celebration. She hid behind a pillar as a drunken knight was carried past her, supported by Captain Theyl. Exzalander could smell the alcohol from her hiding place and found herself frowning with disapproval.

When she was alone once more, she peaked into the hall. She could see no sign of the man she had assisted and concluded that Ardahl must have kept him at the palace. Once satisfied that she was safe, she slipped in and made her way to the king's table. She was quite pleased her entrance was not announced and that they were too deep in conversation, and drink, to notice her.

Standing before the two kings, she curtseyed.

'Exzalander!' Tuâth announced. 'Are you feeling better?'

She beamed at him.

'Yes father, I am most rested now. However, I seem to have missed this evening's festivities—more's the pity.'

'Nonsense,' slurred her father. 'Come, sit with us—eat!'

Exzalander smiled her thanks and took her place next to her mother. She found it difficult to eat with decorum and her stomach growled for sustenance.

Shénnin stroked her daughter's hair and whispered in her ear.

'Are you sure that you are well enough to be here? You look so pale.'

Exzalander had her mouth full, so attempted a smile and nod to brook no pause in her eating.

By the evening's end, the only man Exzalander had bothered to stop eating for long enough to dance with, was Kryepast. As the king took his seat again, he was out of breath, clearly unaccustomed to such an activity.

'Quite the charmer your young one, Tuâth,' he said. 'Won't be long before she's breaking hearts, you mark my words.'

Tuâth *did* mark them and found that by the time he retired for the night, he had a very bad headache.

As Exzalander arrived back at her chamber, she was more than full and began to regret having eaten so much. It had not been an enjoyable evening; her mother had continued to bombard her with questions and she had not the skill of her maid for lying.

She fell back onto her bed and called for Beth. There was no answer and she remembered that she had sent the girl away.

Trying, without success, to reach the hooks on the back of her gown, she soon gave up and lay back on her bed again, resigning herself to stay fully dressed until her servant returned.

Thirteen

As the sun rose, the crowing of a cock awakened Caitul. The sound seemed to thunder through his head and he blinked, wishing he could have stopped the morning light from stabbing his eyeballs so. He groaned and turned over, spying his brother entwined about a naked woman before the dying embers of the fire.

His hangover seemed temporarily cured as he stared at the smooth contours of soft flesh before him. His eyes moved up the length of the woman's body, before he realised that she was awake and staring back at him. She did not seem angry at his intrusion, but rather, was smiling in a way that made him more than a little nervous.

Caitul looked away and the woman detangled herself from Theyl, sitting up, her bare breasts greeting the day.

'Good morning,' she said quietly.

He glanced back to her, expecting her to have reached for some clothes and was both disturbed and fascinated to see that she had not. Try as he might, he could not avert his eyes from her breasts. She seemed to be enjoying his attention and began to toy with herself.

Part of him was appalled by her behaviour, yet his instincts as a man kept his mouth firmly shut, and his eyes fixed. She got to her feet, after what seemed like an age to the young knight, and began to dress. Theyl turned over and snored. Caitul watched the woman silently, as if judging a threat. He followed her approach and was horrified when she lifted her skirts and straddled him. She laid a finger across his lips, which opened too late to speak his protest. Her other hand found the involuntary bulge in his breeches and rested there.

'I will try and return later if I can,' she said. 'Stay sober tonight and I will please *both* of you.'

She slipped out of the door and Caitul sat unmoving, until he could breathe once more. Reaching for the bucket, he vomited. The sound was enough to wake his brother at last.

'You all right, brother?' Theyl asked.

Caitul heaved, as he came back up for air. 'Yes,' he replied.

Theyl sat up and glanced about him. 'Beth gone?'

'Yes.' Caitul grimaced, feeling ill once more. 'Please put some clothes on, man. Am I not sick enough?'

Theyl laughed and the sound was like glass shattering inside Caitul's skull.

'It's not my fault you can't take your drink, little brother,' he said.

Caitul ruffled his hair and went in search of water, trying to put thoughts of the odious woman from his head, cursing his body for being so weak.

Beth found her mistress asleep, fully clothed. She smiled and lit the fire, preparing the water before gently awaking the princess.

'You should have sent for me, Your Highness,' she said. 'Here, let me help you out of that gown.'

Exzalander was insistent that her decision was the right one and wanted to hear all about Beth's excursion. She felt herself blushing as Beth described Theyl's talent in bed. But she seemed less than amused at the teasing of the brother, once she was informed of his position in the house of Kryepast.

'You should not have done that, Beth. What if he were to tell someone? We would *both* be in trouble.'

Beth laughed harshly, as if thinking her mistress silly.

'He was terrified, Your Highness. I doubt he will even tell his brother, let alone the court.'

'Still, he is a knight and you should have shown more respect.'

Beth laughed, taking the princess's hands in her own. 'He is but a man, Your Highness, and what are men, but playthings for our amusement,' she said. 'One day you will learn how your body can be used in such a way. Maybe you should introduce yourself to the knight. I am sure that he could give you much pleasure.'

'Beth!' Exzalander pulled away, abashed.

'I was only teasing you, Milady. Come, let us get you dressed.'

Exzalander chose a deep red gown, encrusted with rubies and pearls at the neck and girdle. She walked out and down to breakfast, the words of Beth still playing through her mind.

It was only her mother and King Kryepast at the table when she arrived. She smiled in greeting.

'Exzalander,' Shénnin said, 'come break your fast with us. Your father has had to meet with a messenger, on a matter of some import apparently, so we may start without him.'

They only got halfway through eating when an old servant entered and bowed low.

'Forgive my interruption, Your Majesty,' he said, 'but the king has requested Princess Exzalander's presence immediately.'

Shénnin looked at Exzalander, who shrugged, genuinely confused.

'Can it not wait until after breakfast?' Shénnin snapped.

'I am afraid not, Your Majesty. The king was quite insistent.'

The queen was staring hard at the old man, as if considering whether to assert her authority. Exzalander stood, deciding that it was better to obey than cause a disagreement between her parents.

'It is all right, mother,' she said. 'I will see you later.' She curtseyed to them both and followed the man as he wound his way through the castle.

'Where are we going?' she asked. 'This part of Brëgwela is not even used any longer.'

'I am taking you to the king, Your Highness,' the man replied dryly. He stopped at a doorway, bowed, and then left.

Cautiously, She opened the door to see the room had been lit. There was a musty smell in the air that spoke of the room's neglect. Her father stood in the corner, his back to her.

'Father, I am come as I am bid,' she said. 'Is everything all right?'

As he turned, she saw the look of fury on his face and was suddenly fearful.

'No, everything is not all right,' he seethed. 'How do you explain this?'

As he thrust the message into her hand, she noticed the broken seal of the Council of Shénnin. Her heart sank, as she guessed only too well what it was about.

'You were seen!' the king hissed. 'Now the Council is calling for Ardahl's head.'

Exzalander's eyes widened as the contents of the letter made one thing clear. 'It does not mention me ... you *knew*! You knew that I visited. Why have you not said so before? If you know it is me, then you can inform the Council and they will see that things are not how they say.'

'Yes I knew,' Tuâth said. 'Of course I did. Do you take your father for a fool? You did this before we left. I saw the effects of the majick. I knew you would try again, but kept quiet for your mother's sake. She needed to believe that you were safe and I knew I could not separate you from Ardahl without allowing such a thing. But now ... you are caught. Why did you leave the safety of the tower? He is being accused of treason, Exzalander ... treason! Do you know what that means? Do you even care?'

'Oh course I care,' she snapped back. 'How can you even ask me that? This is all a misunderstanding. Just tell the Council that it was me ...'

'You were not announced. Your visit did not follow the laws of protocol. Your presence there cannot be made known without it seeming like some plot against the Council ... or me.'

'You make the laws father; you can change them,' she replied flippantly.

The king shook her by the shoulders and she felt tears stinging her eyes at the sign of his anger toward her.

'You fool,' he said. 'You understand nothing. My law applies to everyone, including myself. I cannot just break or change a law and expect my people to accept that! A royal visit must be official, must be announced. You were staying in the tower ... you must understand how it will appear. The people will think that you plot the downfall of the Council, perhaps even your king, in order to bring back majick to the land.'

'But this is all a misunderstanding,' she protested. I was only visiting a friend.'

'Your friend, who is the only true wizard remaining in the kingdom, not to mention that majick was employed in order for you to enter the palace ...'

He seemed shrunken beyond measure and Exzalander felt her guilt set in.

'I am sorry, father, truly I am.'

'You will be sent to apologise to the Council for not announcing yourself. You will kneel before them and beg their forgiveness. Is that clear?'

Exzalander felt her body stiffen and she glared back at her father.

'I will *not*,' she seethed. 'I am a princess, not a servant!'

The blow came without warning—a sharp sting followed where his hand had struck her cheek.

'You are a servant to the law, as are we all; you *will* obey me in this.'

She clenched her jaw and continued to glare. Her face was red and hot and her hands hurt from where her nails dug into her palms. She knew he was expecting an answer, but was too angry to speak.

I will visit the Council all right, she thought, *and I will make them beg **my** forgiveness.*

Without another word, she flounced from the room, her father's voice raging after her.

Gailon was tired of waiting for his master's summons and decided that enough time had passed for which Ardahl's temper to cool. He made his way to the entrance to the catacombs and was startled to find a guard posted. He slipped back behind the corner and breathed slowly, wondering if Ardahl was aware of what was happening. *The guard could have been placed there for me,* he considered. He backed away, scared. *Would Ardahl have me arrested for what I did? No, it would mean revealing Exzalander's presence here and he seemed rather keen to avoid that. Besides, it is not his way. Ardahl is quite capable of administering his own punishment and the wizard would need no guard to locate me if he's a mind. No — this is something else.*

Gailon had become so lost in his thoughts that he was unaware of someone approaching from behind, until it was too late. He turned suddenly, gasping as his eyes met those of his master.

Ardahl put his fingers to his lips, beckoning his apprentice to follow him. He led Gailon down passageways unfamiliar, until the apprentice felt quite lost. Ardahl stopped so abruptly, that Gailon banged into the back of him.

'Idiot!' Ardahl cursed. He reached out and pulled aside an old tapestry to reveal a hidden door. It was old — old as the palace itself. It had no handle or lock, but opened to Ardahl's command.

The wizard ushered Gailon into the darkness beyond, closing the door behind them. It was not until they reached the safety of the tower that either dare speak.

'It is well that you came when you did, young Gailon.'

He called me by my name; it must be serious, Gailon realised. 'What has happened, Master? Why are there guards down there?'

Ardahl unwrapped the bundle he was carrying and Gailon noted at once that it was food—enough to last many days at a stretch.

'I have been accused of treason. The Council see in Exzalander's visit, a way to rid themselves and the kingdom of majick, once and for all. As long as we remain up here, we are safe. As far as they're aware, I do not yet know of their summons. It gives me time to think at least.'

Ardahl related what had occurred between Katahl and the princess and smiled wryly at his apprentice's look of dismay.

'Do not fear,' he said. 'We will think of something ... cheese?' he offered.

But Gailon had never felt less like eating in his life. He found himself wondering why he had not become a painter, as his mother had wanted for him.

* * * * *

Exzalander flounced into her chamber, slamming the door behind her. Beth was at her side in moments.

'What is't Milady? What is the matter?'

'Everything ... I hate that I am bound by so many rules. I'm expected to comply without complaint. My father hit me, Beth; he has never done so before.'

'I'm sure you did not mean to anger him ...'

'I do not care if he is angry,' she snapped back. 'I am angry too! I will not do what he demands and he cannot make me,' she finished sulkily, sitting on the bed.

Beth climbed up behind her and began gently brushing Exzalander's hair. With each stroke, the princess could feel her fury dissipate, but that which remained was not calm, but calculation, and she smiled slowly.

'I have a task for you, Beth,' she said. 'It is not an easy one and I give you leave to refuse, if you wish. I shall not think any less of you if you choose to do so.'

Beth stopped brushing the princess's hair and sat beside her, intrigued by what her mistress intended.

'I am to travel to Ealdorbold in a few days,' she explained. 'I have an errand there. I suppose that I will be sent with our visitors. I want you to take my place. You can wear a veil and you will be in my carriage for the journey. Keep the illusion up as long as you are able, Beth. Are you willing to perform this task?'

'Do you not wish to visit the palace, yourself?'

'No, I need you to buy me time.'

'Time for what, Your Highness?'

'Time to get away.'

Beth's eyes widened and she took Exzalander's hands in her own.

'Your Highness, you have a duty. You may not like it, but you are heir to the throne. You cannot simply disappear.'

Exzalander pulled her hands away, and paced toward the window, annoyed that Beth had dared to question her.

'I am not running away forever,' she said. 'I know my duty well enough, but I also know that my father is wrong in what he asks. I must consult with a friend before I concede to his command. Please Beth.' She smiled. 'You are always saying that I should have more adventure in my life—well here is my chance.'

Beth raised her eyebrows. 'Very well,' she said. 'I will do as you ask. I will gain you as much time as I am able.'

Exzalander hugged her servant. 'If anyone can do it, you can, Beth. You will be suitably rewarded, that I promise you.'

Letting her frown fall, Beth offered her most dazzling smile, deciding that it was going to be an interesting journey.

Fourteen

Exzalander purposely did not show her face at court for the remainder of Kryepast's stay. She sent only a one-word reply to the king's note regarding their conversation. Tuâth remained angry at his daughter's conduct and refused to speak to her directly until his command had been met. His wife could do nothing, but try and calm him and her headstrong daughter, her conversation with Exzalander ending in tears.

The princess lay awake each night, fuming over her father's actions, counting the days until she could get away. Beth had brought her servant's clothes from Kryepast's household. The boys wore skullcaps, which would make hiding her hair a lot simpler. She sighed with frustration and anger as she replayed her father's blow back in her mind.

In the adjoining room, Beth turned over and pretended she was asleep. She was in no mood to pander to the princess; all the secrecy had meant that she had been prevented from revisiting Theyl's bed.

On the morning of King Kryepast's departure, Exzalander assisted Beth into her travelling dress with veil, and tucked the girl's brown hair under her pearl headdress.

'Good luck,' she whispered, as she departed to join the king's entourage. She kept reminding herself to look to the floor, not hold her head high as she was accustomed to. She approached a young knight in the corridor and bowed her head as he passed, before hurrying on her way.

Caitul was uncomfortable with being made to escort the princess, deciding that he would prefer the company of his new companions. His head was sore, yet again, from the farewell drinking session with his brother, during which, he had voiced his disapproval of Theyl's taste in women.

As he knocked on the door, he realised that he was holding his breath. The little luggage Exzalander was taking had already been loaded; there was only the princess to go. Most surprised was Caitul, when the princess herself opened the door to him. He immediately bowed, remembering his manners. She seemed amused and he felt sure that he heard a quiet laugh from beneath her veil. Uncomfortably chewing his lip, he led her outside to the waiting carriage.

Exzalander tucked herself in with a handful of servants to the rear of the luggage cart. She watched with apprehension as her father approached Beth and spoke to her. As instructed, Beth completely ignored Tuâth. But the king suddenly gripped her arm and spoke again.

Exzalander held her breath, believing her escape to have been foiled, but was amazed as Beth yanked her arm away and stepped into the carriage. She smiled at the audacity of the girl, making a note to herself to ensure Beth was rewarded remarkably well.

Tuâth, eager that the conflict between himself and his daughter remain private, stepped away and waved to his friend as they began to move away. Caitul nodded to the king, as he kicked his horse into action. He waved goodbye to his brother and was startled when he noticed that the princess had drawn her curtain across, seeming to watch him too.

After the first day's travel, Exzalander began to question what she had been thinking. Her feet were too sore to concentrate on her pride, and she longed for a warm bath and her soft bed.

Beth was enjoying watching the serving boys putting up her tent, especially when she realised one of them was her mistress. She beckoned to Caitul to sit with her and keep her company. The knight obeyed without question, but sat in silence. There came a laugh from beneath the veil and Caitul faced her, frowning.

'Something amuses you, Your Highness?' he asked, trying not to sound terrified.

'You are not used to keeping a lady occupied, are you, Caitul?'

Her voice was warm and rich, feeling oddly familiar to him.

'Tis true, Milady. I am trained to fight, not to converse. I fear I may lack the skill.'

Beth laughed again and Caitul found himself swallowing.

'Then I shall have to give you plenty of practice on this trip. Is that acceptable to you, knight?'

'Of course, Milady.' He bowed. 'Whatever you wish; I am at your service.

She reached out to him and to his shock, she lifted his chin with her hand, so that she could see his face. He froze with fear, unsure how to react, but every cell in his body knew what she was doing was forbidden and he felt a strong desire to run away.

'I am glad to hear it, knight,' she said. 'I will make good use of you during our time together, trust me in that.'

He blinked, wishing he could see her face to judge how much she was jesting with him.

'Tell me about your brother. He is our Captain of the Guard, is he not?'

She released him and he breathed a silent sigh of relief, glad to have been given a subject on which he could comfortably speak.

As the tent was completed, Caitul felt as though he could converse quite freely with the princess. She felt a lot less stuffy than he would have believed her to be, and her positive reaction to him put his etiquette at ease more than he should have let it. Had she been the real princess, he might have been confronted about his casual manner, but Beth enjoyed the fact that he was beginning to trust her.

Exzalander wandered away from camp, eager for silence. Unaccustomed to such close company, she dragged herself to the nearest stream, in which to bathe her weary feet, deciding then and there, to pay more attention to servants; she had gone only one day in service and that was one day too long. She began to wonder if she should just transport herself to Ardahl. Sighing, she realised it was such behaviour that had caused the problem in the first place, besides which, she still felt weak from the last time she had used the spell and Ardahl had warned her not to make regular use of it.

She lay back, allowing her feet to dry in the coolness of evening and drifted to sleep on the grassy bank, her exhaustion allowing her to do without the luxury of her bed.

It was a shout in the middle of the night that awoke her and she sat up suddenly, wondering where she was, until her memory kicked in and she groaned. Getting to her feet, she made her way back to camp.

Things were being packed in a hurry. Whatever had distracted them all allowed Exzalander to edge closer to the princess's tent and slip inside.

'What is happening, Beth?' she asked.

'I don't know, Milady,' Beth replied, with a yawn. 'Help me get this veil on straight and I'll find out.'

Exzalander obliged only just in time as Caitul's voice sounded outside the entrance.

'Your Highness, may I enter?'

The princess ducked behind the screen and Beth smiled beneath her veil.

'Of course, Knight Caitul. What is all the commotion out there?'

'Your Highness, I regret to inform you that a messenger arrived, requesting our immediate aid. Dragons have attacked Ichnaarim and we are called upon to assist. King Kryepast has sent the messenger on to your father to urge him to make haste. Our knights are to offer aid at once.'

'And I?' Beth asked. She was beginning to regret agreeing to Exzalander's scheme. No reward in the world would convince her to face dragons.

'I am to escort you back home. King Kryepast says that you will be safe there.'

'I will do what King Kryepast thinks is best. Thank him for allowing you to accompany me, Caitul.'

'Of course,' he replied, bowing before making his exit.

Exzalander came out of hiding, her eyes fearful. 'Dragons?' she said. 'You cannot return to Brëgwela. The knight will be needed to fight. Tell them that you will continue to Ealdorbold, alone.

'I doubt that they'll allow that, Your Highness, besides, I imagine that they will travel directly to battle. Perhaps you should accompany me back to the castle. This jest is no longer sound.'

'It is no joke, Beth! I am not returning to my father. I will go with the company and help as I may. It is my duty to do so, besides, the friend I seek will surely be there,' she finished regally.

Beth curtseyed to the princess, deciding it was best not to argue; it was clear she meant what she had said—still, the ruse seemed no longer as fun as it had. She had not expected to ride into such danger.

Exzalander left the tent and was grabbed immediately by First Knight Caitul. She silently cursed herself for her stupidity, and stared down at her feet.

'Boy, what were you doing in Her Highness' tent?'

To Exzalander's relief, Beth opened the flap and dismissed the servant.

'All is well, Caitul. I asked him to fetch you. I have decided that it is best you should not be kept from your duties. You will be much needed if there are dragons to be fought. I will continue to Ealdorbold and from there you can more easily join the fight.'

'But Your Highness.'

'There is no discussion to be had on this matter,' Beth cut in. 'If you will not accompany me, then I must continue on my own. But saddened will I be to be deprived of your company, Caitul.'

He looked down and realised that she held his gauntleted hand; without thinking he bowed and swiftly kissed hers, a tingling sensation running the length of his body.

Knight Nimrïn watched with amusement, his friend's clumsy attentions to the princess, and devised ways in which to torment him.

'You, boy,' he ordered Exzalander, as she dashed away from the tent.

'Yes Milord,' she squeaked.

'Take this, will you.' He passed her a drained goblet. 'And find my squire. Tell him to make ready my horse. We ride within the hour.'

Exzalander bowed, grateful that the knight did not pay too close attention to a servant's face. It took some time for her to locate the young squire and as she did so, she was enlisted to help in preparations. The advantage of assisting with the luggage, she realised, was being able to hitch a ride on the wagon. *Pretending to be a servant will be easier if I do not have to work too hard,* she decided.

Ardahl watched from his tower as the troops filed out of the gates.

'What is happening I wonder?' he said, to his young apprentice.

Gailon sat with his chin rested on his hands. Being branded a traitor was not his idea of career advancement.

'You must go and find out.'

Ardahl's words took a moment to sink in, before Gailon looked up, startled.

'I'll be arrested if I'm caught, Master,' he protested.

'It doesn't look as though there's anyone left *to* arrest you, boy.' Ardahl chuckled, then seeing Gailon's face, he shook his head.

'Deary me, anyone would think I'd asked you to murder your mother. Very well, *I* will go,' he said, making his way to his portal.

'What is this?' He paused to stare at the painting that covered the majick device.

Gailon shrugged, embarrassed. 'Just one of my paintings,' he muttered.

Ardahl looked closely and turned to frown at Gailon.

'This is a non-commissioned picture of Her Highness,' he said. 'As if we were not in enough trouble, boy!' He raised a bushy eyebrow at the clearly embarrassed apprentice.

'It's not what you think, Master. It's a dream painting. It depicts an event that hasn't happened yet.'

'Yes I know what a dream painting is,' Ardahl snapped. 'I just don't see the point in it—foolish pastime. You'd be better off practising your basic spells, rather than augury, boy.'

Gailon's mouth twisted into a grimace and he thought better than to protest. The old wizard tutted and stepping behind the painting, he disappeared.

King Kryepast gathered his and his son's knights about him, informing them of his intention that they should ride ahead with all haste. Nimrin's squire fixed his master's bridle, his hands trembling. Exzalander passed him a water flask for the journey and he took it, thanking her.

'Are you all right?' she asked.

All colour had drained from the boy's face. 'Yes,' he whispered. 'It's just that … well, I had hoped never to see another dragon as long a I live. My family lived in Pentref for many years.'

Exzalander was unsure how to respond. She was unaccustomed to such conversation with servants.

'Well, you will have useful experience of them then,' she offered, smiling. 'I am sure that it will prove most beneficial to your master.'

'They were all eaten!' he cried. 'I'm the only one left. The only advice I could honestly offer is, don't go,' he said, tears stabbing his eyes.

Exzalander's mouth twisted awkwardly and she patted him on the shoulder.

'Maybe he will let you stay behind,' she said.

The squire's eyes met hers and he blinked away the tears, trying to harden his expression, but his lips wobbled again.

'Nimrïn needs a squire. I cannot remain. It is my duty … unless … *you* could go in my place. You could inform my master that I have been injured and that you are replacing me.'

Exzalander stared at the boy, his pathetic expression reaching her in a way that she had not experienced before.

'Very well,' she replied. 'Stay here and I will go in your place.'

The boy issued his thanks as she led the horses off to meet the knight of the house of Kryepast.

'Bloody fools!' Ardahl yelled, as he crashed into his tower.

Gailon, who had nodded off, awoke with a start. 'Master?'

'Dragons! The dragons have attacked Ichnaarim. What in Taiohãhn's name did they expect? They've been allowing, even encouraging, the sale of outlawed dragon artefacts for over a year now. The illegal dragon trade was flourishing in the heart of Ichnaarim. Did they honestly think Morgothal would not retaliate?'

Gailon stared, dumbstruck at his master.

'Close you mouth, boy; you'll catch flies sitting there like that, besides, it's most unseemly.' He paced about the tower and Beaky opened a sleepy eye to assess if the old man was about to do any damage.

'We can only hope that they don't learn of the Council's hand in this, or we're next,' he continued. 'They'll level Ealdorbold without a second thought.'

'Should we not do something?' Gailon said.

Ardahl stopped pacing and eagerly eyed his apprentice.

'I'm not sure that we should. If your family was slaughtered and their body parts sold as trinkets, would you not think that you had a right to revenge?'

Gailon's head hurt; Ardahl's pacing and his own lack of a proper meal were sending his mind into a spin. He could not bring himself to feel sorry for the dragons.

'Besides,' Ardahl continued. 'What would you suggest that we do? The moment any guard recognises me, I'd be arrested for treason. Damn that boy and his hormones! I wonder who he consulted ... I bet it was Sohãhn, that conniving little turd!'

* * * * *

'Where's Seb?' Nimrïn barked.

Exzalander swallowed hard before answering. 'I regret to inform you that he has met with an accident and will be unable to attend you, Sir. I will ride in his place.'

The knight regarded her for a moment. He was a skinny boy and not much spirit it seemed; he didn't even look up from his boots. From what Nimrïn could see, the boy looked more female than male and he had little doubt that he would make a good jest to that effect, in the days to come. He took the reins from the boy's hands.

'Come on then, pretty boy. Let us not tarry. We've dragons to slay and glory to gain.'

'It's Tam,' Exzalander protested. To her surprise, the knight guffawed.

'Maybe more to you than I thought, pretty boy. Come on then, *Tam*; duty and glory won't wait for your pride y'know.'

Exzalander bowed low and mounted the horse. She wobbled as she sat astride the beast, unaccustomed to being anything other than side-saddle. Nimrïn laughed at her expression, assuming that his temporary squire was unused to horseback.

Dahal rode over and joined him. 'Hardly a laughing matter,' he said. 'The dragons have not attacked on mass before. I don't know how we can be expected to defeat them'

Exzalander was feeling distinctly uncomfortable; her new position was gaining more attention than she wished and she was affeared that one of the knights of Starigorat might actually recognise her.

She watched as Knight Aarnon signalled that the company was moving and she fell behind. Taking a final glance back to Beth's tent, she hoped that she could reach Ardahl before Beth met with the Council of Shénnin.

Fifteen

As soon as the news of the attack reached the palace, Katahl rode out with the Shénnin Guard and Ealdorbold's reserve. It was two days ride to the city and he held little hope that it would still be standing by the time aid arrived.

'It is good to see you up and about, Lord Katahl.'

Katahl smiled at the Captain of the Shénnin Guard.

'Thomn-the-Cleaverhand,' he said, 'glad am I to be on the road, but I wish it could have been in happier circumstances.'

Thomn nodded grimly. 'At least we will not be alone in this. Your father and Tuâth's troops will join us soon.'

'Indeed, and with them, your son.'

A shadow passed over Thomn's face as he realised that both of his sons would have to face such danger.

There came a distant boom, causing the horses to rear and splutter. All eyes in the column gazed ahead, as black smoke curled high into the sky.

'We must make greater haste, lest there be no city to save,' Thomn shouted, and spurred his horse onward.

Exzalander rode as well as any man, and once she had got used to riding astride the horse, the equal distribution of her weight made it even easier. She smiled, thinking it was best not to like such a thing too much; her father would be cross if her saw her thus. Thinking of her father triggered darker thoughts—memories of Tuâth's anger, directed toward herself. She kicked her horse a little too hard and it raced ahead of the knights, making for the king, until one of his older knights grabbed her reins.

'Woah, where are you heading?' he said.

Exzalander glanced ahead, terrified that Kryepast would turn and recognise her. She lowered her head meekly.

'Forgive me, Sir,' she said, 'I lost control of the reins for a moment.'

The knight frowned at her, a look she mirrored at the roar of laughter from Nimrïn. She felt herself tense. She was not accustomed to being the source of another's amusement and found that she did not enjoy the experience much. Clenching her jaw, she fell in behind Nimrïn again, but her expression only served to amuse him more.

'What a lucky fellow that Caitul is ...' Nimrïn beamed, forgetting his new servant at last.

'How so?' Aarnon asked.

'Time alone with the princess—whilst we ride to battle.'

Exzalander felt her cheeks growing hot. She wanted to put a stop to such gossip, but knew that it was not considered her place. Her eyes bore into Nimrïn's back, almost daring him to besmirch her good name.

'Caitul will join us when he is able,' Aarnon said. 'He has no desire to be babysitting longer than is necessary.'

Nimrïn grinned. 'I don't know ... he seemed pretty cosy with Her Highness to me, and who can blame him? I hear she's quite the beauty.'

Exzalander wanted nothing more than to unhorse him, she was so furious.

'She is,' Dahal agreed. 'I saw her at the welcome feast.'

Exzalander breathed slowly, her fury changing to fear at Dahal's words.

'I don't recall her,' said Nimrïn.

Aarnon laughed. 'That's because you were too drunk!'

Nimrïn sniffed, seeming offended and then roared with laughter. 'I can't imagine Caitul will be in much of a hurry to join the battle if she's happy to keep him company.'

Exzalander frowned, opening her mouth to speak her protest, but luckily, Aarnon did it for her.

'Enough Nimrïn, you go too far. Remember that you are speaking of the daughter of the house of Shénnin and Tuâth; you should show more respect.'

Exzalander breathed once more as the subject was changed, but knew that the journey was going to feel like a very long one.

Beth slept soundly for what remained of the night and ate her breakfast in silence, thinking of the handsome Caitul and his pretty manners.

As if in answer to her thoughts, Caitul's voice sounded outside.

'Your Highness, we are making ready to leave. Are you almost ready? Do you need help dressing?'

She tore the flap aside and saw that he was blushing.

'You are offering to help me dress?' she asked.

'Nnno,' he stuttered, 'I only meant, I could fetch a maid. Indeed I am surprised that you did not bring your own lady-in-waiting to assist you.' He stared awkwardly at the floor, his face returning to its normal shade.

'I like the adventure, Caitul. Now walk with me whilst my tent is packed away.'

Caitul nodded and smiled, offering his arm. As they walked together, he found himself conflicted. Part of him was most gratified at her attentions to him, but there was a voice inside him warning she was deliberately toying with him, that she merely found him a source of amusement— something to be laughed at later on.

His opinions did not sway during their day's ride. He found that she wanted to know all about him, but was most reluctant to speak of her own life. As they made camp for the night, she asked him to join her for supper, to which he apprehensively agreed. She ate very little and Caitul wondered whether her veil made it difficult.

'Forgive my impertinence, Your Highness,' he said, 'but would it not be easier to remove your veil whilst you eat?'

'Alas, my dear Caitul,' Beth sighed. 'It is not permitted.'

Caitul felt his cheeks warm at her term of endearment.

'You can rely on my discretion—I will tell no-one.'

She moved closer and poured him a goblet of wine.

'Indeed? Well, that is good to know.'

Caitul tipped back the wine; her words seemed almost suggestive to him and he found that he was annoyed by it, believing royalty should not behave so.

'I must go,' he said sternly, turning away.

'Must you?' she breathed, and grabbed his hand.

He froze. None of his training or experience had prepared him for such an occurrence.

'If you must go, then you must,' Beth sighed. 'But first ... I need you to assist me.'

'What is it that you require, Your Highness?'

'I cannot unclasp my gown alone,' she said matter-of-factly and turned her back to him.

He stared at the hooks down the length of her dress; his anger was fleeting and confusion set in again.

'I will fetch ...' he began.

'No, I trust you, Caitul,' she breathed. 'Please assist me.'

His hands shook as he unclasped the top hooks of her gown, and he wondered if he could be punished for disobeying her, as he was not a member of her household.

She sighed as his hands worked the length of the fastenings, and she shrugged off the gown, turning to face him.

'Highness ...'

'Shhhh,' she replied, placing a finger to his lips.

Part of him wanted to run away, but that part was held captive by his desire, as she began to unbuckle his jerkin. The sensible voice in his head questioned why he had not worn his armour, but the other voice was only too pleased that he had not. He raised a hand to her veil, but she grabbed it to prevent him.

'I told you, I'm not permitted,' she said.

Taking his hands, she placed them onto her breasts, willing him to fondle them. He took little coaxing and felt the tightness in his groin increase as she moaned at his caress. His head swam with desire, as it battled with honour and duty.

'I cannot do this,' his voice strained.

She reached for his fly.

'Do you not desire me?' she asked.

Her voice sounded childish making him angry rather than aroused.

'Of course I do, but you are Princess Exzalander,' he replied.

'No I'm not,' she cut in. 'Tonight, I am just a woman, a woman who needs you, Caitul, a body that yearns for yours; you would not deny me? Especially when I feel that you share my desire.'

She was touching him where no woman had ever touched him before. He could feel the hardness of his penis in her hand and as she closed her fingers around it, he trembled. She pulled him toward her and standing on tiptoe, she ran his member between her legs and the wetness of her waiting pudendum rid him of his last doubts and worries. He reached out with his hand, finding the soft opening of her womanhood and he played a while. His lack of experience did not seem to matter, as her breathing quickened. Instinctively, or as a result of boyish stories, he dipped his fingers inside her and sighed at the velvety warmth that greeted him.

'You're so wet,' he panted. Realisation struck, it was no jest—she truly wanted him; her body demanded it and he was happy to acquiesce to her.

Despite their best efforts to be quiet, many of the servants heard the sounds of copulating coming from within. By morning it seemed common knowledge that the First Knight to Katahl, had bedded the Princess Exzalander.

Caitul's eyes were reluctant to open; having had the most incredible dream, he was unwilling to face reality once more. As he felt soft lips brush against his own, his eyes flicked open and a grin spread across his face.

'It wasn't a dream,' he sighed.

'No, my beautiful knight, it was no dream, but you must help me dress if we're to be on our way.' Beth stared down appreciatively at his naked body, wishing that her veil did not obstruct her view so.

As he obeyed her, he could not help running his hands across her skin. It was smooth, but browner than he would have expected. As he fastened the final clasp of her gown, he bent to kiss her neck.

'Now you promised me discretion, remember?' she said.

He backed away with a smile, ruffling his hair. As she watched him leave, Beth could not help wonder that with a little training, he might be a better lover than his brother.

Although nothing was said, Caitul realised immediately that they all knew. It was only at that moment his happiness turn to cold fear.

'What have I done?' he whispered to himself. 'Tuâth will have my head on a spike for this.'

As they continued to approach the palace, it was difficult to tell if it was getting cooler, or his fear was getting the better of him. *The sooner I arrive to battle, the better,* he thought. *Perhaps I shall be lucky and a dragon will eat me—rather that, than have to face the wrath of Tuâth for having despoiled his only child.*

Sixteen

The smell of burning reached the guards from Ealdorbold, long before they sighted any dragon and the horses grew increasingly uneasy, as they approached the danger. Ugly clouds of black smoke hung in the air and all signs of life had scattered, leaving an unnatural quiet, which set the men's nerves on edge.

A sudden sound on the road ahead caused all guards to draw their weapons. It was not, however, the roar of dragons, but approaching horses.

'Father,' hissed Katahl, too wary to raise his voice to a shout.

'King Kryepast,' echoed Thomn's voice. 'Your arrival is most timely. You must have already been on the road to arrive so soon.

'Yes, it is true,' Kryepast agreed. 'But we sent your messenger onward to Tuâth, so reinforcements are sure to follow.'

'That is well,' Thomn replied. 'Shall we go down together and see what can be done?'

Exzalander recognised the face of the newcomer at once and watched as the man, whose life she had helped to save, approached and linked arms in greeting with the knights. She could feel her heart pounding in her chest and had to remind herself to breathe.

'Well met, my friends,' Katahl said quietly, as he joined them.

Exzalander felt a thrill at the rich voice, returned to good health. Colour was back in his cheeks and his skin no longer clung to his bones. His eyes sparkled like jets, as he greeted his friends.

'Greetings Milord, we have much missed you. I hear dragons were summoned to make us meet that much sooner.'

'You are aright in that, Nimrïn and very like you to make light of so dire a situation. But tell me, where is my First Knight? Where is Caitul?'

His First Knight? Milord? Exzalander thought. *So this is Katahl. I tended the son of King Kryepast. How could I not have realised as much before? Well, I shall just have to hope that he was too fevered to notice me.*

'We regret to inform you, Lord Katahl, that your First Knight had to accompany the princess. She was on some private errand to the palace and since her envoy now only consists of servants, your father deemed it best to let her keep your First Knight, as you had little use for him we thought.'

Katahl frowned at the news and Exzalander tried to edge closer whilst staying obscured from view.

'She must be sent to meet with the Council with regard to a matter of treason. The wizard Ardahl is so accused and the council are calling for his execution. I am surprised that he did not attend to the matter personally—still, it cannot be helped. We can only hope that Caitul will join us soon.'

'Ardahl, a traitor? Surely not...'

Their voices grew quieter as they moved down the hill toward the city. Exzalander did not move, her thoughts halting her advance. *How can I have been so foolish? Of course Ardahl will not be here if he stands so accused.*

She felt a shudder of trepidation at the sudden realisation and the roar ahead did not ease her alarm. Her body trembled with fear, as the sound vibrated through her. Her horse began to panic too and threw her from the saddle. Running into the trees, she followed the path of the knights and guards—not knowing what else to do.

As the company reached Ichnaarim, they saw nothing but ash, smoke and flame; no sign of human life was discernable.

Where once the great city had stood, there sat an enormous crater, filled with the remains of buildings and population alike, now nothing more than a fine ash, as the result of dragon fire. Exzalander heard the sounds, as though from far away; the smell of burnt flesh invaded her nostrils, whilst the shock of the scene ahead took over completely. She almost tripped over charred remains and was caught by Nimrïn.

'There you are, Tam,' he said. 'Stay close to me.'

She saw several soldiers vomiting at the sight of the remains of what could have been family or friends, and she was sure that the acrid smell of vomit reached her nose along with the dead. She gripped Nimrïn, unable to move—his strong arms her only comfort in the madness. He took her face in his hands and she looked up into his eyes, feeling tears trickle down her pallid cheeks.

'Come now lad, keep it together,' he said. 'You don't want me to make a mockery of you later, now do you? Stay with me!'

Exzalander nodded and felt as though her actions were slow—out of phase with the thoughts screaming in her head.

'Your horse?' she mumbled.

'Threw me—the bastard. So you see,' he slapped her on the arm, 'you can get your own back later. All you have to do is stay alive, pretty boy.'

She could hear his words and one hand still gripped his bear-like arm. It was sturdy; his voice was sturdy too. It helped her feel grounded—feel real.

'It's Tam,' she stuttered.

He slapped her again.

'That's the spirit, lad. Come on!'

Once her senses began to function properly once more, she longed for the shock to return. *This is real, it's really happening,* her mind screamed. *Yes it is really happening and if you do not pull yourself together right now and start acting with some decorum, you are going to wind up a pile of bones and seared flesh, like these poor souls,* she told herself, making the decision then and there that, although she might die, she would refuse to be afraid.

Remaining close to Nimrïn, she made her way down to the crater that had once been the great city of Ichnaarim, on the main trade route through Maldahl. All races went there to sell their wares. Many races had dwelled there peacefully for hundreds of years. Indeed, it was the only place in the known lands that did not have its own indigenous race.

Looking out across the crater, it was as though Ichnaarim had never even existed. No buildings remained intact and those dragons that remained were obliterating the final ruins jutting out of the fine grey ash.

Great beasts swooped gracefully down from the darkness above, moonlight glinting off their scaled bodies before a burst of flame was released and the ruins were gone … just gone, exterminated one by one like the people before them and leaving only the strange alien landscape of desolation—a reminder of the strength of one of the world's oldest and most powerful races.

Exzalander had drifted again and Nimrïn was nowhere to be seen. Shouts to her left drew her attention from the ash crater; screams and a great roar followed a burst of flame. It was not the same sound as before, but a pained cry of a beast in the throws of death. As she dashed forward toward the knights, Exzalander could see the dragon, still breathing, despite the many spears thrust into its hide. Swords were thrust again and again whilst Exzalander watched the death dance with morbid fascination. The knights jumped away from the creature's thrashing tail, stabbing repeatedly until the breathing slowed and then stopped altogether.

The cheers that followed did not fill Exzalander with joy; she felt sick, weary and more than a little saddle sore.

'What am I doing here?' she asked aloud. Turning away from the celebration, she made her way back into the trees, toward the road that would lead her back to Ealdorbold.

A single knight noticed the squire as he retreated into the trees and he moved away from the celebration, to pursue him. He felt sorry for the boy, seeing the desolation and facing such creatures, was not for the faint-hearted and yet it did not change the fact that the boy was a squire to the knights of his house and as such, was not permitted to desert his post for any reason; his oaths and duty were clear and he, Lord Katahl, would be sure to remind him as much.

'Will you not join me, Caitul?' Beth asked innocently.

Caitul winced, knowing better. 'With regret, Your Highness, I must decline. I think it best to stay on guard tonight.'

Had he been able to see her eyes, he would have noted the flash of anger that preceded her smile.

'As you wish,' she said. ' You know where to find me when you change your mind.'

She stepped into the tent and Caitul felt nothing but relief at her absence. He cursed his body for having given in to her and continued to dread what the future would bring for him.

Beth flounced over to her camp bed, with a huff. *Even as the princess he's rejecting me,* she thought. *But last night ... last night was sensational. He was afraid, that much was plain to see. If only there was a way to let him know that I'm not actually who he thinks I am. Then I could have him again.*

Caitul continued to fume, glaring at any who came near him, as if daring them to challenge his behaviour. He played over the events of the previous night in his mind. Parts of his memories were sweet, having finally learned the touch and pleasures of a woman and yet ... the more he thought about it, the more he was convinced that it had not been her first time. *She seemed far too knowledgeable,* he thought. *Knowing better than I, what went where, and I'm a man!* The thought of the princess behaving like a common whore, sickened him to the core, and he vowed that he would never touch the woman again. He wished he could ride off and meet his brother knights. *I'd rather be fighting dragons than in the company of that harpy.*

'Caitul? Would you please come here?' Beth crooned from within the tent. 'I wish to speak with you on a most urgent matter.'

Stiffening with resolve, he entered. 'Yes Your Highness, what is it?'

She was naked, all but her veil, and beckoned for him to join her. Caitul barely glanced at her and gritted his teeth, wishing he had never met the woman.

'Have you no shame?' he seethed. 'You are a princess. You should be chaste. You ought to be pure. Torture me no more, woman!'

She laughed then and it was a harsh sound that made his flesh crawl.

'You did not seem to concern yourself with such things last night, Milord,' she said. 'You made good use of me, as I recall. What do you think King Tuâth would say, if he thought you had bedded his daughter?'

'I think he would have me hanged and you whipped. Is that what you want?' he returned icily, his mind racing with fear and questions. 'Why did you just call me Milord? Why did you refer to your father by name?'

She remained silent.

'Answer me!' he hissed.

She laughed again. 'Oh come, do not fear me; I will not tell anyone how much you enjoyed me.'

Without warning, Caitul paced toward her. Beth, thinking he meant to bed her, lay back as if surrendering to him, but he did not mount her, as was clearly her desire, instead, he snatched her veil away. Too slow was her reaction and only resulted in a scratched face.

'You!' Caitul hissed, as realisation struck.

Beth reached to where he had caught her and saw specks of blood on her fingertips.

'Well I hope you're happy now, knight. Look!' she said, shoving her scratched face toward him.

'Where is the Princess Exzalander?' he demanded.

She lay back again and to his horror, she smiled. He felt sick to his stomach at the depth of her manipulation.

'I don't know why you're so angry, Milord,' she said. 'Now you can enjoy me without fear of consequences.'

'You fool woman. They *know*; they all know and they think that you're the princess. You have belied Her Highness.'

Beth's eyes flashed, suddenly worried by his words.

'Now tell me what you're doing here and where the real princess is, or so help me, I will run you through.' He drew his sword and held it to her throat, noticing the vein that protruded, beating heavily beneath the skin.

Beth's eyes filled with sudden fear and she wished she were not naked.

'The princess asked me to go to Ealdorbold in her place. She rode out with your king's men. She said that it was her duty to help.'

Caitul almost dropped his sword in shock at what the impostor was saying.

'She's dressed as a servant,' Beth continued, 'and is passing as squire to Knight Nimrïn.'

Caitul sheathed his sword once more and commanded her to get dressed. As she reached for her veil, he yanked her away, dragging her from the tent. Several servants nearby saw his actions and made to intervene.

Caitul, First Knight to Katahl, ripped the headdress from Beth's hair and her brown locks fell down to her shoulders.

'This woman is an impostor!' he shouted to the camp. 'The real princess rides into danger. Continue to Ealdorbold and take this *harlot* with you.'

Beth fell to her knees, aware of all eyes upon her and she did not like it. For the first time in her life, she felt ashamed.

'You're not leaving me?' she screamed at him, as he mounted his horse.

'My duty is to protect the princess, not a whore,' he replied coldly. Without looking at her, he spurred his horse and rode away toward Ichnaarim.

Seventeen

By the time Katahl had caught up to the squire, the boy was running to get away, seeming oblivious to his pursuer. Katahl dived at the boy, knocking him to the ground beneath him. To his surprise the squire gave a high-pitched yelp and struggled to get free.

'It's all right, boy,' Katahl said. 'I'm not going to hurt you, but I cannot let you wander off.'

To Katahl's dismay, the squire continued to squirm and struggle against him; the boy managed to turn, trying to push him away. Katahl grabbed the squire's tiny wrists and forced his arms to the ground behind him. He sat astride the boy, his breath heavy with the struggle, and his eyes widened in surprise as the last face in the world he had expected to see, glared up at him.

Exzalander could feel his body heavy upon hers and realised that it was Katahl who had caught her. *Why is he staring at me like that?* she wondered. It felt an age lying there, his face close to her own, until she could endure it no longer.

'Get off me!' she ordered.

To her surprise and relief, he complied. She began to walk away, but he yanked her about, pinning her against a tree. She looked at him, horrified for a moment as his hand pushed into her shoulder, before gently tracing the line of her face and pulling away her skullcap. Her red hair tumbled down her back and she realised that he had recognised her.

'It *is* you,' he said. 'I thought that I would never see you again. Why are you dressed like a squire?'

He was still holding her and Exzalander pushed him away.

'You must not touch me like that,' she ordered. 'It is not permitted.'

Katahl tried to relinquish his smile, to no success. 'Forgive me,' he offered, as he stepped away from her. 'I only wished to prevent you from running again.'

'I have to go.' She scowled back at him. 'I came to find Ardahl, but I find that he is not here. Please do not delay me, Lord Katahl.'

'You have me at a disadvantage, Milady,' Katahl said, stepping into her path.

She felt her skin burning as he stared at her and wanted to order him to stop it.

'You know my name, Milady,' he explained, 'but I have yet to learn yours.'

'It's Beth,' Exzalander lied. 'Now let me go. I have done nothing wrong.'

Katahl's face beamed back at her and he looked more handsome than ever.

'Nothing wrong? You disguise yourself as one of my servants. What mean you by it?'

Exzalander huffed in frustration, growing increasingly impatient with the man's casual manner. 'Your knights would not let a woman accompany them,' she said. 'I had no choice.'

She tried to walk around him, but again he sidestepped into her path.

'Do you not you have a dragon to slay?' she snapped at him. The sound of his laugh immediately brought butterflies to her stomach.

'On no Milady, I must now accompany you to safety.'

'There really is no need,' she said. 'I will be quite all right on my own.'

'I insist.' His voice hardened, but if he had expected her to comply with the command in his tone, he was very much mistaken.

'Do not be ridiculous!' she said. 'Your father will worry where you are. Return to him at once!'

'You are very free with your orders, Milady. You do realise that I am the son of a king?'

'All the more reason to return to him then,' she said smugly.

She strode away, but he caught her by the hand and spun her about to face him. This time as she opened her mouth to protest, he pressed his lips to hers.

She froze.

She could feel his lips against her own as they urged her to return that which he offered. She felt the warmth of his hands as he held her in tight embrace and it felt wonderful. Yet, she could not return the gesture.

'Forgive me, Beth,' he breathed, his eyes glittering as he pulled back. 'I have been looking for you. I wanted to tell you …'

'Well, now I know why he was such a pretty boy.' Nimrïn laughed, as he strode toward them. 'Tam is it? If I'd known what sweet delights you were hiding, Tam, then Katahl here would never have gotten a hand on you.'

Exzalander looked horrified and wrenched away, storming off into the darkness. Katahl frowned at his knight, with obvious distain at the man's choice of words.

'That is the girl who saved my life,' he explained. 'The one I have been searching for. Tell my father that I am escorting her to Ealdorbold. She should never have been here!'

'But what about the dragons?' Nimrïn protested.

Katahl turned to his friend and shrugged.

'Most of them have returned to their home; there is nobody left to save. Send my apologies to the king, will you.'

Nimrïn shook his head, bemused as Katahl set off after his beloved.

Exzalander could feel the tears forming in her eyes at Nimrïn's words. Katahl had spoken to her as if she was some easy wench to be passed around like a tankard of ale. She gritted her teeth and wiped her eyes as she heard him approach.

Grabbing a fallen branch in her frightened hands, she span to face her pursuer.

'Stay away!' she spat at him.

Katahl stopped suddenly, raising his hands as if surrendering to her.

'I will not harm you, Beth,' he said, taking a step closer.

She swung the branch with all her strength, but he caught it and wrestled it from her grasp, causing her to back away, wide-eyed.

'You need not fear me. I meant what I said; I am going to escort you to safety, whether you like it or not.'

He could not help but stare at her; even in boys attire she was beautiful. He felt his heart quicken once again, but fought to control his desire. She was afraid of him and that was the last thing he wanted.

'Come,' he coaxed, almost in a whisper, 'let me take you to safety.'

'And what would you expect in return?' she spat viciously at him again.

Curse Nimrïn, he thought, *and curse my own impetuousness.* 'Nothing Beth ... forgive my actions before. I have searched for you and I was lost in the moment when I realised I had found you once more. It will not happen again.'

She watched him closely for signs of deception, but could detect none.

'Very well,' she said, 'your assistance is acceptable to me. You may escort me to the palace.' Her voice filled with confidence, but her eyes showed only confusion.

He gestured for her to move on and followed close, able to admire her form from behind, without fear of reproach.

They walked on in silence for a while, but after a time, Exzalander dared to ask the question that had been running around in her mind.

'What did you mean you have been looking for me?'

Katahl swallowed hard; he had tried being direct with her and she had reacted badly. He considered that he needed to give her time. If she had no feelings for him at present, then it was up to him to woo her.

'I wanted to thank you … for saving my life.'

She risked a glance back to him and the corners of her lips twitched upward for a moment.

'There is no need,' she said. 'Anyone would have done as much.'

He grabbed her arm, forcing her to face him.

'But they didn't. *You* did.'

She stared down at his hand and then glared at him until he released her again.

'You provided me with comfort,' he explained, 'and I know that you told Ardahl how to cure me. I *know* it was you.'

'Nonsense. You cannot possibly know such a thing. You were not even conscious!' She tutted, and moved on once more.

Katahl dashed in front of her, walking backward, so that he could see her face.

'That, I note, was not a denial,' he said. 'Who are you that you can order the court wizard thus?'

She quickened her pace, forcing him to turn and stride beside her.

'You were fevered,' she said. 'It is a wonder that you remember anything and you seem to have imagined much! I helped make you more comfortable. For that, I accept your thanks, though they are not necessary. It was certainly no reason to go seeking me out.'

The land ahead levelled out and the moon shone pale above them as they clambered onto the main road heading southwest to Ealdorbold. Katahl offered his hand to help her and lingered for a moment as she stepped up before him.

She felt the heat rise to her cheeks again as she saw his eyes shining back at her own.

'I must confess something to you, Beth,' Katahl said.

She cringed at the name, wishing that she had not lied to him.

'You are the most beautiful woman that I have ever beheld. I *needed* to find you.' He smiled. 'My heart demanded it.'

She was holding her breath and could swear that she could hear her own heart fluttering in her chest. Then the anger struck.

'You think me a fool?' she said. 'Am I consort? Am I harlot for you to use me this way? Keep your flattery—I will not hear it!' She clamped her hands over her ears.

Even in the moonlight, Katahl could see that she was blushing. His anger at her words, cooled within him as he looked upon her, for he realised that she had probably never been spoken to in such a way before. Her entire reaction displayed only innocence in matters of the heart. He smiled and she removed her hands from her ears, staring back at him defiantly, despite her blush.

'I speak only the truth, my dear one,' he said. 'Now that I have met perfection, how could I settle for any other?'

She frowned at him and walked away again.

'I do not think you harlot,' he called after her. 'I think you are a beautiful and powerful woman. All I ask is that you let me know you better.'

'You are mistaken, Lord Katahl. I am not what you think I am. I thank you for your compliments, but you have bestowed them upon someone who is not free to return such affections. I am sorry.'

Her heart thundered and her breathing quickened. *This handsome son of a king has as good as declared that he loves me,* she thought, *and yet I am rejecting him. Why? Because despite my foolishness of late, I am aware of my duty; no such attachment can be formed without the consent of father.*

Katahl's head was bowed and she wondered what he was thinking. Suddenly, she wished only to see his smile again. She shook herself; such thoughts were foolish. She was not free to even desire a smile from his lips.

'Are you and Ardahl?' he muttered, without looking at her. He did not want to finish the question. He was sure that she was a maid and suddenly wished he had not spoken.

'Are we what?' Exzalander repeated.

'Nothing … I withdraw the question.'

'Are we what?' she demanded.

'Are you lovers?' he answered. Feelings of both gratification and guilt rose at the horror of her reaction.

'Of course not!' she said. 'How can you even suggest? I … how dare you!'

'It was just that you said you are not free. It made it sound as though there was someone else.'

She planted her hands on her hips and scowled at him.

'You are wrong to make such an assumption. I am not free to be with anyone. What sort of woman do you take me for?'

Katahl could not help the corners of his mouth twitch and he resisted the urge to smile. 'So you are not attached to any man and you have made no denial whatsoever at finding me attractive … it's a start; I can continue to hope then …'

She huffed and quickened her pace once more, leaving him grinning behind her.

'You presume much,' she called back, glad that he could not see the beginnings of the smile that touched her lips.

It was difficult to get Katahl to talk about himself when all he wanted to hear about was her. Exzalander had no desire to lie to him any more than she already had and so insisted on hearing about his life at Starigorat. To her surprise and secret delight, he did not boast, as many young men were wont to do to impress a woman; he spoke modestly, his love for his land and his father clear from his words.

The moon had long since disappeared and the skies had begun to lighten as they stopped for a rest. Exzalander stretched and lay back, looking up at the fading stars. Katahl found that he could not resist the urge to watch her as her hair sprawled about her.

'Have I you to thank for this mess with Ardahl?' she asked, turning her head to look at him.

The sheepish look on his face amused her.

'I … yes … is that why you need to see him?'

She raised herself up so that she was leaning on one elbow. 'Yes. The Council have got a lot to answer for!' she seethed.

He lay back so that he was level with her and she gazed back at him, no longer uncomfortable in his presence, it seemed.

'They think that you are a sorceress he's been training.'

She laughed at his words, making his entire body tingle.

'Me, a sorceress?' she said. 'What a ridiculous notion!'

He touched her hair and was pleasantly surprised when she did not flinch or back away.

'*This* is indicative of majick potential, as I am sure you are well aware. What else were they to think? Especially when Ardahl went to such lengths to conceal you ever being there.'

She bowed her head, ashamed of the trouble she had caused. 'He had his reasons,' she muttered. She looked up at him once more, her eyes sharp and full of feeling as they met his. 'None of which are any of those that you have speculated or been informed of. I will speak to the Council and set matters to rights.'

'You?' Katahl said. 'But you will be lucky if they do anything other than throw you in the dungeon. What makes you think that they will listen to you?'

Her mouth twisted awkwardly. She wanted to tell him why he was wrong, but selfishly wanted him to think that she was an ordinary woman so that she might truly know how he felt about her.

'I cannot tell you ... not yet,' she said. 'You are going to have to trust me, Lord Katahl.'

He smiled lazily at her, willing to submit to anything, as long as he could remain at her side.

Caitul urged his horse forward; glad he had put so many leagues between himself and Beth. He promised never let desire come before his duty again.

What was the woman thinking running off with Kryepast's company like that? he thought. *She could be killed ...*

He kicked his horse a little too hard and silently cursed all women for their foolish ways.

The stars had all gone and the rosy haze of dawn bathed Exzalander and Katahl with a welcome light.

'We should move on, Beth,' Katahl said. 'I do not like the thought of us being out in the open like this.'

Jumping to his feet, he reached out, helping her up. His hand felt warm about hers and she smiled pleasantly. His eyes lingered long after she had turned away from him and walked on. She had gone a dozen paces before she turned back and laughed at him.

'Why are you standing there gawping?'

He joined her laugh, feeling as though his skin was the only thing stopping him from floating off in all directions at once. But as quickly as that feeling of elation came, it changed to dread when he saw her expression change to one of sheer terror.

He had been careless; so caught up in his new emotions, that he had thrown caution to the wind. He was aware of it now, the great beating sound from above them, as the dragon swooped overhead. Drawing his sword, he ran to protect Exzalander, wondering why she had not tried to escape.

The dragon landed before her—a great blue and silver beast, beautiful and terrible to behold. Still Exzalander had not retreated and Katahl leapt forward, knowing there was nothing more he could do, other than to die at her side. He thrust his sword at the beast and was knocked away with no more thought than one would swat a fly. Scrambling about for his blade, he yelled up at the creature, hoping to draw its attention away from his love.

The dragon, unperturbed by the noise, curled its long scaled neck until it was face to face with the princess. She was still frozen with fear and her lip quivered as the beast's eyes met her own. She could feel its breath, hot against her trembling body, and although she willed her body to move, she found that it would not.

Katahl's fingers found his sword and turned to face his doom, however, the sight that met his eyes, caused him to pause.

'Get away from her!' he screamed.

'Child of destiny,' the dragon breathed.

Katahl found that he could no longer function as the beast's majick took effect.

'I smell the gods on you, human. I *know* who you are.'

Exzalander blinked away her tears, her eyes pleading. *Let it be quick*, she hoped.

Katahl fought against the majick that held him, but to no avail; his sword was frozen in his grasp, unmoving as his limbs.

'Please! Do not hurt her. Take me … only … leave her. She has done you no harm.'

The dragon turned to regard Katahl for the first time.

'I am Syphr; no human makes demands of me. If I allow her the destiny that is mapped out for her, if I let her keep her life—my death will follow. That, I cannot allow. I see our end and I will prevent it, cost what it may when I face Taiohãhn in the next life.'

The dragon raised its head and smoke plumed from its nostrils. Exzalander wanted to scream, wanted to run, anything to avoid becoming one of those blackened bits of meat and bone. She considered transporting herself … *it might not kill me*, she thought. *It is a risk, but to stay is certain death. But what of Katahl? He has offered his life to save me. Can I leave him so cruelly?* She looked to him and tried to smile. *I would have liked a chance to know him better. I would have liked …* But whatever her thoughts, they dispersed the moment Syphr's flames sped toward her.

Eighteen

Katahl cried out as the flames came and at the same time the dragon's spell broke, he felt his heart breaking also. He did not know why the majick no longer held him; he only knew the hatred in his heart for that which had killed the woman he loved. He leapt forward with unbridled fury, plunging his sword into the dragon's side.

Syphr roared with anger and turned his head toward Katahl. The flames sped toward him and he closed his eyes— welcoming death.

But death did not come.

Neither did the agony of the fire.

Syphr screeched and stomped about. Katahl opened his eyes and saw a man pulling his beloved away from the angry dragon.

She was alive.

More men surrounded the beast. They were chanting and its majick did not affect them.

Wizards, Katahl thought. He was too grateful for the intervention to be fearful and ran back to retrieve his sword from the dragon's side, letting it find its mark repeatedly, until the angry beast was no more.

As Syphr gave his death rasp, Katahl rushed and swept Exzalander up into his arms, holding her tight to him, pressing his lips to her head.

'I thought I had lost you,' he murmured. Almost immediately, he let her go, remembering his promise to keep his distance.

She stared at him, her eyes full of shock and disbelief. She felt herself stumble, as though her legs were no longer her own. He caught her as she fell and swept her up into his arms.

'I've got you, Beth, it's all right.'

The wizards gathered about Exzalander as Katahl set her down, looking to each other at the young lord's words. Their strange glances were not beyond Katahl's notice.

'What is it?' he demanded. 'Why do you look to each other in such a way?'

The man who had dragged Exzalander to safety, knelt at her side and took her hand in his own. Katahl tensed and made a move to stop him.

'Stay yourself, Katahl; I do not harm her,' said the man. 'We only wish to help.'

'Who are you and how do you know my name?' Katahl demanded.

He smiled, his eyes meeting with Exzalander.

'My name is not important,' he said.

She gulped, realising that the wizard knew precisely who she was.

'We long ago foresaw this encounter and so made preparation to save you. Fear not. No harm will befall you now.'

Exzalander felt dizzy and she breathed too quickly. A sound rushed in her ears and she was vaguely aware of Katahl's questions about why they had not saved Ichnaarim. The wizards seemed to display no emotion over the devastation whatsoever, she observed. Slowly, she got to her feet and faced the man who appeared to be their leader.

'You have our thanks, sir, but may we not know to whom we are indebted?'

The wizards smiled and began to turn away; only their leader remained.

'You are not indebted to anyone; we were never here. If you speak of our assistance, it will not go well for you. We are banished and our aid could only place you under suspicion. Let the young lord here take credit and do not speak of our intervention.'

'I am not afraid of the Council,' she said defiantly.

'No? But they are afraid of you and that makes them very dangerous … until we meet again.' He bowed low and walked away to join his brethren.

The sun had risen and the whole incident seemed a dream to her. Katahl, however, was not of the same mind. Though grateful for their lives, he held nought but suspicion for wizards in hiding, wizards powerful enough to break a dragon's spell. He took a hard look at the woman before him. *She has many secrets*, he deemed.

'Everyone seems to know you, but I,' he said. 'Even the dragon knew you. What did he mean by touch of gods though? I am not sure I even want to kn …'

His words stopped abruptly, as she threw herself at him. She clung to him as if to convince herself of reality. He did not care about her reasons for doing so; all the questions he had been ready to ask, simply melted away. He wished he were not wearing his armour, as he wrapped his arms about her. She did not try to pull away, but pressed her head against his shoulder and wept.

'It's all right, my love,' he said softly. 'All is well,'

He took her face in his hands; her tear-filled eyes, looked greener than ever, and he found himself smiling at her.

'I should not have come,' she said, trying not to splutter.

He stroked her head and was gratified when she closed her eyes at his touch.

'I am glad that you did. How else would I have found you?'

She looked at him then, the last of her tears forming streaks down her ivory skin. Her lips parted slightly, as if she wanted to say something, yet could not find the words. Her hand reached out and touched his face, grimy from recent battle.

'You could have got away,' she said. 'When Syphr held me, you could have run. He was not aware of you; you offered your life in place of mine. Truly, I think knights would be a welcome addition in the house of Tuâth and Shénnin. I have never really understood what nobility was, until today.' She did not look away as his eyes bore into her own.

'That is praise indeed, for any knight,' he replied, 'and yet it was not my knight's nobility that made me offer my life.'

She frowned as his meaning escaped her understanding. He smiled and gently took her face in his hands once more, so that she had nowhere to look, even if she wished it.

'I did it because I love you,' he breathed.

The fear hit him then. He had said it and knew that he should not have. He could not bear to hear her reject him; rather to suffer a last kiss before subjected to such pain.

His mouth met her own and held her there. She did not struggle, but rather, leaned into him, drawing him closer still, her lips parted, as she tried to emulate his movements.

Her inexperience was clear to him, but it only made him want her more. All the inexperience in the world, however, could not conceal her passion as she returned his kiss. In the end it was he who drew away, aware of his body's reaction and understanding the need for control.

She smiled and blushed, dragging her glance downward, yet showing no sign of regret.

'Oh Beth,' he breathed. 'I love you, and soon the world will know it.'

Her eyes snapped up to him and she felt her common sense begin to win out over the giddy sensation that had momentarily taken over her senses.

'My name is not Beth. I lied to you,' she said flatly.

He stared at her, confused.

'I don't know why really,' she continued. 'I panicked. I felt it was for the best ... I am sorry.'

He smiled and his lips found hers again. She fought to keep hold of her senses, but his passion was too strong for her to fight for long.

'NO!' a voice seethed from behind them.

They had been so caught up in the moment, that the horse's approach had not even registered.

'Father.'

Katahl smiled up at Kryepast, but Exzalander was loath to turn about and face him.

'Katahl, you will return to Starigorat *immediately*. Take your knights and go!'

Katahl's face faltered, clearly confused by his father's anger.

'Father, I wish you to meet ...' he paused, realising that he still did not know the name of his love. 'The woman I am going to marry,' he finished, without a glance to her.

Kryepast's face lost its colour, but his countenance remained. 'You will return to our home at once. There will be no talk of marriage. Leave, now!'

Exzalander bit her lip as Katahl looked at her; his face was red with both fury and embarrassment.

'Must I repeat myself a third time and have your knights take you home in chains?' Kryepast said.

Exzalander reached for Katahl's hand. She saw his jaw clench and was afraid what his next move would be. The last thing she needed, when she was already in so much trouble, was to cause a rift between her father and his oldest and most powerful ally.

'You must go, Katahl ... please,' she whispered.

He looked at her then, her eyes pleading with him.

'I will go, if you so order it,' Katahl said. 'But I have vowed to see this lady to Ealdorbold ... on my honour,' he ended, his voice full of hope.

'*I* will escort the princess; *you* will obey your king,' said King Kryepast. 'Come Exzalander. I will take you to safety.'

Katahl was too shocked to say anything. She wanted to speak to him, to apologise again for her deception, but she felt all too keenly, the eyes of so many upon her. A squire stood by with the horse she had rode in on and she took the reins with a mumble of thanks. Kryepast glared at his son, before riding off, his knights and Exzalander behind him.

She turned before they were out of sight and saw that Katahl was still stood—unmoving. She sighed, wondering if he had truly meant anything of the sentiments he had spoken to her.

The journey back to her ancestral home, was an uncomfortable one, with King Kryepast refusing to even acknowledge her. She was glad of the silence—better that, than have to answer questions about her conduct.

She played back the events of the past day in her head, from the wizard's intervention to the feel of Katahl's lips as they had pressed against her own. She smiled as she recalled his words regarding marriage. *He really is too headstrong,* she thought. *Still, he will probably not speak to me again now, so it is foolish to dwell on it. Better to let it be but a happy memory, to recall from time to time.*

Exzalander drew up to Kryepast's side and glanced over to see his stony features fixed upon the road before them.

Why is he so angry? Surely I would be considered the perfect match for his precious son, she thought haughtily, and looked away again, trying to recall the surrounding landscape from her childhood—a time when life was less complicated and she did not have to concern herself with the wrath of dragons or visiting royalty.

Even Nimrïn resisted the urge to tease as the king left them; his Lord was clearly in no mood for jests.

'Forgive the intrusion, Milord,' said Dahal at last. 'We were following the last of the dragons and your father was concerned as it was heading in your direction.'

Katahl blinked, still unable to turn away from the road where Exzalander had ridden away.

'Lord Katahl, are you quite well?'

Nimrïn stepped up, suddenly slapping Dahal on the shoulder.

'Well? Of course he's well. He killed a dragon single-handed. His tale will be sung the length and breadth of the land.'

Katahl winced, wanting to correct the misunderstanding, but remembering the wizard's words of warning. Ordinarily, he would not have cared, but he seemed to be in enough trouble with his father, without compounding it with such news as him consorting with banished wizards.

'Lord Katahl, we should not tarry here,' Aarnon said. 'Let the carrion birds have this beast and we to put as much distance between us and this fell creature as we can, lest any of its kin find us and wish to exact revenge.'

'Why did she not tell me?' Katahl whispered, still rooted to the spot.

Nimrïn smiled sympathetically at his friend and lord.

'What man has ever been able to fathom the female mind, Milord?' he said. 'They all say one thing and then do another. They seem to live only to test our patience. But come, Aarnon is correct. We should begone from this place. Let us return home.'

Katahl nodded, dreamlike, and took the reins of his horse.

At the crossroads, which joined Ealdorbold to the road toward Starigorat, the knights saw a figure approaching at speed. Defensively, they reached for their weapons, but as the man drew nearer, they relaxed once more.

'Well met, Caitul,' Nimrïn called.

Caitul smiled and greeted them warmly.

'My Lord Katahl,' he said, 'good is it to see you well again.

Katahl gave the ghost of a smile in return.

Nimrïn spoke cheerfully, trying to brighten the mood. 'You arrive too late to make a name for yourself as dragon slayer, my friend.'

Caitul's eyes flashed to the company, as if searching for someone amongst them; he seemed distracted, even panicked.

'Milord, I regret to inform you that I failed in my duty,' he said. 'I was ordered to keep the Princess Exzalander safe, but ...'

Katahl's eyes snapped away from his brooding at the mention of his love.

'She was an impostor,' Caitul continued. 'I was informed that the real princess disguised herself and accompanied the knights, but I fear that I see nobody amongst your company whom I do not recognise. I fear ...'

Katahl managed a wry smile. 'Do not trouble yourself, Caitul, ' he said. 'She is safe and rides with my father, back to Ealdorbold. All is well.'

'So who were you babysitting then?' Nimrïn asked, as they set off together.

'Her name was Beth,' Caitul replied, through gritted teeth.

Nimrïn laughed at his friend and Katahl listened eagerly.

'I feel a story coming on, young Caitul. Come, tell us what this Beth did that would make you so venomous toward her.'

Caitul related all, knowing that if he did not then all would be made known from the mouths of servants. Better the truth was heard from his lips before events became idle chitchat.

By nightfall, they encamped in Freya Valley at the village inhabited by the Daleena people. Caitul finished his account and Katahl listened patiently, growing angrier by the minute.

'She should be punished!' he said at last.

The tribe's people looked warily over to him and his display of anger. Their hunting weapons were of little use against 'the men of metal', as they called them, but they gripped them tightly nonetheless.

Katahl seethed. 'This Beth is clearly a servant of the princess and she has committed many offences.'

Nimrïn laughed and the Daleena relaxed once more.

'If young Caitul was so offended, he didn't have to bed her.'

Caitul grimaced, but Katahl jumped to his defence.

'This woman, Beth, clearly understands how to seduce a man and the fact that she did so in the guise of the princess is not only distasteful, but akin to treason. Caitul bears no blame in this.'

'The women of the house of Tuâth and Shénnin are manipulative,' offered Dahal, with obvious distain.

Katahl took to silence at the comment, and gazed sadly into the flames of their campfire.

The Daleena were an ancient people, who had little to do with the outside world. The knights were eager to share tales, songs and of course, food with them and they revelled well into the night.

Katahl sat with Caitul; little did he feel like making friends with the strange people with their oddly coloured skin and lack of clothing.

'She was not trying to manipulate you, Milord,' offered Caitul. 'Princess Exzalander has been friends with Ardahl her entire life. My father said that the queen found it impossible to keep them apart. He believes that to be the main reason for their family moving back north, to the house of Tuâth.'

Katahl listened sombrely as he continued to watch the flames rise and fall.

'But why did she not tell me who she really was? Why lie?'

Caitul added a few more sticks to the fire and warmed his hands gratefully. 'It is not for me to say, Milord, but if I were to hazard a guess, I would say that she was trying to keep her presence at the palace a secret; she would have lied to anyone. From what I can gather, the only reason she was even seen, was because she took time to help *you*.'

'So it really is my fault that the wizard stands charged with treason ... but ...'

'Yes Milord?'

'When I described the princess to Counsellor Sohãhn, he said he was aware of nobody of that description. Would he not have known her to be Exzalander?'

Caitul's brow furrowed; he disliked the Counsellors and had no desire to become embroiled in their devious dealings. 'Yes Milord,' he replied, with reluctance. 'All Council members would have met the princess many times. Why he lied to you, I cannot say and I would rather not guess.'

Katahl's eyes reflected the flames before him and his face was set to steel. 'Why else? To get rid of the only legal majick user in Maldahl. And I handed them the method of their downfall ... Her oldest friend? She will never forgive me if he is executed ...'

'I doubt it will come to that, Milord.'

'Oh, but it may, Caitul.'

Exzalander felt a quiet thrill at the sight of the palace. Many years had it been since she last beheld it from the outside. She was glad the journey was over; she was tired, saddle sore, and could think of nothing she would like more, other than to bathe and sleep.

Bugles sounded at their approach and she felt the ache in her head begin to pound. Entering the courtyard, she noted the entire Council had gathered to greet them and as she dismounted, all eyes stared at her dishevelled form. She still wore boy's clothing—as dirty and unkempt as *she* was.

'Princess Exzalander?' queried Counsellor Hondar.

'Yes Counsellor,' Kryepast said. 'I thought it best to escort her here, to avoid any harm or further mishap.'

'I can speak for myself, King Kryepast,' Exzalander said. Her tone was regal and she was pleased that she had resisted the urge to snap. She had never felt less royal in her life, but her pride was enough to pull her through the awkward meeting. 'Counsellors,' she said. 'I am come here to speak with you on a matter of import, however, it is a concern that can wait until the morning. Kindly see to it that my room is prepared for me.'

High Counsellor Danah gave a stiff nod, his eyes fixed on her odd attire, while his hand beckoned a servant.

'Of course,' he said, 'it is an honour to receive you, Your Highness. King Kryepast, you got our message I deem. What news?'

Exzalander walked off into the palace—a servant rushing ahead to see her needs were met. Once food had been brought and a bath prepared, she was pleased to dismiss them. She sighed with relief as the bustle and noise vanished behind the door. Undressing, she smiled, recalling the last occupant of her chamber and how sweet his touch had been. Sighing, she sank into the warmth of the water and pushed pleasant thoughts from her head, to be replaced by what she might say to the Council.

'It's her, Master, I'm certain of it,' Gailon cried, as he peered down to the courtyard below.

'Come away, boy. If it is Her Highness, then we'll know soon enough. Meanwhile, feed Beaky. He's famished.'

'Aren't we all,' muttered Gailon unhappily.

Nineteen

The sound of a fanfare woke Exzalander from deep slumber. The morning light streamed through a gap in her curtains, and she groaned, pulling a pillow over her head. As the fanfare sounded again, she sat up abruptly. Two fanfares could only mean one thing.

'Father is here,' she said.

Grimacing, she got out of bed, the night having done nothing to ease her weary limbs. Fresh water and a light meal had been left for her; an ice-blue gown was draped across her chair—the chair in which she had placed Katahl. She ran her finger along the arm, before examining the gown.

It was more complex than she liked. Once she had washed and eaten, she summoned a servant to assist her.

'I know you,' Exzalander said, as the girl entered.

The woman looked terrified at the words, but Exzalander was undeterred.

'Yes, you were one of the women who helped me tend to the Lord Katahl.'

The girl fixed her eyes on Exzalander's hair for a moment, then nodded fearfully.

'Forgive me, Your Highness; I have no memory of that time, as Master Ardahl took it away using majick.'

Exzalander breathed in as Hettle tightened the back of the gown.

'It is *I* who should be begging your forgiveness,' she said. 'If not for me, then you would never have been placed in such a position.'

Hettle gave a low curtsey and Exzalander dismissed her. The look in the girl's eyes made it clear that she wanted nothing more than to be away from the woman who had caused her so much trouble.

Exzalander stared at her reflection. The pale colour of the dress did not suit her and only seemed to accentuate the dark circles about her eyes. She took some deep breaths before going down to face her father's fury.

As she entered the throne room, she was dismayed to see that Tuâth was deep in conversation with Kryepast. His face was ghostly white at his friend's words and as his eyes met hers, he seemed several years older. She curtseyed to him, a sign of respect, yet a gesture too late.

'Come here daughter,' he said.

His voice was not angry as she had expected and yet neither was it the voice of her loving father; she heard the voice of her king and felt humbled. Stepping forward, she could not help fixing her eyes on the floor. She heard shuffling about her and glanced up; to her horror, she saw he had summoned the entire Council.

Her cheeks burned at the indignity. *Surely he does not mean to bring up the matter of Katahl in front of them*, she thought. Her mouth felt dry and she had the sudden desire to run away, to keep running, never to return.

'Ardahl the wizard is charged with treason,' King Tuâth said formerly. 'He is believed to have been plotting to bring down our great house by conspiring against us, by training a sorceress without sanction of the Council or myself. What say you to this, Exzalander?'

Exzalander gazed about her. The Council watched her like a hawk might watch its prey. She swallowed, trying to ease the dryness in her throat; all her anger and bluster had gone and she felt keenly, the embarrassment of her father knowing of her behaviour with Katahl. The Council leaned in as she cleared her throat to speak.

'It was me,' she mumbled, as she stared at the floor.

'Explain!' barked her father.

Just for a moment, she hated him for putting her in such a position. She glared up at him and the sudden burst of anger was enough for her to find herself again.

'Ardahl is no traitor! There was no sorceress. I visited Ardahl without my father's permission, without the knowledge of the Council. I broke protocol and I am the one who should suffer, not Ardahl.'

'Yet Ardahl did not inform us of your presence here, Your Highness,' oiled Sohāhn. 'Why is *that* do you think?'

She looked at the counsellor and in an instant she knew that the situation was all his doing. Defiantly, she held his gaze and felt herself appalled when he had the nerve to smile back at her.

'He was under royal command. He had no choice,' she answered, refusing to be the one to look away first.

'But why keep your presence here a secret, Your Highness?' Craibon asked. 'It might make us question what you were doing.'

'I was visiting my friend, that is all,' she cut in. 'I disobeyed my father; this is hardly the Council's concern.'

To her dismay, Sohāhn rose from his chair and approached her.

'Oh, but it is our concern, when your father happens to be the king.'

His eyes were glittering with triumph as he stood beside her—too close for her liking, yet she refused to look away.

'It appears so,' she conceded. 'I was in the wrong. I should have announced my visit.'

To her relief, Sohāhn's eyes moved away from her. He gazed about, seeming to judge the mood of the Council.

'If you deem it necessary to punish me for not following protocol, then that is what you must do,' she said, 'but still Ardahl is blameless in this matter. He is a loyal subject ... and useful. Maldahl is not yet ready to abandon majick altogether.'

Sohãhn's eyes snapped back to her.

'Interesting that you should bring up the subject of majick, Your Highness,' he said, 'when it is truly one of our concerns here.'

'Concerns? I do not see how. Ardahl has done much good. Without his majick, The Lord Katahl would be dead,' she concluded. Her eyes pleaded with Kryepast to back her up.

Sohãhn watched Kryepast's reaction and observed how the king of Starigorat grimaced as she mentioned his son's name. He, however, continued to smile and that disconcerted Exzalander all the more.

'There seems to be some debate on that regard, Your Highness,' Sohãhn said. 'The Lord Katahl believes that it was *you* who cured him.'

'He is mistaken, Counsellor. I merely assisted Ardahl.'

'Indeed? Assisted? By your own admission, Ardahl used majick. Are you therefore admitting to having assisted in the use of majick?'

Exzalander felt her nails digging into her palms and she forced herself to stop.

'Not unless holding a bowl is considered majick use, Counsellor,' she replied dryly.

The sound of several chuckles coming from other Council members was gratifying to hear, and helped her courage to return.

Sohãhn inclined his head, as if conceding to her, but the slow smile that spread, was unnerving.

'Are you denying ever having used majick, Princess?' he asked.

She could feel her cheeks warming again and was unsure she could find the nerve to lie. He saved her the need, however.

'The thing I find difficult to determine, is just how you got home ahead of King Kryepast ... or indeed how you entered the palace unbeknownst to us, if not by use of majick. Do you deny it?'

Tuâth went pale and his hands clasped the arms of his throne.

'I do not deny it,' Exzalander replied. 'I am able to convey myself instantly. It is a skill I have had since I was a child and it is not majick that was *taught* to me.'

There was outcry at her admission. King Tuâth stood, raising his hand and instant silence followed.

'Thank you, Exzalander,' he said. 'You may leave us now.'

She looked back to Sohãhn, who was still smiling at her, the look of triumph emanating across his entire being. Turning back to her father, she nodded and left. Unsure as to why she was being sent away.

As the door was closed behind her, she could hear her father's voice rising and falling beyond it. She longed to try and listen in, but the guards at the door stared menacingly ahead and she did not want to risk them telling the Council. As she walked away, she heard quite clearly the name of Taiohãhn being spoken.

She stopped, recalling the words of the dragon, wondering what Taiohãhn had to do with her. She sat down with her back to a pillar, determined to wait until she could discover what was being discussed. Once or twice, she could make out a particular voice that she recognised. Kryepast spoke and she found herself questioning how any of it was the concern of a foreign king.

'I will not allow it!' Kryepast said flatly.

'But King Kryepast, if His Majesty does not disapprove then why should you?' Counsellor Lachlan asked. 'A match between the great houses would only strengthen us all.'

'On the one hand you're all happy to accept Exzalander as a child of prophecy,' Kryepast said, 'that she can no more help that she has majick than she can help the sky is blue. If you truly believe that she is the chosen one of the gods, then I am right to reject their match. I do not want my son to be a puppet. I will not have him destroyed. Better to suffer a broken heart than ... well, who knows? I have heard many disturbing theories and some of them seem to have very unhappy endings for him. I will not allow it!

'Tuâth, you say something. You of all people should wish to avoid her making a match. To do so would be to bring about your death and Shénnin's. Is that what you want?'

'No of course not,' Tuâth said, with a sad smile. 'I do not want that, my friend, but neither do I want to see my daughter unhappy. I tried to keep Exzalander from knowing her destiny. I told her long ago, and when she seemed to have forgotten, I did everything in my power to ensure that she could lead a normal life; it was all I could offer her, for I learned back then that it was a foolish task to try and avoid fate. What will be will be, Kryepast—that much is sure. Counsellors what say you?'

Almost all of the Counsellors were in agreement with their king. They heard the talk of their sovereigns' demise and their thoughts seemed to lead them to a similar conclusion. All accept one—one whose ambitions were higher still.

'I disagree,' Sohãhn said. 'Exzalander's husband should be chosen from within the house of Shénnin and so strengthen the existing bonds between north and south.'

'Are you suggesting that she should marry a member of the Council?'

'I am,' Sohãhn said.

'Yes ... let her marry one of you,' Kryepast said, 'only please ... not Katahl. I beg you, Tuâth.'

King Tuâth sat back into his throne, sighing. She was his little girl and there they were talking about selling her off to the highest bidder.

'My daughter's happiness is my primary concern here,' he said. 'If she has formed an attachment with Katahl, then I am loath to forbid it. Yet, I do see sense in Sohãhn's words. Whilst she is here, she might be wooed away from your son, if that is your wish.'

'It is,' Kryepast replied.

'Is there any among you who might wish to apply for this suit?' Tuâth asked.

Sohãhn stepped toward the king and if Tuâth disapproved, then he did not show it.

'Very well, you will have until we return to resolve this matter. We will continue to Dragon Mountains, to eliminate their threat, once and for all.'

'My Lord King, is it really necessary to obliterate an entire race?' Counsellor Tyrian asked. 'The dragon trade has proved so lucrative and your treasury has indeed benefited ...'

The stony face of the king moved the young counsellor to silence, causing him to nod in agreement with his king.

'I shall require Ardahl to accompany me,' Tuâth said. 'There is a task I would have him perform.'

'We have not been able to contact him, Your Majesty.'

The king closed his eyes for a moment. 'Now that the charge of treason has been dropped, I'm sure it will prove a lot easier. Let us move onto the final matter of business before we adjourn for refreshment. Send for the prisoner!'

'Beth!' Exzalander exclaimed, as she jumped to her feet. 'What do you here? Are you well?'

The servant's eyes were sunken and she appeared to have lost her fullness of form.

'Beth?'

The doors opened, and the servant was taken in. Exzalander dashed in after her.

'You were not sent for,' said her father. 'You will leave.'

Exzalander thrust out her chin, in defiance. 'No I will not,' she said. 'This is my lady-in-waiting. She is only guilty of following orders. I told her to impersonate me!'

'That is enough! It is not the matter of her impersonation that she stands accused. It is what she did in your name for which she shall receive punishment; you have no say in the matter. Go seek Ardahl if you will; he is cleared of all charges and surely would be happy of such news.'

'May I not be permitted to speak on her behalf?' Exzalander protested.

Her eyes fell on Beth, who gazed fixedly at the floor. The woman's fire was gone and she seemed sunken in the presence of such powerful and forbidding men.

'No you may not. Now leave.'

Exzalander looked about her and her eyes met Sohähn. She realised that if she did not submit to her father's order, then she would be seen to be disobedient again. For the sake of Ardahl, she complied. Curtseying, she gave one final glance to Beth, before leaving the room, Sohähn's eyes haunting her every step.

Twenty

It was a beautiful morning and the knights of Katahl had been permitted to spend it at their ease. Katahl was in no hurry to return and hoped that his father might yet send for him, once his temper had cooled. A little after noon, a messenger arrived from the palace that made Katahl believe his hopes had been realised. The news, however, was not to his liking.

'We are to make for Forest of Iyes, there to await the entire force of our combined guard. We are to march to Dragon Mountains; Tuâth and my father have officially declared war on the Dragon race.'

Nimrïn whistled between his teeth. 'That's going to be some battle. What of your woman? Does he mention her?'

'No,' Katahl replied. Throwing the message aside, he rose to his feet and walked away from them.

'A lot of fuss over a woman … a fight is just what he needs to help put her out of his mind,' Nimrïn said cheerfully.

'Yes, or get him killed,' Dahal interjected.

Caitul watched as his new friend stripped to the waist and waded into the lake.

'She must be something special,' he pondered.

Nimrïn laughed. 'Ah well, all women have something special, my friend. She certainly is a beauty. But that's no reason for him to languish so. It's unmanly!'

Aarnon began to ready their packs and tutted at Nimrïn's words.

'Hardly a fitting way to describe our lord.'

'Bah!' Nimrïn replied, unperturbed by his friend's chastisement.

'Inform Katahl that I'm going to ride ahead and speak to the Ptee Tsa tribe,' Dahal said. 'They will need to be informed of our approaching armies. As I know them well, it is only right that I should do it.'

When Katahl returned to camp, Aarnon spoke with him about Dahal's whereabouts. Nimrïn frowned and took a swig from his flask, immediately spitting out the contents.

'Water!' he cried.

Caitul laughed at his friend's expression.

'You finished the ale last night, remember?'

'No I don't remember,' Nimrïn grumbled. 'It wouldn't have been much of an evening if I did, now would it?'

Caitul shook his head, laughing. 'I suppose not,' he replied.

'Your Highness!' Ardahl exclaimed, as she entered the tower. 'So Gailon here has keen eyes it seems. He said he saw you yester-evening. You are most welcome, as always. What news do you bring? It must be good, for I see no soldiers at your heels.'

Exzalander embraced him.

'Cleared of all charges,' she said. 'Forgive me, for having placed you in that position, Ardahl.'

The old man placed a hand on her cheek and she smiled then, the child of old appearing in her features.

'It is no matter. I knew all would be well. Now, pleasantries aside, you must forgive Gailon and I, as we have an important appointment in the palace kitchens.' He laughed, turning to Gailon, whose relief was clear.

Exzalander accompanied them, telling Ardahl all that had happened since she had left him. She spoke animatedly and seemed lost in her recount. Gailon clearly saw the change in his master's features as she told him of Katahl's declarations of love. He put down his food, as if his appetite had fled. Exzalander continued on, telling him about Syphr and how the wizards had arrived.

'Fahl? It must have been,' Ardahl mused.

'Who is he?' Exzalander asked.

'The wizards you met were called The Order of Vivianne, named after Shénnin's great, great grandmother who founded them, to help her keep order and protect the realm. They were banished years ago—you are probably too young to remember them.' Ardahl took a deep draught of ale and seemed lost in memory.

'But why were they banished and why did they return to help me?'

A servant entered and bowed to the princess. He wore pale grey velvet, the uniform of the personal servants to the king.

'Forgive my intrusion, Your Highness,' he said, 'but I am sent to request Ardahl's presence at once. The king wishes to speak with him on a matter of great import.'

Ardahl waggled his eyebrows at Exzalander, who laughed in return.

'Back in demand,' he said. 'Now Gailon, you can finish your chores when you're done here; don't think about taking up Exzalander's time.'

'Yes Master,' Gailon groaned, as the old wizard left.

Exzalander smiled and finished her drink. 'Do not mind him, Gailon. Take your time. I am going to see if I can find what is happening about my lady-in-waiting.'

Gailon stood as she swept away, scarcely believing that the princess had addressed him, by name too.

As she reached the old throne room, she was dismayed to find it empty.

'Beth,' she whispered, as her concern grew. She turned and headed back down the hall toward the Council Chamber. The door was open and she entered, trying to stay composed.

'Your Highness,' Sohāhn said, smiling. 'This is an unexpected pleasure.'

Exzalander looked dismayed as he offered her a goblet of wine.

She glanced over the empty chairs. 'I thought the Council would be here,' she said.

Sohãhn frowned, as she ignored the cup he had offered. 'You find only me. Everyone is about their duties.'

'And you Counsellor?' she asked, turning to face him at last. 'Do you not have duties too?'

'I do. My duty, Princess, is to you. It is my sad task to inform you that your servant has been sentenced to death.'

He watched as the changes came upon the princess; her skin paled and her hands began to tremble; her lips parted to speak, yet no sound issued forth. He moved toward her then, guiding her to a chair, where she received the wine at last. She held it in her shaking hands, but did not drink.

'It cannot be,' she said, in barely more than a whisper. 'It's all my fault.'

Sohãhn took the opportunity, whilst she was in shock, to observe her; He found her face was even more beautiful in its sorrow. *She will make a fine queen,* he decided.

'Princess Exzalander, forgive my impertinence, but you are blaming yourself when you do not even know of what the woman has been found guilty.'

She looked up at him, not the defiant wilful child from mere hours before, but defeated, broken, her eyes pleading with his own to find understanding and he found that he was excited by her vulnerability.

'She seduced the First Knight to Lord Katahl,' Sohãhn explained. 'She had carnal relations in the guise of your royal person. She sullied your good name and the name of your house, reducing you to nothing short of whore.'

The cup fell from her hands and clattered on the floor— the hem of her dress soaking up the contents and she glanced about, as if in a panic.

'Forgive my language, Your Highness,' Sohãhn said. 'I only wish you to understand the seriousness of her crime.'

'It is most shocking,' Exzalander said. 'I can scarcely believe it.'

She stared down at her wine-soaked dress, biting her lip. All the while, Sohãhn watched her—fascinated.

'Can nothing be done for her?' she asked, after a moment's silence.

Sohãhn made a sound in his throat, which she barely perceived, and picking up the empty goblet, he placed it back on the table.

'You do realise what the woman has done?' he said, his back to her.

'I know,' she pleaded. 'But Beth is not a *bad* person. She made a foolish mistake that's all ...'

The Counsellor whirled around to face her again, his large eyes full of feeling. She could not bear to face those eyes for too long; the intensity of his gaze made her feel uncomfortable.

'The Council did not see it that way,' he said, 'and neither do I.'

She clenched her jaw. *Why am I even bothering to discuss the matter with him?* she thought. *He is the one who had accused Ardahl. It is pointless trying to reason with him.* She got to her feet, summoning the courage to face him.

'Of course you do not see it that way,' she said. 'Why would you? *You* tried to have me arrested for using majick. Why would you look kindly on anything I now say?'

She made for the door, but as she passed him, he grabbed her wrist and pulled her back to face him.

'You're mistaken, Your Highness. It was *I* who defended your use of majick and got the charges against you dropped.'

She stared at him for a moment, unable to believe her ears.

'Everything I have done has been in defence of *you*. I cannot allow his woman, no matter how dear she is to you, to sully your reputation.'

She realised that he was still holding her wrist and pulled herself away.

'Do you not see?' he continued. 'By trying to defend her, you draw attention to your actions again. You must not be seen to stand against your father's decision and ours ... *please.*'

She frowned hard at him. 'But it's all my fault; had I not made her pretend to be me, then this could never have happened.'

Sohãhn raised an eyebrow at her, considering that she was beautiful to be sure, but her defence of a servant left a lot to be desired.

'Whatever the circumstances, her wanton behaviour causes shame to you, Princess,' he said. 'You need to disassociate from her actions, lest your own be brought into question.'

She drew herself up to full height and he saw the fire in her once more.

'Are you threatening me, Counsellor?

He smiled at her and shook his head. 'No Princess, I most certainly am not. Why do you persistently misunderstand my intent?'

She did not know what to say to him. He continued to smile, despite her insult.

'I ... I do not mean to ... I ... I should go. My father would be most displeased if he saw the state of my attire.'

'Very wise, Your Highness,' Sohãhn said, with a bow.

She nodded nervously back at him and left the room. By the time she had reached the safety of her chambers, her heart was fluttering.

She found several maids unpacking her trunk, and her mind strayed to Beth. She was angry at Beth's conduct, but despite Sohãhn's protestation, still felt responsible for the woman's fate.

Pleased to have her own attire once more, Exzalander chose a deep copper colour gown, which brought out the colour of her eyes. She arrived in the courtyard, as her father made ready to depart. Ardahl seemed withdrawn as he greeted her; it was clear that he had no desire to travel with the company. Tuâth was already horsed, armoured and ready for battle.

She wanted to defend Beth, to demand that the sentence be quashed, but seeing him there, about to ride to war, all she felt was fear, and she ran to him.

'Father, please be careful,' she beseeched him. 'I am sorry for my behaviour, truly I am. I cannot lose you ...'

He bent down from his horse to kiss the top of her head.

'There child, do not distress yourself. We all have our duty, even the king; remember that.'

His words did nothing at all to comfort her and she shivered as the company rode away. Long time she stood after they had departed, fear freezing her heart.

'Come, Your Highness, you must be cold standing there. Let us get you in the warm.'

She turned, expecting to see Beth and then she remembered ... she was alone. The woman before her, held out a finely embroidered shawl to warm the princess, but Exzalander pushed her away and fled back to the palace.

Sohãhn, who was watching, smiled.

As evening came, a servant knocked on Exzalander's door, delivering a request from High Counsellor Danah, that she should join them for dinner. She did not want to go. The only thing she wished was to be left alone with her melancholy, but her father's words regarding duty, haunted her and she followed the servant down to the banquet hall.

She winced, as she was announced, wary of her unbrushed hair and creased gown. The assembly stood as she entered and she wished, more than anything, she could be back home with her family, with no stain upon her name and no threat of dragons to darken the day.

The lords and ladies beamed at her presence there, but she could not return their attentions; her smiles were all spent, lost in a time when things had been simpler. A chair had been set next to the High Counsellor and she was relieved when she finally sat and the company returned to their conversation.

The discourse was polite and trivial, much to her relief; she had no desire to discuss her recent actions any further. Feeling exhausted and emotionally drained, she looked down at the food before her and could not help but think of Beth, alone in a cell, awaiting execution.

'You are not hungry, Your Highness?' asked Counsellor Baruch.

'I am afraid not, Counsellor,' she said. ' It has been a long day and I am weary. I desire nothing more than sleep.'

'Is that so? Danah droned, 'but the night is yet young and the company have been eager for your visit. You would not deny them a chance to meet you, surely?' He clearly had no intention of allowing her an early exit.

She forced the corners of her mouth upward into what she hoped resembled a smile and picked reluctantly at the plate of food before her.

Sohãhn watched in silence, as the princess forced herself to eat. She was pale and distressed, that much was clear to him. Yet it pleased him; in the limited time he had been given, her vulnerability would only make her more susceptible to forming an alliance and hopefully more.

After the banquet, the company retreated to the Great Hall. As a child, Exzalander had never been permitted to attend the evening's revelling at Ealdorbold, so it was a new experience for her. The music began to play and drinks were distributed seamlessly by the servants, moving about the throng.

Exzalander wondered if she might slip into a quiet corner until it was all over. She was disappointed to discover that such a wish was impossible as many of the company made directly for her.

'Duty...' she whispered to herself. She gave them a regal greeting, as they lined up before her, trying to forget the soreness of her limbs and exhaustion of too much riding and not enough sleep.

The hours seemed to drag as she conversed with people who eagerly watched her, yet did not really see her. After refusing the fifth dance request, she gazed about desperately, considering how long she would need to endure. Her eyes met with Sohãhn; he leaned against a pillar and appeared to be watching her. *No doubt amused by my discomfort*, she thought. Tearing her gaze away, she forced her attention back to the couple before her.

'Forgive my interruption, Your Highness, but I was wondering if I might have the honour of the next dance.'

The man before her was so young that he could scarcely be called a man at all. She looked into his eager eyes, about to refuse, when she heard the grumble of complaint from the couple with whom she had been conversing.

'Yes, I accept,' she heard herself say, enjoying the look of restrained contempt from the faces of the couple. 'If you will excuse me.' She smiled to them.

The boy took her hand and led her toward the dance floor, clearly terrified. Exzalander concluded that he must have asked her as a dare, not thinking for one moment that she would agree. But whether or not he would prove a worthy dance partner, she never got to discover.

'Your Highness,' interrupted Counsellor Sohãhn, 'I am afraid that I must claim you for an important matter of state.'

She raised an eyebrow. 'Indeed Counsellor, in that case,' she turned towards the boy. 'You must forgive me; perhaps another time.'

The boy bowed low, but by the time he stood straight again, the Counsellor was steering the princess toward the doors.

'A matter of state?' Exzalander mused, as Sohãhn led her away.

'Indeed Your Highness ... an important one, do not forget.'

She nodded as guests bowed and curtseyed as she passed and left the hall with the Counsellor.

'Why is it then, if it is so important, that the rest of the Council remains within?'

'Ah, well,' Sohãhn said, as he walked beside her. 'They are not bored by such tedious company. I felt that it was my *duty*, to remove you from the hall, lest we suffer a diplomatic incident.'

'I see,' she said. As she spoke, the ghost of a smile touched her pallid lips. 'In that case, I am most grateful for your intervention. But tell me, what type of diplomatic incident were you afraid of?'

She lifted her skirts as he led her down the steps and out into the cool night air.

'The type that consists of you assaulting one of the guests.'

Exzalander laughed; it was a sound that warmed him to the core.

'Indeed? Am I really that transparent?' she asked.

He was smiling at her and his eyes locked on her own. The intensity of his gazed caused her to look away almost instantly.

'You have been cooped up all day. A turn around the gardens is just what you need,' he suggested.

She looked up at the moon, beautiful in its purity; the cool breeze felt refreshing after the closeness of the hall.

'Very well,' she agreed. 'But we must remain in plain sight at all times. It would not be prudent to wander off. I am in enough trouble already.'

Sohãhn bowed his head in concurrence with her terms, and offered his arm. She took it warily, her mind questioning his intentions. She had thought him her enemy, and yet now he appeared her only friend.

Perhaps a friend on the Council is exactly what is required, she decided.

Twenty-one

Katahl stared up at the papery moon, wondering if Exzalander saw it too. He had no desire to go to battle; his only wish was to hold her in his arms once more. He knew what Nimrïn would say and he didn't care. *Let the whole world laugh at me if they will,* he thought, *but I will not be deterred from my love. I cannot understand why my father is so angry. Exzalander is the daughter of his oldest friend, it is true, yet surely that is a reason to rejoice. I might have understood such anger had she been a commoner ... it just doesn't make any sense.*

The trees of Iyes towered over them. Nowhere in Maldahl were there trees as mighty. They had been likened to Taiohãhn's realm—the Forest of Forgetfulness. Not that Katahl could directly compare. No mortal had ever been to the Underworld and returned.

He shuddered.

The trees made him uncomfortable and the Ptee Tsa even more so. To him, there was something wholly unnatural about their winged mutations and lack of clothing. *I hope that we will not have to remain here long,* he thought. *When my father arrives, I will set about changing his mind about my choice for a bride.*

Gailon closely watched Ardahl, as they journeyed south. Something was clearly weighing on the wizard's mind.

'Master, what is the matter?'

Ardahl frowned at the intrusion of his solitude. 'Apart from the fact that we are to attempt to wipe out an entire race, why nothing!'

'I know it's more than that,' Gailon muttered. 'Whatever the king has ordered you to do, has upset you.'

'That may be so, Gailon, yet you need not concern yourself with such things.'

'How can you say that, Master? *Your* burden is my burden.'

Ardahl stared out from beneath his bushy eyebrows as they knitted together. He laughed suddenly. 'How very noble of you, boy,' he said. 'Well I suppose I had better teach you something of the spell I'm to perform; if anything goes wrong, you'll be expected to fix it after all.'

Gailon gulped. The only reason *he* would be expected to step in, was if Ardahl was unable to, and the only reason Ardahl would be unable to complete his work was if he was dead.

'Surely I'll not be needed, Master ...' his words trailed off, as he considered how dangerous their mission could prove to be.

Ardahl fixed his eyes ahead and began to tell his apprentice their true reason for being there.

As Exzalander accompanied Sohãhn about the gardens, she began to regret her decision. He was so intense, so very serious, that she wondered if he could ever really be a friend to her. *Yet I have seen a lighter-hearted side to him*, she considered.

'You miss your home, Princess,' Sohãhn remarked.

'I have not really had chance to think about it. Besides, *this* is my home too, you know.'

'I am glad that you think so, Your Highness, and know that it is only truly home when you are in it.'

She stopped, unlinking her hand from his arm. The counsellor silently cursed. *Too much, too soon ... fool.*

'I do not rightly understand you, Counsellor,' Exzalander said. 'Are you teasing me?'

He smiled, his relief well hidden. 'Perhaps a little, Princess,' he replied.

He saw her shiver and frowned as she tried to disguise her teeth chattering. Removing his overcoat, he draped it about her shoulders.

'You are cold, Your Highness. Allow me to return you to the palace.'

He offered his arm and she held it gratefully as he walked her back to the ancient building. At the foot of the steps, she shrugged off his coat and held it out to him. His hand brushed against her own as he received it back from her, and she found herself blush at his touch.

'My thanks, Counsellor,' she said. 'I bid you goodnight.'

Without warning, he clasped her hand in his own and kissed it with a feather-light touch. She turned and almost fled back into the building, leaving him staring after her. Lifting his coat, he took in the scent of her and began to whistle to himself.

At the first landing, Exzalander broke into a run. She could feel the surge of panic rise within her. She did not stop until she was safely in her own chambers—door locked firmly behind her. She stood before the mirror and stared long at her reflection, noticing how her hands still trembled, how her skin was flushed. She also noted how she was no longer a child.

'I must be more guarded,' she whispered, and her fearful reflection mirrored her words. She was unsure of the counsellor's intentions, but was suddenly fearful, rather than grateful, by his attention toward her. *I was without chaperone and walking with a man after dark,* she thought. *Such a thing could be easily misconstrued. I am a fool—a stupid, naïve fool.*

She tugged off her gown and clambered into bed, pulling the covers up over her head, as if to keep her fears away. Outside, she could hear the call of a nocturnal bird on its nightly hunt and she found herself wishing that she had wings, so that she might fly away from the attentions of men.

But Katahl's attentions were so sweet. If she thought hard enough, she could recall the press of his lips to hers; she could remember his declaration of love. *Oh, but I am a fool,* she decided. *Love indeed! Beth warned me of such things, besides, can I love him after so short an acquaintance? Is it not simply the excitement of such a dangerous encounter that I found most thrilling? In the same way the counsellor's eyes penetrate my own, excites me.*

Excites, or terrifies?

Perhaps both.

She drifted off to sleep to such thoughts and had a restless night of dreams, where Beth was trying to teach her about satisfying a man, as she was undergoing her own execution.

Exzalander awoke late and felt as though she had not slept at all. She could hear servants bustling outside her door and rose to open it.

She yawned, as she let them in. 'What time is it?' she asked.

'It is gone ten now, Your Highness. It's warm out too, so I'll lay your silk dress out; it's better for hotter weather,'

'Thank you,' Exzalander said. She tried to stretch out her weariness, as more servants entered, filling her bath and setting out her food.

'You may leave,' she said, when they had finished.

'As you wish, Your Highness.'

To save time, she bathed and ate together, deciding that it would not do to not show her face until after lunch. She combed her hair by the fire, hoping to dry it sooner. The sun blazed through the window and she closed her eyes, letting it warm her face.

Hair still wet, she slipped on the lime green gown. It was sleeveless, not the fashion of the palace and Exzalander thought it likely she would set a new trend. The dress accentuated her slender arms, and the scoop at the neck drew attention to her breasts. She combed the last of the knots out of her damp hair, and went off to greet the day.

In the Forest of Iyes, Dahal returned to his lord with the king of the Ptee Tsa accompanying him. Katahl felt a shudder of revulsion as the small king embraced him as an equal.

'You are welcome here, Lord Katahl. We are happy to escort you through our lands to meet the mighty Kryepast.'

Katahl could feel his jaw clenching and forced his face into a smile. 'We thank you for your hospitality, King Auk. My father is already here?'

'Yes indeed; he awaits you at Sciatháin. He rode hard yesterday and night seemingly. I will take you to meet him.'

The king beat his wings and rose into the air, signalling for them to follow. Katahl could not help staring at the bony protrusions where wing met body and he fought a wave of nausea.

Auk and his guard, led the way through the ancient forest, flitting through the trees above, clearly more comfortable in flight than on foot. Eventually, the trees opened out and looking up, Katahl and his knights saw houses in the boughs above them.

'They live in the trees,' marvelled Caitul.

'Of course,' Dahal said matter-of-factly.

Katahl said nothing. *The sooner I'm away from the abominations, the better*, he thought.

His father was sleeping on their arrival, and Katahl decided it best not to disturb him, despite his eagerness to depart. If Kryepast had ridden through the night, likely he would be in a foul mood if awoken and Katahl had no intention of having to suffer another outburst of his father's temper, in front of his men. Instead, his knights gathered at the foot of the King's tree and gratefully received a late breakfast.

Caitul appeared quite taken to the Ptee Tsa and found their way of life fascinating. Katahl watched with increasing vehemence as his First Knight engaged in conversation with Auk, *the so-called king*. He himself, ate nothing—suspicious of their food, in case their condition was catching. Closing his eyes, he allowed sleep to claim him, rather than have to witness any more.

It was Kryepast who woke him.

'Father? Is it time to leave?' Katahl asked. His voice was filled with caution and he was pleasantly surprised when the king smiled and affectionately squeezed his shoulder.

'It is good to see you, my son. Yes, it is time that we move on. We are indeed honoured, as King Auk sends his best warriors to aid us in our fight.'

Katahl felt his heart sink and he gave his father an awkward smile in acknowledgement. His eyes flitted toward the face of King Tuâth and he felt a surge of fear, as he considered another obstacle that would need to be overcome if he was ever be free to love Exzalander.

To his surprise, Tuâth did not seem angry to him at all. He embraced him, offering his thanks for saving his daughter's life. It was most unexpected and Katahl found himself without words. It was Nimrin's snigger that brought his wits back again, understanding full well what amused the knight so; he wondered if Tuâth had been informed of the whole truth.

'Let us be gone,' Tuâth ordered.

As the army marched on toward Dragon Mountains, Katahl could still hear his knight chuckling, and turned, giving him a warning look to silence him.

'This should prove an interesting journey,' Dahal whispered to Caitul. 'Tuâth knows about Katahl's attentions to his daughter and has, as yet, said nothing. How long before he pulls Katahl aside I wonder? Poor Katahl, he thought to have a tumble in the hay, but the object of his affection turned out to be none other than the High King's daughter. He got more than he bargained for, that is certain.'

Nimrïn could feel the urge to laugh again at the predicament of his lord, and it took all his willpower to suppress his mirth once more.

Exzalander was keen to get outside and greet the sun. Her fears from the previous night were almost forgotten. It was not until she spied Counsellor Sohãhn that they returned. He was deep in conversation with Counsellor Tarim, and Exzalander retreated behind the fountain to observe him, unnoticed.

He was striking to look at, tall with features that appeared to be carved out of stone. His sandy hair shone and swept cleanly about his freckled face. His Counsellor's attire was beautifully tailored, showing his broad shoulders and long legs to full advantage. His pale blue, green eyes, also contrasted perfectly against the black velvet of his clothes. He was almost twice her age and yet still comely.

She sat at the fountain's edge, feeling confused about men, love, growing up and life in general. Kicking her feet up and down, as she had as a child, she found herself craving that innocence back, to be able to return to a time when life was less complicated. The voice of Sohãhn tore her away from her thoughts. It was deep, rich and resonant, making her heart skip a beat.

'Princess Exzalander,' he said, 'I thought that was you I saw. May I say how remarkably fine you are looking this morning? That gown becomes you well.'

She wanted to run away from him, run home and never return. She wasn't speaking and knew that he would expect a reply, but she could not tear her gaze away from the ground.

'Your Highness, does something ail you?' he asked.

She could see his shiny, black boots and let her gaze lift a little to the hem of his robe where his boots and his tight velvet trousers, began.

'I ...' she stammered, forcing herself to face him.

His eyes bore into her as she had expected and she felt more like prey than princess. Yet, despite the severity of his features, his eyes *did* convey worry.

'It is nothing, Counsellor,' she said. 'I thank you for your concern. Please do not let me keep you from your duties.' Her voice was nothing more than a mumble and her gaze fell to his feet again almost immediately. To her dismay, they moved and he sat, uninvited, beside her. Her heart was thumping in her chest and she struggled to breathe.

'Really, I am quite well,' she insisted. 'There is no need to trouble yourself, Counsellor,'

'Sohãhn,' he replied, with a note of finality. 'You always call me by my title and not by my name. Please Exzalander,' he breathed.

His informality startled her and she wanted to tell him how inappropriate his behaviour was, but she could not find the words. Looking up at him, her eyes conveyed the terror that she felt.

'I am concerned about father,' she said a little too quickly. 'I wish he had not ridden to war ...' It was the truth, but not the reason for her odd behaviour.

To her horror, Sohãhn took her hand in his. Her eyes snapped up and he saw in an instant that he had gone too far.

'You must not do that, Counsellor ... Sohãhn,' she finished as an afterthought.

'And why is that, Princess?'

She pulled her hand away, placing it into her lap, her face becoming all defiance.

'Because I am the king's daughter and such familiarity is not permitted,' she snapped. It was all bluster; she felt neither brave nor true anger.

'Can a friend not offer comfort and support to a troubled soul?'

She held his gaze, hoping that she did not blush or tremble.

'I am indeed most grateful for your offer of friendship,' she said, 'yet feel compelled to recall aloud that it was *you* who reminded me about duty and honour. I must be above reproach.'

Sohāhn's eyes narrowed slightly; his mouth lifted into a sly smile as if commending her for trapping him with his own words.

'It *will* please your father to see us friends,' he said delicately.

'Indeed? Well, a good friend would know the rules regarding the king's daughter. A friend would know the title by which she must be addressed and what physical contact is appropriate,' she concluded.

The sun went behind the clouds and Sohāhn's features seemed to follow suit. Exzalander felt suddenly guilty for having upset him.

'You were not quite so adherent to such rules when you were caught in the arms of Katahl,' he replied.

Her hand moved to strike him; it took all her self-control to prevent her from doing so. He had seen the movement and was surprised when the blow failed to land.

'How dare you!' she said.

Her words and her manner were icy as she walked away from him. He wanted to follow her, challenge her, but knew it was not the time, not while the eyes of the court were about them. He watched her retreat back to the palace, taking the opportunity to admire her form as her gown accentuated every curve.

As the princess passed people in the hallways, she felt as though all eyes were on her. Her cheeks burned with anger at

Sohãhn's words. The Council had obviously been informed about what occurred between herself and Katahl. She stormed into the Council Chamber without waiting to be announced. The counsellors present, bowed.

'Your Highness,' droned the High Counsellor. 'How may we assist you?'

'I wish to return home, High Counsellor,' Exzalander replied.

There were nervous glances between the men in attendance and Exzalander knew instantly what their response was about to be.

'I am afraid that will not be possible, Your Highness. Your father left strict instructions that you were to remain here ... protected, until his return.'

'And if he does not return? What then? Shall I remain here forever?'

'Please Your Highness, you seem upset. Is there ought you require to ...'

'I require to return home!' she snapped back at him.

'That we cannot grant you. I am sorry.'

She looked about her; six Counsellors were present and they all *knew*.

Her face burned with both anger and shame, and she flounced from the room. She made for her chamber, but Sohãhn's approach prevented her. She could bear no more; hot tears ran down her cheeks and, turning, she broke into a run, retreating to the only place where she could be away from everyone.

Twenty-two

*S*he had almost struck him for his impertinence. *Perhaps I should not have mentioned the young lord,* Sohãhn considered. *I let emotion overtake me for a moment—my anger that the Lord Katahl should prove so adept in matters of love play, and it has cost me dear.*

Deep in thought, he walked slowly toward the Council Chamber, when he spied the princess storming toward him. She was clearly distressed, her face reddened and her eyes set hard. As she saw him, she stopped and he saw the tears as they began to form, just before she ran from him.

He pursued.

It was more of an instinct than a conscious decision. When a mouse dashes past, the cat has no choice other than to chase it; it's in his nature to do so.

As Exzalander turned the corner, Sohãhn picked up his pace, unwilling to run in case it should draw unwanted attention; as he turned the corner, she was gone—the only way out being …

'The catacombs … of course.' *She knows the way to Ardahl's Tower and has retreated there,* he realised. *Still, she has to eat sometime!*

Beaky seemed pleased to see the princess as she entered the tower. She sniffed quietly as she fed the hungry bird.

'Oh Beaky, I wish Ardahl was here.'

The bird squawked as she walked away from him. She lay down on the bed, crying herself to sleep.

The evening banquet came and went with no sign of the princess. The High Counsellor was furious when Sohãhn informed him where she had gone.

'Technically, she hasn't left the palace; she is not disobeying her father,' Serin offered, to which Danah growled.

Tyrian tutted and took a draught of his wine. 'Well let her sulk,' he said. 'She can't stay up there forever.'

'She won't need to,' said Hondar. 'There's many ways out of that rat hole Ardahl calls home. How do you think he managed to stay up there so long when he faced his charge of treason? If the princess knows her way up there, she most likely knows other escape routes too. She could hide up there indefinitely.'

Sohãhn felt his stomach turn. 'That does it!' he said, rising. 'I'm going to fetch her down.'

Briam laughed. 'Don't be ridiculous,' he said. 'You'll never find her; you'll only get yourself lost and there's nobody here who'll be able to find you. It's suicide to even try, so sit down.'

'*She'll* be able to find me.'

'Huh, only if she wants to, and from what I hear, it was your fault that she came asking to leave in the first place!'

Sohãhn sneered, his eyes narrowing. 'And if I discover who told you that, Briam, I will ensure that he is rewarded with the removal of his tongue.'

Many of the company stared after him as he walked out; Serin stood as if to go after him.

'Oh let him go, Serin,' Danah huffed, 'if the fool is stupid enough to enter the catacombs, then he deserves his fate! His ambitions are disturbingly high. This could be a fine opportunity to gain a new brother, one who shares our vision of things to come.'

Counsellor Serin took his seat once more to the many nods of agreement from his fellow counsellors.

It was dark when Exzalander awoke. The moonlight bathed Ardahl's Tower in an eerie glow. Beaky seemed sound asleep and all was silence. She stretched and got to her feet, walking over to the window. She could not guess what the time was, but reckoned it was late.

'Wonderful,' she sighed, 'in trouble again.'

Resigning herself to the fact that she would have to apologise to the Council, she headed for the door and down the corridor. The way to the tower was guarded by majick; only those who knew the way were certain of safety. The first thing to remember was, although the tower was the highest point of the palace, the route to it always led downward. Climbing would only lead to a labyrinth of blackness and most likely death—unless you were lucky enough to be heard by one of the few people who knew the way. Two of those dwelt in the north and had moved when their king returned to Brëgwela; two were on route to Dragon Mountains; that left Exzalander.

She was about half way back when she heard the voice in the darkness.

'Princess *please!*'

She started at the sound of a voice from where there should have been only silence. She stopped—listening, wondering if perhaps she might have imagined it.

'Your Highness, I am lost.'

It was Sohãhn's voice, alone in the darkness. She had not recognised it at first; although resonant still, it had lost the velvet confidence and desperation had set in.

Should I help him? she questioned, then cursed herself for her deliberation, knowing that to leave him stranded in the catacombs was nothing short of murder. She heard his call again and her feelings clarified in that moment of his desperation. She feared *because* she was so drawn to him, attracted to him even. But beyond that, she did not ponder.

'Stay where you are!' she shouted. 'I am coming to you.' She dashed up the stairs and called out to him again. 'Keep talking to me and I will find you.'

'Forgive me,' he called back.

She found herself struggling to concentrate as his words from earlier in the day came back to haunt her.

'Not now, Counsellor, I must focus without distraction of conversation. Tell me a story,' she suggested. 'Anything, but keep talking.'

'Very well,' he replied, pushing back his fears. He began to recite a story from his childhood, a tale of a Mo-rye and a mermaid. As he spoke, he closed his eyes and his fear began to melt away.

Exzalander heard the change in his voice, as he recited his tale. His rich, confident tone returned and she smiled, drawing closer. Surprisingly, he was not as far away from the path as she would have expected.

'I can see a light!' he called out.

'That's the path. Can you make your way toward me now?'

'Yes, I believe so.' He held out his hands and felt along the wall, heading toward the faint glow before him. As he drew closer, the corridor began to narrow, until he was uncertain that he would be able to reach the light beyond.

Exzalander saw a hand reach through a tiny gap in the walls and stepped up to touch the stone. Before him, the very walls rumbled as they dragged themselves apart to reveal the face of his saviour, bathed in torchlight.

Sohãhn stepped into the corridor to join the princess, wanting to ask about majick walls, but finding himself unable to speak.

'What were you thinking coming here?' she scolded him. 'Do you have a death wish?'

He saw the concern in her features then and he was glad that he had taken the risk.

'I had to find you,' he breathed.

She tutted and turned away from him.

'Why?' she asked. 'Did you come to insult me some more? Have you not said enough? You malign me, without knowing *anything* about what happened! I did not seek Katahl out; he discovered me!'

Sohãhn took a step toward her and she turned to face him once more, as if defensively keeping an eye on his movements.

'Why were you in Ichnaarim then, if not to see Katahl?' he asked. He could tell from her eyes that she was getting angry with him again.

'I went to find Ardahl,' she snapped. 'I knew of the charges against him and was concerned. Stupidly, I thought to find him there and do not look at me like that. Yes I know I should have spoken to the Council first and I have already apologised for my actions.'

'And Katahl?'

'I did not even know who Katahl was. He recognised me as the woman who had helped him, and insisted on escorting me here.'

'Indeed? And why was it then, that you failed to mention who you were? Why not declare it at once?'

'I was not supposed to be there; you know that. It was one of the reasons I was made to defend myself to you and the rest of the Council. I was disobeying father's orders.'

'You were found kissing him, Exzalander! Do you think me a fool?'

She winced at the use of her name again. 'Yes,' she snapped back at him, taking him by surprise. 'Yes you are a fool. I don't even know the Lord Katahl; he seemed very nice and, had I been able to spend more time with him then perhaps … We had just been attacked by a dragon; it was terrifying and exciting and … I don't know what else to say. I was caught up in the moment and I behaved wrongly. But so did you! You go on about my behaving as is fitting to my station and yet you treat me with no more respect that he did.

And Katahl did not know who I am. *You* do! You should know better.'

He stared at her, her tiny fists beginning to clench, her face flushing with anger, and he laughed.

'I fail to see what amuses you, Counsellor Sohãhn,' she said, through gritted teeth.

'Oh my Princess, anger becomes you well.'

'Stop that … it is not funny.'

He stepped toward her again and she instinctively tried to retreat, but found herself backed up against the wall.

'You made it clear that a public display was unwanted, yet here we are, not another soul near or within even hearing distance.'

'Stop it … please,' Exzalander ordered, as he closed in. The anger was gone in an instant to be replaced by fear.

One hand rested on the wall behind her, the other stroked her hair along its length until it reached her breasts. She gasped as if to protest again, but words eluded her.

'Your father chose me as a suitor,' he said. 'You must put all thoughts of Katahl out of your pretty head.' Gently squeezing the breast nearest his free hand, his remaining hand left the wall and worked along her back, gently pulling her hair, so that she was forced to look up at him.'

'Please … stop,' she whimpered, her heart racing. She wanted to run, but fear froze her to the spot.

'There's no-one to hear us …'

His mouth hovered above her own and as he closed in, she caught the aroma of sandalwood. At that moment, her body yearned to surrender to him. As his lips crushed against her own, she felt his hand squeezing her bottom as the other groped her breast. Her breath came in gasps as she offered further protest. His eyes were blazing as he continued to fondle her, his mouth moving to her ear, where he thrust his tongue inside.

She felt giddy and lost all focus and control. The sensation of his tongue as it pushed into her ear was almost too much to bear. She was panting between protests and the noise only excited him more. Pushing against her, he allowed her to feel the hardness below. He manoeuvred his foot so that he pushed her legs apart; she did not even notice.

Kissing her neck sent her into a frenzy of moans that was making him lose all control. His hand left her breast and began to pull up her gown; still she remained unaware, as his lips caressed the base of her neck. It was not until his hand touched the inside of her thigh, did Exzalander become conscious of his new intrusion and as he began to gently stroke upward, he felt her tense.

'No!' she protested, and began to struggle.

His free hand held her against the wall, as his other continued to climb.

'Stop,' she whimpered.

He gazed at her, her neck reddened from where his mouth had done its work.

'I am not going to hurt you, Exzalander,' he said.

He spoke quietly and his hand found its target. His fingers ran along the smooth velvety folds of her skin and smiled as she gasped. The hardness in his pants was almost painful, but he knew that would have to wait. He forced self-control again, moving his fingers up and down then circling.

'What are you doing to me?' she gasped. Her eyes closed as her mouth opened and she licked her lips.

'Does that feel good?' he smiled, enjoying the power he held over her.

'Please stop; this is wrong,' she said breathily, between her gasps of pleasure.

'Do you really want me to stop?' he asked. His voice was half-hearted, as he moved a little faster, stopping abruptly as he waited for her reply.

Her eyes snapped open and she held his gaze, the intensity of it finally matching his own and he could see that she was losing all control. She knew what she wanted, he considered, whether she had experience or not. However, it would not do to let that moment pass. It would not do for her to order him to stop.

He gently dipped the end of his finger inside, enough to wet it and began to tease her clitoris again. Her eyes were still blazing into his own and he enjoyed the fire he found there, challenging him to satisfy her.

'I shall take that as a no then, shall I?' He smiled, as he felt her getting slicker.

Her head was swimming; part of her was screaming for him to stop. The problem was, the voice was inside her head, being drowned out by her desire to surrender to him. His lips touched hers once more and she met his kiss with her own — enjoying the taste of dessert that still lingered on his tongue. He seemed surprised by her sudden ferocity and fought for dominance again. Drawing away, he held his mouth close to her own, his eyes glittering in the torchlight.

'I will taste you now,' he stated. His words were not whispered, but clear and resonant as was his wont. They seemed to bounce off the walls back at her. She didn't understand, naively mistaking his intent for what he had already been doing. To her fascination and growing unease, he slowly placed his wet fingers into his mouth, all the while watching her reaction, daring her to look away. The fear was returning to her eyes — exciting him all the more.

She opened her mouth to protest again.

'Shhhh,' he whispered directly into her ear, sending shivers down the length of her body.

Seamlessly, he bent until he knelt before her, savouring the sight of her erect nipples on his way down, as they pushed against the silk of her gown. One hand still held her gown up and he brought his other to join it, giving him a view of that which no man had been permitted to see. He drew closer, taking in the scent of her. She was driving him crazy. All he wanted to do was place himself inside her and relieve the desire. *Now is not the time,* he fought to remind himself.

She began to struggle again and he pushed her back, breathing slowly at her opening.

'I told you; I want to taste you.'

'No,' she cried. 'You must not … please.'

She was pushing at his shoulders, making it difficult for him to concentrate.

'Soha …' she began to cry, but failed to order him to stop as he thrust his tongue inside her.

The shock of what he was doing, left her feeling violated, until the waves of pure pleasure drove away such thoughts and she surrendered completely. He thrust his tongue as deeply as it would go and moved it slowly in a circular motion inside her. As he flicked in and out, he felt her resistance to him melt away.

'Sohãhn,' she breathed. It was a plea for mercy.

She couldn't take much more, he realised and was delighted as her hands began to play with his hair and he sucked, driving her moans to a crescendo. Pushing two fingers deep inside her, he felt her body protest in pain for a few moments. Thrusting hard into her, slowly at first, he leaned in and built up speed. Her eyes closed and she looked beautifully dishevelled to him.

'Do you want me to fuck you?' he breathed, watching her reaction closely.

Her eyes flicked open and she seemed to fight the building ecstasy for a moment. Her breath came in short snatches. 'I know not what that means,' she struggled to say.

'It's like this, my Princess, only better,' Sohãhn explained, with a leer.

'Yes,' she surrendered. 'Fuck me Sohãhn. Fuck me, if you will.'

The words sounded delightfully strange coming from the lips of the future queen, but Sohãhn enjoyed hearing them — enjoyed seeing her beg him to please her. Suddenly, he pulled away and let her skirts drop. The look of alarm in her beautiful eyes made him want to give in to her demands, even though she had no concept of what it was that she asked of him.

'I must stop,' he said. 'Forgive me, Exzalander; my passion for you carried me away. It is not something that you should experience before your wedding night, besides it will be painful, unless ...'

Her eyes seemed hurt and confused. *It will not do to let the throws of ecstasy wear off too much*, Sohãhn thought.

'Unless what?' she whimpered — helpless.

He smiled slowly. 'Unless I prepare your body beforehand,' he said matter-of-factly.

'How would you do that?' she murmured.

'Why, by what we have just been doing, of course.'

'Oh,' she replied, appearing embarrassed.

'Would you like that?'

'I ... no ... you should not have done that to me!' she cried.

'Lift your skirts.'

'What?'

'You heard me, Exzalander. Lift your skirts and let me finish what I started. You were almost there and I don't intend to stop again until you come.'

'Come where?''

He smiled slyly, lifting a solitary eyebrow at her misunderstanding.

'Lift, your, skirts!' he demanded.

He saw the merest glimpse of tears in her eyes as she obeyed him and he thought that he might burst when she opened her legs to him.

'Oh Exzalander,' he breathed.

Closing in, he thrust his fingers inside her, once more. His other hand danced upon her clitoris sending her reeling again.

'You're mine … say it!' he ordered.

'I am yours,' she whimpered.

She felt the sensation within her peak and she cried out, the muscles within her contracting in waves against his fingers. He cried out too, and they leaned against each other for a moment of perfect silence.

He had climaxed. She had made him come with only her voice as it cried out to him. He wondered if she realised; he didn't think so. Gently sliding his fingers from inside her body, he kissed the top of her head. She looked up at him then, her eyes glassy with post ecstasy and tears.

'Sohãhn,' she breathed. 'I …'

But whatever she was going to say, he stopped with his kiss. His touch was gentle as he held his lips to hers for what seemed like minutes.

'Marry me,' he said, as he pulled away from her.

Her body felt alive at that moment … wonderful.

'I must speak to father …'

'He has already given his consent, Exzalander,' Sohãhn cut in.

'So you say, but I have yet to hear that from him.'

She began to walk away from him, back in the direction of civilisation. He strode up behind her and held her by the shoulders.

'You do realise what we just did, do you not? How can you hesitate with an answer after that?'

She turned to face him, her features stern.

'What *you* did,' she snapped. 'I tried to stop you!'

He reached out and drew her closer to him, staring down into her eyes.

'Are you saying that you did not enjoy it?'

She could feel a tingling sensation, as she stared up at him.

'Whether I did or not is irrelevant; it was not permitted. I should not have succumbed to such pleasures!'

He smiled warmly and kissed her forehead.

'I didn't give you much of a choice,' he said.

She stiffened in his arms.

'No you didn't, Sohãhn,' she retorted. 'Now, I am returning to the palace. I suggest that you follow, unless you want to spend a night in the dark of the catacombs.'

She turned and stormed away from him. He followed closely behind her, his smile wider than usual. As the light of the palace was about them once more, Sohãhn caught hold of her hand.

'Please say that you will think over my proposal, Princess,' he said quietly.

'I will give it careful consideration, Counsellor Sohãhn. Goodnight.'

'Good night, Your Highness,' he murmured, as she strode away from him. He smiled, making for his bedchamber and a clean change of clothing.

Exzalander stood with her back to the door for a long time, considering what had occurred. She felt a surge of embarrassment at how easily she had surrendered to him. *I should have struck him ... called for help*, she reflected. *Ah, but he chose his hunting ground wisely, and I (fool that I am) walked straight into his trap.*

I should report him. He should be made to pay ... but whom can I tell? I cannot possibly face the Council and accuse him, because I could never speak of such a thing to them ... I wish mother were here.

Pulling off her gown, she stared at her naked reflection; her skin about the neck still appeared flush, her nipples definitely larger and pinker than usual. Her eyes went lower still and stared at the plume of hair between her legs. She had paid no heed to it before. Tentatively, she allowed her hand to touch herself, finding the wetness that remained. Her fingers played a while, recalling what he had done to her, before she ran to the water bowl and scrubbed herself clean.

Twenty-three

That night, Exzalander's dreams were confused; she relived the experience over and over; sometimes it was with Sohãhn and others it was Katahl who committed the same sweet invasion of her. In her last dream, both of them played with her together and she awoke to the memory of the sound of Sohãhn's grunt as he called out in ecstasy.

It was early, too early to be up and about, but she had no desire to be haunted by men any longer. Avoiding the water from the previous night, she got dressed, deciding to venture downstairs. It was quiet, only a scattering of servants, certainly no Counsellors or members of the court. It gave her an idea. She headed toward the rear of the palace down into the deep recesses—to the dungeon.

Only one guard was on duty, and he was half asleep. She was almost past him before he spluttered.

'Halt! Who goes there?'

Exzalander stood tall. 'Princess Exzalander, to see the girl Beth,' she said authoritatively.

The man blushed for a moment, before bowing low.

'I'm sorry, Your Highness; nobody is permitted access to the prisoner. Orders of the Council.'

'The Council?' she scoffed. 'I am the future queen! I *shall* pass.' She walked by him, knowing that he would not dare to physically prevent her, giving a sly smile, as she realised she had got the better of him. It was a sensation that turned quickly to revulsion, as the smell of faecal waste and urine burned her nostrils.

The guard had not followed her and she wanted to run back and demand that he explain the appalling conditions. She held a hand under her nose, shouting Beth's name.

'Milady, is that you?' came a reply.

Exzalander heard the cry and saw Beth's tiny fingers poke out from the grate of a nearby cell door. She ran and touched fingers to the much-stained hands of her former lady-in-waiting.

'Oh Beth, what have they done to you?'

The girl peering out from the darkness, was barely recognisable. She had lost weight; her hair was lank and greasy; the glow in her face and sparkle in her eyes were completely gone.

'Milady, I am so sorry,' she wept.

'Hush Beth; none of that now,' Exzalander said. She spoke sternly, but did so to fight her own tears, wondering if Beth knew that she was to be executed.

'I bedded the knight, Caitul; I was so foolish. I did not think about what could happen. I am so sorry,' she sobbed, and the sound was of deepest desperation.

Yes she knows what is to happen to her, thought Exzalander. 'I am not here to chastise you, Beth. I just wanted you to know that I was thinking of you.'

Beth's sobs stopped abruptly. 'Can you get me out of this, Milady? Is there ought you can do?'

Exzalander felt suddenly angry that Beth was asking her, even if she would have put herself in such a position freely.

'How can I speak for you, without your behaviour reflecting on me?'

'Oh Milady please!' Beth pleaded.

'I will try,' Exzalander relented.

Beth gripped her hand, her cries reaching a terrible crescendo.

'Release Her Highness at once!' came a commanding voice.

Exzalander saw the fear in Beth's eyes as she backed away, before retreating to the darkness of her cell. She turned, anger fuelling her, and was surprised to see Sohähn stood in his bedclothes, before walking back up the corridor. Her anger was tempered with the sudden urge to laugh, as she followed him back to the guardroom.

'Wait outside!' he barked at the guard.

'Stay!' Exzalander ordered.

The unfortunate guard stood still, perplexed by the opposing orders from his superiors. He looked back to Sohãhn, his eyes pleading.

'I gave you an order, man,' Sohãhn growled.

'Do not trouble yourself,' Exzalander snapped. '*I* am leaving. If the counsellor wishes to converse with me, he may do so away from this pigsty!'

As she flounced from the dungeon, the counsellor followed her and the guard sighed with relief, counting the minutes until the approaching shift change.

Sohãhn was slightly out of breath, Exzalander noted. She concluded that he must have run to catch her in the dungeon.

'You should not have been there,' he growled under his breath.

She felt the corners of her mouth twitch into a smile. He looked furious at her reaction and it only made her want to laugh even more. Such a reaction was hysteria, though Sohãhn did not realise. The man who terrified her, mere hours before, had degraded and molested her was stood before her in his nightgown, his hold over her seeming suddenly castrated. It was the shame over what had occurred that left her with the options to cry or laugh; she chose laughter.

'Counsellor Sohãhn, if you wish to say something to me regarding this matter, might you leave it until you are more suitably attired,' she chided. Walking away, she giggled childishly.

The counsellor stood for a moment, in shock. Of all the reactions to him that he had expected that morning, laughter had not been one of them. Pacing back to his quarters, he fantasised ways he would make her pay for her mirth.

On her return to her room, Exzalander found the servants making her bed and setting out her breakfast.

'Forgive us, Milady, we did not know you were to rise early...'

'Do not trouble yourselves,' Exzalander said, 'it is of no matter.'

'We've prepared you a bath. Would you like it now, or shall we remove the water?'

Exzalander smiled as she picked a strawberry from her plate. 'No, I shall take it thank you.'

'Is there ought else that you require, Your Highness?'

'No, thank you; you may leave.'

She set the breakfast on a stool next to the steaming bath, and removed her gown. The warm water caressed her skin as she sank down, sighing. Steam filled the air and she closed her eyes, reaching over to pick a grape from her plate and popping it into her mouth.

A click sounded from behind the screen and she called out.

'Is anyone there?'

Silence.

She sank back into blissful warmth, reminding herself to lock the door in future. Closing her eyes again, she began to drift into a light sleep, dreaming almost the same dream again. She could feel the pressure between her legs, as Katahl caressed there. It felt more real this time. Her eyes snapped opened and she saw Sohãhn at her side, his sleeve rolled up and his hand ...

She started.

It wasn't a dream.

'I hope you don't mind, but I helped myself to some of your breakfast,' he said lazily. Dipping a strawberry between the soft folds between her legs, he ran it along, before removing it and placing it between his lips, savouring each bite with an appreciative 'mmm'.

'Stop that!' she hissed.

He smiled slowly and she felt the familiar tingles of excitement and terror combined.

'Get out!' she ordered.

He leaned over her, savouring the sight of her breasts beneath the water.

'Shhh Princess, you would not want anyone to find me here, would you?'

'You have no right to be here,' she whispered. Sitting up, she wrapped her arms about her legs, to disrupt his view.

'Maybe so,' he said, 'but you had no right to visit the dungeon.'

'I had to see Beth.'

'I warned you why that was not prudent. Can you not see that I am trying to protect you? What that woman did was wrong. You cannot associate yourself with that.'

Exzalander stood suddenly and the counsellor was stunned into silence by the naked body before him. His eyes were level with her navel, but could not help but rove across ever inch of her. She stepped from the water and swiftly wrapped herself in a towel.

'How am I any different?' she hissed, her voice little more than a whisper. 'What you ... what we did last night ...'

'It *is* different, Princess and you know it.'

'I do not see how,' she snapped back at him. 'I cannot simply stand by and watch her burn.'

'Then I suggest you do not look,' Sohãhn said.

His tone was flippant, her defence of the servant starting to annoy him. The last thing he expected was the slap that followed.

'Get out!' Exzalander ordered. This time there was no mistaking she meant it. She glared at him when he remained unmoving.

'This really means that much to you?' he said.

She felt a tiny jolt at his words—the flames of hope.

'It does,' she answered carefully.

'What if I were to arrange for her to escape?' He watched her closely, judging her reaction.

'Escape? But can you not revisit her sentence?' she asked.

'Not possible; I am willing to help her escape, but you must have no more to do with the woman from this moment on.'

'But if you were caught …'

'Then I would join her in death,' he said. 'I take this risk for *you* and hope that you will remember as much when you give me your decision on my proposal.'

She considered if that meant he would not help Beth if she refused him, but was too affeared to ask.

'This is what your father wants, Exzalander,' he coaxed. 'Katahl was refused consent by the court and Kryepast. He is not an eligible suitor to you.'

'And my father?'

'I told you, he gave *me* his blessing, and I will do this for you, my Princess, to prove myself a worthy suitor.'

She sank to the bed, her sheet starting to slip. *It is clear that he despises Beth; he has made no attempt to hide the fact,* she thought. *But he has said that he was willing to help.* She had never felt so conflicted. Part of her was disgusted with herself; she felt used, yet part of her relished the sensations he had aroused within her. Her feelings toward him were equally as conflicted and she thought about letting her father down again. *If this is really what he wants then …*

'Yes,' she whispered.

He looked down at her, the marks from where she had struck him, beginning to redden.

'Yes? I do not comprehend you,' he said.

'Help Beth escape and, as long as father approves … I will be your wife.'

The triumph in his eyes shone out as he smiled at her.

'You have made me so happy, Exzalander and I will endeavour to make you so.'

He moved toward her and she stiffened.

'How now Exzalander?'

'You should leave,' she suggested, 'before someone barges in.'

He sat beside her and she felt goose bumps form as he breathed near her neck.

'I locked the door.'

'But you said …'

'I lied.'

His hands caressed her bare neck and shoulders and she felt tremors of pleasure across her body.

'We cannot do this,' she said pathetically. 'I know this is wrong. We can wait until we are wed.'

His lips brushed the nape of her neck and she sighed.

'Practice remember; I need to prepare you. Now lie back.'

'I will do no such thing.' She tutted and shook him free, fighting to gain control of her senses once more.

'Tired of me already?' he asked, his voice playful.

'No … I … Sohãhn please. You need to leave.'

'Not only rejection, but you struck me also,' he ended.

His eyes seemed to harden and she looked ashamed.

'I am sorry,' she offered. 'I should not have hit you.' Reaching up, she dared to touch his reddened cheek.

His eyes glittered as she stroked his face and hair. She had agreed to be his. She was handing him the entire kingdom along with herself.

'Beautiful,' he breathed, overwhelmed by his sudden good fortune.

She smiled at him then and her tender touch warmed him.

'I love you,' he said, and for that moment, he meant it.

She kissed him; the touch of her lips was soft and warm; more caring than any woman he had taken before. *Servants, whores, all of them,* he thought. *But she is my lady and will give me everything that I desire.*

He returned her kiss with a ferocity that took her by surprise, his weight pushing her back, until she was lying on the bed. Climbing on top of her, his lips never left her own and as he pushed the hardness in his trousers against her, he was delighted to see her eyes open in terror.

She could feel him as he rubbed against her and again, her fear filled him with desire. She knew what men had down there; Beth had told her all about it. She also knew that she was not ready to experience such a thing for herself.

'No,' she struggled.

The anger in her eyes made him climb off her.

'Do not fear me, Princess. Some things must wait, I know. But for now...'

He peeled open the already loosened sheet and stared down at her perfect body. Her pert breasts stood to attention as her arousal grew.

His silence unnerved her. 'What are you doing?' she whispered.

'I am looking at my bride to be.'

'Only when you free Beth,' she protested.

'Do you think that I would fail to do so when I have been offered such an incentive. Do you think that I would wish to give up this?' he leered.

Leaning over, he began licking one of her nipples, enjoying how it grew harder as he placed it into his mouth.

'You've had lots of women I am sure,' she panted. 'So it must merely be my position that attracts you.'

He stopped, holding her eyes for what seemed like an age.

'It is true,' he said.

She seemed hurt beyond measure; the pain in her eyes, the greatest aphrodisiac to him.

'I *have* had lots of women,' he affirmed.

Her relief was clear.

'But none compare to you,' he continued. 'I will not lie to you, Exzalander. Your position and power are an attractive dowry, but you must also know how beautiful you are, how amazing and how you make me feel.'

She was silent, staring up at him, mesmerised by his words. He had not denied that he wanted to marry her for power. If he had, then she would have disbelieved him anyhow.

He saw the confusion in her eyes and decided to make things clearer. His eyes ran along the length of her milk-white skin and stopped at her most private place. He had seen a glimpse of it before, in the flicker of torchlight, but now, the pink soft folds of her flesh called out to him, wet and begging.

She watched as he examined her form; seeing where his gaze fell, she instinctively began to close her legs. Both of his hands shot out to prevent her; with a hand on each knee, he gently pushed her legs apart and climbed between them.

'Beautiful,' he said again, taking in the scent of her. 'Now you'll need to stay as quiet as you can. You wouldn't want to be heard now, would you?' he breathed.

Delighted, he saw her body react as the heat of his breath, caressed her. He held the tip of his tongue to her clitoris, its hardness mirroring his own. He dabbed it a few times and her back arched in pleasure. Smiling, he licked the length of her, his saliva mixing with her wetness.

'Now, let us see how tight you are today.' He let a hand slip down from one of her knees and his fingers slid into her.

'That's good; easier than yesterday,' he said, as he pushed his fingers in and out. 'Let's try one more, shall we?'

He pulled his hand away and she watched as he smoothed the slick wetness on his middle fingers, across a third.

'Open your legs, wider,' he leered. His eyes glittered with such intensity that she obeyed him without question—compelled.

He gasped as she pulled her legs open as wide as they would go. She could feel the damp between her legs as it began to trickle out of her.

'Exzalander,' he breathed, as his arousal grew.

'Sohãhn,' she answered.

He placed three fingers at her opening and pushed. She stifled a cry, as the pain hit her and he shushed her as softly as a mother would her child.

'There now,' he said, 'let us go gently at first. This is only training after all.'

He eased his fingers out a little and then back in; she whimpered, clearly in pain. Placing his tongue on her clitoris he played, holding his hand still, allowing her to get used to the sensation of him inside her. Her whimper turned to a low moan and he was delighted when he felt her hips rock against his hand. She was wetter than ever and he let his hand join in once more, in counter rhythm against her.

The pain was gone and she struggled to keep her moans quiet when he began sucking her clitoris, as he thrust his fingers in and out.

He wanted her so badly, wondering if she would have the strength to protest if he opened his pants. *Will she cry out for help if I push my dick deep inside her?* He struggled to keep hold of his sanity. *She tastes so good; she's so wet*, he thought. *By Taiohãhn, I so desperately want to fuck her, to hear her scream as I push as deeply as I can go.*

She could hear his moaning, as his arousal grew. She could feel his thrust become more urgent and battled to keep from crying out as she climaxed.

Her back arched and her muscles tensed and Sohãhn felt another ripple within her before he pulled his hand away. Her vagina looked dark, inviting, and so very wet.

She lay back, her eyes closed and she held a sweet smile across her face. 'Sohãhn,' she sighed.

It was too much for him to bear. Unbuttoning his fly, his penis burst out, looking hungry. She sighed, as he gently touched her again, the feeling different.

'Mmm,' she murmured.

Her eyes opened slightly to see him. However, he was not looking at her but down between them, where his hand held …

'No!' she protested. She saw the huge member protruding from his open trousers and tried to sit up, but his weight prevented her.

'I just want to feel you,' he whispered desperately, running his penis along her opening.

'It is wrong … you could be executed. You need to wait.' She tried to soothe him into stopping, but he continued to stare down as the wetness between her legs coated one side of him.

'I know,' he breathed. Holding the tip of it outside her body, he wet it, as he moved it around. 'Let me inside you, Exzalander,' he asserted. 'I won't do anything, please, just let me put it in you.'

'You said it would hurt,' she pleaded.

'I think you have trained enough; time to let me in.' His eyes snapped up and locked on her own.

'No!' she began to command.

Her protest was stifled, as he covered her mouth with his hand. Holding himself over her, he pushed. There was a beautiful resistance at first and then he felt himself slide into tight velvet heaven. She struggled under him, and the screams from beneath his hand only made him swell within her. Her eyes were full of fear and pain, as he sank as deep as he could go.

'Now does that not feel good?' he breathed over her. 'I am going to take my hand away if you promise not to call out. Do you promise?'

Tears formed in her eyes and she nodded.

'I didn't hurt you, did I?' he asked half-heartedly.

'Please stop this,' she entreated. 'You know it's wrong,'

'I'm not doing anything. You cannot expect to have all the fun now, can you?'

'You are right.'

'What?' he questioned.

Her reaction drew him away from his desire to continue, long enough for her to reason with him.

'Free Beth and we will continue this,' she said. 'You will teach me how to please you, but for now ...'

Part of him wanted to show her that *he* was the one in control, not her. *But there is too much to lose for just one fuck,* he considered. *She is right; this will have to wait; besides, she's not only agreed to wed me, but to do whatever I want. It is certainly enough of an incentive.* He slid slowly out of her, gratified to hear the sound of pain that escaped her lips.

'Forgive me, Exzalander. My passion for you took over ...'

She kissed him then, and he returned it as chastely as he was able.

'I must go,' he said.

He wrapped the sheet delicately about her. Her eyes shone and her rosy cheeks were a give away, he thought.

'I shall leave you to finish your bath.'

'It will be cold by now,' she said.

'That might not be a bad thing. ' He gave a sly smile, but the comment was beyond her understanding. He kissed her forehead and drew away from her.

'I will see you at dinner, Your Highness.'

He walked out so formerly, that she wanted to run after him and demand that he kiss her once more. She considered that he should have been on his knees begging her forgiveness, and yet she was the one feeling as though she should have been sorry. She lay back and sighed, part post pleasure, but mostly relief.

I have agreed to be his bride, she thought. *Is that what I really want? He makes me feel so good, yet humiliated.* The memory of his penis thrust deep within her, brought a flush of shame to her face. *Marriage will soothe away such concerns. Marriage will mean that we can pleasure each other without fear of deadly reprisals, and hopefully the feeling of degradation will desist. Since father has rejected all thoughts of Katahl, it seems that Sohāhn is my only choice. I can endeavour to keep him happy, but do I love him? Will I ever?*

'It's a bit late now,' she said aloud.

Letting the sheet fall, she returned to the bath.

Twenty-four

The army took little rest on the approach to Dragon Mountains. Katahl got the distinct impression that Tuâth was deliberately pushing them onward, to avoid having to speak with him regarding his daughter. The kings rode at the head of the army and Katahl was loath to approach them together, keeping to the company of his knights.

It was the largest army ever amassed in Maldahl and each man knew that the loss of life would be high when pitted against so terrible an enemy. How many dragons still dwelt there, was unknown. It had been said that while the gods still ruled over them, many had passed to another world. But the gods had been absent a long time and such gateways had been closed; the dragons that remained were going nowhere.

The air grew colder on the mountain's approach and Katahl shivered, drawing his cloak about him. He recalled the dragon, Syphr, and felt a sudden fear grow within him. Spurring his horse, he made his way to the front of the column, in search of Ardahl. Caitul followed close on Katahl's heels, his duty being to stay at his Lord's side, unless commanded otherwise.

Ardahl was riding to the rear of the kings. *Perhaps it is time to speak to Tuâth as well*, Katahl thought.

Auk turned on Katahl's approach and Katahl gritted his teeth, trying to disguise his loathing as he nodded in greeting.

'Lord Katahl,' King Auk said, in a friendly manner. 'I was wondering when you were going to join us.'

'I am here to speak to Ardahl,' Katahl replied curtly.

His father turned to frown at his son's lack of manners toward their ally.

'I see,' Auk said. 'Please join us when you're ready. I'm beginning to think you're avoiding us for some reason.'

Katahl was not oblivious to the glance between Tuâth and his father, and he tightened his jaw, attempting to ignore it.

He smiled, as genuinely as he was able. 'Not at all, I assure you,' he said.

As King Auk turned back to speak with his father, Katahl shuddered with revulsion. Turning his own attention to Ardahl, he saw the wizard watching him, expectant.

'Ardahl, I wanted to warn you; when we were attacked by a dragon, it used majick to restrain us. Are you prepared for that?'

Ardahl smiled knowingly. 'Us?' he said.

Katahl frowned back at the wizard. 'I am glad it amuses you, Ardahl,' he retorted. 'She would not have been there had it not been for you!'

Kryepast glanced over his shoulder and scowled at his son.

'Is that so?' Ardahl said, with a smirk.

'If you had told me who she was when I asked, then I never would have gone to Sohãhn.'

Tuâth reined his horse suddenly and the entire column came to a halt behind him. The king turned to face the young lord, his gaze steady, revealing nothing.

'What do you accuse my counsellor of?' he asked

Katahl felt suddenly uncomfortable, not wishing for a public confrontation. 'Sohãhn *knew*,' he said quietly. 'He lied to me about Exzalander. He knew who she was all along. He accused Ardahl of treason, knowing that there was no sorceress.'

The king's face seemed to turn a shade of crimson at Katahl's words.

'It cannot be,' he said. 'He must not have realised ...'

Ardahl huffed, his opinion on the matter made clear.

'That is enough, Katahl!' ordered Kryepast. 'The counsellor merely made a mistake, I am sure. Why would he even suppose that you were talking about the princess?'

Ardahl huffed again. 'Dragonspit!' he said. 'Of course he knew. He's known the girl her entire life. Even the barest of descriptions would have brought her to his mind.'

Auk stretched his wings, as if to shield them from prying eyes. 'Perhaps you should continue this conversation in a more private capacity,' he offered.

Tuâth looked about him, seeing the faces of the company, as they pretended not to be listening.

'We will rest here for a while,' he called. 'Kryepast, Katahl, ride ahead with me, if you please.'

The company took rest while Tuâth headed off. When he was out of earshot of the army, he wheeled around, furious.

'Ardahl is right; the accusation can only have been made to damage him and my daughter.'

'But why would he wish to do that, Tuâth? He wants to marry her after all,' offered Kryepast.

'What!' Katahl exclaimed. He backed away, not wanting to believe what he was hearing.

'This is no concern of yours, Katahl. I said no to you and I meant it! Tuâth has given Sohãhn consent.'

'No! Father, I love her. Does that mean nothing to you?'

'You don't understand, Katahl; I am protecting you. You don't know what she is …'

'This is not the time, Kryepast,' Tuâth said. 'My concern is for Exzalander. If, as you say, Sohãhn has orchestrated the charge of treason, knowing full well that the charge was false, then he is being playing a dangerous game and his prize—my crown. What have I done, old friend?'

Tuâth fell forward and Kryepast caught him, steadying him for a moment.

'I should return to the palace,' Tuâth said, gripping his friend's shoulder.

'You know you cannot.'

'Let *me* go,' Katahl jumped in.

Kryepast glared at his son, but Katahl would not be silenced.

'I *know* Sohãhn; he has no respect for women. He manipulates and beds them for his amusement. Let me go to her *please*. He cannot be allowed to get away with this.'

'He won't, believe me, Katahl,' Tuâth said. 'But we ride to war; there is nothing can be done at present.'

'But if he sullies her, Tuâth, then she will have to marry him; honour will dictate it.'

'He would not dare! It would mean his execution,' the king raged.

'Not if you've openly given your consent. I'm going; I will not let him touch her!'

'No! You'll obey me, boy,' his father said. 'Tuâth can send someone else. I will not see you killed over this.'

Desperation in his eyes, Tuâth sank to the ground, supported by his friend.

'Does your son know the prophecy regarding my daughter?' he whispered.

'Of course I know it,' Katahl said. 'It's one of the first things we learn after the history of the gods, but I care not. I love her. Nothing anyone does or says will change that and I certainly refuse to be ruled by an old story.'

'It is no story, boy!' interrupted his father.

'I don't care.'

Tuâth buried his face in his hands.

'King Tuâth, I ask permission for your daughter's hand in marriage.'

'I will not allow this,' Kryepast seethed, 'you are *my* son.'

Tuâth looked at the young lord, blinking the tears from his eyes. 'You really think he plans to seduce her?' his voice cracked.

'It's what he does,' Katahl said, too desperate to sound sympathetic.

'And I gave him leave to do it.'

Kryepast put his arm about the king to comfort him.

'All will be well, my friend,' he said. 'Just because the man's habits are questionable, does not mean his intentions are not honourable when it comes to your daughter. Calm yourself. Katahl here is too overcome with his feelings to think clearly on this matter.'

Tuâth patted his friend's hands. His eyes were glassy and it seemed unlikely he was registering very much now the shock had set in.

'You speak wisely, Kryepast; I must trust your counsel in this. Perhaps you see more clearly than *we* do. He would be a fool to risk so much ...'

Katahl threw his hands up in the air in frustration. He was on the verge of disobeying his father and perhaps the High King as well.

'We will discuss Katahl's suit, Kryepast,' Tuâth said. 'I think that he should be heard in this matter, once we have done what we came here to do. Is that acceptable to you both?' Tuâth finished. His voice gained strength, as he seemed to gather his wits once more.

Neither answered.

'Katahl, your sword is needed here. Kryepast, your son is a man now. We can sit down and give him all the details of the prophecy as we know it, but in the end, he must be allowed to form his own decision in this. You must see that.'

'I do not see it,' Kryepast grumbled. 'But as you say, we have more pressing matters at hand. Let us wait until we are safely returned from battle. Besides—I may be killed in this campaign and then there will be no stopping you, Katahl.'

'Do not say such things, father!'

'Are we agreed then?' Tuâth asked.

The king of Starigorat and his son, nodded their heads, but inside, Katahl was a raging turmoil of emotion, as he thought of his love in the clutches of the ambitious leech he had once called friend.

As they walked back to join the company, Katahl made a silent promise that Sohähn would find welcome on the point of his sword if he dared hurt Exzalander, and damn the consequences.

As Katahl joined his knights once more, he apprised them of the situation.

'That sneaky little toad!' exclaimed Nimrïn. 'I'll deal with him for you, Milord. It would be my pleasure.'

Katahl stared darkly at the road ahead. 'Trust me, Nimrïn, if anyone is to deal with Sohähn, then it will be me.'

Nimrïn saw the seriousness of his lord's countenance and responded appropriately.

'As you wish, Milord.'

'What say you, Caitul?' Katahl said. 'Sohähn is one of your people, yet you give no opinion on the subject.'

Caitul shook his head, frowning. 'Nor would I, unless asked; it is not my place to do so,' he said.

'Come now Caitul, I *do* so ask. What think you of Sohähn? Will he harm her do you think?'

Caitul's face reddened as he answered. 'I dislike the Council. I think their interests do not lie in the interest of the people, as they ought. I do not know Sohähn personally; I did not move in such circles, but his habits and … *appetites* are generally known.'

Katahl's eyebrows furrowed as he pondered the First Knight's words.

'It is as I feared then. Can nothing be done?'

'Not at present, Milord,' Aarnon said. 'But the sooner we complete this business, the sooner we can deal with the counsellor.'

The mountains loomed overhead and the trees thinned out, until disappearing altogether. Their cover gone, there was no going back. As the sun rose, the company began the long climb up to the abode of dragons. All was unnervingly quiet—expectant, as if nature awaited the clash of two great powers, both ancient and new.

Speech along the column ceased and the army climbed in silence. Ardahl and Gailon worked a spell of courage upon the men and yet many still shook, convinced that there was no way to defeat so terrible an enemy on its home ground.

It was not knowing that was the worst; not knowing how many dragons there were to face or whether it was the last day that they would ever see. Tuâth sent no scouts ahead, feeling their best form of attack would be surprise. Better that they remained ignorant about the enemy's numbers, than forewarn the dragons of attack.

Dragons were quite solitary and nested only with a mate. Tuâth hoped that he could take out a nest or two without their presence being known to all. But despite their lack of voice, a thousand tramping feet was enough for a lower nester to notice. He poked his head from his cave and turned his ears, trying to determine the strange noise; it was no dragon, and there was a smell … he sniffed the air again.

Days of marching in armour and mail produced a distinct sweaty odour, which Ahini was only too familiar with. Poachers had taken his mother whilst he was still small, and it was a scent that was forever etched in his sense memory. He growled and stepped from his nest, promising that he would not be caught sleeping as his mother had.

Ahini was still very young in dragon terms. Had he not been so young, he might not have been so headstrong; he may have considered raising the alarm, rather than rushing in for attack.

The approaching army was ready for him, having been on the alert since they left the safety of the trees. One young dragon against over a thousand armed soldiers was hardly fair. Ahini realised his mistake too late and died cursing all men, as the netters and archers brought him crashing down to the ground to be hacked to pieces by axes and swords.

Captains struggled to keep their men quiet after such an easy victory. Smiles spread between them and so many at the rear were eager for their share of blood sport.

Tehtra started in her sleep and awakened suddenly. Her mate stirred beside her.

'What is it, my love?' he asked.

She turned to him, her eyes wide with fear.

'A dream, Morlech; I must speak to the king at once.'

Morlech stretched and smiled, showing an impressive array of canines. He closed his eyes and began to drift off again. Tehtra, to his surprise, was on her feet, thundering toward the cave entrance. Her scales shone different colours as the midday sun bounced off them.

Morlech was snoring by the time she beat her wings and rose into the air, heading for Morgothal's nest, high at the mountain summit.

The army spied her from a distance and gripped their weapons in readiness, but she was not making for them; she flew upward.

'Do you think it spotted us?' Auk asked.

'There's no way,' assured Kryepast.

Morgothal, the great dragon—the Stormbringer, was fast asleep as Tehtra made her entrance.

'Lord King Morgothal, I bring grave news.'

The great dragon opened one eye and growled at her in annoyance.

Morgothal was the largest and strongest of the race. His green scales were thicker than plate mail and even less penetrable. It was *he* who had ordered that Ichnaarim should be wiped out and he had done so on a whim—tired of complaints about poachers from dragons too weak to defend themselves against so puny a race.

'You grow tired of Morlech already, Tehtra. Come join me if you will, but no more noise. I will see to your needs later.'

Tehtra flashed red and the king's pupils narrowed at her display of anger.

'The humans are going to attack, Lord King. I have dreamed as much.'

Morgothal moved more quickly than a creature of his size should have been able. Not for nothing was he lord of them all.

'Your dreams are never wrong.' He roared then, a terrifying sound that shook the mountainside, waking all remaining inhabitants to his call.

The men gazed up in dread, to see the mighty Morgothal climb to the rocky pinnacle above his abode and there cling with dreadful claws as he surveyed his domain.

Dragon upon dragon awoke to his call, crawling out of a warren of caves to face their lord—the Stormbringer.

Down below, Maldahl's army gazed up in despair as a dozen or more dragons appeared on the mountainside. All hope of surprise was gone; Tuâth had no choice other than to signal for a charge.

Ardahl's role was crucial; he and Gailon would hold off the dragon's majick, which included the flames.

The men broke off into their prearranged units, and the battle began. The dragons who relied upon fire as a weapon were the easiest to subdue. It was Galgard the wingless who proved most effective in the initial stage of the battle; he simply trampled his attackers and the taste of their flesh spurred him on to the aid of others.

Morgothal was furious; no king of men had ever dared declare war on his kind. Nobody before had brought an army to his home. *I will kill every last one of them for their impertinence,* he decided. *I will …*

His thoughts were interrupted as a spear pierced his chest, lodged between two scales. He fell, crashing on top of a fellow dragon and its attackers. The dragon was dazed—the men, dead.

'Excellent shot, Caitul,' shouted Katahl, as he ran toward the falling dragon.

The ground shook as the Stormbringer came crashing down and those standing near, struggled to keep their footing. Morgothal, the largest and most powerful of the dragons, was no more. As he passed beyond, his majick died with him. Those dragons closest to their lord as he fell, quailed and panicked.

'If one man can bring down Morgothal, what hope do any of us have?' some wailed. It was the panic that brought about the highest casualties. Hundreds of men were trampled underfoot, as the dragons struggled to get clear enough for flight.

Morlech had seen the fall of his king and a cold fear filled his veins. He searched for Tehtra, determined to get them away from the danger. Morlech was a scholar; he had played no part in the killing of humans, and their affairs held no interest for him. But now … Tehtra was at risk and he planned to destroy any who stood in his way of getting her to safety.

Caitul tore his spear loose from the dragon's armpit, shaking the dark blood off its tip as he went in search of his next quarry. His lord was climbing once more and hurried to his side.

'Onward and upward, Caitul, until battle be done,' Katahl called savagely.

'Indeed Milord,' Caitul answered, with a grin.

Tuâth and Kryepast surveyed the battle, barking orders until they could no longer be heard. Once the dragon lord had fallen, a wild madness spurred the army to seek further blood.

'No more spells for morale, Ardahl,' ordered Tuâth. 'The men will be fine now. Can your apprentice hold the fire at bay without your assistance?'

'Yes Your Majesty. I believe that he is strong enough.'

'Good, then he can wait here with Kryepast. You and I have another task that must be accomplished this day.'

Tehtra saw the men as they climbed toward her. Instinctively, she threw flames their way, but they dispersed into the air without making contact. The humans had a wizard amongst them and the dragon's majick was no aid to them until their wizard was no more. Unlike her mate, Tehtra had taken an interest in human society and had actually conversed with majick users of their kind on many occasions. Long time it had been since a visit had been made; long time in the lives of men at least. They all looked alike to her, but their smell … human majick had a very unique odour, potent enough to track even amongst the stench of the horde who invaded her home.

As Katahl and his knights clambered up onto the rocky ridge at the summit, their quarry took to the air. Caitul thrust his spear forward, but the creature lashed out with its tail, knocking him to the ground.

Aarnon knelt beside the stunned Caitul and offered him water.

'We will rest here a moment,' Katahl said, as he surveyed the crawling mountainside below them.

Tehtra rose into the air, as the humans clambered up to her. The spear that sped toward her, still held the scent of

Morgothal's blood. She lashed out with her tail, angry with the slayer and angry with herself for predicting the attack too late. Circling at a distance, she tasted the air for their majick user; he was lower, near the roots of the mountain. She dived suddenly, determined to bring him down, even if it were her last act.

Morlech saw her speeding toward him and found himself distracted by her beauty, momentarily forgetting the soldiers about him. He roared as the chains were fired over him and snapped at the nearest netter, breaking him in two. He could taste human blood and spat it out, the taste not at all to his liking. He was aware of cheers among the screams and roars. His race was falling to man. They were too few; the more they slaughtered, the more men stepped up to take the place of the dead.

As Tehtra dived in for the kill, she saw Morlech as they attempted to bind him. It was then that she understood the remainder of her vision. At that moment she knew that they had lost, but she saw also, a way to save her love.

'Stop!' she screamed. 'Do not harm him. I offer myself in exchange for his life.'

Morlech roared for her to slaughter them, but she hushed him.

'I have seen what is to happen, my love. I can prevent losing you. Wizard,' she turned to Ardahl, 'I know what it is you intend and I offer myself freely if you allow Morlech to live. Your spell will go much easier if I am willing.'

Ardahl stepped from the shadows, awed by the magnificence of her scales as the colours shifted and changed.

'We cannot do that, dragon,' shouted the king. 'None shall survive this day!'

The dragon stared down at the wizard, her intelligent eyes, pleading.

'No Your Majesty,' Ardahl argued, 'it must be her. She is the worthy choice,'

'Then kill the other one,' Tuâth ordered.

Spears and swords were thrust toward the dragon, but bounced off as Ardahl protected him and he was left unharmed.

'No Your Majesty,' Ardahl said. 'I agree to her terms. If you wish me to perform this majick, then you will as well. He cannot breed on his own and if he chooses to seek revenge, *then* will we deal with him. But I deem that he will not, for he may yet get to see her again.'

'You are my servant, Ardahl and yet you refuse to follow my order!' the king seethed.

'You may punish me later, but still your wish shall not be met,' Ardahl retorted. He was too tired to care about the reprisals regarding his decision.

'If you will not do this for your King, then do it for Exzalander. The power of a dragon will help protect her when I am gone. Please Ardahl.'

'Only if you agree to the female's terms. She is not the only one with far sight. I can see a time when the mercy you show to the male, will also aid your daughter.'

The king glared at his wizard, but Ardahl did not look away and met Tuâth's gaze with patience.

'So be it,' Tuâth conceded.

Ardahl turned and immediately began the spell. It was long and complicated transformation majick, but Tehtra was pleased for the delay as it gave her time to say farewell to her love. Morlech was so tightly bound, that all he could do was stare desperately up at her, his eyes all questions.

She could feel it, painful at first, then oddly pleasurable. As the warmth inside her grew, no more words escaped her. The world about grew larger and the tingling reached a deafening crescendo. Then nothing.

She felt nothing more. There was a vague awareness, but not what could be described as sentience. A clear image of the King's daughter imprinted on that limited consciousness and the knowledge that by protecting the woman, she may yet live again. But now it was time to sleep, to let the darkness take her until she was needed.

The king's men made their way down the smoking ruin. Over a thousand had arrived, only hundreds would return. As for the dragons, they were no more. All dead, except for one—tightly chained on the mountainside that he had called home; one male who cried dragon tears as he witnessed the destruction of his love. The men about him withdrew and the king went down to join the joyful crowd. Ardahl raised his hand and all restraint fell from the dragon's body.

Morlech longed for death and yet they all walked away from him, as if he was not worth the effort of putting to the sword. He thought of roaring and pursuing them, but his sorrow made him numb and unable to move. Ardahl stood before him, a beautiful dragon hilted dagger in his hand.

'I am sorry, Morlech,' he said. 'I have done what I could for you and your female. If Exzalander fulfils the prophecy, then the spell I have placed on your love will break and she will be free once more.'

Morlech stared down at the tiny weapon, his eyes continually losing focus as his great tears fell. Ardahl turned away sadly thinking, *he is of an ancient and mighty race and it is tragic that he's been given so undignified a fate.*

Gripping the weapon in his hand, he staggered down the mountain, to face his king.

It had been the prophecy that had informed the king of the existence of such a weapon. Ardahl was full of questions. How would any of them thought to have performed such majick, if they had not at first read it in the CODM prophecy? The prophecy was to speak of things to come, not guide them to their future. For the first time in his long life, the wizard felt a creeping doubt and suspicion of why the prophecy actually existed.

Twenty-Five

There was blood on the sheet, Exzalander noticed as she dressed herself. The servants were at the door and she thought quickly, cutting her hand on the knife, hoping to fool them and holding the bloodied sheet to her wound.

Sphene rushed to Exzalander's side. 'Milady, what have you done?' she cried

The princess smiled. 'I cut my hand on the fruit knife. It is nothing, really. Do not concern yourself.'

Looking down at the cut, Sphene seemed satisfied that it had been the cause of the blood and ran to fetch a bandage.

The princess breathed a sigh of relief, as they took the bloodied sheet away, silently cursing herself for her stupidity. *Why did I let him do that to me? He was out of line … now I have struck a bargain and so must honour it. Still, I am determined that he will not so much as look at me suggestively until after he has freed Beth.*

She allowed the servants to fuss over her for a while, letting them bandage her hand and plait her hair in the fashion of the ladies of Ealdorbold. She frowned at her reflection in the mirror. The navy, high-necked gown, along with the new hairstyle, was too austere for her liking; it made her look older. She felt older that morning. *A few days ago a girl and now …* She tried to push thoughts of Sohãhn from her head as she made her way back downstairs.

Sohãhn was late for the Council meeting and many seemed surprised to see him at all. He gave a slow smile and offered his apology, unnerving those who had wished his downfall the night before; the princess after all, could not hate him that much if she was willing to guide him out of the catacombs.

The High Counsellor felt his mood darken as he considered what it would actually mean if Sohãhn was successful in his ambition. *No, something has to be done*, he thought.

* * * * *

On his ascent, Ardahl presented the dragon blade to his king. The tiredness hit him then and he swooned. Tuâth held him steady, summoning assistance.

'Rest now old friend,' he said. 'You have done Maldahl a great service this day.'

The wizard's eyes closed and he collapsed into oblivion. Soldiers carried him to one of the provision carts, to rest alongside his apprentice.

Tuâth held the dagger in his hand. It was a cruel looking weapon, strangely warm to the touch, with a razor sharp curved blade; the miniature of Tehtra's face and body was so life-like, it looked as though it might move at any moment. The king placed it in his belt and wrapped his cloak about him.

Katahl and his knights were last down from the mountain and were met with a heroes welcome.

'Caitul!' came a shout from the crowd.

'Theyl!' Caitul cried, running to greet his older brother. 'I did not realise that you were here.'

'Well it was a big army,' Theyl replied, embracing him.

Caitul noticed how few of them remained and his face grew grave, knowing the loss of so many men would have repercussions for years to come

'Glad to see you're still alive, big brother. Come, I'd like you to meet Lord Katahl.'

Katahl grimaced as men patted him on the back. It was Caitul who had killed the dragon's leader, and he was a getting tired of receiving credit for the deeds of others.

'Milord, may I present my brother Theyl,' said the First Knight.

Katahl gripped Theyl's arm in greeting. 'A pleasure Theyl,' he said, 'but forgive me, you must excuse us. We are heading to Ealdorbold at once.'

Caitul's disappointment was clear and Katahl told him to stay with his brother whilst he consulted with King Tuâth.

Such celebration when so many lay dead on the mountainside, jubilation in the sight of such horrors enough to haunt the dreams of even the steadiest heart, might seem distasteful to any who had not taken part in the battle. Bodies lay four deep in some places and yet, below the fires were being lit and the store of ale distributed. Tomorrow would be for mourning the dead. At dawn they would deal with their lifeless friends.

Katahl saw his father in the distance, deep in conversation with King Auk. Tuâth was nowhere to be seen. He did not feel like celebrating.

'Lord Katahl, you should take your rest,' Dahal said, in his ear.

Katahl turned to find Dahal smiling and Nimrïn holding out a tankard. It took him moments to make up his mind.

'I'm leaving … now.'

'I'll fetch Caitul,' Aarnon offered.

'No, leave him with his brother. If he leaves now then Theyl will probably inform Tuâth. Aarnon, Nimrïn, you will be with me. Dahal stay here and create the illusion of my being here as long as possible. A day's head start would be nice, but do the best you can. Most of all, once it is discovered that I am gone, keep those cursed Ptee Tsa off our tails. Understood?'

'Yes Milord,' Dahal said, bowing.

They walked through the camp, returning waves when greeted. Luckily most of the army was too deep in victory celebration to care about Katahl's movements or whereabouts. The three men led their horses away from the crowd, before mounting.

Nimrïn kicked his horse into action. 'Let us go and save your lady fair,' he said.

Katahl wished that he could feel so cheerful, but he was less afraid of dragons than the thought of losing Exzalander.

The princess found herself brooding and made up her mind to try and lift her spirits. She knew so few people at the palace. Sohãhn was in his Council meeting and although she had the right to attend if she wished, she decided that it would be even more tedious there. She walked across the courtyard and through the gates to the outer ring of the palace.

The town of Haesburg was situated within the outer walls and yet it could not have been more different. The moment Exzalander stepped over the threshold, she felt her depression lift. Haesburg was livelier and the people there held genuine smiles, not the stiff faces existing at court.

Chickens clucked as she passed and there were cows being led out to the pasture beyond the palace confines. Women drew up water from the well and sang a local song, which she recalled from her childhood. She smiled in greeting to them as she strolled on.

'Your Highness, you should not be out here,' said a gruff voice, coming from a doorway to her right.

She stared at the man for a moment, before realisation reached her.

'Thomn!' she squealed, running to embrace him. 'Captain Thomn, so good it is to see you. It has been too long.'

The old captain carefully removed her from his person, clearly uncomfortable with her show of affection.

'I am honoured that you remember me, Princess,' he said formerly.

'Nonsense Thomn, how could I forget you? Is this where you live?'

'It is,' Thomn replied, with a frown.

'But I thought that you were made lord of Haesburg. Should you not reside in the manor house?'

'That is true, Your Highness, but I prefer to stay here. Allow me to escort you back to the palace,' he offered. 'There are too few guards left, should you require one.'

Behind him, a woman appeared, clapping flour from her hands. On seeing Exzalander, her eyes widened in fright and she sank into a curtsey.

'You must be Thomn's wife,' Exzalander said, pushing past the captain.

Elsbeth did not rise until Exzalander took her hands in her own.

'It is a great pleasure to meet you,' the princess said.

The woman froze with confusion and fear at Exzalander's lack of ceremony.

'As you guessed, Your Highness, this is my wife, Elsbeth. Elsbeth, may I formally introduce you to Her Highness Princess Exzalander.'

'It is a great honour to meet you, Your Highness,' the woman said, curtseying again.

'Enough of that now,' Exzalander said. Smiling, she looked about her, thinking how cosy it was, despite the lack of the luxurious trappings she was accustomed to. 'You have a very lovely home. What are you doing here?

At first, Elsbeth froze to the spot, until Thomn nodded for her to respond.

'I'm baking bread, Your Highness,' she replied.

'Oooo really? Will you teach me?'

Thomn stepped up and gestured toward the door. 'I really must insist that I escort you back to the palace, Your Highness,' he said.

To his annoyance, the princess laughed at him.

'You always did make me smile, Captain Thomn. But I would like to remain here if that is all right with Elsbeth, besides, your reasons for having me return were for my safety. I am quite sure I shall be safe here. Might I stay, Elsbeth, please?'

'You may do as you please, Your Highness,' the woman replied.

'I will only stay if you want me to. I have no desire to make you feel uncomfortable. It is just that I have nothing to do and know so few people here. I would very much like to know you better and learn how to make bread.'

'Your Highness,' Thomn pleaded, 'please come with me to the palace.'

'It's all right, Thomn,' Elsbeth said. 'Her Highness can stay with me. She'll be quite safe here. You get to your duty now.'

Thomn glared at the princess, who smiled at him, offering him a wave goodbye. Elsbeth turned back to the princess and smiled.

'I will teach you how to make bread, but I will only show you; we can't have you messing up your clothes.'

'Very well,' Exzalander agreed.

Her heart lifted as the woman smiled. She felt a jolt inside, a sudden longing for her mother. *So much has happened,* she realised. *How will mother feel about my getting married and moving back south? It is unlikely to make her happy.* She shivered, trying to push thoughts of marriage and feelings of abasement from her head.

The Council meeting seemed even more formal than usual. Discussions about the new tax had reached an impasse, and all the while Sohãhn was left with the distinct impression that they were focused on him. The final business was sentencing and scheduling execution.

Beth's was set for two days hence. *If I am to get the wench out, it had best be done tonight,* Sohãhn thought. *Besides, the sooner the woman is free, the sooner I can announce my betrothal.*

'You seem distracted today, Sohãhn,' remarked High Counsellor Danah.

'Forgive me.' Sohãhn respectfully bowed his head. 'I have other matters on my mind.'

'The Princess? Can we expect an announcement any time soon?' Danah asked.

'Let us hope so,' Sohãhn replied. He grinned, showing his too, too, white teeth.

Yes, something will indeed have to be done, and soon, thought Danah. *I have no desire to bow to that upstart.*

Exzalander was not in her chambers, or the gardens. None of the servants had seen her in hours. As Sohãhn headed back into the building, a sense of panic overcame him. *What if she's changed her mind and run away? If that is the case, then I am a dead man,* he thought. Shaking himself, he pushed such thoughts to the back of his mind. He headed for the dungeon. *If she isn't there at least I can begin making escape plans for the whore-in-waiting.*

* * * * *

It was early evening and Exzalander still could not be found. Sohãhn, assuming that she had gone to the catacombs again, used her absence as a means to assist in Beth's escape. There was only one guard in the dungeon, and the Counsellor sent him to join the search for Exzalander. He put a few drops of sleeping draught into the guards drink and then headed off to Beth's cell.

'Woman!' he hissed. 'Come here.'

The miserable, yet comely, face of Beth appeared at the bars.

'Here is a key to the door of the cell.' He produced a package from beneath his robes and handed it to her. 'Wait until the moon is high. Put on these clothes and make for the forest. Two miles southwest, is a cabin that we sometimes use when we're hunting. Make for that and I or Exzalander will meet you there as soon as we can.'

The girl's eyes were on fire with gratitude and Sohāhn let his gaze stray down.

'The guard?' she asked.

'Will be asleep by then; I have given him something to ensure as much.'

Beth fell to her knees, wrapping her arms about him and offering her thanks. Sohāhn pushed her off and looked down with a razor smile.

She is likely to be very grateful, he considered and walked away without another word.

By the time evening came, Elsbeth was far less guarded toward Exzalander and was treating her more like the daughter she never had, rather than the princess.

'It smells so wonderful,' offered Exzalander.

'Well it's not just for smelling, you know. You'll be able to eat it too.'

The princess glanced to the window. Noticing how dark it was, her heart sank.

'I wish that I could,' she said. 'But it is late and I have probably been missed by now. Thank you so much for a lovely afternoon; I would like nothing more than to come and visit again.'

Elsbeth dismissed protocol and hugged her.

'You'll always be welcome. It's so nice to hear laughter in this house once more.'

As Exzalander left the house, she heard a shout ahead of her.

'They're looking for you everywhere.' Thomn said gruffly. 'I didn't tell them where you were. The last thing I need, is for you to get my wife into trouble.'

'Thanks Captain Thomn,' she replied, offering Thomn her most dazzling smile.

Thomn huffed, disliking how she always found the lighter side of everything. He watched as she skipped off toward the palace and shaking his head, went home to greet his wife.

Despite her efforts to keep clean, Exzalander still found that she was covered in flour. As she came into the Main Hall, the Council turned to face her. Her smile faded as she took in their stony demeanour.

'Your Highness, we have been worried,' offered Lachlan.

Exzalander gave a laugh and tried to walk past them, as if nothing was amiss.

'Worried?' she said. 'I know not why. I will see you at the feast, Counsellors.'

Sohãhn stepped out, and in front of all, he spoke to her.

'What have you been doing?'

'Baking bread,' she said, grinning up at him.

He raised a solitary eyebrow, but decided not to question her further.

'Your Highness,' he said, 'I would be most honoured if you would permit me to escort you to tonight's feast.'

The richness of his voice made her feel suddenly warm.

'I would like that Counsellor,' she replied. 'But be prompt, as I have no wish to be late. I would not want anyone to worry at my absence again.'

With a tinkling laugh, she ran up the stairs, leaving Sohãhn smiling. He turned to face the concerned faces of his fellow Counsellors and got the distinct impression it was not bread making that was troubling them.

Exzalander met Sohãhn at the foot of the main stairs, at precisely one minute before the feast was due to begin. She was gratified by the look on his face as he watched her descend. She was well aware of how complimentary her deep red velvet gown was. Her favourite dressmaker had created it and he designed to perfectly suit her form. She wore her hair part up, part down, pinned to simulate curls and the servants had been hard at work with the hot irons in order to curl the lengths of it. Her headdress of rubies and opals glittered much like her escort's eyes as she placed her hand to his.

'May I say Your Highness, how astounding you look this evening,' Sohãhn said.

Exzalander tried not to smile and stared ahead. 'You may say, only when we are out of the hearing of others.'

'Then may I take this opportunity, while I may do so, to tell you …'

'Your Highness,' greeted Hondar.

Sohãhn bit his lip.

She smiled and greeted all the guests, seeming much more comfortable in her role. There were whispers about her escort, but she was doing nothing untoward accompanying a Counsellor to the feast, so she continued to smile back at them, undisturbed.

Sohãhn helped her into her seat and immediately began conversation with his fellow Counsellors. She listened for a while, stifling a yawn. Glancing at Sohãhn, she wondered if he was deliberately leaving her out. She smiled and turned her back on him, to speak to the man on her left.

Within seconds, he was at her side again, unwilling to share her it seemed. She felt aglow, as the first course arrived. Staring down at the meats, she found that she had little appetite. She picked at a few pieces so as not to attract attention, but food was the last thing on her mind as her thoughts strayed to the morning and what Sohãhn had done to her.

'Your Highness, you appear a little flushed,' Counsellor Craibon said. 'Are you quite well?'

Sohãhn turned to her again, holding her gaze for the briefest of moments, seeming more than a little amused, as if her had guessed what occupied her thoughts.

'I am well, Counsellor,' she replied. 'It is the wine I fear, a little heavy for my taste.' She reached for the water, with a pleasant smile upon her lips, crushing the desire to kick Sohãhn beneath the table.

Exzalander was once again relieved as the company retired into the Great Hall. She was unaccustomed to such feasts every night. It was a tradition introduced for and by the Council.

She began to make for a comfortable chair to settle in, but Sohãhn had other plans. He took her by the hand and half dragged her onto the dance floor.

'Dance with me,' he said, with a smile.

It was no request and she did not smile back at him; to reject him would draw too much unwanted attention. He moved gracefully about her and leaned in as he held her, whispering in her ear.

'She is escaping tonight.'

Exzalander tried not to react to his words. It was most unexpected news. *Still, he was hardly likely to have made a public announcement,* she mused. She tilted her head in acknowledgment of his words, and suddenly felt lighter. *Perhaps I might enjoy the dancing, after all,* she thought. *At least whatever arrangements Sohãhn has made—we both have the perfect cover.*

Counsellor Tyrian took a pause in the music to request the next dance. Exzalander saw Sohãhn's jaw clenching as he handed her to another man. She, however, enjoyed seeing him not get his own way for once. As the music began, she smiled at her partner, taking his hand.

Tyrian was a relatively new Counsellor, consequently the least familiar to her. He was more than ten years Sohãhn's junior and their appearance could not have been more different. Tyrian was dark skinned and platinum blonde—his mother having been from Golstur. He was the only man of half blood, ever to have been appointed counsellor.

'You must be worried about your father,' Tyrian said, as he moved back into hold.

'Yes, I am … I am worried for them all. The dragons are a fierce and dangerous foe. I wish that they had never gone to meet them.'

Tyrian's mouth thinned into what she assumed was a smile.

'Many of us wish that very same thing,' he said. 'The dragons are better left alone.'

They drew apart once and into a circle for the mid-section of the dance. Exzalander found that she was biting her lip. As he took her hand and pulled her out of the circle, he observed the effect of his words.

'Forgive me, Your Highness,' he said.' It was not my intention to upset you. I was merely making conversation.'

She tried to smile at him, but the memory of Syphr consumed her thoughts and she felt a sudden shortness of breath as the panic within her, rose to the surface.

'Your Highness, I am sure that all will be well.'

'You cannot possibly know that, Counsellor. You are just saying what you think I want to hear. I have been in the presence of one of those creatures; I would be dead if not for …' she paused, not wanting to risk telling him of the wizard's intervention and having no desire to lie. 'Well, perhaps it is best not to dwell, rather indulge in more pleasurable diversions … such as dancing.' She smiled, but her hands were shaking.

Tyrian's brow furrowed as the music came to a close. Glancing up, he saw Sohãhn working his way through the couples toward them.

'Your Highness,' he said, with some urgency. 'I wasn't sure whether to warn you … but with your father away, I feel that it is my duty…' he trailed off, knowing that if Sohãhn reached them, his opportunity would be lost.

Exzalander took the Counsellor's hand and half led him from the floor.

'Tell me Counsellor Tyrian,' she urged softly.

He leaned in and whispered in her ear.

'Beware Sohãhn; he is not what he seems. He is a dangerous man and I wouldn't want to see you manipulated or …'

'Your Highness,' Sohãhn interrupted, with a scowl at the closeness of Tyrian. 'Might I steal you for the next?'

Tyrian nodded swiftly and turned away, leaving Exzalander wanting to demand an explanation from him. She felt as though she couldn't breathe; the fear for her father and the shame of her actions with Sohãhn, overwhelmed her and she felt the desire to run after Tyrian and plead for his help—report Sohãhn's abuse. *But Beth will die if I do so*, she thought. *I am trapped and there is no escaping the marriage now.*

She swooned and the faces about her faded with her panic, giving way to velvet blackness.

Tyrian turned back as he heard the cries, just in time to see Sohãhn catch the princess as she fainted. The counsellor carried her to one of the couches positioned about the outside of the hall, laying her down, holding her hand.

He is already too familiar with her, Tyrian thought. *Danah is right; Sohãhn cannot be allowed to realise his ambition. If he does, then none of us will be safe.* Tyrian stared at the unconscious princess as Sohãhn tried to coax some wine into her. *Too pale she is—pale and frightened. What has Sohãhn done to her? Most likely he has compromised her to force her into marriage.*

He felt sympathy for the girl, but there was no more that he could do. Sohãhn was unlikely to let him anywhere near her again.

* * * * *

As Beth turned the key in the lock, the answering click sounded deafening. Creeping along the corridor, she felt sick with fear and tried not to breathe too loudly. Sohãhn had been true to his word; the guard was sprawled upon the floor, his tankard knocked over next to the last of his dinner.

She made her way up to the main level and felt an ache at the sound of revelry, wondering if she would ever be part of that world again. Sadly, she turned away, slipping through the great doors and out into the chill night air. Drawing her shawl up over her head, she walked determinedly toward the gates, fighting the fear as it built to a deafening crescendo inside her head.

The gate wards barely glanced her way as she slipped outside. As there were no laws of curfew, she was not prevented, or even questioned. She headed toward Ánweald, the forest that shielded the north of Shénnin's domain. Resisting the urge to break into a run, she remained convinced that the alarm would sound at any moment.

It didn't; she was free.

The darkness of the trees loomed ahead and she dare not risk waiting until dawn to continue. If she were to make it to the cabin, she would have to do so without light to guide her. Glancing up into the sky, she took in the positions of the stars, and then taking a large breath in, she plunged into the darkness of the forest.

Twenty-six

Sohāhn did not take kindly to being shooed away by anyone, but he deemed it prudent to leave Exzalander to the care of the healers. He did not want his presence in her chambers to come into question. Taking one final look at her pale face, he turned on his heel and returned to the Great Hall. Going to his room was unwise; until Beth's escape was discovered, he considered it sensible for his whereabouts to be known. He sat in the corner, his face like thunder.

The room came into view; familiar blue, velvet drapes tied about the bed in Exzalander's room.

'What happened?' she croaked.

A face she did not recognise appeared at her bedside, smiling.

'Don't try to sit up yet, Your Highness. You fainted. Just lie still and get your wits back.'

The healer made her drink and she sipped, lying back and closing her eyes

Too many people, she thought. *I just want calm and quiet.* When she opened her eyes again, only one of them remained. The woman sat in a chair, reading a book.

Exzalander felt tired and sick. The more she ran events through her head, the worse she felt. *The moon is high by now; Beth must be free*, she thought. *And I am bound by honour to marry Sohāhn—a man who has shown no honour in his treatment of me. Perhaps all will be well.* It was the words of Tyrian that had made her doubts so much worse. *Sohāhn says he loves me … who is Tyrian to say that Sohāhn's word is worth less than his own?*

She didn't know how, but she fell asleep. She realised that she must be asleep as she could see Katahl and knew that he was far away. She watched him from afar as he rode hard through the night—the knights Nimrïn and Aarnon at his heels.

'What have I done,' she whimpered in her sleep, and turned over.

The healer checked her forehead and pulse, satisfied that the princess was merely dreaming and not running a fever.

Exzalander stirred again, reaching out to Katahl, the grim determination on his face, more serious than she had ever seen. *He offered his life for my own and I cast him aside so easily.* She cried out once more and fell silent. The healer frowned and wondered what matters might be the cause of such a nightmare.

Tyrian, who was more than a little curious by Sohãhn's behaviour that night, noticed that he purposely did not retire, despite it being evident that he did not want to be there.

A bell sounded, which brought a halt to the music and dancing. Danah stood and called the Council to him, to meet in chambers. The company dispersed, many concerned by the alarm and its implications.

'A prisoner has escaped,' Baruch said, without emotion.

'Who?' Gerum demanded.

'The lady-in-waiting,' replied the High Counsellor. 'The guards are searching the palace now, but from what I have been told, it is clear that she was assisted. The guard fell asleep, but remains adamant he was drugged and there is the matter of how she got out of her cell …'

Tyrian heard every word and could not help but watch Sohãhn's reaction. The man did not seem concerned or surprised. *If he has assisted in the woman's escape, it would explain his odd behaviour*, he thought.

There was much debating; some even questioned if the princess had been involved and if her faint had been for real.

'Milords, she has had a healer with her at all times, unless you are suggesting that good woman Pyrope is under suspicion too,' Tyrian found himself saying. His eyes met Sohãhn's for the briefest of moments and they exchanged a scowl. *Yes, Sohãhn definitely had something to do with it,* Tyrian decided.

Thomn-the-Cleaverhand entered, looking sleepy.

'Report!' barked Danah,

'No news as yet, High Counsellor,' the Captain said. 'But the gate watchers say several people have left the palace grounds this evening and as we only question people on entry, they cannot be much help. It is likely that she is long gone. We have few guards to expand the search and it would leave Her Highness and yourselves undefended. I am not comfortable with that. A likeness of the girl will be issued and sent abroad. We may yet recapture her,' Thomn concluded.

'Make it so, Captain,' Danah sighed. 'I want the woman found and I want to know who aided her.'

If Sohãhn was concerned, then he did not show it. He looked as confident and smug as ever.

'Well gentlemen,' he said, 'there is little else that can be done. A drink before we retire?'

'Are we to question Exzalander?' cut in Hondar.

Danah winced at the younger Counsellor's words.

'I fear that we would be on very dangerous footing to do so. She is the king's daughter and obviously did not have a direct hand in this. We cannot accuse her and must assume that she remains above suspicion.'

'But she is the only one who cared about the woman. Who else would want her freed?'

'Hondar, we cannot accuse the princess of this. We will leave things as they are. However, should we find the accomplice then he or she will join the maid in death; be assured of that.'

Hondar seemed far from satisfied at the conclusion, but said no more.

Tyrian felt shivers of excitement as he began to comprehend what the knowledge of Sohãhn's guilt could mean. He was handing the Council their means of disposing of the troublesome counsellor—legally. It was certain promotion for him. *No more Liaison to the Poor,* he considered. *Sohãhn's position will do nicely. I can see myself in charge of infrastructure ... no, I am getting ahead of myself. I still need proof. To accuse Sohãhn without it is suicide, no matter how much he is despised by the others.*

At the foot of the mountain, Ardahl continued to sleep. The pyres were lit and a deathly quiet settled upon the army, as they watched their fallen comrades burn. King Tuâth bowed his head. He had done much in his life of which he wasn't proud and the recent battle, the loss of life, would weigh heavily upon him. Such were the burdens of kingship. More than anything, he wished to hurry home, but the men needed time, a chance to say goodbye and despite his own troubles, he owed them that much.

It was noon before they finally made ready to leave and Tuâth promised himself, never to lay eyes upon the mountains again.

'King Tuâth?'

The king looked up from his dark brooding to see Kryepast before him.

'Yes my friend, what is it?'

'It is Katahl. I cannot find him anywhere,' Kryepast said. 'I questioned his First Knight, but the man has not seen him since last night. I fear he may ... I believe he is ...'

Tuâth gripped his friend's shoulder.

'Do not distress yourself,' he said. 'We ride now. Send for Katahl's knights. We will dispatch them ahead; they will stop him from taking foolish action and they will be able to ride much quicker than the entire army is able.'

'I will do as you ask,' Kryepast replied. His face was grey and his voice, barely a whisper.

Exzalander felt stiff and heavy as she awoke; sitting up brought only dizziness.

'Your Highness, please lie back. You are not well,' Pyrope said.

'I am fine,' she lied. 'I need some air.' She tried to get out of bed and the healer rushed to her side.

'That is inadvisable, Your Highness. I really must insist that you rest,' Pyrope said, with a note of finality.

'Indeed?' Exzalander raised an eyebrow at the woman's order, her features stony.

'Milady, it is my duty to protect your well-being,' Pyrope explained. 'I am answerable only to the queen and she would heed my advice in this.' The old woman spoke with calm authority, refusing to be intimidated by Exzalander's manner.

The princess huffed in frustration. 'Nonsense,' she said. 'You are being over cautious because of who I am. I appreciate your diligence, but I am quite well. It was merely lack of sustenance that caused my collapse.'

'That may be the case, Your Highness, but one would have to ask why you've not been eating and ensure that you take food before you rise from your sickbed.'

Exzalander felt her lips draw tightly together. She was tired of being treated like a child. 'I have not been eating because I have no appetite,' she said curtly.

A knock at the door brought welcome release from the tension in the room.

Hettle entered and curtseyed, placing a tray of food down. 'High Counsellor Danah has requested to speak with you, Pyrope,' she said.

The healer held the gaze of the princess for a moment.

'Well let us hope that your appetite has returned. I shall be back shortly.' She gave a stiff nod to Exzalander and left.

'Help me get dressed,' Exzalander ordered. She was pleased there was one servant who would not answer her back.

Tyrian eagerly waited for his manservant to return. He paced about the courtyard, his impatience growing.

'Is something amiss, Counsellor? You seem most distracted.'

Tyrian stopped pacing and turned. 'Your Highness,' he said and bowed low. 'Are you quite well? We were informed that you would be resting today.'

'Yes, everyone does seem to be so concerned for my welfare,' she said.

'Is there a reason why we shouldn't be?' Tyrian asked, his smile retreating.

'You tell me, Counsellor,' she said. Her words were abrupt, and she bit her lip at her rudeness. 'Forgive me, I am tired and I feel as though everyone is an enemy today.'

Tyrian stared at her and she looked away, not wanting to face any more questions.

'Milord, might I have a word?'

'Chael! You have returned. Princess Exzalander, please excuse me for a moment.' Tyrian bowed and walked away.

The servant was quite animated in what he was saying and the counsellor listened with interest. Exzalander retreated, having no curiosity as to their subject of conversation, and Tyrian had to run to catch up with her.

'Your Highness, I was about to take a ride. Since you are obviously feeling better, I wonder if you would like to accompany me.'

Looking at him for a moment, she hoped her surprise did not show. She opened her mouth to refuse him and an image of Pyrope ordering her back to bed, sprang into her mind.

'Counsellor Tyrian,' she said, 'I believe some fresh air and time away from the palace are just what I need. I gladly accept your invitation.'

'Excellent,' Tyrian replied. 'Chael, fetch our horses.'

They followed along toward the stables. By the time Pyrope's search for the princess extended outside the palace, Exzalander was already long gone.

It felt good to be outdoors; the sun shone overhead and a cool wind blew over the trees, whistling a song that Exzalander had not heard in a long time. She paused to look up at the branches swaying overhead.

'I miss them,' she sighed.

'Your Highness?'

'The trees, Counsellor Tyrian. There are no trees in the north, unless you count those twisted monstrosities in the swamp. They are pale imitations, barely clinging to life. Here … well, it is not just the trees; *everything* is so …' She met his quizzical gaze and laughed. 'Oh well, it is of no matter. I would not expect you to understand.'

Tyrian frowned. 'I was born in the desert, Your Highness; I think I understand better than anyone,' he protested.

They rode on, speaking of many things. Chael guided them deeper and the forest floor became darker. Exzalander learned about Tyrian's life in the desert, before his mother took him to Golstur. Exzalander stopped suddenly, a wave of dizziness overcoming her.

'Your Highness?'

His words sounded distant and she was aware of supporting arms then soft ground beneath her.

'Drink, Princess.'

Exzalander obeyed, becoming more aware of her surroundings. Chael tethered their horses and the moss beneath her fingertips felt more real with each sip of water she took.

'Forgive me, Counsellor Tyrian,' she said. 'I believe it was my stubborn pride that allowed me this excursion today. I feel a little weak. I should have eaten ...'

Tyrian smiled, holding up a spice cake under her nose.

'Then eat, Your Highness,' he said.

Taking the cake, she gratefully took a bite, its hot sweetness bringing focus back. She silently cursed for not having taken better care of herself; she was too used to Beth seeing to such needs.

She smiled. *Beth,* she thought. *She is safe.*

Tyrian spoke in a whisper with Chael and Exzalander got unsteadily to her feet.

'Your Highness, take my arm,' Tyrian said. 'Let us stretch your legs a little before you try your horse again. Come, this way.'

Chael remained with the horses and Exzalander felt her suspicion grow. She was alone and unchaperoned again. Although she did not suspect Tyrian's intentions toward her to be untrustworthy, there was something ... he seemed so focused on the path ahead, that he almost dragged her through the trees. She began to feel trapped and fear closed upon her.

'Please slow down, Counsellor.'

'Almost there,' he said.

A cold shiver ran through her. 'Almost where?' she demanded. 'Where are you taking me?'

When he did not answer, she yanked her arm free. He turned, distracted from his goal, to face the furious woman.

'I've discovered something that I want you to see,' he said, trying to calm his breathing.

'I will not take another step until you tell me what is going on!'

'It's about Sohāhn,' he said.

Exzalander remembered his warning then, just before she had fainted.

'What about him?' she asked. She was careful to display no emotion.

'Please, let me show you,' he urged.

She felt the dizziness again, but fought it away. 'Very well, but Sohāhn will not take kindly to your trying to stain his good name.'

'Shhh,' Tyrian said. 'We're here; you must be very quiet.'

Exzalander saw the cabin ahead and stepped closer, still confused. Tyrian was almost at the window when he beckoned her to join him. She took a few steps then heard it— a noise coming from within, a low grunt and a moan. Human sounds.

Trembling, she moved alongside Tyrian. She could not look, did not want to know what they were doing. She justified her reluctance by deciding that whatever was happening in the cabin was not her business.

'Look,' Tyrian ordered. His voice was cold, showing no respect for her rank and his eyes glittered in a way that made her realise it was futile to refuse.

As she feared, the scene before her was not meant for prying eyes. A man stood behind a woman, his hands squeezing her breasts, whilst he rammed into her. The act looked violent, yet the woman clearly enjoyed herself, and she cried out for more.

'Beth,' Exzalander whispered. The full horror of the scene hit her, as the man's eyes looked up and met her own. He smiled.

'Sohāhn,' she choked.

Tearing herself away, she broke into a run. She didn't care which way she was running; all she knew was she had to escape what she'd seen.

Strong arms held her and she struggled. Fury took over and she struck out with her fists, pounding, until she realised that it was not Sohāhn who held her, but Tyrian. Collapsing at his feet, her eyes were wide and tearful. He knelt before her, feeling a pang of guilt at what he had put her through. She looked broken.

'Your Highness,' Tyrian whispered.

As he held a hand out toward her, she slapped it away, shaking her head, as if to deny what she had seen.

'I don't know what hold he has over you, but let me help you. Let me help you be free of him.'

She heard his words and part of her wanted to throw herself at him, beg him and thank him. But the trust was fleeting and she withdrew, holding her head against her knees.

Tyrian watched as her breathing gradually changed, from gasps to even and steady breaths; her eyes hardened and the lips stopped trembling, setting into a thin, determined line.

'We should return to the palace at once,' she said. 'Beth is an escaped prisoner and must be retrieved. The counsellor— *her lover*, is clearly guilty of harbouring her and possibly assisting in her escape. His position means nothing here. The full extent of the law should be dealt in this case.'

Tyrian had never really understood men's attraction to the young princess; she had seemed more child than woman to him, but at that moment, he could have kissed her.

Sohãhn had seen the horror on his betrothed face. It had aroused him more than the whore was able. He smiled as she ran from the window, feeling that it was good she knew what would be expected from her. As he climaxed, he pushed Beth from him and reached for his trousers.

'Get dressed and get out' he ordered. 'Avoid the larger towns. Change your appearance. Remember, if you are caught, I am not to be mentioned.'

'But what will I do, Milord? I have no money.'

'Judging by your performance just now, I doubt that you will starve,' he sneered.

Beth glared up at him and he stared back, daring her to retaliate. She didn't. Grabbing her clothes, she slipped them on. By the time that she was dressed, he was already gone.

Exzalander rode astride the horse, for speed. She wanted to make sure that she arrived back to the palace before the fire within her had time to abate. On entering the gates, Tyrian called to the guards and told Chael to show them to the cabin.

She strode into the Council Chamber, Tyrian at her side.

'We've found the escaped prisoner,' Tyrian said. 'Sohāhn has her hidden in our old hunting cabin in the forest.' The sound of triumph in his voice could not be hidden.

Exzalander saw their faces and the fire within her died. She was no longer angry; she felt used and a fool.

'Your Highness, you saw the girl too?' Danah asked.

She opened her mouth to speak only to find that her voice had fled. Tyrian glanced sidelong at her.

'It's all right, Your Highness,' he urged. 'Tell the Council what you saw.'

'But he is one of you,' she said, uncertain.

Danah stood and approached her, his eyes straying to Tyrian in wonderment at what he suspected he had achieved.

'He *is* one of us it is true, Your Highness,' Danah said, 'but if he is guilty, then no title will save him let me assure you.'

She could not shake the image of Sohāhn copulating, and it made her feel sick.

'He was there ... they were ... they ...' she trailed off.

Her knees felt weak. Tyrian's arms were steadying her.

'Forgive Her Highness, fellow Counsellors,' he said. 'She is still unwell. I should escort her back to the healers.'

Exzalander stood tall, her stubbornness giving her strength.

'Thank you for your concern,' she said. 'I will return when I have said this. Counsellor Sohãhn has shown himself to be disloyal, untrustworthy and a criminal. His sentence gentlemen, I leave to you.' She curtseyed then—a sign of deep respect to the Council.

As she left, Danah smiled.

'I do not know how you did it, Tyrian, but Sohãhn is as good as dead. Issue a warrant for his arrest immediately.'

But there was no need. Sohãhn sauntered into the Council Chamber, with a wide grin on his face.

'Sohãhn, you are under arrest for aiding in the escape of a convicted prisoner. You are hereby stripped of land and title.'

'What!' he yelled, his smile fading to a vicious sneer.

'You were *seen* Sohãhn. The girl will be apprehended soon enough, but you may escape death if you admit your part in this now.'

'Who accuses me?' Sohãhn spat. His mind raced with fear and anger. *She wouldn't have had the nerve to say anything. To do so would be to implicate herself,* he thought.

'I do,' Tyrian said. 'My manservant and the Princess Exzalander also. Do you wish now to make denial or confession?'

'She made me do it!' he cried. 'It was a royal command.'

Hondar laughed. 'Oh dear, using Exzalander's own argument for defence. You were none too kind when she told you the same thing in regard to Ardahl. Besides, you cannot tell me that she ordered you to have sexual relations with the girl.'

'The princess is my betrothed,' Sohãhn said defiantly. 'She has agreed to be my wife.'

'Indeed?' Tyrian said. 'Even if that were so, I believe after what she witnessed you doing to that girl ... by the way she reacted, I'd say the wedding's off!'

'You!' screeched Sohãhn, as he took a swipe at Tyrian.

The guards began to drag him away.

'She's a whore!' he screamed, as he was removed from the chamber.

From the second landing, Exzalander heard his words as he was taken away. She felt sick again and retreated back to her room, refusing to see anyone. Thoughts of what else Sohãhn might have said about her, plagued her mind.

It was Hettle who brought her the news that Beth had been found and had told the Council how Sohãhn had helped her escape in payment for sex.

Perhaps my own reputation may yet remain intact, Exzalander hoped. She found that she still had little appetite, but forced herself to eat something. Blowing out the candles, she sat gazing at the firelight, trying not to allow the image of Sohãhn and Beth to take over her thoughts.

She felt used. *I let him touch me when I should have fought him,* she thought. *But I did not know how; it is not the kind of thing I have ever been taught. He knew that of course — had counted on my innocence being my downfall, knowing that if he could force me to surrender just once, then I was lost.*

A wave of nausea hit her and she retched, but there was not enough food inside her to bring up.

'Well, well, feeling guilty?'

She jumped to her feet, her heart thundering in her chest.

'Sohãhn!' she cried. 'How did you get here?'

'You will tell them that we are betrothed,' he hissed. 'You made a deal. Honour dictates that you see it through.'

His eyes were like vipers, but her anger left no room for fear.

'Honour? How dare you speak of honour! Such a word is utterly meaningless to you.'

The slap was unexpected. She was stunned for a moment and he dragged her to her feet by the hair.

'I liked you seeing me,' he breathed in her ear. 'Now you know what I expect from you.'

She cried out as he pinned her to her bed, pulling up her skirts.

'No!' she screamed. Part of her wondered if such a protest had only been in her mind.

'You will recant what you said. You will take the blame.' He was tearing at her clothes, opening his trousers.

No, no, no, her mind cried out. *He is going to rape me and if I do not pull myself together, he will take me without a fight.* She struggled then—biting, scratching and screaming. He had not expected that.

'Quiet, you trollop. Do you want people to know what you're doing? I like to be watched, but do you?'

She could feel his member against her body. She cried, begging for him to stop, but that only made him want her more. She tried to take her mind away—think of anything other than what he was about to do to her.

Did it work? Is it over?

There were the sounds of a fight and she struggled to turn, Sohãhn's weight no longer pinning her.

Tyrian, she realised. *He is here; he has saved me.*

She grabbed for her skirts and pulled them down, trying to cover her shame. She froze, unable to move or even blink. No words came and time seemed to hold no meaning. The fight before her seemed slow and she saw every punch land, yet heard nothing.

As Sohãhn was dragged away by Thomn, she did not hear his words of insult. As Tyrian approached, she could not hear the words of comfort, which were spoken.

Another Counsellor trying to befriend me—to use me, she thought. She shook violently, clearly terrified.

'Princess Exzalander, it's all right,' Tyrian said, trying to soothe her. 'He can't hurt you.'

She backed away from him, scrambling into the corner. He held up his hands as he approached, trying to show that he meant no harm. But he did not know that she couldn't hear him, did not know how lost she was and as he reached toward her, she vanished.

Twenty-seven

'We must rest,' complained Aarnon.

'No,' Katahl replied, with a scowl.

'Milord, the horses are tired and so are we,' Aarnon pleaded. 'If they collapse from exhaustion then we'll not get there. Please Katahl.'

Katahl could feel his breath coming in short bursts. The horse he had taken was slimy with sweat and he reined it to a halt.

'Thank you,' Aarnon said, with relief. He dismounted and immediately went in search of water.

Nimrïn looked over to Katahl with growing concern. Never had he seen the young lord more determined in anything. He shook his head and began to rub down his horse. Katahl dismounted and stood staring up at the stars. Part of him wanted to remount, to ride on come what may. What happened next, neither he nor Nimrïn were prepared for. The princess appeared from nowhere.

'Exzalander!' Katahl exclaimed. He saw her torn clothes and bruise upon her cheek and felt anger begin to boil.

She was vaguely aware of the sound of a sword being drawn and saw Nimrïn hold Katahl back. She didn't care anymore. *Let the darkness take me,* she thought. *What does it matter?*

'Let me go, Nimrïn.' Katahl pulled his arm away and ran to catch her as she fell.

'She is real, Nimrïn—no evil apparition. Find Aarnon; bring that water quickly!'

'I am here' came Aarnon's voice, as he stepped back onto the path. 'What happened to her?'

Katahl took another look at her appearance. 'I'll kill him,' he said, and held her to him. 'Sohãhn is a dead man! Oh my love, you are safe now; you are safe.'

For over an hour, he cradled her in his arms, coaxing her to wake. He bathed her wound and wrapped his cloak about her. She did not stir, however, and seemed all but dead.

'We are close to Starigorat, Milord. We should take her there,' Aarnon suggested.

Katahl looked pale and his eyes, distant. 'Yes, yes,' he said, 'let us take her home. Nimrïn, hold her for me while I mount my horse, then pass her up.

'Of course, Milord,' Nimrïn said. All his mirth had left him. *I liked her*, he thought. *She showed spirit, but now ... well, to do that to a woman ... if Katahl doesn't kill that bastard, then I will.* He carried her over to his lord. Too pale and much too light she seemed to him as he passed her up into Katahl's waiting arms.

'Thank you, Nimrïn,' Katahl said. 'I have a task for you.'

The knight straightened, his eyes steely in anticipation.

'I want you to ride to King Tuâth. Tell him that I have his daughter. Tell him all that has occurred here and that I am taking her to Starigorat. Ride back with him to the palace and make sure that he does not execute that son of a whore. I want the pleasure of doing it myself.'

Nimrïn nodded. 'Consider it done,' he said, as he grabbed his reins.

'Aarnon, you are with me,' Katahl ordered.

'Yes Milord,' Aarnon said, secretly wishing that he hadn't been saddled with babysitting the half dead princess and his sombre, love-struck lord.

Thomn-the-Cleaverhand steadied Tyrian.

'She disappeared!' Tyrian cried. 'She must be somewhere.' He scrambled about the chamber, seeming to babble to himself. 'She just vanished, Captain ...' He stopped and looked at Thomn. 'I heard that she was able to, but I never thought ... where has she gone? She's the king's daughter; he entrusted her safety to us ...'

Tyrian seemed to have aged within the last few minutes. Thomn may have found the man's behaviour amusing, if not for his own concern for the missing princess.

'Sohãhn is secure again, Counsellor Tyrian and we've ceased all servants from taking food down to him,' Thomn said. 'High Counsellor Danah is questioning the girl who let him out. I expect he will want to make an example of her.'

Tyrian felt the air in front of him once more, ensuring that the princess was really gone.

'She may have returned home,' suggested Thomn.

'She was terrified of me,' Tyrian whispered. He recalled how she had backed away. 'But I saved her; you saw that, right?'

Thomn's eyes narrowed, thinking that the man seemed more concerned how events would affect *him*, rather than the well-being of Exzalander. He huffed and left the room, not sure who he detested more—the king for turning him into a celebrated murderer, or the Council who had manipulated the king into such a course of action.

He had been on his way home when Tyrian had called for his aid. *Elsbeth will be worried*, he thought. *What will she say when I tell her? Well at least we got to the bastard in time.*

As Thomn descended the stairs, he saw Molly standing tearful, surrounded by angry Counsellors.

'I had to,' she wailed. 'He said he would have my mother evicted if I didn't ...'

It was all Thomn could bear. He wanted to see Elsbeth, wanted simply to be away from the sorry mess ... first the girl, Beth, and then Molly; he had never seen women imprisoned in the dungeon before. The usual vision of the women he had killed years before, flashed before him.

He shuddered.

It doesn't matter how many times that I tell myself they were monsters or that I was doing my duty, he thought. *I can recall every scream, every dead face as though I killed them only yesterday.*

Maybe it is best that I don't face Elsbeth, just yet. She struggles to cope when my black mood descends. Better to lose myself at the bottom of a pitcher of ale, than have to face the sympathy in her eyes one more time.

It was past dawn before Katahl arrived home. The great black rock fortress jutted up out of the earth, as though it was cut from the landscape. He had always detested the architecture of Starigorat, finding it slightly disturbing—a mutated creation. But now, home had never felt more welcoming to him.

Despite his weariness, he insisted on carrying Exzalander to his room, deeming it the only fit one in which to house her.

His servants fussed about him, as he laid her gently onto his bed.

'Send for the healers,' he demanded. He wished that he could lie down beside her. She barely seemed to be breathing and the bruise on her face had swollen to distort the symmetry of her lovely face.

'My Lord Katahl, I am healer Cairn.' The man bowed low. 'My assistants will cleanse and dress the lady, but you must tell me all that you know of her affliction. Come, let us give them a little privacy.'

Katahl gave one last look to Exzalander's unconscious form, before allowing Cairn to lead him away. He placed himself in the room next door, allowed the servants to wash and clothe him, while others made up the bed and fire. He ate whilst he talked, not because he was hungry, but because he knew that he might not have the opportunity to do so for some time and was determined to keep his strength up.

He related all that he knew to Cairn—who she was, what he believed to have happened to her and how she appeared out of nowhere. Cairn listened patiently, his eyes closed, leaning against his fingertips as they pressed together.

'It sounds like majick,' he said. 'I have little experience of such things you understand, but if the girl is Exzalander, then it would make sense that she is that powerful.'

'Powerful! She's half dead!' Katahl retorted.

'It's the majick. Such potent majick would require enormous energy. She has used hers up. I believe with rest, she will recover. As for the other ... injuries, well, I shall speak to my assistants now. She may or may not have been violated, but there was certainly an attack, a struggle. Rest may heal her body, but as for her state of mind, we won't know until she awakes. It is likely she will be fragile and fearful of company, especially male company.'

'Even I?' Katahl asked.

Cairn grimaced and nodded. He had no intention to upset the young lord, but felt it best that he was prepared for the worst.

Katahl felt his eyes involuntarily close and forced himself into waking once more. He stared down at his charge. If Cairn had not told him that she was still breathing, then he may have believed otherwise. Cautiously, he took her hand in his own; it was cold, but warmed easily.

He smiled, considering how circumstances had turned on their head. She had nursed him and now she was the one who required care. *But I had fought,* he considered. *Did she? Well, Sohāhn is a large man. What sort of a fight could she have given him?*

He closed his eyes, his chest tightening as he considered what she had endured. He tried to push such thoughts away. *I must be strong—she needs me to be strong.*

Nimrïn met up with Caitul and Dahal before he caught sight of the king and the army. After a fond greeting, he related what had occurred. Dahal complained at his orders having to go back and forth, saying he felt more like a child's toy, than a knight.

'Well wait here then and I'll ride back,' Nimrïn said. 'We'll collect you on our return.'

'What about me?' Caitul asked.

'Up to you. Take a rest if you will. The king will give you orders soon enough.' Nimrïn offered an apologetic shrug and spurred his horse onward.

'I have said it once and I will repeat myself if I may,' Dahal said. 'The women of Ealdorbold seem to be most troublesome and manipulative; I cannot understand all the fuss!'

Caitul gritted his teeth at the knight's words. 'My mother is a woman of Ealdorbold,' he said.

The knight sucked in his cheeks for a moment, trying to judge if Caitul's next move would be one of violence.

'Forgive me, I just meant that ...'

'You know nothing of Ealdorbold or its women, Dahal, so I suggest that you drop this right now. What Sohãhn did to her ... *nothing* can excuse his actions; even if she was the cheapest harlot, he should be made to pay.'

Dahal bowed his head, as if to concede.

When Ardahl finally awoke, he was disorientated. The mountain was the last location that he recalled. The grief-stricken face of Morlech sprang to his mind, and he sat up.

'Master Ardahl, you're awake!' Gailon cried, springing to his side.

'Yes boy, don't fuss. Where are we?'

'On our way back home, but something has happened. One of the knights of Katahl has just arrived. He's talking with the kings and they seem very angry.'

'Enough,' Ardahl said. 'Help me to my feet and I will discover what I may.'

As Gailon assisted his master, he could not help but notice, how much older the wizard looked.

'You need your rest,' he said. 'King Tuâth will send for you if he requires you.'

Ardahl groaned, as he clambered down from the cart. 'He will not, unless he knows that I'm back in the land of the living.'

Tuâth, paced about the tent. 'It is as I feared, Kryepast. What more remains to be said?' he growled

Nimrïn interrupted, speaking with as much diplomacy as he was able. 'The Lord Katahl wishes me to accompany King Tuâth back to the palace. He requests the killing of the vermin himself.'

'I must see my daughter, but I must ensure that Sohãhn is punished. For all we know, he could be strutting about, pretending nothing has happened.'

'Then allow me to go, King Tuâth,' Nimrïn cried. 'You can write a warrant; I will lead your army home and see your will be done. You may go with King Kryepast to Starigorat.'

Ardahl stepped into the tent, unannounced. 'Am I interrupting?' he asked.

Tuâth's eyes seemed to lose focus for a moment and he sank into his chair. 'Ardahl, good it is to see you with us once more,' he said. 'There have been some … developments. I wish you to return to Ealdorbold; Nimrïn here will accompany you.'

'And you, Your Majesty?'

'I will visit Starigorat. My daughter is there.'

Ardahl raised an eyebrow in disbelief. 'Exzalander … is she quite well?'

Tuâth placed his head in his hands, fighting the tears that threatened.

'If she is not, Your Majesty, then perhaps I should accompany you,' the wizard suggested.

'I doubt even your skills will aid her,' Tuâth said, his voice barely audible. 'No, return to the palace. Nimrïn, I will write my orders, though whether I allow Katahl the killing blow, I cannot promise. My daughter is my priority for the present. Please send for Captain Theyl. I must also convey word to the queen.'

'Will you tell her of Exzalander?' Kryepast asked.

'Not as yet; I am hoping that she will never have to learn.'

Ardahl looked confused, having joined the conversation too late. As the wizard opened his mouth, Tuâth put up his hand to keep him silent.

'The knight will fill you in, my friend. I cannot. I have not the strength for retelling as yet. Please leave me to ready myself.'

The wizard bowed and left the king to his black mood.

Within the hour, all parties were on their way once more. At the crossroads from the main road to Kryepast's home, the two kings gave their thanks to Auk, bidding him farewell. Tuâth no longer had the energy to meet Nimrïn and Ardahl's knowing gaze. He turned his horse and followed Kryepast towards the stronghold of Starigorat.

Twenty-Eight

It was the afternoon of the third day since their arrival that Exzalander finally stirred. The first thing she became aware of, was that the room she was in, was not her own; the second was the pain in her head.

'Where am I?' she groaned. As she tried to sit up, she was aware of a supporting arm, but struggled to focus to the face at the end of it.

'Easy there, Your Highness; take it slowly.'

She heard the voice … so familiar. She blinked hard, trying to clear the haze from her sight.

'Katahl?' she croaked.

'Yes my love,' he beamed.

'Am I dreaming?' She did not remember falling asleep. In point of fact she struggled to recall anything. It was as though she had used majick …

Her eyes widened suddenly, as the memories came flooding back.

'No,' she struggled, and her tears fell freely. 'Sohãhn … he …'

'It is all right, my love. He is not here. You are safe now and I will not let him harm you again.'

She shuddered and pulled her knees up to her chest. He saw her hand slip away, but made no move to recover it.

She no longer met his gaze. 'Where am I?' she mumbled.

'Starigorat,' Katahl replied quietly. Every instinct told him to take her in his arms and hold her close; he had to remind himself what Cairn had told him and that it was wrong to do so.

'I had to get away,' she stammered. 'I thought to be with loved ones … I thought to join up with father.'

Katahl felt warmth throughout his body, understanding the significance of her words, even if she did not. It gave him reason to hope.

The door burst open and Katahl was surprised to see the face of the High King of Maldahl.

'Exzalander?' Tuâth said.

Katahl caught sight of his father, loitering in the doorway.

'She is awake,' he said. His voice was quiet as he considered what thought lay beyond Kryepast's gaze. Fury? Disappointment? Resignation even. He was at a loss to interpret.

Kryepast beckoned him and walked out of sight. Tuâth took his child in his arms and they both wept. Katahl felt like an intruder and slipped away, unnoticed by the pair as they clung to one another.

As Katahl made to follow his father, the healer, Cairn smiled in greeting as he passed them, heading for his charge.

'Your chamber, Katahl?' Kryepast grumbled, as he paced away. 'Hardly appropriate.'

'I did not need it, besides it was the most suitable for someone of her rank, at such short notice.'

'Mmm,' Kryepast grunted, leaving Katahl wondering if it was an agreement or a growl at his son's impertinence.

Without warning, King Kryepast stopped and faced his son, examining him closely as if he was something wholly new, something that above all else, he needed to understand.

'Cairn said that you have not left her side, have not slept and barely eaten.'

Katahl shrugged at his father, wondering where his words were leading.

'You smell; go bathe, eat, rest! That is not a request, Katahl. The princess will take it as a kindness—believe me. You are more likely to win a lady's heart if you look and *smell* presentable,' Kryepast growled, but his eyes twinkled mischievously.

A slow smile spread across Katahl's face, as the meaning behind his father's words became clear.

'Truly father? I have your blessing?'

'Ai,' Kryepast replied. 'If she'll have you. I am counting on you to keep her out of trouble though. Her poor father cannot take any more excitement.'

Katahl caught his father in a bear hug and Kryepast choked.

'Bath … now!' he ordered and walked away.

Katahl ran to the baths, feeling as though he could fly. Kryepast's smile faded as he turned away from his boy, believing he had just signed his son's death warrant.

As Tuâth drew away from his daughter, he saw that her eyes fell straight to her lap, refusing to meet his gaze.

'Exzalander, I must know all that occurred. It will be my task to sentence him and I need to be aware of the extent of his crimes.'

Exzalander shot a look to the healer and shook her head, fresh tears running down her cheeks.

'Perhaps I should wait outside, King Tuâth,' said Cairn. 'If you could make sure the princess drinks this; it will help rejuvenate her. Food is being prepared, just send for it when she's ready.'

'My thanks to you,' Tuâth said, with a nod. All the while he watched his little girl. As the door closed he whispered, 'It is all my fault.'

Exzalander wiped her tears away, trying to keep her lip from wobbling. 'I am *used* father. He told me he loved me … he made me …'

'Has he taken you daughter? You must tell me.'

'As good as,' she wept. 'He made me do things … and he tried to take me by force … I am so ashamed, father.'

She broke into sobs and he tried hard to console her, all the while, his anger brewing within him. She cried until she fell asleep in his arms. Gently, he laid her back onto the pillows. Her face was red and blotchy, yet still beautiful despite the bruising and distress. The king eased himself off the bed and wearily left the room.

Cairn waited without, and the king explained that she was sleeping. The healer nodded and escorted him to a nearby room, which had been prepared for him.

'I will watch over her, King Tuâth; do not worry yourself.'

'Perhaps I should have brought my wizard with me,' Tuâth said. 'He might have been able to make her forget.' He turned away, closing the door behind him.

Exzalander woke late in the night. Her dreams had been terrifying visions of marriage to Sohãhn. In them, he was king and she, one of his many consorts. His abuse of her was horrific.

Feeling sick, she reached for the pitcher of water, hoping to calm the waves of nausea, which threatened to overcome her.

'Princess Exzalander, may I suggest that you eat a little,' Cairn whispered from the darkness.

She looked alarmed for a moment, until she saw a glimpse of his healer's robes.

'I ... I am not hungry,' her voice cracked.

'You won't start to mend unless you build your strength,' he coaxed.

She nodded, relenting; she had no energy to argue. She could not remember the last time she had eaten. Memories of approaching the cabin came to her mind and she pushed them aside. 'A little food then,' she agreed. 'I will follow your guidance, healer.'

'It's Cairn,' he said smoothly.

She nodded in acknowledgment, but no smile touched her pallid lips.

One step at a time, considered Cairn, as he handed her some food.

Once she had eaten all that she was able, she fell asleep again and slept until past dawn.

A knock just after nine, stirred Cairn from his dozing.

He smiled. 'Lord Katahl, you appear much rested.'

'Thank you, Cairn; I will relieve you now. You must be exhausted.'

'As you wish,' said the healer. He bowed and left Katahl with his charge.

Katahl observed that Exzalander had more colour in her cheeks. The bruise had turned a greenish brown colour and did not look as angry as it had. Her hair sprawled out across the pillow—lank and greasy; perspiration clung to her body, dribbling down her forehead; her breathing seemed laboured as her chest rose and fell in unsteady rhythm; her eyes flickered and moved beneath the lids and she moaned, her head turning away.

Katahl sat beside her, wondering whether to wake her from the nightmare or no'. She thrashed and his hand hovered over her, unsure what to do.

'No you must not ... please,' she mumbled.

As she lashed about again, Katahl felt the anger rise within him. He stormed over to the open window, taking gulps of air in effort to calm himself.

She awoke with a start, the dreams dispersing in the sunlight that filled the room. Sitting up, she noticed Cairn was no longer there, in his stead stood Katahl, his back to her as he gazed out of the window. He wore a deep purple velvet doublet over his black trousers and his hair was combed neatly behind his ears.

'Lord Katahl,' she said.

He turned in an instant; his haunted features made her wish that she had remained silent, suddenly conscious of how unkempt she must appear.

'It is very kind of you to look in on me,' she continued. 'Really, there is no need for you to be here; I am sure that you have more important things to be doing.'

He stared long at her then. Part of him wanted to know every detail of her dealings with Sohāhn; he wanted to demand to know and yet, another sensible voice whispered that it was better not to know such things and certainly unwise to ask. As his eyes fixed upon her, she began to pull the covers over herself and comb her knotted hair with her fingers.

'M,might I request a bath?' she stuttered.

'We have a heated bath chamber on the lowest level. I will fetch someone to attend you,' he offered.

She wanted to cry again. *His voice is so level and controlled,* she thought. *Of course it is. Sohāhn has stained me forever. I can no longer belong to anyone, least of all the son of a king.* Bowing her head in shame, a jolt of misery ran through her, as Katahl left her without another word.

She was still crying when the servants arrived and they asked if they should come back later. Swiftly, she dried her eyes, assuring them it would not be necessary. She felt unsteady on her feet and the room span for a moment.

Smoothing down the white robe that the healers had placed her in, she stepped into the waiting shoes. Two women stood by to change her bedclothes and she found herself finding a parallel to her care for Katahl. She sighed, wishing she could return to those days, convincing herself that she could have avoided so much suffering, if she had but done things differently.

Shuffling along behind her guide, Exzalander was vaguely aware of richly decorated tapestries and detailed paintings, ornate furniture and high ceilings with beautiful pictures, detailing anything from events in Maldahl's history, to birds and flowers. The staircase she descended was of a rich dark stone, intricately carved.

'The baths are along here, Milady,' the guide said, breaking the silence. Her voice was high and nervous, with the same accent as the Lord Katahl. 'Would you like me to attend you?'

'No,' came Exzalander's hasty reply. 'I wish to be alone.'

She closed the door, leaving the girl outside the room. The bath was built into the floor and beautifully tiled to depict Mo-Rye at play. It was so large that Exzalander thought it more suitable to swimming, than bathing. She noticed that clean robes had been placed next to towels on a decorative, tiled bench beside the steaming pool.

She was grateful for the momentary distraction the grandeur of the room allowed, before sinking back into depression once more. Glancing nervously about, she ensured that she was truly alone, before removing her robe and stepping into the welcoming water.

As she waded to the middle, the water reached above her breasts. She sighed, allowing the grime of the past few days to wash away and the water to soothe her aching limbs.

She swam back to the bath's edge and lay back, her head resting on the side. Closing her eyes, she tried to push away the constant flashbacks of Sohãhn. The tears ran again and she welcomed the chance to cry freely without witnesses.

Katahl pressed his ear to the door; Exzalander's sobs were pitiful to hear. He sank to the ground, feeling utterly helpless. *Had I been able to reach her in time, then I could have prevented such suffering,* he thought. He closed his eyes, allowing the sound of her misery to enhance his own.

'Help her.'

He jumped, believing that he had drifted off to sleep for a moment. A voice had woken him up; he had never heard anything so commanding—so clear. He shook himself, widening his eyes and forcing the tiredness to flee.

'Help her,' the voice commanded again.

He was not asleep, had not dreamed it. Jumping to his feet, he peered about him. All was still; all was completely quiet ... too quiet. The sobs had stopped. Fear gripped him then and he fought to quench it as he ran to the far entrance where the maid sat waiting and still.

'Is she in there?'

The girl curtseyed. 'Yes Milord,' she said.

'Check on her,' he demanded.

'Yes Milord.' She bobbed another curtsey before opening the door.

Katahl held his breath for what seemed like an age. He knew that his fears were unfounded, but for the voice he had heard on the edge of sleep. A scream pierced his being and forgetting decorum, he ran. The woman shrieked and pointed, but Exzalander was not there.

'She's drowned,' the girl wailed.

Katahl jumped into the bath, reaching down for the shadow beneath the water and heaving her to the surface.

'Don't you dare die on me!' he yelled, as he shook her.

Exzalander spluttered and coughed; opening her eyes, she froze with fright.

'I thought I had lost you,' Katahl breathed. His eyes filled with relief. 'Here,' he said, wrapping his overcoat about her to cover her modesty.

'Do not touch me!' she rasped. Clambering out of the bath, she reached toward the towels.

'I am sorry, Princess, I thought ... you were trying to kill yourself,' Katahl finished awkwardly.

'And what if I was?' she snapped. Trying to sound forceful brought on another bout of coughing. 'My welfare is no concern of yours. It never was, and now it never can be.'

'Leave us!' Katahl commanded the terrified servant.

The girl forgot to curtsey as she fled the room.

'I know what you have been through must have been awful,' he said. 'But if you think I am going to let you harm yourself; you can think again.'

'Just leave me be,' her voice cracked. She turned away, and as she wrapped a towel about her, fresh tears streamed down her face.

'I cannot do that,' he said.

He took a step toward her and she froze, her body went rigid when he stepped closer. He gritted his jaw, his hatred for Sohãhn bubbling to the surface.

'He is a dead man, Princess. He will die by my hand, I swear to you.' He rested his hands on her shoulders.

'Do not touch me,' she hissed and swivelled about to face him. 'Do you not understand anything? I am ruined! No man will ever touch me again. My bloodline will end with me. I am shamed and it is all my fault.'

'He raped you, Exzalander; that is not your fault,' Katahl protested, feeling helpless.

'No ... he didn't. He tried, but I got away from him.'

Katahl's relief was clear, but it only served to make her feel worse.

'He got me alone and unprotected and he ... touched me. I tried to protest; he would not listen. He continued his attentions until I actually enjoyed it. I asked him for more, Katahl. Afterwards, I felt too ashamed to report him. I was angry because he should not have done what he did, but I was even angrier with myself because I could not stop him. Afterwards, I was so scared that he would reveal my shame, that I allowed him to do it again.

'He trapped me and I let him. So you see, his attempted defilement was not the worst of it and I have nobody to blame but myself. I am not worthy of your sympathy or your aid, Lord Katahl.

'I am nothing.

'You should have let me drown.'

Katahl's face went from red to white, as she spoke. He looked as though he might vomit and when she left the room, he made no attempt to follow her.

Twenty-nine

Exzalander walked away from him, deep down hoping that he would follow her. When it was clear that he did not intend to fetch her back, she searched for a dark corner to hide in, waiting for him to leave so that she might recover her robe. She tried to convince herself that telling him all, had been more important than her own feelings.

When the maid found her over an hour later, she urged Exzalander to get dressed and return to her room, where a fire had been lit. Tuâth was there when she arrived and she could not face him, could not bear to see the disappointment in his eyes.

'When do we return home, father?' she asked wearily. 'The sooner the better, do you not think?'

Tuâth's face was grave. 'We are not going anywhere until I know that you are well, child,' he said. 'Now, do you want to tell me what just happened? Katahl said that you tried to kill yourself. Is it true?'

She sat on the edge of the bed, staring down at her feet. The words of her father were distant, the memory of Katahl's horrified face, less so.

'Exzalander.' Tuâth shook her.

She blinked and looked up. 'I am fine,' she muttered.

'That is not what I asked,' he growled.

The arrival of Cairn was timely in dispersing the tension in the room. Tuâth whispered to him about the latest development in his daughter's condition. She no longer cared what they said. *Let them utter what they will,* she thought. *I just want to be away from Starigorat, away from anyone who can remind me of what I am and that which I have lost.*

Tuâth had left the room and she failed to notice. Cairn sat beside her, his face revealing no emotion.

'Father is angry because I told the Lord Katahl what happened to me,' she explained. 'I am sure that he was hoping to pass me on to whoever would have me, in the circumstances. Well, I have saved him the trouble of trying. Nobody will have me now, so he may as well start thinking who is to be his successor. He can hardly have a harlot for a queen.'

'Drink this, Princess,' said Cairn, his voice calm.

She complied. *A servant of a foreign house commands me and I obey*, she thought. *I am no longer of rank; I am less than servant, as I cannot even earn a living.* Her eyes grew heavy and she stared at Cairn with horror.

'It will help you to sleep,' he explained.

He removed the goblet from her failing grasp, and she lost consciousness.

Katahl paced about the throne room, his anger reaching boiling point.

'Father, may I have your permission to go to Ealdorbold?'

King Kryepast watched his son as he turned again and retraced his steps.

'For what purpose?' Kryepast asked.

'To kill Sohãhn. He must pay for what he has done.'

Kryepast stepped down from the dais and reached out for Katahl, forcing him to stop pacing.

'He *will* be punished, but you cannot override Tuâth's laws.'

'He has ruined all, father. She tried to kill herself! She is broken … she is ruined,' he finished, in a whisper.

'Do you love her?'

Katahl looked at his father for a moment then closed his eyes.

'Yes father,' he replied, 'but she will have none of me. I have never felt so helpless in my entire life as I do now. She blames herself completely for that manipulating bastard's actions.'

Kryepast held his son in a tight embrace, concerned by the emotions threatening to overwhelm the young lord.

'She needs time that is all,' he said. 'Which do you think that she will be more grateful for … you riding off to murder Sohāhn, or knowing that you are here for her when she needs you? Anyhow, I am not sure why I am encouraging you. If I had my way, I would rather you not make her your bride at all, and you know why.'

'The prophecy.'

'Exactly, such a match is the herald of very dark times ahead m'boy. It could mean your death.'

'The prophecy does not say that at all y'know. I have checked.'

'There is more than one version, Katahl.'

'Well, it really should not be taken too seriously then,' Katahl said flippantly. 'Do you honestly believe some dark presence from across the stars will threaten to destroy Maldahl, because our gods are no more? Honestly father, the whole thing is ludicrous!'

Kryepast sighed and climbed the steps to his throne. He used to believe as Katahl did, until Tuâth told him of the contents of the book of CODM, before he had seen the evil book with his own eyes and knew that it was a thing not of their world.

'Let us hope so, for all our sakes,' he said, as he sank back onto the throne.

Whatever Cairn had given her was working. She did not remember falling asleep, but she knew that she was. She wandered through a great palace of white and green marble, feeling serenity for the first time in so long. She did not want the peace to end and be forced to return to the fear and guilt that awaited her.

'You cannot stay here forever, Exzalander.'

She looked behind her for the voice, startled to see a balcony where before had been only wall. Outside, an enormous forest grew, stretching as far as the eye could see. She rushed over to look out at the vast blanket of green, feeling a sudden apprehension.

'You will not try to harm yourself again,' said the voice, directly in her ear. 'That is not a request.'

Turning again, she found herself back in the room at Starigorat. She blinked, the final image of trees, still in her vision. Sitting up, she expected the usual ache and dizziness, but they were gone. She felt healed. Beside her bed was the last person whom she expected to see. Katahl slept—his head at an awkward angle.

Why is he here? she wondered.

The guilt and shame, which had blissfully departed for a moment after waking, came crashing back and she wanted to get away. Creeping over to the door, she turned the handle.

Locked.

Turning back to Katahl, she noticed the large ornate key sticking out of his belt. His breathing rose and fell slowly, seeming to be in deep slumber. Approaching cautiously, she reached out to touch the metal of the key. She pulled as gently as she could and yelped as a hand grabbed her wrist and the key clattered to the floor.

Looking up, she saw Katahl's eyes, bleary with sleep, yet still blazing back at her.

'Where do you think you are going?' he asked.

Her heart pounded as she fought for her voice. 'Let me go,' she said.

He obeyed at once, the fear in her eyes sickening him for a moment. She backed away and he bent down to retrieve the key, thrusting it back into his belt.

'I was tired,' he explained, 'and I did not want you trying to run off. Cairn needs rest, besides, I cannot assign him to you indefinitely; we have a lot of wounded men returned from Dragon Mountains who are in need of his skills.'

'Let me out,' she tried to demand. The spark of defiance and command was gone and she seemed a shell of what she was.

'No,' Katahl replied. 'You have nowhere to run to this time. You are going to sit down and you are going to talk to me properly.'

She backed away, running for the door, banging on it and rattling the handle, frantic to get away from him and his officious manner.

'Somebody let me out!' she wailed.

'*I* command here, Princess,' he said matter-of-factly.

As soon as the words escaped his lips, he regretted them, as he saw her eyes fill with sheer terror at contemplation of what that could mean.

'I have said all that I am going to say to you, Lord Katahl. There is nothing else to speak about, other than to congratulate you on your escape.'

Katahl remained still, aware of how erratic her breathing was as her panic increased. He observed how her body trembled and did not wish to frighten her further. Her eyes darted about the room, as if searching for a means of escape—or possibly a weapon.

Backing away as far as the window, she glanced behind to see she was too far up to have any hope of a safe landing. Keeping her eyes on him, she reached back for the handle.

'What are you doing?' Katahl asked slowly. 'You cannot escape that way.'

Ignoring him she turned, closing her eyes. She wanted to find the peace again—*peace and the palace in the trees*, she thought. *But the voice said that I must not harm myself.* She took a breath, hoping the voice would be forgiving and started to climb out of the window.

Katahl rushed over and pulled her back.

'No!' she cried. 'Let me go … I cannot take anymore … please, have mercy.'

He pulled her to him and fought to hold her as she struggled. She thrashed about crying, and the wailing broke his heart. Still he clung to her, until her energy waned and she stopped fighting and let him rest her head against his chest. She did not attempt to struggle, but closed her eyes, allowing the warmth of his body to soothe her. He stroked her hair and she flinched for the merest of moments then … nothing. It was clear that he desired nothing more than to hold her close.

'I will not let you hurt yourself,' he said.

'It is not your concern,' she whimpered.

He pushed her away, holding her at arms length and she felt suddenly cold, away from his embrace.

'Of course it is my concern,' he said. 'If you want to blame anyone, then blame me. I should never have let you go that day. I should have disobeyed my father and accompanied you to Ealdorbold as I vowed I would. If I had been there then that snake would not have stood a chance.'

'But I …' she tried to protest.

'You do not know him as I do, Princess. If you did, then you may have been able to guard yourself against him. Your father threw you at him it seems—not realising what he was. *None* of this is your fault.'

Katahl caught the tears as they fell, trying to smile at her.

'*Nothing* will make me stop loving you,' he said. 'I only hope that you will be able to forgive me.'

She blinked. 'It is not your fault,' she spluttered.

'Mmm, I will tell you what; I shall agree that it's not my fault, only if you agree that it's not yours.'

'I cannot do that.'

'Shhh,' he soothed. 'I will hear no more of it.' He moved toward her once more and gently picked her up in his arms. She did not protest, but seemed far from at ease there. As he laid her in bed, he leaned forward and saw her flinch. He kissed her forehead, realising that she had expected something else and silently cursed Sohãhn.

A knock at the door gave him the opportunity to turn away so that she did not see the pain in his eyes.

'I am not Sohãhn,' he said coolly.

As he unlocked the door, she closed her eyes, trying to remember the place in her dreams. She was aware of voices as they spoke in whispers and when she opened her eyes once more, Katahl had gone. She was glad. He had said a lot and she needed time to think on his words.

A male servant sat with her, staring at the floor in obvious discomfort. She realised then, the purpose of such a choice and she felt her self-pity retreat as annoyance took hold.

'You do not need to be here, you know. I am quite well and am no longer in need of supervision,' she said haughtily.

The man winced at having been spoken to. As he answered, his eyes never left the spot on the floor.

'That may be so, Milady, but I have strict orders and have no choice.'

'Oh for goodness sake,' she replied.

She got to her feet and the man looked up, terrified, assessing what she meant to do.

'I wish to get dressed and go outside. I am feeling a lot better and I am tired of being cooped up. Please find out if there is anything other than this healing robe for me to wear.' She tried to sound commanding; the man's timid manner made it easier.

'I'm sorry, but I'm not allowed to leave you, Milady.'

Exzalander huffed and paced over to the door. 'Very well,' she said, opening it with a swift motion. 'Coming?'

She left the room, barefoot, with an embarrassed servant in tow.

Tuâth enjoyed his bath and joined Kryepast in the sunroom, marvelling at how it had been constructed almost entirely out of glass, giving a wide view of the gardens.

He sat beside his friend. 'Simply marvellous,' he breathed.

'I know,' agreed Kryepast. 'My wife's idea. I try to sit here at least once a day to remember her.'

'She was an extraordinary woman.'

'That she was,' Kryepast agreed with a smile, and looked out.

Katahl was pacing about the garden, swinging his sword from side to side.

'What has Katahl got against the flowers?' Tuâth asked.

'He is worrying about your daughter, I fear.'

Tuâth nodded knowingly. 'He is young … more difficult to hide emotions at that age. Now I know that she is out of danger, I find it easier to maintain a more regal countenance.'

Kryepast laughed. 'Truly?'

'Absolutely, besides, he has nothing to fear. We have both given our consent. We just need to make arrangements for the wedding. I am more concerned with what I am to tell Shénnin.'

Kryepast poured two glasses of wine and handed one to Tuâth.

'But Exzalander sounds unwilling to take any husband after her ordeal, old friend.'

'She has little choice in the matter, Kryepast. Your son has proven the most worthy suitor. She clearly has some feelings for him—the rest will follow in time.'

Katahl swiped his sword from side to side, his frustration getting the better of him. He decided he would prefer to face another dragon than the fear in her eyes again.

I know that she cannot help it, but damn it, I would never hurt her—she must know that, he thought. *She is to be my wife. My dearest wish has been realised and yet I cannot feel happy.* He did not want an unwilling bride and try as he might to tell himself that what happened with Sohãhn did not matter ... it did; the thought of her with him made his skin crawl.

He swiped higher with his weapon and turned to pace the other way, his sword swinging mere inches away from Exzalander's chest. He almost dropped it in surprise.

'Invisible enemies?' she asked.

'Forgive me,' he breathed. Sheathing his weapon a little too quickly, he almost injured himself. Staring back at her then, he thought she looked more like her old self. The burnt orange, high-neck gown was of the fashion of Starigorat and seemed to make her neck look very long and her even taller. He glanced behind her, spotting her guard.

She gave a half smile. 'My shadow,' she said, as if she was introducing him. 'I suppose that I have you to thank.'

'My father—well both our fathers,' Katahl replied, grimacing. 'I suggested that a male was hardly appropriate, but they insisted.'

'In case I needed to be restrained,' Exzalander suggested.

He bit his lip, looking awkward. 'I would hope that you would not need to be ... I mean ... again,' he trailed off.

'Well, perhaps my shadow might be relieved for a while. I am sure that *you* are quite capable of dealing with any foolish attempts that I might choose to make,' she said evenly.

Katahl nodded and signalled the man away with a single look. Once he was out of earshot, Exzalander fixed her eyes on Katahl.

'I have no intention of harming myself,' she said. 'I have come to my senses. I am the daughter of the High King and I will behave accordingly.' Her voice sounded almost haughty in tone.

Katahl wanted to smile; he had heard the front from her before and it made him want to tease. He restrained himself though, unable to believe she was truly feeling better.

'It must feel good to be outdoors. Do you wish to sit?' he asked. His tone was polite, making it clear that he felt the need for a change of subject.

'No, Lord Katahl; I wish to walk, to stretch my legs.'

He smiled slyly. 'You are not planning to run away again, are you?

'In these shoes?' she said, raising an eyebrow.

He saw the corner of her mouth flick up briefly in the beginning of a smile. Looking down, he noticed that the dress she was wearing was too short for her, the hem falling well above her ankles. It was not the dress that made her appear taller; the women of Starigorat were short in stature and favoured a heel to increase their height; being tall was considered a sign of beauty. He smiled at the borrowed shoes, hoping that she would not get too used to them; he was barely taller than her without them.

Acknowledging Exzalander's words with a polite tilt of the head, he fought back the grin as he considered her trying to run in such heels. She seemed suddenly interested in flowers, as if not ready to face a humorous comeback from him.

'I will see to it that you are made clothes to fit you, Princess.'

'Really, there is no need, Lord Katahl. I will be returning home soon I expect. I am certain that I can manage with borrowed gowns until then.'

'But,' he broke in, 'you do not know?'

Exzalander stared down at the flower in her hand. Like Starigorat itself, it had a bizarre extravagance to it; the petals were rosettes of deepest purple, appearing almost black.

'Know what?' she asked, bending to smell it.

No scent …

No answer.

She stood, reluctant to turn. His silence unnerved her.

'It matters not,' he said, at last. 'Good it is to see you are doing so well.'

He stared awkwardly into the distance; his face was brooding she noticed, but his eyes … they told a different story; they glittered with concealed excitement.

'What are you not telling me, Lord Katahl? I demand on knowing the truth at once!'

'Demand indeed?' He smiled. 'Might I remind you where you are and who rules here.'

'Not you!' she snapped back.

'No … my father.'

'And *my* father is High King,' she retorted. 'You are just stalling.'

'I see,' he said, with a casual smile, 'we are competing over who has the most authority here, are we?'

'You started this,' Exzalander pouted.

He could bear it no longer; in one swift motion, he grabbed her and pressed his lips to her own. Despite the initial force, his lips touched hers with feather lightness. She stepped away from him, her features all confusion. He opened his mouth to speak, but she turned and fled back to the fortress.

She can run in those heels after all, he thought sadly.

Tuâth watched as his daughter ran from the Lord Katahl. The guilt inside threatened to consume him. He knew that she was lucky Katahl still wanted her. If she did not accept him then there was unlikely to be another. The prophecy stated her mate would help restore the balance to Maldahl. A pool of regrets swept over him—what ifs that he knew were pointless asking …

What if I had not given Sohãhn consent?
What if I had never driven her away?
What if I had not named her Exzalander?

Defied Taiohãhn, a god? Still, what would have happened? Taiohãhn has long since abandoned Maldahl. Does He even have the power to have made me?

Too many what ifs … irrelevant now.

'Are we doing the right thing, Kryepast?' he asked.

The king of Starigorat placed a hand on his friend's shoulder.

'For the sake of Maldahl, yes.'

'And for them?'

Kryepast stared out at his grounds. Katahl had gone and all was quiet.

'We do what we must for the benefit of all. If we do not, then all will perish — that is what is written.'

'But your son?'

'He offers himself freely. I almost lost him once; I will not do it again. He is a man now and I must allow him to make his own choices. I will continue to live in hope that all will be well.'

'The Princess Exzalander,' announced a servant at the door.

The kings turned in unison. Exzalander paused for a moment, gazing at each of them in turn; they looked as though they had been caught doing something they shouldn't.

'I wish to return home, father,' she said. 'Mother will begin to worry and I have been gone longer than expected.'

Kryepast moved back to his seat, sipping his wine in silence.

'That will not be possible, daughter,' Tuâth said. 'Besides, I have already sent word to your mother. She will not be worried.'

Exzalander's gaze fell beyond Tuâth's shoulder and she felt her face flush, realising that he had a perfect view of the garden and had likely witnessed her encounter with Kryepast's son.

'I do not want to stay here, father. If you will not return with me, then I shall go on my own.'

'You will do no such thing!' Tuâth boomed. 'You will learn to obey me for once. If you had shown any level of obedience then ...'

Exzalander sucked in her cheeks, trying to control her anger. She let out the air in a long hiss and narrowed her eyes at Tuâth.

'Then what, father?' she said. 'Then I would not have been prey for your counsellor? Or I would have been his wife by now? That is what you wanted, was it not?'

Tuâth winced at her words, another wave of guilt washing over him.

'I am as much to blame for that as Tuâth,' Kryepast intervened. He felt suddenly glad that he hadn't a daughter. 'I refused consent to Katahl. I have, however, removed that objection.' He spoke as if he truly believed that his words would make everything all right.

She stared at them, incredulous, her eyes questioning what Kryepast meant.

Her father fought to compose himself. 'You are to marry the Lord Katahl,' he confirmed.

Exzalander shook her head, backing away.

'It is not a request, child. For once, you will do as you are told! The announcement will be made tonight and I will write to Shénnin.'

'Congratulations Exzalander,' Kryepast offered.

She forced her mouth to close, aware that it was open. Her father's face was fierce and threatening, as if daring her to disobey him. Kryepast sounded genuine, but something in his countenance made him seem far from happy.

There was no more to be said. She turned on her heel and stormed from the sunroom, Tuâth calling her, demanding that she return. Katahl waited for her at the foot of the stairs.

She scowled at him for a moment, before sweeping past him and back to her room, without a word.

Thirty

Dressmakers had been hard at work, adjusting gowns to fit the new royal guest. Frills of petticoats were sewn in layers, to add length to the short gowns she had already been given. Exzalander stared long at her reflection in the mirror. The dress was an odd shape since the additions—extremely fitting all the way past the knee, where it opened up into layers of bright colours, similar to dancing gypsy girls she had seen back in the towns near home.

She had been presented with fabrics so that new gowns could be made to fit her properly and she had chosen the brightest emerald as her favourite, it reminding her of the great forest and the marble palace from her dreams. Her hair was scraped back off her face and pinned into a tight bun. She did not argue as the women fussed over her; she had barely spoken a word since her father had given her the news.

She was late down to dinner, but found that she did not care. There were fewer nobles at the fortress of Starigorat and the celebratory banquet was a small affair. She was glad of it—*less people to have to smile at.*

As she entered the chamber, the company stood and clapped. With horror, she realised that the announcement had already been made. Katahl walked around the banquet table, stepping up to meet her. He held out his hand and she stared at it, unmoving.

Too late to run, she considered.

Her father glared at her for her hesitation and she relented, taking hold of Katahl's fingertips, as he escorted her to the table.

There was a cheer from the company and Exzalander swallowed, feeling as though her throat was dry. His fingers felt warm and she could feel his pulse thumping against her skin.

As they reached their place, Katahl let go of her hand and pulled out a chair for her. She held her fingers tight against her palm, feeling suddenly cold. She did not thank him; she did not speak to him or even acknowledge his existence. She was angry.

Reaching out, she placed food onto her plate, not wanting to give Katahl the opportunity to offer her anything from the table. The company resumed their chatter and she stared down at the cold meats, unwilling to acknowledge anything else.

'You are upset,' Katahl whispered.

She almost choked on a piece of ham as if he had made the understatement of the year.

'I suppose I understand,' he continued, 'but I had hoped that you would be happy.'

She turned slowly and glowered at him—a look of sheer fury.

'You loved me once,' he said. He spoke carefully, not wanting to enrage her further.

'I cannot believe that you agreed to this,' she hissed. 'I told you *everything* and still you are fool enough to take me on.'

Katahl glanced nervously about; her anger made her louder than he would have liked.

'Perhaps we should continue this conversation when we are alone,' he suggested.

'Alone?' she spat. 'I do not intend on being alone with you, *Milord*,' she said. Her emphasis of his title sounded nothing short of condescending.

'You are the most stubborn woman I have ever met, do you realise that? I *know* you had feelings for me. I *know*. I also know you have been through a lot; believe me I have no intention of rushing you into anything—despite what our fathers have said. I think that you are angry because they told you. I would have preferred to ask you in my own time.'

Her features softened a little. She still looked furious, but not in a way that made him want to remove sharp objects from her reach. She turned away, continuing to eat in silence for a while.

Dessert was a surprise; Exzalander had never seen anything like it. The entire course was presented with such intricacy and beauty that it was more akin to a work of art than food.

'Try some,' Katahl coaxed.

He removed a piece of pastry from the display and she almost sounded a protest at the destruction.

'It's for eating,' he said. 'Try it.'

She took a nibble; it was sweet and oozed syrup, the like of which she had never tasted before. After the sweetness came the almost earthy, savoury nut paste, making her smile.

'Mmmm,' she said, and then set her face to scowl again.

'Here, try some more,' Katahl said.

He broke her off another piece. She did not smile again, but she did not argue either, so Katahl considered it an improvement.

After the feast, the music began. The instruments were strikingly different to those she was familiar with; a staccato array of fast high-pitched notes sounded, which seemed to hold no discernable melody. Drums made her feel as though her heart was beating along with them, accompanied by the strange wind instruments.

She watched as the couples joined each other in the centre of the room. The dancing too was unique; the couples stayed together—no lines or circles formed or swapping partners. The men held the women closer than seemed appropriate and at several crescendos in the music, they lifted them off the ground.

Exzalander held her breath, fascinated by the strange intimacy that seemed commonplace at Starigorat.

'Would you like to dance?' Katahl breathed in her ear.

She turned to see his black eyes twinkling, yet he wore no smile. She shook her head and turned back to the floor.

'I do not know this type of dance,' she said. 'I fear I would make a poor partner.' she took a long draught of wine, as if to hide from his attention.

'Nonsense,' he whispered. 'Besides, the company will be expecting it.'

She felt a tingle along her spine as he whispered to her. Shaking herself, she wondered if it was his close proximity or the sudden memory of Sohãhn with his tongue in her ear that had been the cause.

'Come,' he insisted.

He stood, his hand held out, but she hesitated, debating how long she could delay before people would notice, before they began to make comment. Without looking, she knew that her father's eyes were glaring in her direction. She let out a breath she had been holding and without another thought and without looking at Katahl, she took his hand, allowing him to lead her to the floor.

His arm slipped about her waist and she gasped, looking up at him in alarm. She fought to control her breathing, trying to remind herself that everyone was dancing in the same way; it was perfectly normal.

He almost dragged her about the floor at first, until she grew used to the steps. As she found a pattern in what they were doing, he felt her relax and drew her in closer. Her eyes met his briefly, before falling back to his chest. She seemed to have discovered a rather interesting piece of embroidery on the front of his shirt to examine, rather than have to hold his gaze.

He smiled, lifting her without warning. He felt her struggle and she slapped awkwardly back to the floor, glancing nervously about her, before looking at him.

'You should have warned me,' she scolded.

He was smiling and his eyes blazed into hers.

'Stop that!' she ordered.

'What?'

'Stop looking at me like that!'

He grinned, his smile both wolfish and boyish, a mischievous combination that he had down to an art.

'Like what?' he asked.

'Like I am one of those pastries.'

'Are you affeared that people will talk?'

'Yes,' she said, glancing about her again.

'We are to be married; people expect me to look at you like that. We are doing nothing wrong.'

He could feel the tension returning to her and he huffed in frustration and looked away. As the music stopped, he bowed formerly and left her to escort herself back to her own chair. Approaching a lady who was seated near the floor, he asked her to join him for the next.

Exzalander stood for a moment, taking in the woman's raven black hair and stunning features, then she stormed away into the sunroom beyond. She stood in the darkness, her head pressed against the glass and watched as her breath formed on the window, like ghosts in the pale moonlight. The sound from the banquet chamber drifted in, leaving her with an ache in her stomach.

She thought of Katahl and the woman whom he was holding, and her insides seemed to flip inside her. *Who is she?* she thought. *A lover? Is she to be what Beth was to Sohãhn? Does marriage mean nothing to men?*

She collapsed on the floor, unable to breathe properly as her thoughts overcame her.

'I will not ... I will not let him see that he has hurt me,' she whispered to herself. 'I will not be used again!' She let out a long breath, feeling her composure return. Getting to her feet, she smoothed down her gown, held her head up high and took a breath in, releasing it as she joined the company once more.

'*Don't look. Don't look*', she ordered herself, but still could not help glance at Katahl as he lifted the woman high into the air. The woman smiled, gripping him tight as she landed. As Exzalander watched him turn her about, she made a silent promise that she would never trust another man as long as she lived.

Katahl was not smiling, 'though Exzalander failed to notice; he seemed to look through his partner to something beyond.

'I am surprised that Lord Katahl did not insist on dancing with you all night, Milady.'

Exzalander jumped, turning to face the man who had spoken.

'I fear that I am a poor dance partner,' she said, trying not to sound too feeble. 'Our dances are very different to those of Starigorat.'

The man was smiling at Katahl with the woman, yet Exzalander could feel his focus upon her and she did not like it.

'Allow me to educate you then,' he said.

Without warning, he slipped his arm about her waist.

Katahl had seen the princess escape to the sunroom and felt a pang of guilt for leaving her on the dance floor. However, he was almost disappointed when he observed her return, her head held so high and her eyes harder than the rock of Starigorat itself. He turned back to his partner; her smiles held no joy for him. *What am I thinking trying to incite jealousy?* he thought. *I have probably driven her further away than ever.*

Lord Darrack was speaking to her; he tried not to stare, but moved his partner about so that he could get closer. He saw Darrack's hand as it moved about Exzalander's waist and the look of terror that followed. The colour drained from her face and with a cry, she shoved him away. Katahl let go of the girl and ran to calm the situation, deciding in an instant that he would make something up about difference in customs— *no need for them to know the real reason for her reaction,* he thought.

It was Kryepast himself who uttered such words and Katahl found himself utterly speechless. Exzalander stood behind him, using him as a shield, her hands clinging to his back. Thankfully, Darrack's attention was on the king and he did not see how the princess held so desperately onto Katahl. Unfortunately, others in the company did observe her behaviour. Katahl heard the whispers forming and he immediately led her from the room, hoping to calm the situation.

Closing the door, he turned to face her. She was trembling and pale, appearing more spectre than living at that moment.

'What happened?' he asked.

'He touched me without permission,' she said, her voice desperate. 'I cannot let that happen again … I will not!'

'Shhh,' Katahl soothed. 'Darrack meant no harm; things are not quite as conventional here. I am sorry, I should have warned you.'

The colour returned to her face in an instant. 'Had you not better get back to your woman?' she spat.

'My woman?' He laughed suddenly.

'I agreed to marry Sohãhn; I did not tell you that.'

His smile vanished in an instant. 'What!' he hissed.

'He gave me little choice, having compromised me in such a way; besides, I thought we could have been happy.

That was until I saw him copulating with my former lady-in-waiting. I turned him in to the Council. That is why he was so angry with me and why he tried to take me by force.

'I will not marry you. I do not care if I have to relinquish my title and live my life as a peasant. I will not marry a man who keeps other women.'

'I don't even know that woman's name,' Katahl protested. 'I only danced with her to make you jealous. Had I known what you had seen ... well, I never would have.'

Her expression was difficult to read.

'Did you really have Sohāhn arrested?' he asked.

'Yes,' she replied. 'My only regret is that I did not do it sooner.'

He smiled then, and although she wanted to return it, she found that she could not. She pondered whether she was being stubborn, or had genuinely forgotten how.

'I do not care what your customs are,' she said, 'that man should not have just assumed that a lady always says yes.'

'You are right. But I am glad it happened,' Katahl concluded.

She looked as though she was about to throw something at him and he quickly tried to explain.

'Now I know that despite your outbursts and your scowls, when you feel threatened, you turn to me. That shows trust; it means a lot.'

Colour flooded to her cheeks, as she considered his words.

'Shall I tell you something else?' he said.

She nodded her head with a nervous gulp.

'You told me that when you vanished, you thought to appear with a loved one.'

'I meant father,' she said quickly, her words almost one.

'But Tuâth was not there; it was me.'

He stepped toward her and she seemed too deep in thought to bother backing away.

'I ...' she said, and fell into silence.

He tilted her chin up so that she had to meet his eyes and was shocked when her hand reached up to touch his cheek. He smiled and stroked her hair.

'I had not thought of that,' she said.

His eyes shined, as he leaned in closer. She could feel the thumping of her heart, yet no desire to run away. Her breathing quickened and her eyes closed. He needed no more encouragement; his lips met hers, and he pulled her close to him. She did not freeze and to his pleasant surprise he felt her hands run along his back as she welcomed him.

She felt a familiar heat rise through her body as her desire grew, but there was not the accompanying feeling of shame. She surrendered and felt as though she would melt into him.

It was the cheering and whooping from the room beyond that brought her reluctantly back down to the ground, before she floated off altogether.

Too loud, she thought, and opened a wary eye.

The guests were stood at the door and had seen enough to know that their king's son was to be a very happy man. Exzalander blushed, but smiled at Katahl.

'It is our way, sorry,' he said, with a boyish smile.

'Don't be,' she whispered in his ear.

Her eyes flashed suggestively as she pulled away, making him feel weak. She did not relinquish hold of his hand as he led her back to the table.

Tuâth seemed half happy, half disturbed at the public display. But Kryepast slapped him on the back with a grin.

'Let's drink!' he cried, and there was another cheer from the company.

Thirty-one

Tuâth smiled at his daughter's approach. She seemed a different person to him, no longer his little girl, but no longer broken at least. Over the past few days, the colour had returned to her cheeks and for the most part, she appeared happy. The shadows that haunted her eyes became less frequent and he held hopes that they would eventually disappear altogether.

She smiled and took his hands as he offered them.

'Father, you wished to see me?' she said.

'Yes my child. It is time that I returned home. I need to stop off at Ealdorbold on the way. I have some urgent matters I must attend to.'

Her features darkened. 'You mean Sohãhn,' she said.

'Yes,' Tuâth replied quietly. He had no desire to pain his daughter, but he refused to lie to her either. 'I need to be there for his sentencing. But *you* need not come. Kryepast has agreed that you should spend time with his son. So good it is to see you accept him.'

Exzalander bowed her head as if weighing up what it would mean if she did not go.

'Father, I think I need to be there. What that man did to me … the way I handled it … it will haunt me to the end of my days.'

Tuâth winced and Exzalander squeezed his hands.

'But if I hide away and pretend that it never happened, then I shall never learn from my mistakes; I will never move on, and that is what I want; it's what I need. Father, please allow me to go with you. Besides, I need to see mother again.'

Tuâth sighed and shook his head. 'Your betrothed will not let you out of his sight, you know. He is very protective of you.'

Exzalander gave a half laugh. 'That's not necessarily a bad thing,' she said. 'I seem utterly incapable of staying out of trouble for any length of time.'

Tuâth tried to smile, tried to see the lighter side to his daughter's words, but the truth was, he felt old. She *did* need looking after and he felt that he no longer had the strength to face more adversity.

'Anyhow,' she continued, 'Katahl is not that protective. I have not even seen him since yesterday.'

She pouted and Tuâth touched her face, enjoying seeing the child for a moment. Rising, he kissed her forehead and walked slowly away. She watched him with a frown of concern. Something was different; he seemed so tired.

His sword, she thought. *Where is his sword?* For her entire life, she had never seen him without it. It was as much a symbol of his authority as the crown on his head. Her mother had once joked that he would wear it to bed, if she let him. Exzalander felt a wave of dread come over her and she stood to go after the king.

'There you are. I have been looking all over for you,' Katahl said. He paced over to her from the direction of the rose garden and she turned to face him, her features were such that he broke into a run.

'What is it?' he asked.

'I … Oh Katahl, something is the matter with father. I must go,' she said, turning away.

Katahl had other ideas and grabbed her hand, preventing her escape. She took deep sips of air, trying to keep her breathing calm.

'It is my fault, is it not?' she said. 'I have done this to him … How will I ever face mother?'

Katahl pulled her into his chest and held her there.

'He has been through a lot. You must not blame yourself. As soon as he is home, he will pick up, you'll see. Anyhow, there is nothing like a wedding for lightening the mood.'

Letting her go, he sank to one knee before her. His absence suddenly made perfect sense when he slipped a wedding bracelet on her wrist. She had stopped breathing—she knew that she had.

I have no choice but to marry him, she thought. *It has all been arranged. Why is he pretending as though it hadn't?* She stared at the bracelet and gasped for breath.

The most beautiful emeralds she had ever seen adorned her wrist. She was reminded of her safe haven—the dream palace and the great forest. But something else stirred in her mind—an almost forgotten childhood memory of a sword ...

'Will you, Exzalander of the house of Shénnin and Tuâth, accept this my bond?' Katahl breathed. 'Will you marry me?'

The memory was gone, even as she had reached out for it; the shock of his words dispersed it once more.

'There is no need to ask, Lord Katahl,' she said, feeling uncomfortable.

His smile began to fade. 'Is that a yes?' he asked.

'I have no choice; why are you doing this?'

His face fell and his eyes grew cold. Clambering to his feet, he stormed over to the seat that she had shared with her father, and placed his head in his hands. She took one last look toward the fortress; her father was out of sight. Unsure how to react, she took a seat beside Katahl and remained silent.

'I wanted you to have a choice,' he mumbled to himself.

She put a hand on his arm and he glanced up at her, his expression unyielding.

'I need to go home,' she said carefully.

The hurt he felt was clear. She placed her hands either side of his face and kissed him.

'I am saying everything all wrong,' she said. 'You surprised me ... our marriage is already agreed and I did not expect or require your proposal.' She kissed him again. 'But it was a lovely gesture and the commitment bracelet is beautiful. I did not mean to appear ungrateful. It was just your timing, it was …'

He stopped her mouth with a kiss and her hands slipped behind his neck as he drew her in closer.

She dragged herself away, her forehead resting against his. 'I need to go home,' she breathed. 'I cannot let father make this journey alone. I am genuinely concerned for his health. He goes to Ealdorbold to oversee Sohãhn's punishment and I need to be with him; can you understand that?'

'Yes,' Katahl sighed. 'Call me selfish if you will, but I cannot let you go from my side.'

She held him at arm's length, staring at him in disbelief.

'I do not require your permission,' she said incredulous.

He laughed at her. 'I would not dream of ordering you, my love. It is more than my life is worth.' He took her hands again and smiled. 'What I meant was, you must go of course, but I am coming with you. Besides, do you not want to introduce your mother to the man you plan to marry?'

Without warning she threw her arms about him. He pulled her up onto his lap and held her there.

'Thank you,' she sighed, allowing her lips to meet his once more.

It was Katahl who removed her from him and caught his breath with a lazy smile dancing upon his lips.

'You should go and prepare. There are a few new gowns for you.'

She slipped off his lap and held out her hand. 'Coming,' she asked.

He grimaced. *It really was the wrong thing to ask,* he thought. He forced a smile. 'You go ahead; I will follow you shortly.'

She nodded and smiled—not a smile of understanding as he had expected. *Perhaps some of her innocence has been retained after all,* he mused, and tried to think non-arousing thoughts.

It was to be their final evening at Starigorat and the young couple made the most of it, joining in the revelry and dancing as if they would not see the place again.

'So, my son follows you to Brëgwela,' Kryepast remarked.

'Mmmm,' acknowledged Tuâth. 'I fear he would not be parted from her again. I would rather they had both remained with you, old friend, but Exzalander is determined to see her mother and I could not deny her that.'

Kryepast closed his eyes and nodded in understanding.

A cheer went up from the dance floor and the two kings looked up to see Exzalander in Katahl's arms as he span around in circles; she was laughing and happy.

Tuâth felt his mood lift at the sight of the young couple. 'Katahl has worked majick upon her. Never did I think to see such joy in her eyes again. It does me good to see it. I only wish it does not dissipate when she sees Sohãhn once again.'

Kryepast choked. 'Surely there can be no cause for her to see him,' he said.

'She has insisted,' Tuâth groaned. 'I doubt that it can be avoided anyhow. I will need her to give evidence against him.'

Kryepast blew air out with a hiss. 'Well, take my advice and avoid it if you can. Above all, keep Katahl away from him. I do not think he would wait for sentencing—he is likely to run him through and I do not want him getting himself into trouble. I know how headstrong he can be.'

'Do not concern yourself, Kryepast. I will look after him—that is until he meets Shénnin. You will likely never see him again after that. She will mother him to death!'

They laughed and clinked goblets together, then turning, they watched their children as they continued to dance the night away.

The journey to Ealdorbold, though uneventful, took longer than it should. Tuâth set a slow, yet steady pace and would not be deterred from it. Exzalander did not seem to mind and took every opportunity to enjoy the new scenery. She remained quiet for the most part, making conversation only when the company stopped for the night.

Only a handful of servants had been sent to escort them. Along with them were also Aarnon and two of Kryepast's own knights. It fell to Katahl to arrange travel formation and he and Aarnon rode up front, whilst Kryepast's knights protected the rear.

Exzalander was glad to have the opportunity to be alone with her thoughts. So much had happened that it felt good to be able to think on everything in solitude for a while. She knew that they were getting closer to the palace, when the temperature became noticeably cooler. The trees, though shorter, grew closer together, making it increasingly difficult to see the road ahead. Branches twisted overhead, reaching across the path and joining so closely with those about them, that it was impossible to tell where one tree ended and another began.

Exzalander shivered and drew her cloak about her, suddenly wishing that the journey were done so she might complete the task she had to perform. She wanted it over.

Katahl sat with the knight Aarnon, watching Exzalander as she spoke with her father. As she warmed her hands by the fire, Katahl resisted the urge to go and wrap his arms about her. He was worried. *She seems too calm about having to face Sohāhn again,* he thought. *I do not understand her need to do so, unless she intends on putting a knife between the man's ribs—it would be no less than he deserves.* He gritted his teeth in frustration. *Of course she isn't considering such a thing—I am.* Stoking the fire, he fantasised he were the hand that performed the execution.

The company heard the bugle blasts in the distance and knew their approach had been spied. By the time they arrived at the palace, it seemed that the entire household was there to greet them. There were cheers of welcome and flowers were thrown. Exzalander remembered that it was the first time her father had been there since they declared war on the dragons. So much had been happening in her own life that she had forgotten the danger they had all been in.

How many died? she wondered, and felt a pang of guilt, realising that such thoughts should have come sooner.

She noticed the tears and sorrow among the joy, women clutching belongings of husbands and sons, brothers and fathers, never to return. The more Exzalander gazed about her, the more grief she observed — silent, bitter faces amongst the heroes' welcome, dutifully greeting their king's return from victory.

She wanted to look away; she did not want to see their pain. Her father smiled and waved to the crowd, making her feel as though it was her duty to respond to them. The ride to the palace courtyard seemed to take an age, and she felt drained from gazing into the eyes of so many, offering silent acknowledgment of their loss. As they halted the horses, she noticed that the Council had also come out to greet them and her stomach lurched at the sight of them. A quick perusal of those gathered revealed that Sohãhn was not among their number, yet she still struggled to contain her panic.

She did not want to face Sohãhn. She did not want to face any of them. In fact, Ealdorbold, which had always felt more like home than Brëgwela, now seemed a place to be feared. She looked about, feeling helpless; everyone was dismounting. She knew Katahl would come to her aid and it was the thought of his hand, his sympathy, all the while the Council looking on and judging her, which made her swing suddenly down from the horse and fall in step beside her father.

'Greeting Counsellors, I have much to discuss with you,' said the king. 'I would like us to meet in the Council Chamber, in one hour.'

Exzalander knew that she was looking at the floor and forced her eyes up. Counsellor Tyrian was staring at her and she felt her cheeks grow warm. All she could think about was how he had been there when Sohãhn had tried to ravage her; he had seen how weak and humiliated she was. As the king finished speaking and moved away, she stepped forward to follow him into the palace.

'Your Highness, might I speak with you a moment?' Tyrian asked.

'Not now counsellor,' Katahl said. His manner was abrupt and protective as he stepped between them, guiding Exzalander indoors. 'The princess needs food and rest.'

She did not know whether to be angry or grateful for his intervention. She did not have the energy to argue. As she passed Tyrian, she saw his eyes fall to her commitment bracelet. A bracelet on the right wrist could mean only one thing. He glanced up at her with shocked realisation, suddenly eager to run after his fellow counsellors.

Wearily, she made her way up to her old rooms, pleased on her arrival, to hear water being poured into her bath within.

'Do you need me to stay with you?'

She jumped, not realising Katahl was still with her.

'You need rest too,' she said. 'No doubt my father will wish you to attend the meeting. Go, I will be fine.'

She tried to smile as he kissed her hand, but the mischievous glint in his eye was more than she had patience for.

'I know not where to go,' he grinned. 'It seems that you have my room.'

She shook her head, too tired to banter. Opening the door to her chambers, she called a servant over to her.

'Please see that Lord Katahl is given suitable chambers and that he is fed.'

'Yes Your Highness,' the girl replied, with a curtsey. She began to walk away, but paused, waiting for Katahl to follow.

Katahl held Exzalander's hand for a moment.

'I will see you later,' he promised, and followed the girl up the corridor.

As Exzalander entered the room, memories of the last time she was there came flooding back. She dismissed the servants and locked the door. She did not trust that Sohãhn was in the dungeon. *He was locked up before and managed to get out easily enough,* she thought. *This room—my room, which I always loved, now sickens me. Everything is contaminated by his presence.* Before removing her clothes, she gazed nervously about as if the very walls were watching her.

As she stepped into the bath, she found that she could not lie back and close her eyes. She felt as though all the water in Maldahl would not get her clean. By the time she had gotten dressed and headed out, the meeting was well underway. Since her father had not requested that she attend, she decided it would be all right to visit Elsbeth.

As she made her way across the courtyard, she felt as though all eyes were upon her and her pace increased with her desire to be away from people.

'Milady!'

She heard the shout over the clash of swords, but assumed it was not directed at her.

'Princess Exzalander!'

Perhaps it had.

She turned to see Knight Nimrïn, pacing across the yard to her—sword in hand. She glanced nervously at the weapon, relieved when he placed in into its scabbard.

'You remember me, I deem,' he said, with a grin.

'Yes Nimrïn, how could I possibly forget? I did not take too kindly to being named 'pretty boy'.'

Nimrïn guffawed and his laugh was so loud and clear that she found herself almost smiling.

'Good it is to see you well,' he said. 'I was there when you …' He saw the horror in her eyes and abruptly stopped. 'This great lug is Caitul, First Knight to Katahl,' he said, as way of introduction.

Exzalander inclined her head in greeting and found the knight was staring. She swallowed, suddenly concerned that she may not have washed her face properly, yet she knew had that been the case, Nimrïn would have relished telling her as much.

'You must excuse me,' she said, and hurried on.

Nimrïn clipped Caitul about the head.

'Ow!' he complained. 'What did you do that for?'

'She's princess of your house; you're supposed to bow, you idiot. She thought you were being rude.'

'I …' But whatever he was going to say, trailed into silence, as he watched her walk away.

Nimrïn waved a hand in front of Caitul's eyes, trying to regain his attention.

'Do you think that she should be wandering off on her own like that?' Caitul murmured.

Nimrïn huffed, drawing his sword. 'What are you, her keeper? Come on, I want you to show me that move again.'

As Exzalander stood at Thomn and Elsbeth's door, she could not bring herself to knock. Doubt filled her mind.

Does everyone know? Surely not … so, what do they know?

The door opened and Elsbeth beamed at her.

'Your Highness!' Without warning, she caught Exzalander in a motherly embrace and held her there. 'Come in, you're freezing. Warm yourself by the fire.'

Exzalander obeyed and breathed in the stew cooking over the flames. 'Smells wonderful,' she mused.

'It's nothing like you're used to, but you're welcome to stay later,' Elsbeth offered.

'Thank you, but I am not sure what father's plans are. Is Captain Thomn on duty?'

Elsbeth took off her apron and sat next to Exzalander, stirring the stew for a moment.

'He's with the Council and your father ... giving an account,' she finished carefully.

'You know?'

Elsbeth's lips tightened and she could not meet Exzalander's gaze.

'Yes, but don't blame Thomn, Your Highness. I *made* him tell me. I knew that something was wrong and I was worried about *you*. I'm sorry.'

Exzalander waved away Elsbeth's apology.

'Does everyone know?' she asked. The moment the words had left her mouth, she immediately wished that she could withdraw the question, feeling quite sure she would rather remain ignorant.

'There have been rumours—nothing more,' Elsbeth said. 'They certainly won't hear anything from me!'

Exzalander stared into the flames, enjoying the way the heat made her face feel like it was glowing.

'You poor dear,' Elsbeth continued. 'I hope your father gives him a slow death.'

Exzalander looked up at the woman, shocked for a moment.

'I think my father wishes he had a son,' she mused.

Elsbeth gave a tinkling laugh. 'Take it from a mother of two boys; they can be much more of a handful. Now, when are you going to tell me of your betrothed? Am I to wait for a public announcement?'

Exzalander's head shot up and she saw Elsbeth's eyes twinkle, as they looked down at her commitment bracelet.

'I should have worn it on the left. It's far too conspicuous,' she grimaced. 'Father will announce it today I should think, but I doubt there is any harm in you knowing before then …'

The door crashed open and Caitul strode in.

'Mother, you'll never guess who I've just met,' he said. Unclasping his belt he placed down his weapons.

'Sword off the table, Caitul! How many times must I tell you? Are you even listening?'

But he wasn't. He was staring again. Suddenly, as if remembering his manners, he bowed. 'Princess Exzalander … er …' he stuttered.

Exzalander stared back at him, as if waiting for him to finish his sentence. *What is wrong with him?* she thought. *Why does he keep looking at me like that?*

The silence and Caitul's staring became too uncomfortable for her to bear.

'I had not realised that your son was First Knight to the Lord Katahl,' she said. 'How did such a thing come about?'

Elsbeth helped her son off with his armour and it was Exzalander's turn to stare. She felt as though she should look away, but found herself transfixed, as each piece of black metal was removed to reveal the man within.

'Caitul will tell you the tale, I'm sure,' Elsbeth urged her dumbstruck son.

He blushed as he saw Exzalander's eyes upon him, but held her gaze, before he pulled on his waiting shirt.

'I should be heading back to the palace,' she said rising. 'I am not sure whether I might be needed to speak.'

Elsbeth smiled. 'Of course.'

'I will escort you back,' Caitul said quickly.

'Very well,' Exzalander agreed, with a half smile. 'It was lovely to see you again, Elsbeth.'

As the two women embraced, Caitul gave the strangest look, confused as to when such a friendship had blossomed and how he could have been ignorant to it. Waiting his turn, he stooped down to kiss his mother on the cheek.

Exzalander took the long way back to the palace, enjoying seeing the gardens once more. Caitul did not comment, but walked silently beside her.

'We have met before, you know,' Exzalander said at last.

He seemed stricken for a moment. 'Surely not, Your Highness, I would remember ...' He trailed off as he met her gaze, noticing how green her eyes were—as green as the gown that she wore, reminding him of grass on a spring morning.

'Indeed we have,' she insisted. 'I bumped into you coming out of a tent, on the way here. I was dressed as a servant and you spoke to me—quite forcefully, if I recall.'

Caitul's eyes widened at her words, his mind catching up to what she referred to.

'How could I not notice that it was you?' he asked himself in astonishment.

She smiled wryly. 'One does not notice servants, Knight Caitul. I have come to observe that, especially of late.'

Caitul bowed his head. 'How you must hate me, Your Highness ... I cannot ask for forgiveness.'

Exzalander took his hands and kissed them.

'You need not ask. Indeed, it is I who should beg forgiveness from you and I who thank you. I owe you a great debt of gratitude. Without you, I may never have been saved.'

She knelt before him and Caitul pulled her to her feet in disbelief.

'No Your Highness, you must not kneel—not to me.'

'Why not? I freely acknowledge that Beth's indiscretion with you led to my escaping a terrible fate. I honestly do not know whether to hate Beth or be grateful to her too.'

'So ... you're not angry with me?' Caitul asked incredulous. 'She was your friend.'

'No Caitul.' Exzalander lifted her chin, as if she had remembered her place. 'She was not my friend; she was a servant and perhaps had I treated her as such, she would not have done such a terrible thing.'

Caitul stepped closer and Exzalander felt small, as he towered over her.

'But if I'd realised who you were, then *none* of this would have happened.'

She smiled up at him and he felt as though he should look away, but found that he could not.

'I think Katahl might have something to say about that,' she mused. 'Come, I really must return now.'

He walked beside her, too afraid to speak, for fear of saying something foolish and inappropriate, instead he was left to his thoughts. *This is the woman that my Lord loves and she is perfect.*

Thirty-Two

Exzalander tried to face lunch, but found that she was unable. More than anything, she longed to visit Ardahl, but thought it prudent not to be beyond reach, in case she was summoned. She found herself moving in the direction of the Council Chamber, wondering if she should request to be there and get it over with.

As she reached the outer chamber, she paused. There were several raised voices coming from within; whatever discussion took place was heated. She stepped closer, the guards at the door glancing nervously at her. Hearing Tuâth's voice call them to order, she hesitated. Her limbs refused to move as fear took over. She wanted to turn back, but knew if she did not at least offer to face the Council, then she could never hope to command their respect again. She forced her legs forward, trying to retain a princely countenance. The guards stiffened to attention as she reached them.

'You haven't been summoned, Your Highness,' said one.

'I am aware of that thank you. Kindly announce me. If the king does not wish me to attend, then I will leave.'

The guard nodded and opened the door. All talking beyond abruptly ceased, and as her name was issued, the whispers began. She held her breath, hoping she would be sent away.

I have done my duty and shown myself willing to face them — surely that will be enough, she thought.

The guard returned. 'You may enter, Your Highness,' he said.

She knew all eyes would be on her and she took small steps, keeping her gaze fixed on the floor ahead of her. She knew where the throne was and risked a glance to her father. His face was troubled and he met her eyes, with sympathy.

She wondered if Katahl was there, yet had not the strength to look for him.

'Your Highness, we are pleased that you felt you could join us today,' High Counsellor Danah said. 'The accused proclaims his innocence and your words here could bring an end to all debate.'

Debate? she thought. *What is there to debate?* She intended to meet the gaze of the High Counsellor, but started, as she realised Sohãhn was in the room. His eyes were fixed upon her and she felt the hatred emanating from him. Feelings of shame threatened to overwhelm her, but the memory of betrayal kept her from crumbling.

'What is it that you wish to know?' she asked. She hoped more than anything that her voice did not waver.

'Sohãhn claims that the relations he had with you were consensual. Is this true?' Counsellor Baruch asked.

She played the attempted rape over in her mind and opened her mouth to speak, only to find that her voice had flown. She shook her head to indicate her answer.

'She lies, Milords!' Sohãhn cried.

'The prisoner will remain silent,' Tuâth ordered.

However, Sohãhn knew he had nothing to lose. 'She agreed to be my wife. It was my right!' he yelled, his voice cracking with desperation.

Exzalander felt the room spinning. Her eyes searched for Katahl and found him staring calmly, lovingly back at her. She was glad then that she had been honest with him, realising that nothing she could say there would shock him, or hurt him any more than she had already done so.

'Is this true?' Tuâth asked, enraged that she might have been stupid enough to keep such a thing from him.

She said nothing, causing the king to repeat himself.

'Yes,' she replied too quietly.

'What was your answer?'

'Yes,' she said again. 'I did agree to marry him. He told me that *you* ordered it; I felt I had little choice.'

There was an outcry in the chamber at her admission and Sohāhn looked triumphant. Katahl continued to stare calmly at her, as if willing her to remain composed.

No matter what happens, she thought. *I know now that Katahl is all that matters.* Her eyes shone back at him and he gave a slight smile of understanding. It was a gesture missed by the arguing counsellors, but not Sohāhn.

'I demand to be released immediately,' he barked. 'Exzalander is to be my wife and you cannot charge the husband of royalty.'

Tuâth brought them to order. He seemed wearier than ever; it was as though his life was being sucked out of him.

'Exzalander, I think that you will need to explain why you felt it necessary to accept his proposal … I am sorry.'

She couldn't—not because of the Council's reaction to *her*, but rather their reaction to her father. She was worried the king would lose their respect should they discover how deeply his daughter had been compromised. She shook her head and felt the panic set in.

'Take the prisoner away,' Danah ordered.

'She's mine!' Sohāhn screeched, 'you heard her. Everything I did, I did because she asked me to!'

His voice sounded maniacal, making Exzalander's skin crawl. She cursed the day she ever met the manipulative, selfish and sadistic former counsellor.

'Do you wish to give further evidence before you are dismissed, Your Highness?' Baruch asked. His tone was exasperated; clearly the proceedings were not heading in the way he had hoped.

Exzalander met Katahl's eyes, taking in his concern. She tried to breathe the panic away, allowing it to dissipate once Sohāhn was removed from her sight.

'Counsellor Sohãhn told me he could help Beth,' she said. 'He made me agree to marry him to bring it about, stating that my father would force me on his return anyhow. The fact that I agreed to be his wife did not give him the right to betray me with the prisoner he released and it certainly did not give him the right to take me by force.

'Had Counsellor Tyrian not arrived when he did ...' she stopped and gulped for air, as the tears streamed down her face. 'Had Tyrian not arrived when he did, then this matter would not be in debate. Sohãhn would have been executed without a thought.

'Ask Tyrian if I sounded as though I consented to Sohãhn's actions as I screamed for him to stop.' She took one last look to Katahl, to give her enough strength to walk, rather than run, from the room.

She considered her words; she had omitted a lot, but found that she could not feel guilty for having done so. Katahl would not mind, or her father. It was all of their reputations that she was sparing. She hoped it was enough. She never wanted to face Sohãhn again.

None of the Counsellors were at the evening feast, neither was her father or Katahl.

As she sat down, Exzalander's stomach felt like an empty pit. Joyous nobles, seemingly ignorant to events, surrounded her. In a way, it was a relief. It gave her reason to hope that her shame was not generally known as she had suspected. Yet their joviality made her angry; she realised how wholly unconnected they were to the real Maldahl. None of them were grieving for lost sons in the battle with the dragons. They sat eating and drinking to excess, without regard to the suffering across the kingdom. Exzalander promised herself there and then, that things would be different when she was queen.

The music began and she realised that she had barely touched her food. The only thing she really felt like eating was a sweet pastry from Starigorat.

'Come on, mopey, let's get this party started,' Nimrïn said, as he stood before her.

Exzalander stared up at him with an icy expression. *At least he has the courtesy to offer his hand rather than drag me to the dance floor,* she thought.

'You will address me by my proper title, Knight Nimrïn,' she warned.

'My sincere apologies,' he bowed, sounding anything but sincere. 'Dance with me, Your Mopiness.'

She looked as though she might strike him, but he laughed and pulled her to her feet.

'Leave them to their ignorance, Princess,' he said. 'Better to appear happy, rather than everyone question your mood. It's none of their damn business.'

She raised an eyebrow at him. 'You are right,' she said.

'That's the spirit!' he laughed.

As they joined the line, Caitul watched them closely. He envied Nimrïn at that moment—such confidence. *He holds in his arms, the most beautiful woman in the world—so lucky,* he considered.

'I hope this is not to be one of our new duties,' Aarnon complained, as he watched the pair dance.

Nimrïn's movements were clumsy, a culmination of unfamiliarity with the steps and the effects of too much wine.

'I doubt it,' Dahal replied, his expression stern, as was his wont. 'You know Nimrïn, cannot resist a pretty face.'

'Well he'll need to; that one's taken,' Aarnon said. 'The wedding announcement has been made at home. I expect they'll make it official here, as soon as the king arrives.'

Caitul felt as though he had been punched in the stomach. He tightly gripped the goblet in his hand, raising it to his lips, to help hide any loss of countenance, as he fought to appear normal. *Of course she is to marry Lord Katahl,* he thought. *What else did I expect?* But it pained him. He had never expected to experience such emotions and now he wished he never had.

'One of you take over, will you,' Nimrïn said, panting slightly. 'I'm exhausted.'

'I *knew* it,' Aarnon hissed under his breath, convinced that he had been right.

'Come on ... I need to pay a visit, if you take my meaning,' he urged, crossing his legs.

Caitul stood.

He knew that he should not have. He knew that pushing Exzalander out of his thoughts was the honourable and most sensible action he could take. But he could not. He felt the commitment bracelet brush his skin, as he took her hand.

'The colour matches your eyes, Your Highness,' he said as he glanced down at her.

Realising what he had meant, she blushed.

'Oh,' she said.

'Might I offer my congratulations? The Lord Katahl is a worthy man.' The words had been sincere enough, but they had not stopped the burning sensation within Caitul, threatening to consume him if he held her any closer.

'You have not yet told me how you came to be First Knight,' Exzalander remarked, changing the subject.

She passed in front of him, taking his opposite hand and the hand of the man to her right.

'I saved the Lord Katahl's life,' he replied. 'He was attacked by one of the CODM.'

'Oh!' She seemed shocked at the sudden realisation. 'I had not known that it was you.'

He smiled, his eyes shining. As she smiled back at him, she could easily see what Beth had found so appealing.

'May I cut in?'

'Katahl!' Exzalander yelped, losing regal bearing with her excitement.

Caitul smiled. 'Milord,' he said. Bowing, he walked away, before another word could be spoken,

'I need to speak with you ... now,' Katahl whispered in her ear. He pulled her away from the dance and they left the hall. Taking her hand, he led her toward the throne room.

'What is wrong, Katahl?'

'Not here,' he replied. His face was brooding and dark as he continued down the corridor.

The throne room was empty and cold. The fires had not been lit there for some time, making it feel inhospitable and unwelcoming.

'I am so sorry,' he said at last.

She stared up in confusion.

'The Council felt that you agreeing to be Sohãhn's wife, gave him certain ... rights. It was considered that he went too far, but as you said, he did not actually rape you so they cannot charge him with that. Neither can they execute him for releasing Beth, as it seems that you may have instigated his actions.'

'No ...' she murmured. Her knees gave way and she sank to the cold floor.

Katahl was there in an instant, cradling her in his arms from behind; his chin rested on the crown of her head.

'They are not releasing him?' she said panicking.

'No ... do not worry about that. He has lost his position on the Council and has been stripped of his title. He will receive a sentence in prison; they are just deliberating how long.'

'But my father, why did he not sentence him to death?'

Katahl hugged her closer.

'The Council each have a voice of their own. In matters such as this, they must all be heard; all have a vote. The king cannot simply override them. This is the system that he himself put in place, wanting a voice for his people. He cannot break his own laws.'

She scrambled to her feet. 'I must get away from here,' she said. 'I cannot be here when he is released.'

Katahl took her hand, pulling her to him.

'That is not likely to be any time soon. But we will leave as soon as may be,' he offered.

'Thank you.'

She gazed into his eyes and he smiled as she smoothed back a piece of his blue-black hair, which had fallen across his face.

'I know not what I would have done without you this day,' she said. 'I do not think I would have found the strength to even be there, if not for you.' She took in every single feature, as if seeing him for the first time. 'I love you.' After she spoke, she let out a breath she had not realised she had been holding.

'Oh my love,' Katahl sighed. 'Despite everything, today is the happiest of days.'

He beamed and picked her up, turning her about. As he put her down again, she slipped her arms about his neck and kissed him. It was not long before he pulled away.

She frowned. 'You always do that,' she said. 'Do I do something wrong?'

He placed a hand on her cheek and smiled with disbelief.

'No my love, it is just that my desire for you is difficult to control. I will not ...' he trailed off, unable to find the words to put the matter delicately.

She lowered her eyes, as sudden understanding came to her.

'Oh.' She blushed deeply, as she realised what he had been attempting to tell her. 'You know that I desire you too ... if you want ... me ... if ...'

He smiled at her awkwardness.

'My love, it is not a question of desire. Of course I want you; surely that is obvious. But even if you are willing, it cannot happen until after we are wed.'

Exzalander bowed her head, feeling suddenly ashamed that she had voiced her choice. 'Of course; that is proper.'

'No, you misunderstand me. After the meeting, your father made a new decree. No man is permitted to touch you in any way, the only exception being—your husband. Once it has been issued, I will not even be able to lead you to a table until after we are wed.'

'What! I have to put a stop to this. It is going too far, Katahl. I shall not be able to hold you ... to kiss you.'

'Shhh,' he soothed.

'I will not shush,' she barked. 'This is an outrage and I will not stand for it. Why did you not contest it?'

Katahl sagged and sighed. 'How could I, my love? To do so would only make your father think that I planned for us to lie together before we are wed. He has been through enough.'

'But it does not mean that. This is ridiculous. I won't be able to dance with anyone, other than my husband, ever again. I won't even be allowed assistance dismounting a horse for crying out loud!'

'I did not realise that you were so eager to be touched by other men.'

She stared at him, horrified by his words. Katahl realised his mistake, too late. She stormed away from him, but he pursued, bringing her to a halt.

'I did not mean that the way it sounded,' he said.

She gazed icily at the hand on her arm and then back to him.

'Release me at once!' she ordered.

'You are being childish, Exzalander,' he informed her.

'You should not have let him do it,' she spat back at him. 'This is my life it affects. It sets me apart as some sort of freak.'

'I will bring the wedding forward,' Katahl offered.

She raised both her eyebrows in disbelief. 'And what makes you so sure there is even going to be a wedding?'

She could see that he was angry and she was glad, feeling it served him right. He placed his hands either side of her face, glaring into her eyes, as she stared defiantly back at him. Within moments, they were kissing once more and this time he did not pull away. His mouth moved to her neck and she gasped with pleasure.

'The decree,' she whispered, her voice all concern.

'Not even death will keep me from you,' he said. His eyes were like glowing coals, as he pressed against her, and she felt his erection. They parted softly, their mouths hovering near one another.

'You are right, Milord,' she gasped. 'We need to bring forward the wedding.'

Thirty-three

Exzalander could not sleep that night. She got up six times to check the door was locked, but still could not shake the feeling of fear welling up inside her.

How can the Council have done this? I hate them all and I will find a way to be might be rid of them, once I come to power. She sighed. *To act from a need for revenge is petty and unbecoming of a ruler. I will need to put the needs of my people above my own concerns... but if the needs of the people just happen to match my own, so much the better.* She smiled ferociously, the dread inside her retreating a little.

Walking over to the window, she stared up at the stars. There was no moon and all below was quiet and dark. Everyone was abed.

All but I, she sulked.

The sudden clanging sound made her heart freeze with terror. 'No,' she whispered, backing away from the window.

There were many prisoners in the dungeon, but only one had the power and influence to escape. She sank to the floor and placed her arms about her knees, rocking gently, trying to pretend it was not happening.

When the servant knocked after sun up, she had not moved.

'Your Highness!' the girl exclaimed. 'Have you been up all night?'

'I need to see my father,' she said dismissively.

'You can't go like that. Let me dress you first.'

The woman proposed a soft grey gown from Starigorat and Exzalander hastened her away, eager to escape her night prison.

On reaching the king's chamber, she discovered it already empty. She ran down to the Council Chamber and found it bustling with people, not all of whom were members of the Council.

Spying her father, she ran to him.

'Have they caught him yet?' she asked.

'How did you know?'

'I heard the alarm,' she explained. 'Who else was it likely to be?'

Tuâth frowned, noticing the dark circles around her eyes.

'Have you not slept at all?' he asked.

'Not a wink; I am guessing neither have you. What effort has been made to recover him?'

Tuâth pointed towards the foresters and hunters. 'They found tracks that led to ...'

'Yes father?' Exzalander asked eagerly. 'What did they lead to?'

'They led to Counsellor Tyrian's body. We know not why, but it appears that Tyrian released him. Once the body was discovered, no further trace of Sohãhn could be found. Katahl is still out there with all of his knights, but I hold little hope that Sohãhn will be caught.'

Exzalander struggled to allow the news to set in. Worst of all, Katahl was away and there was nobody to protect her.

'Tyrian hated Sohãhn,' she said. 'He had no cause to set him free.'

'None that we can think of at any rate ... Listen, you look dreadful. Why do you not try to get some sleep? I will get someone to wake you after midday meal.'

She gave Tuâth an incredulous nod and his expression softened.

'Worry not, my child.' he said. 'Sohãhn would be a fool to return to the palace after what he has done. He will be long gone by now. I doubt we shall ever see him again.'

He kissed her forehead and her mouth twisted, as her eyes hardened.

'Is that not against the law now, father?' she asked sarcastically.

He appeared abashed for a moment. 'Ah, so you have heard. It is for the best. At least they will be no more ... misunderstandings.'

'Father, we will talk about this when we are both less tired. Believe me, I am not happy about it. I really do not think you have thought ...'

'Sorry child, I have to speak with Danah. Get some rest.'

She glared after the king for a moment, knowing her grievance would have to wait; she was tired and he had his mind on other matters. Leaving the chamber without a fuss, she considered returning to her room. Despite Tuâth's protestations, she felt far from safe. She made her way to Katahl's chamber and entered.

The room was still dark and the curtains had not been drawn. There was no key in the door, but she felt safer in there. In order for Sohãhn to find her, he would have to reveal himself to others so that he might get directions.

She walked over and sat on the bed; it had been slept in, but was cold. Katahl had been up for a few hours at least, she deemed. Slipping off her shoes, she lay back in his bed, drawing up the covers. A yawn escaped her lips and sleep took her almost immediately.

Dreams conveyed her straight to the marble palace and she roamed for a while, feeling the loneliness of the place. A new room greeted her on her wandering; the floor and part of the walls were padded; several weapon racks were stationed to the sides of the room.

She marvelled at the beautiful craftsmanship of the swords, scimitars, daggers and many wooden weapons, the like of which she had never seen before. Picking up a sword, she turned it in her hand, unable to discern the runes that adorned it.

'You are holding it incorrectly, Exzalander.'

She swivelled toward the voice, the sword clasped tightly in her hand.

'Show yourself!' she demanded. The sound of her voice was weak compared to His. 'Where are you?'

The weapon knocked out of her hand and she grabbed her wrist in pain.

'I told you; you grip it too tightly. A sword is like life—the harder you grip it, the easier it is to lose it.'

'Surely everyone holds close to life,' Exzalander pondered.

'Ah, but it is fear of losing it that makes people grip so tightly they forget to actually live—they merely exist.'

Exzalander felt shivers run down her body. The voice was unlike any she had ever heard and she longed to meet the speaker.

'Why do you not reveal yourself?'

'Because, you are not ready to see me. Now, pick up the sword and we shall try again.'

As Katahl entered his room, he was shocked to see the princess fast asleep in his bed. He smiled and sat down besides her, watching her twitch and murmur to the sound of laboured breathing. He stroked her hair for a moment, longing to climb under the covers with her.

A knock at the door drew his attention away from temptation.

'Milord?' Caitul put his head around the door and issued an instant apology on seeing Exzalander.

'It is all right, Caitul. She is sleeping. She looks so peaceful,' he mused.

Caitul could not help but draw closer to stare.

'We should leave her to rest,' Katahl said. 'Perhaps I should carry her back to her room; her father would not be pleased to learn where she is.'

Caitul stepped closer still, transfixed by her hair as it sprawled out across the pillows. Her long lashes twitched, as she shifted in her sleep and her mouth set in a determined line.

'She is dreaming,' he offered, thinking that Katahl was wrong; the princess looked far from peaceful. 'She must have sneaked up here, thinking it to be safer than her own rooms.'

'You are in the right I think, Caitul. I will sit with her a while and see you at dinner. See that you say your farewells. We leave for Brëgwela in the morning.'

Caitul bowed low, his eyes fixed on Exzalander. Katahl did not notice; he settled back in his chair and watched his love until his eyes felt heavy.

When Exzalander awoke, she was unsure where she was at first. Panic ensued, until she spied Katahl at her side. She resisted the urge to wake him and quietly got to her feet.

'Leaving already?'

She turned and smiled at him. He watched her, all signs of sleep removed.

'I thought you were asleep.'

'Just resting my eyes,' he assured her.

She appeared saddened for a moment, considering that he sounded all wrong and she longed for the voice from the marble palace.

'What is it?' Katahl asked, suddenly concerned. 'Did something happen whilst I was gone?'

His voice was filled with worry, making her feel guilty for hanging onto her dream.

'I wanted to feel safe,' she said smiling.

Now it was Katahl's turn to appear guilty. He reached out to touch her face and suddenly withdrew his hand.

'It's all my fault,' he whispered.

As he drew close, Exzalander felt a tinge of anticipation, which dissipated as he moved away from her.

'You cannot blame yourself,' she said. 'It was Tyrian who released Sohāhn, although I cannot even begin to understand why.'

Katahl bowed his head and turned away, gazing out of the window into the distance. She stood staring at his back for a moment; the tension in his muscles was clear and she placed a hand on his back, feeling him stiffen further.

'What is it?' she asked.

He turned and smiled, but his brow furrowed and his eyes were far away. Exzalander put her hands to his face and he tried to pull back.

'Now I know there is something the matter. I do not wish there to be secrets between us,' she said sternly.

'Please do not hate me,' he murmured.

She took a step back from him, wondering what he may have done that might cause her to hate him.

'You have found another woman,' she offered, recalling how easily Sohāhn had strayed. As soon as the words left her mouth, she convinced herself that they must be true. Her knees felt weak and she sat onto the bed, gasping for breath, the panic growing as the pause lengthened.

Katahl watched her for a moment; realising her reason for jumping to such a conclusion only made his guilt deepen.

'Nothing like that, my love,' he assured. 'No other could take your place in my heart.'

She seemed unconvinced by his words and he felt a stab of anger at her mistrust, knowing that he had never given her a reason to distrust him. *I am not Sohāhn*, he thought, *and yet she insists on comparing us.*

'It is my fault that Tyrian's dead,' he said.

She looked up at him, confusion in her eyes.

'I was not the only one who disagreed with the verdict regarding Sohāhn,' he explained. 'Tyrian approached me after the hearing and together we plotted a way to get proper justice.

Exzalander's jaw tightened, as she considered Katahl's words. 'But Tyrian freed him,' she said suspiciously.

'It was part of the plan. Tyrian would assist Sohähn and secure him until I could execute him. But Tyrian must have underestimated Sohähn because ...' His words trailed off as he saw the jaw of his beloved tighten even further.

'You? You had him released? What did you think was going to happen? That he would just allow you to lead him off somewhere to have his throat slit?'

'I am not a cutthroat, Exzalander.'

Her eyes narrowed at his tone and she stood defiantly face-to-face, as if daring him to say something else.

'Murder is murder, Katahl. You have no right to call it anything else.'

He grabbed her, shaking her slightly.

'I could not let him get away with what he did to you. Call it what you will, but I wanted him gone so you would never have to fear facing him again.'

Tear stung her eyes and she felt her lower lip tremble as she spoke. 'Now he is free and I fear to even close my eyes.'

'I am sorry. I am *so* sorry,' he said. 'I will protect you. No harm will come to you. You know that, do you not?'

She nodded her head and blinked away her tears. He held her until he felt the tension ease from her limbs and the initial shock of his admission had been processed.

'Now, do you feel ready to face the world again?' he asked, lightly kissing her forehead. 'I am making arrangements for you to return to your mother. Is there anything you wish to do ere we depart?'

She forced a smile, trying to seem as dismissive as he appeared to be.

'Yes,' she said. 'I want to see Ardahl. I want him to hear about our engagement, from me.'

'Lead the way.'

She hesitated as he held his hand out toward her.

'What is it?' he asked.

'You may come if you wish, but the way to his tower is secret. I will be quite safe there.'

Katahl considered for a moment and then kissed her hand.

'Then allow me to escort you as far as you wish me to.'

She nodded in agreement, but took her hand away, determined to change her father's mind about his foolish new law.

As she sat in Ardahl's tower, Exzalander's thoughts continued to stray to the seriousness of what Katahl had done. She longed to confide in Ardahl, yet held her tongue, speaking rather of how wonderful Katahl was and telling the wizard about Starigorat's knights.

Gailon sat in a corner with his head in a book, but she was convinced that he was listening in and so decided it would be imprudent to reveal Katahl's crime. She continued to overcompensate for fear of revealing something that might damage Katahl or their future happiness. In her mind, she came to the conclusion that Katahl had made a foolish mistake, yet she herself had done much worse and so she had no right to judge.

Ardahl was unusually quiet and listened in silence to all that she said. She did not perceive anything was amiss at first, as her own thoughts were enough of a distraction. After a time, once she had reconciled Katahl's actions, she began to notice the disparity; no fire burned in the hearth; Ardahl's notes, which were always so orderly, were strewn about the room; the wizard himself was pale and seemed too thin, his eyes shrunken and bloodshot.

'Ardahl, have you heard a word I have been saying?' Exzalander asked.

The wizard nodded, drawing his eyebrows together. 'Yes I have and don't take that tone with me, girl,' he grumbled.

She smiled at him, thinking that he sounded like himself, at least.

'Tell me what is the matter then,' she urged.

The old wizard closed his eyes. 'Just tired, Princess, nothing to worry about; I used some hefty majick in the dragon battle and it's taken its toll. It will take a while to recover, that is all.'

But it was not all; she could see that—could feel it in her bones. Something else was amiss; her best friend kept secrets from her.

It was not long before she left, glad to be away from the gloomy atmosphere of the tower. As she headed back to the palace, she felt a jolt as a memory of Sohãhn filled her mind. She had reached the corridor where he had made his move, away from the hearing of all those who might have aided her. She blanched at the thought of him pinning her to the wall.

'I should have left him to rot down here,' she said aloud, and tramped off toward civilisation.

The last day at Ealdorbold, Exzalander did not see Katahl at all. She oversaw her packing and went for a final visit to Ardahl. It was even more unbearable than before and Exzalander found herself trying to fill the silence with everything she had already said. She longed to ask Gailon what was wrong, but he sat working silently, seemingly oblivious to her presence.

'It may be some time before I can visit again, Ardahl,' she said finally.

As he showed her to the door, an overwhelming sense of sadness washed over her. She was unsure whether it was a feeling of impending doom or the atmosphere in the tower that contaminated. Without warning, she threw her arms about the wizard, holding him close.

He rested his chin against her head and sighed. He felt the same sadness as she, although he comprehended the meaning that she did not. This was goodbye—the last time he would ever see her.

'Farewell Princess,' his voice sounded strangled. Each word forced out with the determination not to reveal emotion.

'Please rest, Ardahl,' she said. 'I am worried about you.'

'Well don't be. Worry about yourself.' He drew away, smiling and it was the last time; Ardahl never smiled again, as long as his life lasted.

Thirty-Four

Ardahl's tower was surrounded in fog and Exzalander stared up at it, giving a wave, hoping that her friend was waving back. Her sense of foreboding was so tangible she felt that she could taste it in the air. All the soldiers from the north had already returned home and so the king's entourage was small, but he did not seem to mind. He wore his sword again, but it hung heavy there, as if it did not belong.

There was no cheery farewell. The fog hung thick in the air and those who were up at that early hour, were chilled to the bone as they struggled to see their king clearly on his departure.

Exzalander was glad she could not see the palace that morning; it held so many recent bad memories, she felt that she needed time to build new memories elsewhere before Ealdorbold could feel like home again.

As they passed from the gates, two figures could be discerned at the side of the road.

'Elsbeth!' Exzalander cried. Despite the dampening quality of the fog, her voice seemed too loud somehow, for the sobriety of the procession.

Elsbeth curtseyed and Thomn bowed low.

'We have come to bid you safe journey,' Thomn said. He spoke sternly, but there was warmth in his eyes.

Elsbeth passed up a small package to the princess.

'I thought that you would enjoy some homemade bread on your travels.'

The princess smiled warmly and thanked her.

'You look after Her Highness, Caitul,' Elsbeth ordered.

The First Knight blushed and began to wish that his visor were down.

Nimrin laughed. 'We *all* will,' he said.

It was Exzalander's turn to blush, embarrassed by the attention. After goodbyes were finally over, the party made their way down the road, which wound around Haesburg before leading north through Ánweald, toward the Soturi Plains. Exzalander began to think that her feeling of unease was more than her imaginings. The king was feeling it; she could tell by the way that he glanced cautiously about. Even passing peasants seemed ill at ease. Something was coming; the air seemed charged, as if preparing for the storm of a lifetime, yet the storm did not come.

As the days passed, Exzalander promised herself that she would not travel again for a long while. Tired and saddle sore, she longed for a bath and some privacy away from the watchful eyes of men, although she was grateful for the fact that she did not feel the need to look over her shoulder at the thought of Sohãhn being near. He would be a fool indeed to attack her whilst surrounded by such renowned fighters.

The journey through the swamps, which bordered the lands to Brëgwela, proved difficult. The air was hot and sticky; insects bit incessantly and the closeness made it difficult to breathe. Even the horses struggled to draw breath, as they trudged through knee-deep water and sludge.

'What is causing this, King Tuâth?' Katahl panted, as he waited for the king to catch up. 'I have never felt anything like it.'

'Must be a storm coming, at least ...'

'Yes?'

'I would have expected it at the Ealdorbold, but here in the north, the weather's a lot more stable.'

'I do not like it,' Katahl said.

'Neither do I,' the king agreed, 'but we must keep moving. The swamps are treacherous enough in good conditions, but if it rains well ... we need to keep moving.'

Tuâth chose to ride up front with Katahl, to assist with the safest route. Exzalander glanced nervously about her, convinced she was being watched.

As a child on her arrival to the north, she had been told the stories of the swamp devils. She had always dismissed the tales as parents' invention to keep their offspring away from the dangers of the swamplands. Now, however, she was unsure; she became convinced that their progress was observed and she longed, more than ever, to see the fields of home.

Hours seemed to drag into days and their progress was slow. As their horses stepped onto solid ground, there came a sigh of relief across the company. The sun shone ahead, making their path look welcoming and despite their fatigue, they picked up speed. Exzalander felt her mood lift and the oppressive feeling had gone. She could not resist a glance back to the place that seemed to play with her wild imaginings.

Dark clouds hung over the land behind them. She shivered as she saw how uniform the cut-off point was between the light and darkness. It was not natural, but with the sun overhead and home almost in sight, it was difficult to stay afraid of shadows, which had passed. She turned back to the road ahead and caught up with her father.

'Glad am I to be close to home again,' Tuâth said to his daughter. 'It has been a difficult time, but I look forward to putting it behind me and looking to the future.'

He seemed more like his old self again and Exzalander hoped that her fears for his health were perhaps unfounded.

The welcome procession seemed deafening after the quiet of their journey, and despite her exhaustion, Exzalander found herself smiling as thousands of brightly coloured petals rained down and fell about them, thrown from the hands of children, eager to greet their king's return in a fitting fashion.

Theyl rode at the head of the king's guard to greet them and acknowledged his brother with a cold stare before turning back to his king.

'Problem?' Exzalander said quietly to the First Knight.

Caitul watched his brother for a moment before glancing to the princess. He could not help but smile at her concern.

'I'm not sure,' he said. 'He seems upset, although how I managed to do so when I've been away for so long, I know not ... oh!' Caitul blushed. 'Beth. She was his ... well they ...'

Exzalander nodded, remembering Beth speak of Theyl. Before she could respond, a royal groomsman took her reins and offered his hand. She almost took it and then remembered.

'Hold the reins,' she said. 'I can get myself down, thank you.'

The man nodded stiffly.

'Silly law,' she muttered under her breath.

All thoughts of Tuâth's law vanished, as she caught sight of a deep raspberry pink gown. It was richly embroidered and came in tight at the waist.

'Mother!' Exzalander cried and ran into Shénnin's open arms.

Tuâth, who would normally be the first to remind his daughter about decorum, followed her example. They stood then, all three in tight embrace, much to the delight of the crowds. With one last wave to the subjects of Tuâth, the royal party retreated within.

'Mother, might I present to you the Lord Katahl, son of King Kryepast.'

Shénnin smiled as she kissed Katahl in greeting, making her look years younger. The initial introduction over, Katahl dismissed his knights and sat a while with the reunited house into which he was marrying. He no longer listened to the conversation, but fixed his gaze on Exzalander. She fought to sit up straight, despite her saddle sore and fatigue; her hair was dishevelled; there was even a smudge of dirt on her face, yet she was more beautiful than ever in his eyes.

Shénnin observed Katahl's gaze and how his eyes lit up as he watched her daughter.

'Has a date been set, Lord Katahl?' she asked.

He shook himself, tearing his gaze away. 'No Queen Shénnin,' he replied, 'but I would like to make arrangements as soon as possible.'

Shénnin noticed the blush on Exzalander's cheeks and she smiled at her daughter's happiness, blissfully unaware of what had occurred to arrive at such a point.

'We have a large banquet and dance planned, in welcome of your return and celebration of your pairing.'

Exzalander's mouth twisted and she huffed. 'There is no point,' she said. 'What is the sense of me attending a dance when I am no longer allowed to participate?'

'What do you mean, daughter,' Queen Shénnin asked. She raised an eyebrow at Exzalander's way of conducting herself. 'I am sure that your betrothed will not begrudge you …'

'It is not Katahl, mother!' She huffed again and stood to leave. 'Ask father!'

'Where are your manners, child?'

'Forgive me, mother; I must have lost them on the road. I am tired, dirty, and cross with father's silly law. Please might I be excused?'

Shénnin stood and pulled her daughter down to kiss her forehead.

'Go,' the queen said. 'I will see you at the banquet, my darling. I am most eager to discuss wedding plans.' Almost immediately, she claimed Katahl's ear, with the intention of doing just that.

Exzalander gave him an apologetic smile and paced from the room. She was halfway to her chamber, when she remembered that she no longer had a lady-in-waiting. She turned, about to find some servants and ran headlong into Caitul.

'Forgive me Your Highness,' he said, looking abashed.

'The fault was mine, Caitul. Have you not been shown to your room yet?'

'I wanted to see my brother first and now I cannot seem to find anyone.'

He sounded exasperated and Exzalander remembered the conflict from earlier.

'I should have warned you,' she said. 'If I had not been so focused on my petty concerns, I could have told you that Beth wanted to seduce you. She had many men. Theyl was a particular favourite, but he certainly was not her sweetheart. She told me that she wanted *both* of you … at the same time.' Exzalander blushed and she noticed a vein protruding at Caitul's right temple.

'I told you that I should have been more strict with Beth,' she offered. 'There did not seem any harm in her behaviour at the time, although I did tell her that she should leave you alone. I was not forceful enough and for that I am sorry. I can speak to Theyl on your behalf if you think it will help.'

Caitul's eyes widened in surprise at her words.

'You should not bother yourself with my concerns, Milady.'

'Nonsense!' she said. 'Oh … unless you are angry with me. Of course you are. You have every right to be …'

His eyes blazed at her and he found that any anger that might have surfaced soon drowned in desire. He wanted to tell her not to worry, that he forgave her, but his desire to kiss her made it impossible for him to speak for fear of saying something wholly inappropriate.

'I understand,' she mumbled, 'here.' She thrust a package under his nose. 'I think that you should have this. It might cheer you up … your mother is a lovely woman.'

'She made it for you,' Caitul replied flatly.

Exzalander shrugged. 'I know, but I am sure she would not begrudge you the last of it.'

'It'll be too stale to eat by now.'

'Mmmm, perhaps you are right. Come with me. I know exactly how to remedy such a problem.'

She was smiling at him again making him wonder why she had to do such a thing, and whether she realised what it did to him.

She stopped to talk to the household head—the most important of all the servants at Brëgwela. Caitul kept a distance, but could not help staring at her. The servant left in a hurry and she beckoned him to follow once more.

'Where are we going?' he asked. His mouth felt almost too dry to speak.

'You will see,' she chimed.

'You do know that you have dirt all over you face!'

She rolled her eyes at him and continued down steep stone steps. The smells emanating from the room beyond made his stomach grumble.

'Food first, wash later.' Exzalander smiled. 'Our rooms will be ready by the time we are finished.'

The chef came over and offered a friendly greeting to Exzalander who asked after his family and goings on in the kitchen during her absence. After she had introduced Caitul, she requested some of his stew.

'It'll take hours to make,' Caitul protested.

The chef gave a sly smile, explaining that he always had a pot on the go. He ladled out two bowls and left them to eat in peace. Exzalander broke the remainder of the bread and gave half to Caitul.

It struck him then how lonely she was. *Does she even have any friends?* he wondered. *Everyone bows down to her rank or is awed by her beauty, but does anyone truly know her? It is no wonder she's taken to my mother so.*

'It will get cold.' She frowned, to which he immediately started eating.

'It's good,' he smiled. He felt his heart flip when she beamed back at him.

They talked then, about important events and trivial things. The sun was sinking low in the sky by the time she rose.

'Forgive me, Caitul,' she said. 'I had not realised how long we had talked. I am keeping you from your rest and I believe you said something about my needing a bath.' She laughed briefly, then a shadow passed over her features and she was the princess once more.

As he stood, he felt giddy, it taking all his self-control not to take her hand and kiss it before she walked away from him.

By the time that Exzalander arrived back at her room, her bath was getting cold. She did not mind, having no desire to luxuriate. She winced as the water stung, washing over the bruising and then felt the pain ebb away a little and closed her eyes.

'You must learn to overcome pain in all forms.'

She had not realised that she had been so sleepy.

'Another lesson?' she asked. The dreams were becoming a regular occurrence and she had even come to expect them.

'Pick up the sword; we are going to work on footwork.'

She groaned; as beautiful as the voice might be, she was so tired that all she wanted was to sleep.

Thirty-Five

$\mathcal{A}$s the days passed, it became clear that King Tuâth would not be dissuaded from stopping the new law. As soon as it was announced, Exzalander felt different. Her people stared at her as if she was on a pedestal—a thing so precious, it was not to be touched, or even spoken to. Whereas people used to revel in conversing with the princess, now they could not get away quick enough. Even Katahl was abiding by the law and keeping a respectful distance.

She had to endure night after night of celebrations of her forthcoming nuptials to a man who was not even permitted to hold her hand. She had not realised how much she enjoyed dancing until no longer able to participate. *At least Katahl does not partake either,* she thought. *He spares me that.*

Shénnin sat Katahl next to herself on most nights and mothered him, as predicted. Exzalander was beginning to think that her mother longed for a son.

There had been no news of Sohãhn and the trackers had reported from Ealdorbold, that they found no indication of where he was; he seemed to have vanished. The princess became bolder and took to walking alone in the gardens.

She felt lonely; it was not just her father's law, it was the dreams. Every time she closed her eyes, it seemed that she was living another life. There was no rest and she was so tired that both reality and dream seemed to merge somehow, until she was less sure which her real life actually was.

'Exzalander, there you are. I have been looking all over for you.'

The sound of Katahl's voice pulled her away from her brooding.

'I am surprised that you even noticed I was gone,' she said sulkily.

He reached out to touch her and pulled his hand back at the last moment, the hurt in her eyes making him grimace.

'I am sorry, Exzalander,' he said. 'Your father's law. It won't be long. Two more months and we shall be together.'

'And you intend to avoid me until then,' she said.

'I am not avoiding you.'

She raised her eyebrows and he crumbled.

'Well maybe a little. It's too hard to see you and not be able to hold you. I am going crazy.'

She sighed and walked away from him, silently hoping that he would grab hold of her to prevent her leaving. He paced up beside her, slightly out of reach.

'You are not the one isolated by everyone around them,' she complained. 'Nobody will go anywhere near me. Even *women* are keeping a distance. I cannot bear this!'

'It is not for long and once we are married, I can take you to Starigorat. The law won't apply there.'

'This is my home,' Exzalander said.

'So is Starigorat. Think about it, okay?'

She nodded sadly. 'I will,' she replied.

'Heh, come on. You are supposed to be happy.'

'Kiss me,' she demanded, her face daring him.

He glanced about nervously and shook his head. 'You know I cannot.'

'Then leave me be. Leave me to my *happy* state,' she said sarcastically.

He wanted to comfort her, but felt unable to with words alone. He had always been a man of action, not words. He walked away in search of Tuâth, deciding that it was time they talked about the law. He needed the king to see sense.

Exzalander stomped across the courtyard, feeling as lifeless as the statues that adorned it. She could not believe Katahl had walked away when she had needed him the most.

A stable hand was grooming Tölt, one of her favourite horses. She approached and laid a hand on the horse's neck. His chestnut hair felt silky smooth beneath her touch and he spluttered at her attention.

'Would you like me to saddle him for you, Your Highness?' the stable hand asked.

The man's accent was strange—certainly not local. She stared at him for a moment. His beard and hair were dark brown and his skin too dark to be northern; he kept his gaze downward, making it impossible for her to tell what colour his eyes were; his nose was wide and flat, as if he had been bashed in the face with a shovel.

'You are new, are you not?' she asked.

He gave a half smile that showed a row of perfect teeth. 'Yes Your Highness,' he said. 'How kind of you to notice.'

'Might I ask where you are from?'

He seemed to hunch over at her question.

'I was born in Freya Valley, but I've travelled a great deal, Your Highness.'

She frowned at his reluctance to even look at her. *Damn my father*, she thought. 'That would explain why I cannot place your accent.'

He bobbed his head, without looking up. She noticed his dark hair, as it jutted out at odd angles—wild.

'Shall I saddle him for you?'

She frowned. It was clear that he was uncomfortable speaking to her; *I cannot blame him*, she thought. *Why would he be thrilled about conversing with a woman who might be the death of him by accident?*

'Please,' she replied, deciding that a ride out in the sunshine was just what she needed to rid herself of her gloom.

'It's only two months, Katahl,' Tuâth argued.

'I do not care. Can you not see how unhappy she is? She is sullen and she barely eats. It's making her ill and I cannot do this to her anymore. I am not asking to bed her, I just cannot *not* show affection, not even for another day. Either you lift the law, or we leave here tonight and forget the royal wedding,' Katahl concluded.

Shénnin gasped at the prospect and reached for Tuâth's hand.

'But you can't,' she protested.

'I can and I will,' said Katahl. 'I will not see her hurt any longer. Has she not been through enough?'

Shénnin's eyes narrowed. 'What do you mean?' she asked

Tuâth closed his own eyes in disbelief and Katahl realised too late, the mistake he had made.

'What does he mean, Tuâth?' Shénnin demanded.

'Nothing dear one,' the king soothed, but her glare was proof that she would not be convinced so easily.

'Either one of you tell me what I am missing or I shall summon my daughter and ask her.'

Silence.

'It is something to do with this new law, is it not? Have you behaved inappropriately, Katahl? No … that is not it … tell me!'

Perhaps I should go,' offered Katahl. 'I have upset Exzalander and I wish to try and make things right between us.'

'Katahl,' Shénnin warned, 'you will find that the woman who loves you is likely to be far more forgiving than a future mother-in-law. Now I *insist* you tell me what is going on!'

Katahl glanced to Tuâth, whose face was like stone.

'It is not my place to tell you, Queen Shénnin,' he said.

She was pale. His words had confirmed that something dreadful had happened to her little girl. He considered whether not telling her would be even more damaging.

'Has someone behaved inappropriately towards her? Is that what this new law is about?'

The look on Tuâth's face confirmed Shénnin's fears and she bit her fist, her knuckles shining white,

'Leave us, Katahl,' Tuâth said. 'I must speak with my wife.'

'Will you do away with the law?'

'We will discuss it later,' he replied, with a note of finality.

Katahl nodded and left Tuâth to relate events to his wife. *Will he tell her all? It is not my concern,* he thought.

Returning to the gardens, he searched for Exzalander, wondering whether to tell her about his mistake in tipping off her mother. When he arrived, she was nowhere to be found. As he entered the palace again, he saw Nimrïn chatting to a maid and he called him over.

'Have you seen Exzalander?' he asked.

'No,' said Nimrïn. 'She's probably in her room.'

The girl who he was with, contradicted him.

'She's not, Milord. She went out earlier and has not returned.'

Katahl stormed back outside, scanning the courtyard before running back to the gardens. His search widened to the area of houses near the castle boundary.

Where is she?

He felt panic setting in and forced himself to calm down. *It is a big castle,* he thought. *She could be anywhere.*

Enlisting help, he returned inside and sent servants to join the search.

Caitul strode over to join his lord. 'Try the kitchens,' he offered

'You have heard?'

'I heard a servant running down the corridor, shouting her name.'

'She'll turn up,' Nimrïn said casually.

He followed Katahl and Caitul outside again. The king and queen had been informed of their daughter's absence and panic was starting to spread.

'Have you seen the princess?' Caitul asked, as the stable master stormed past.

The man huffed and stopped. 'No I aint! S'bad enough Karim's gone missin'. Left a right mess over there he did. Now I've got to clean up after 'im.' The man strode off, shaking his head.

Katahl ran his fingers through his blue, black hair, sighing in frustration. 'No-one has seen her, Caitul. She was so upset. What if she has run away?'

'If she has, then we'll find her, Milord,' he replied, with confidence. 'She would need a horse to get anywhere.'

Katahl held Caitul's arm for a moment.

'I bless the day that you came into my life, my friend,' he said, seeming a little more focused.

He and Caitul ran over to the stables, where the man they had just met was still whinging.

'Are all the horses accounted for?' Katahl demanded.

The man scowled at the foreign lord for a moment before making his answer.

'Do you have any idea how many horses there are in the Royal Stables?' he asked.

Katahl's face reddened as his frustration grew.

'Please can you just check,' interceded Caitul, before his lord did something that he might later regret.

The man threw his arms up in the air and stormed inside. Shortly after, he returned—a little po-faced.

'Tölt is missing,' he said. 'I left Karim grooming him. Other than that, I can't be sure unless I check against the records for today.'

'How do you know that Tölt is missing then?'

'Because he won't let no-one ride him but Her Highness,' he said, as if Katahl was an idiot for not knowing such a thing.

Caitul and Katahl exchanged a look.

'Saddle us three horses,' he ordered. 'Caitul, fetch Nimrïn and meet me back here.'

Caitul bowed and ran to call Nimrïn back. He informed the king and queen what was suspected, urging them to mount a search party as soon as possible. As he returned to Katahl, he could see the concern on the young lord's face.

'We will find her, Milord.'

'It is not that, Caitul. It is the stable man, Karim. He's missing! Apparently he has only been working here a few days and he was seen riding out a little while ago.'

Caitul felt his stomach turn. He jumped onto the horse that had been prepared for him.

'Let's go,' he said.

Exzalander loved Tölt, even though he was smaller than most horses. He had a fifth gait that was easy on the legs. He could amble for miles and not break a sweat.

She headed in a northeasterly direction, towards the coastlands, hoping to catch a glimpse of the sea. In the distance, dark clouds hung heavily in the sky and she sighed in disappointment. With such a storm brewing, she would not get the view she desired—not if she wanted to return to Brëgwela before nightfall.

She rode on, heading toward the rocky terrain that climbed high before the long descent down to the waters far below. A sense of unease was growing upon her and she reined in Tölt in order to get her bearings.

The dark clouds spread out for miles and there seemed to be no end. She found herself thinking back to the swamp and shivered as it seemed the darkness closed in upon Brëgwela, slowly creeping inward, surrounding her home as if it intended to engulf it, as if it had a consciousness of its own.

'Silly,' she said aloud, and began to climb. She needed to see back down south. She needed to assure herself that the darkness was not still there—not sneaking forward as she feared.

Tölt stumbled on the rocky terrain and cried out in pain. Dismounting immediately, Exzalander checked the horse's feet. The right foreleg had not been shoed correctly and the horse whinnied in retaliation at her examination.

'Sorry boy, I did not know,' she whispered in his ear and stroked his mane.

The horse rubbed his head against her own for a moment, until a sound beyond his mistress's hearing, made his ears twitch and turn.

'What is it, boy?' she asked.

A horse was coming up the path behind. She smiled.

'It will be all right, Tölt. We are going back now. Hello,' she called down to the approaching figure, 'can you help me, please?'

'Your Highness, I am so glad that I found you. I was worried. I realised after you had gone, that he needed shoeing.'

Exzalander climbed down to meet the stable hand, smiling with relief.

'Do not worry, I am just glad that you are here now,' she said.

He smiled up at her, his white teeth contrasting against the darkness of his skin. She stared for a moment, wondering why she found his smile disturbing and then it struck her. His teeth were perfect. She had never seen a person of that rank with such good teeth.

His eyes watched her closely and she met them for the first time. He saw her jump, as if she recognised him yet was confused from where. His razor smile widened at her look of fear and he reached up to his face, clawing at it, peeling what she thought had been skin, to reveal a sharp pointed nose and much paler complexion beneath.

'Cornstarch and dye—very useful,' he said. 'And this,' he pulled the hair from his head. 'Horse hair.'

'Sohãhn,' she gasped.

'Forgive my poor appearance, Princess. I am a wanted man after all.'

The cheerful tone that he used sent fear coursing through her.

'What do you want?' she half whispered.

'Is that not obvious?' he sneered, taking a step toward her.

Without a thought, her knee raised and struck him in the genitals. He lurched forward in agony and she tried to run by him to get to his horse. He grabbed for her and she fell. Her head struck a rock and then all she knew was pain and blackness.

There was no palace of marble, no commanding voice— just darkness and oblivion until the pain ebbed back and she groaned. She became gradually aware of the thumping in her stomach and the stabbing pain in her head. The sound of hooves pounded beneath her and she fought to open her eyes.

'Ah, you are awake. Good,' Sohãhn said cheerfully.

The deep resonance of his voice that had once thrilled, made her want to vomit. She lay across his horse; a quick attempt to move her arms and legs, revealed they were bound. She gasped for air, trying to find her voice.

'Not easy talking in that position; believe me I know,' he said, in mock sympathy. He told her about his escape, speaking as one might to a child. She felt herself retch as the pain threatened to overwhelm her. He laughed and it was his amusement that gave her the strength to fight back the pain.

She gritted her teeth and concentrated her breath, focusing as she had learned in her dreams.

'Are you even listening to me?' Sohãhn complained. 'Nothing to say? Oh well. I think we will stop here for the night. There are plenty of caves along the coast. I could even risk a fire if you behave yourself.'

He dragged her from the horse and she collapsed forward, her feet numb from where the cord gripped too tightly. Putting his arms about her, he yanked her up, pressing in behind her. To her horror, he sniffed her hair.

'Mmm, I have missed that smell. Now, are you going to be foolish if I cut your bonds, or do I have to carry you?'

She stared blankly ahead, unable to feel her feet at all. 'I won't run,' she said.

He laughed at her icy tone and let her go; she fell to the floor, wincing at the swelling around her ankles.

'Perhaps I was a little fervent with my binding,' he said. 'Here.' Removing a dagger from his belt, he revelled as the fear came to her lovely eyes. He lingered, enjoying the moment, before he sliced through her leg restraints.

She suppressed a cry as the blood went rushing back into her feet and pins and needles of fire, stabbed.

'Put your arms about my neck and I will carry you,' he offered.

'I would rather walk,' she spat back at him. Trying to clamber to her feet, she immediately collapsed again.

'Be carried or dragged—your choice,' Sohãhn sneered, his face close to her own.

She saw the spark in his eyes and had visions of how much he might enjoy pulling her by the hair. She relented and slipped her arms about his neck. The smile that followed was enough to make her crave being dragged by the hair.

'There now, is this not cosy?' he said, as he lifted her. 'Just like old times.'

He set her down in the dark of the cave. The sound of the sea crashing outside made her feel even colder and more miserable. As if responding to an unspoken request, he removed a tinderbox from his jacket and began to light a fire. It seemed to take him an age to do so and despite her fear, Exzalander felt her eyes close involuntarily.

'Unarmed combat.'

She blinked and realised that she was back in the marble palace.

'I have been captured,' she said. 'How could I have been so foolish?'

'Unarmed combat,' spoke the voice again.

'When I wake, I shall just transport myself back home,' she muttered, ignoring the voice.

'No!'

She nearly fell over. Just for a moment she thought she had seen the face to whom the voice belonged, as He had barked the order.

Perfection. The most perfect and beautiful face that she had ever seen. She felt overwhelmed; a sudden urge to fall at His feet, to bask in His glory came upon her.

'You will not do anything so foolish. It is too soon since the last time that you used such majick. You would kill yourself.'

She trembled at His command.

'This is not just a dream, is it?' she murmured.

'No, it is no dream, Exzalander.'

'Why do you not reveal yourself to me?'

'It is not time. The veil between us thins. It becomes difficult to hide my form from you; as your destiny draws nearer, so *you* draw nearer to me.'

She shook her head in confusion at His words.

'Had events played out as they should, you would not have been required to come to me as yet, but your involvement with Sohãhn was … unforeseen. I had no choice but to intervene.'

'How?' she asked, incredulous. 'How have you possibly intervened?'

Silence.

His lack of a reply unnerved her. She wondered if she was missing something, if He might have done something of which she was unaware. She called to Him, but the wind rushing through the forest outside was her only answer. Miserable, she sank to the floor, aware of the cold and pain in her limbs, far away. It seemed hours to her, sitting there on the cold marble floor, waiting for the voice to return.

'Unarmed combat,' the voice said again.

Exzalander gritted her teeth, convincing herself that she was part of a game. He had probably watched her sitting there all that time … helpless.

'I don't know what you mean.'

'On you feet! I'm going to teach you to fight without a weapon.'

'Do you not understand? I am cold and tired and I do not know what this is, but it's not real. I do not know who you are, but you are not real either, are you? So I refuse to play this silly game any longer.'

'On your feet!' the voice commanded, and it held such clarity and authority that Exzalander trembled and cradled her knees in fear.

An invisible hand touched her head and she gasped, her eyes wide, fighting to see His face. His touch was agony and yet filled her with such joy that she wanted Him to hold her forever. She was filled with the deepest fear and exhilaration at the same time, which gave way to obedience and a sense of being humble in the presence of one so mighty.

'Yes Milord,' she conceded. Ignoring the stiffness throughout her body, and the pain in her head, she got to her feet.

Thirty-Six

Tölt limped down the track, toward home. He was upset. His mistress had abandoned him on the rocky hills and now he was hurting and very cold. He did not like the dark and longed for soft straw and the warmth of his stable. The smell of friends was in the air and he neighed loudly, hoping they had brought help for him.

Hoof beats thundered towards his cry and he nodded at his friends' approach. Their riders he did not know, but a splutter from Selka, told him they were men folk who were close to his mistress.

Tölt tried not to flinch, as their leader approached and inspected his foot. He could feel the man's fear grow and it made him respond in kind. More hooves sounded and shouts ensued. His friends grew wary; they did not like being out after dark, either. It was not to be borne, being treated like a soldier's mount.

'I'll lead Tölt back home,' the stable master offered. 'The princess will be furious if he's harmed.'

'If only he could tell us which way the bastard's taken her,' Nimrïn said.

'We don't know for certain that he did,' cut in Caitul. He gave his friend a hard look and a glance to Katahl, hinting that Nimrïn needed to show more sensitivity.

Katahl, however, seemed not to have heard. The king's men spread out and continued the search.

'Any news?'

Katahl did not even acknowledge the king, but Tuâth seemed not to notice.

'No King Tuâth,' Nimrïn replied. 'She has obviously been on this path at some point, but we don't know if she continued on foot or ...' Nimrïn stopped as Caitul's eyes flashed again.

'Your Majesty,' came a shout from above. A white horse with a plaited mane was led down the steep slope ahead, and the rider came to a halt before the king. 'We found these on the trail ahead,' the guard said. He handed the king a pile of hair and a rubbery mess.

'What is it?' Caitul asked.

'Horsehair; it could have been used to disguise someone's true hair colour, and this,' the man said, with a look of disgust, 'is shaped like a nose.'

Katahl's eyes fixed on the items and a cold fury burned in his eyes. His mouth thinned to into a determined line and he kicked his horse forward up the trail. The others needed no prompt and followed behind.

The pain flooded back and Exzalander realised that she was awake. Opening her eyes, she saw the flicker of firelight. Beyond the darkness of the cave mouth, the wind howled and a heavy rain fell. The sea sounded dangerously close as it crashed onto the shore beyond.

'Good sleep?'

She blinked, trying to focus. Sohāhn was crouched by the fire; his face was washed clean and she cursed herself for not recognising who he was back at the stable. When she did not reply, he looked up at her, his piercing eyes roving over her for a moment, before returning to the fire.

He had retied her legs together, but mercifully not as tight. She shuffled closer, not proud enough to miss out on the opportunity to warm herself by the fire.

He was cooking. She was not sure where he had managed to get food. She guessed that he had been planning for such an event since his arrival at Brëgwela.

'You know, I have to thank you,' he said cheerfully.

She wanted to hit him.

'I never dreamed that you would make it this easy for me.'

She gritted her teeth, determined not to react or indeed speak with him.

'But then, perhaps I should thank your father,' he continued. 'His new law was marvellous in drawing you to me. It was heart wrenching watching your own people scrambling to be away from you like you have some disease. I always found your loneliness so attractive.'

'That is because you are twisted!' Exzalander snapped. She glared at him, silently cursing herself for offering him a reaction.

One corner of his mouth lifted into a smile and he picked up a skewer from the fire, offering it to her. She felt her mouth water at the smell and swallowed.

'I am not hungry,' she said, turning her head away.

'Liar!' Taking the meat away again, he sat chewing it, offering a few murmurs and exclamations of how delicious it was, in order to torment her.

She let him enjoy himself; it gave her the opportunity to test her bonds. There was little give. She considered the possibility that she might be able to wriggle free, but knew it was wisest to wait until Sohãhn slept.

'Changed you mind yet?' he asked.

As another offering was made, her stomach growled and she realised that her pride would not keep her strength up. Raising her hands, she took the skewer from his grasp, assessing it as a potential weapon, before nibbling on the meat. She could feel his eyes upon her as she ate.

Where is my fear? What has happened to me? If Sohãhn was going to kill me, he would not have waited, she reasoned. *Every moment that I am held captive is time for any rescue to reach me.*

As she nibbled the last of the meat, she subtly tested the strength of the skewer.

'I'll take that,' Sohãhn said.

As if he had already pre-empted the danger, he reached over to snatch the skewer from her grasp. She slashed at him, disappointed when it did nothing but prick his skin. His eyes were furious at her defiance and she tried to shuffle away from his anger.

He grabbed her wrists with his bleeding hand, yanking the skewer from her grasp and throwing into the fire where it crackled for a moment, before being consumed by the flames. She struggled to free herself and he pushed her backward, forcing her hands over her head, as he sat on top of her.

His eyes roved down to her chest, as if deliberating how much damage she could do if he released his grip on her hands to give him access. He pushed down on top of her, his weight making it difficult for her to breathe.

'You never had this much fight before, Princess. I like it.' Pushing his hips in against her, he rocked slightly, making her aware of what she was doing to him.

'Katahl will gut you for this, Sohãhn!' she hissed.

He stopped. Anger flashed in his eyes and he climbed off her, moving back to his place by the fire.

'That whelp, I doubt it!' He laughed. 'I cannot wait to see his face when we return man and wife.'

She stared at him, incredulous, wondering if she had heard him correctly

'You are completely insane,' she murmured.

'I hardly think so,' he replied, his eyes glinting in the firelight. 'You said yes; such a promise is not something to be taken lightly. Your commitment to me outweighs any subsequent betrayals your father made with the boy.'

'*Lord* Katahl is my betrothed,' she retaliated.

Instantly, she regretted her reply. He was on top of her in moments, his hand reaching under her skirts. She thumped him with her tied hands and he backed off.

'You know how I can make you feel. Why do you resist me?' he asked, his voice smooth and seductive.

'You make me sick,' she said.

'Well, perhaps you are right. Best to wait until after we are wed … keep your father happy.'

'You have lost your mind, Sohãhn. Nobody is going to marry us. As soon as they learn who I am, they will arrest you. Let me go; you can still escape. At least you would be alive. You have broken the new law. If you are caught they *will* execute you.'

He put his hand across his heart. 'Ah such concern, Princess,' he mocked. 'Save it; such a pathetic attempt at manipulation is beneath you. Do you not think that I planned for every eventuality? I knew there was a chance that you might back out of your promise. I made certain that I found someone who was more than willing to see us wed.'

She gazed at him in horror. 'You cannot make me,' she said. Her voice sounded less than certain and she shivered as he leered over her.

'My dear, I think you will find that I can make you do whatever I want.'

She shook her head in denial, the panic setting in.

'Lie back,' he urged, his eyes blazing.

'No.' Her voice was barely more than a whisper.

'Lie back or I'll make you,' he ordered, his voice a little louder than before.

She stuck out her chin defiantly, ready to do as much damage as she could. He watched her, assessing her mood. It was clear she would fight him all the way and he was tired.

'It is no matter,' he said nonchalantly. 'We will wait until our wedding night. If you will not succumb then, I will have the Mo-Rye hold you down while I fuck you. I told you, I liked to be watched. The Mo-Rye share their wives on their wedding night, did you know that?'

Her eyes grew wide with fear and he licked his lips.

'The Mo-Rye … they are our allies; they would never agree …' she trailed off.

'I offered them a very generous trade agreement in exchange for their assistance. As for you ... well you know how they view females. You *know* that they will be only too pleased to help me break you.'

She felt her lip wobble and almost choked at his look of triumph.

'But you are not a Counsellor,' she stuttered. 'You have no authority to make such an offer.'

A solitary tear streamed down her cheek—a sign of defeat. He reached out to her legs and ran his hand up her calf; she flinched, but did not fight back.

'My dear,' he said, 'who else has more authority than the king?'

She felt as though she could not breathe. *Please be a dream—just a bad dream,* she thought. *He has arranged a marriage to be forced upon me, plotted father's demise and to usurp my power. I have to escape before we reach the stronghold of the Mo-Rye. It is pointless waiting for a rescue that might never come.*

'I wish I could trust you not to kick me if I release your legs,' he breathed, as he kissed her lower thigh.

Perhaps if I convince him that I will no longer attack, then I could tempt him to release my legs, she thought. *At least I would have a chance to run.*

He looked up at her. No sound escaped her lips, but she did not struggle either. He smiled and lifted her dress over her hips.

'Tricky, tricky,' he said. 'You're concentrating, are you not? You used to find me so ... distracting. I am obviously not pleasuring you enough.' He pulled himself up.

Can I issue enough force to render him unconscious? she considered. *No. And with my legs bound, even stunning him will not give me enough of a chance to escape.*

She could feel his breath, hot against her body and she fought the urge to struggle. Such actions only seemed to arouse him more and she wanted to avoid that.

He gently kissed her, as low as he could go where her thighs pressed together. Still she did not move. He stopped to look up again, releasing a slight huff at the lack of response from her. His hands pressed open the tops of her slender thighs, giving him enough room to slip his tongue between. He licked the length of her opening and stopped to tease her clitoris.

She could feel the pressure of his head, as it struggled to cope with the lack of space. She could feel the heat rising within her and fought to stop herself drawing her feet up to open her legs a little wider. He was murmuring, making appreciate noises, tormenting her as he had done earlier with dinner.

'Untie my legs,' she said.

He stopped, assessing her face.

'Why?' he asked, smiling.

'I,' she panted. 'I want to open my legs for you.' She felt sick as she spoke the words, sick at the thought of her former obedience to his lewd requests.

He shook his head slightly, as if amused at how easily she had succumbed. He got off her and climbed above her head.

'Give me your hands,' he said. His voice was calm, revealing nothing.

I have to show a level of trust, she thought. *I have to or he might not release me.*

She obeyed.

It was a mistake.

He climbed on top of her from behind her head, pinning her arms with his feet.

'Give me your feet, if you want me to untie you.'

The pain in her arms was immense and she fought to push it away.

Surely, he will not weigh me down for long, she hoped. Bending her legs up toward him, he grabbed her ankles, forcing them to the floor. As she cried out in pain, the sound washed over him. She could see the swell in his trousers increase where it hovered over her face.

'You said you would release my legs,' she cried.

'No I didn't. I said, give me your feet if you want me to release you. Now there is no need.'

He leaned down, pressing against her feet and placing his tongue onto her clitoris once more.

She was glad of the pain then. *I deserve it for being such an idiot*, she thought. It helped to distract her from what he was doing to her. Despite her anger and pain, she could feel herself getting wetter and she heard him murmur appreciatively.

'Taking longer today, but we'll get there,' he said, in a patronising tone.

'I hate you, Sohãhn,' she hissed. 'I will kill you the first chance that I …'

He thrust his tongue inside her and he felt her tighten about him. Believing that she had climaxed, he decided to continue to torment her.

'I suppose that it would be too much to ask for me to put myself in your mouth,' he said.

She tried to struggle, but could not move. 'Not unless you want me to bite it off!' she hissed.

'Mmm … pity. And I do not think that I will be able to get inside you very easily while you are bound.'

He leaned forward and started playing with her, again.

'Stop it!' she screamed. 'No more.'

He reached down, pulled his breaches open and began to masturbate on top of her. His other hand still pressed against her leg, but she continued to struggle to get him off. He began to murmur and grunt while she struggled beneath him. The speed of his hand movements increased and she saw him swell and jerk above her until a pale fluid expelled across her chest. She cried out in disgust and he collapsed forward, keeping his appendage clear of her teeth in case she made good on her promise.

After what seemed like an age to Exzalander, he rolled off her and fastened his breeches. She stared down at the sticky white patch across the front of her dress.

'You are a mess,' Sohãhn said.

Her nostrils flared as she glowered back at him with sheer hatred at what he had done.

'Don't look at me like that!' he said. 'I gave you the option of putting it in your mouth. If you had, then your pretty dress would not have been spoiled. You only have yourself to blame.'

She drew her dress back over her knees and down toward her ankles. Feeling the bonds, she realised how easy it would be to release her feet. *All I need to do is wait for him to sleep,* she thought.

'You could always take your dress off, if it bothers you,' Sohãhn offered. 'The Mo-Rye women do not wear clothes.'

She tried not to look alarmed at his comment.

'I wish to sleep,' she said. 'Or did you intend on boring me to death with talk of the Mo-Rye all night?'

He laughed and she cursed herself for not being able to fool him.

'You are right,' he agreed.

He pulled her to him and wrapped his arm about her waist.

'Goodnight,' he whispered in her ear.

She tried not to tense up. *Wonderful,* she thought. *Now, I will have to wait until he is in a deep sleep before I can even attempt to loosen the bonds.*

Hours passed, but every time that she tried to slip away, he held her tighter. She tried to relax and slow her breathing, hoping to convince him she was asleep, in the hope that he would drift off.

He did.

Unfortunately, so did she.

When Exzalander awoke, she felt exhausted. The voice in the palace had been angry by her pathetic attempt at escape and drilled her hard in ways to incapacitate. She forced her eyes open, to see that the fire had gone out and a few embers still glowed in the crisp morning air.

Sohãhn was not there and she did not hesitate. Untying her feet, she ran from the cave. A blast of cold sea air hit her and the waves crashed onto the shore before her.

'Ah good, you are up and you have untied your feet,' greeted Sohãhn. 'Excellent, saved me a job. I need you to ride today—quicker and more comfortable for you.' He was saddling the horse, whistling happily.

No point in running ... 'I want to bathe,' she demanded, thinking quickly.

He stopped what he was doing and turned to appraise her.

'Where?'

She gave him a look of contempt at his stupidity and pointed toward the sea.

He smiled slowly. 'It is freezing; besides, your skin will be caked in salt. You will burn when we head further east.'

East—toward the stronghold of the Mo-Rye, an amphibious people whose home stretched out into and under the sea. She had longed to visit the place, hearing of the vastness of the structure and beauty of the decoration, using pearls from the sea to add to their intricate carvings. It was said that one of the Mo-Rye had helped build Starigorat long ago—an ancient king taken slave by Kryepast's ancestor.

She no longer wished to see the stronghold and she hoped never to meet the Mo-Rye. Turning, she fled, struggling to release her hands, as she went. The rope burned and cut into her skin, but she did not care. *Better to be dead than a slave to a mad man,* she thought.

She was a fast runner, and despite the distraction of her hand ties, Sohāhn took a while to catch up to her. Diving at her, he knocked her to the sand. A scream escaped her, not a cry of terror, but the sound of pure fury and frustration, a determination that she would not give into him again.

Her arms thrust back and she elbowed him in the jaw. It was not a hard blow, due to her position, but it was enough to knock him back. The last rope came free and she ignored the burning pain in her wrists, allowing it to wash over her, helping to fuel her anger.

Jumping to her feet, she prepared herself for his counterattack. He laughed and she seethed at his reaction.

'What are you doing?' he said. 'You look as though you actually intend to fight me.'

She gave a savage grin, causing his smile drop a little.

'Yes, that's the plan,' she said.

Thirty-Seven

$\mathcal{C}$aitul heard the scream and forced his exhausted horse onward. Katahl was on the cliffs above and the First Knight hoped that he had heard it too. Two figures were on the beach ahead—a long way off still, too far to be sure if it was Exzalander. His horse sweated and panted beneath him and he felt sure that the pounding of her hooves would distract the altercation ahead.

As he drew closer, he was left with no doubt that it was her; he saw her red hair flowing like fireweed in the sea's breeze. Relief filled him and he urged his horse on. Sohãhn moved to hit her and Caitul winced at the thought of her in pain. To his surprise and relief, however, he saw her block and strike back.

Pride filled his chest at the fearless way that she battled Sohãhn. Her moves were flawless and showed obvious training. There was no time to wonder about it though; Sohãhn had managed to get hold of her and part wrestled, part yanked her back to the waiting horse.

Disbelieving his stupidity, Exzalander reached out and grabbed Sohãhn's sword. At the sound of his blade being unsheathed, he let her go.

He laughed. 'Do not be ridiculous, Princess,' he said. 'You do not even know how to hold a sword.'

She did a figure of eight and pointed it toward his neck, her grip unwavering. Fear was in his eyes and for the first time, she could understand why he enjoyed it so much.

'Your Highness,' Caitul called, as he caught up to them.

As he sprang down from his horse, she swung about, holding her sword out toward him, expecting a new enemy. He gazed at her in alarm.

'It is I, Caitul, you're safe now,' he soothed. 'Katahl's here, and your father. Give me the sword.'

Her eyes narrowed. 'No,' she hissed.

Sohãhn used the distraction to have his dagger at her throat. He dug the knife in, until a droplet of blood could be seen to demonstrate that he was serious

'Drop the sword, Princess, and back off, knight!' he ordered.

Caitul put up his hands and took a step back, but Exzalander still clung onto the weapon.

'Do it, Sohãhn,' she goaded. 'I told you; I would rather be *dead* than forced to marry you. Do it. I care not.'

'But *I* do,' blurted Caitul. 'Please Your Highness, put down the sword.'

The hard look in her eyes, softened a little at his words and she blinked, as if seeing him for the first time.

'Listen to him, Exzalander,' Sohãhn hissed.

He pulled the dagger across her neck, leaving a trickle of blood, making Caitul take a sharp intake of breath. Exzalander, however, seemed unmoved.

'It's over Sohãhn,' Caitul said. 'You'll never get away; you know that. Let her go.'

'I am dead either way,' Sohãhn spat. 'I have nothing to lose and *everything* to gain.' He yanked Exzalander's hair back, exposing more of her throat.

'Look how concerned he is, Princess,' he continued. 'I do believe that the boy has feelings for you. How pathetic! As if you could possibly satisfy her, knight. Still, you had that whore Beth to train you and she knew something about pleasing men.

Caitul drew his sword, shaking with anger.

'Ah, ah, ah,' Sohãhn said, shaking his head. 'Exzalander drop your sword. This is the last time that I will tell you.'

She felt a sense of calm; the sound of the sea was gone, her breathing was steady and she moved quicker and with more fluidity than even the voice in her dreams had trained her to. She turned the sword, pointing it toward herself, stabbing between her armpit and her torso. Sohãhn gasped and fell back.

She turned, sword hovering over him.

'You will address me by my proper title,' she said.

'You bitch,' he spat.

He nursed the wound. It was not mortal, but enough to have defeated him. Caitul kicked the knife out of reach and tried to coax Exzalander away once more. He moved around behind Sohãhn, so that she was facing him.

'It's over now. Give me the sword,' he urged. 'You don't want to kill him.'

Tears formed in her eyes. 'Do you have any idea what this man did to me?' she said.

Caitul grimaced and tried to speak, but his imagination ran wild. It was then that he saw the stain on the front of her gown and felt something snap inside him. He unclasped his cloak and held it out to her, his hand trembling.

'Your Highness, put this on. Do not let my lord see you like that,' he whispered, his eyes haunted.

She realised what he had seen and felt shame flood her cheeks; spluttering, she threw the sword away, wrapping the cloak tightly about her.

'Thank you,' she said.

Her voice sounding strangled and Caitul could not bear to meet her eyes.

'Exzalander!' came a voice from the base of the cliff.

'Katahl!' she cried.

'Go to him,' Caitul urged. His voice was level, but deeper than was his wont.

She ran as if the wind carried her. She ran and she did not stop until she was in Katahl's arms. He held her to him and smothered her with kisses, breaking Tuâth's law a hundred times over in a matter of moments.

Tuâth came forward and embraced them both. It was the terrified scream that drew them apart. Katahl looked up and then pulled Exzalander to him.

'Do not look,' he ordered.

'What is it?' she asked, her voice muffled against his chest.

Caitul stared up at his lord and former king. Wild hatred was in his eyes as his bloody sword hung at his side, the tip of it still close to Sohãhn's severed head.

'Take my daughter away. I do not wish her to see that,' Tuâth said gravely.

'See what?' Exzalander asked. She tried to turn her head, but Katahl prevented her.

He is angry, she observed. 'Katahl, what is it? What was that scream? Is Caitul all right?'

Katahl held her concerned eyes for a moment, but whatever thoughts came into his head, he did not voice them.

'Milord, forgive me,' Caitul said, as he joined them.

Exzalander turned swiftly, smiling with relief and her eyes followed the trail across the sand to where Sohãhn lay, his lifeless eyes staring out in horrified disbelief. She tried to pull her gaze away, but could not. It did not seem real somehow.

'Exzalander please!' Katahl yanked her about. 'You had no right, Caitul,' he spat furiously.

Exzalander remembered what had made Caitul lose control and drew his cloak tight across her chest.

'First Knight Caitul did us great service this day,' she said. 'He saved my life.' She hoped that her words would appease Katahl.

He glared at his First Knight. '*I* was going to kill him—I needed to,' he hissed.

'I am glad that you did not, my love,' Exzalander said. 'It would have seemed too much like revenge. You must not be angry with Caitul. *I* ordered him to finish the task. I did not want to risk Sohãhn escaping again.'

That stung. She knew that it would, but felt it necessary to remind Katahl that it was his fault Sohãhn was freed to begin with. She saw the shame in his features and drew his eyes back to her. As he opened his mouth to speak, she placed a finger to his lips then drew his mouth to hers.

It took a couple of coughs from Tuâth and a mumble about his new law being broken, to draw them apart. She kissed the king on the cheek.

'Father,' she said, 'I do hope that you are not intending on executing my future husband.'

Katahl gripped arms with Caitul and drew him into an embrace, offering his apologies and thanks. Caitul seemed too stunned to reply. His eyes flicked to Exzalander; a strange light was in them. He blinked silent thanks for her lie that had saved both his friendship and position. She smiled back, but her eyes slipped past him, distracted by the bloody mess beyond. She felt her knees buckle and Katahl caught her, sweeping her up into his arms.

'Allow me to escort you home,' he said.

As they reached the cliffs, Caitul built a signal fire to bring the other soldiers and Nimrïn back to the castle.

Tuâth did not complain when Exzalander sat with Katahl on the same horse. It was only when they were far away from the beach that Exzalander began to tell them of Sohãhn's alliance with the Mo-Rye. She felt Katahl tense and the horse spluttered beneath him.

'If it is true then it means war,' Tuâth said.

'I am not lying, father,' Exzalander protested.

Her father smiled grimly over to her. 'Of course not, my child, but Sohãhn might have been. I will need to look into this matter.'

'But how will you prove such a thing?' Caitul asked.

'That is why Sohāhn should not have been killed,' snapped Tuâth, gazing ahead.

'I have no regrets about that,' Caitul mumbled, understanding his father's dislike for the king, all to well.

Katahl remained silent, his body tense as a bowstring. Exzalander knew that investigating did not matter to him; he would have rode off alone to the stronghold of the Mo-Rye, if he had the chance. She turned and kissed him.

'I love you,' she whispered.

The affects of her words were like majick. He instantly relaxed and a glorious smile brightened his features as he snuggled against her.

Soldiers from all directions gradually joined them on their road back home. Clinging to Katahl, Exzalander stared up at the blackening sky. He did not seem to notice—none of them did; they did not see how the darkness was closing in on Brëgwela.

'It is almost time.'

She started and Katahl kissed her head.

'You fell asleep, my love,' he said. 'Look, we are nearly home.'

The sun blazed about the castle, making it appear on fire. She shuddered.

'What is it?' Katahl asked.

She smiled back at him. 'Nothing,' she replied.

Almost a week passed since Exzalander's abduction. No news had yet returned regarding the Mo-Rye plot. Exzalander grew increasingly restless. She tried to explain how she felt to her mother, who put it down to pre-marital jitters.

'It is nothing to do with Katahl, mother,' she said. 'It is that damn storm. It draws ever closer; it never dissipates. Sometimes I feel as though I cannot breathe.'

'What storm, child?' We have not had bad weather in months.'

Exzalander moved to the window, gazing out toward the marshes. 'That one,' she pointed. 'It just hangs there. It's not right.'

Shénnin's eyes widened for a moment before regaining composure. 'I see nothing, daughter, nothing but blue skies. I think everything you have been through has taken its toll. It is understandable, my poor darling.'

She reached out and stroked her daughter's hair, causing Exzalander to frown.

'Father told you.'

As her mother nodded, Exzalander saw the disappointment in her eyes. She snapped at her for feeling such things.

'My daughter, my loved one, you are upset,' Shénnin soothed. 'It is understandable. Being with Katahl is not a thing to be feared; he would never hurt you and I know that his greatest desire is to see you happy. You are seeing things that are not there and it is because you are anxious. I know what will make you cheer up. Ardahl has sent word; he arrives next week. I know how much you wanted him to come to your wedding.'

Shénnin kissed her daughter on the cheek, but Exzalander's face hardened and she looked out toward Ardahl's tower. On a clear day, she would be able to see it. Now the darkness pressed close, blocking all views beyond the plains. *Can Ardahl see it?* she wondered and clenched her teeth in frustration. *Maybe when Ardahl arrives, he will know how to help me.*

That afternoon, she attended a celebration in Caitul's honour. He was to receive reward for her rescue. She hung onto Katahl's arm, basking in his love.

Nimrïn dismounted and paced toward them. 'Milord, apologies for my lateness,' he called.

Exzalander felt suddenly odd. It was as though she was viewing the scene from afar and for a moment forgot who she was. She shivered.

Katahl's eyes filled with concern. 'My love, are you well?' he asked

She wanted to tell him that she was not, that for a moment, she had been in another time and place, seeing through the eyes of someone else—Nimrïn in fact. But he had seemed so different, so lost and empty. She stared at the knight for a moment.

'I am fine,' she said, trying to stem the tide of panic.

Caitul spoke to them then, but whatever he said, she did not hear. She could smell burning. Gazing about in alarm, she saw dead bodies littered about the courtyard. She gasped, wanting to scream.

'My love?'

Katahl's arm was about her; the bodies were gone.

No fire.

Just a perfect day.

She forced a smile and began counting the days before Ardahl would arrive and fix her.

It was that night the dreams started. There was no marble palace, no beautiful voice, only death and destruction, the ending of her house, the fall of so many good people. Sohãhn's dead eyes mocked her from his severed head. Horrified, she ran, searching for Katahl. She could feel the sand, cold beneath her feet.

Cold like a fish.

Looking down, she saw hundreds of Mo-Rye, dead beneath her.

'My wedding gift to you, my love,' Katahl said.

She stared up in horror as he sat on a throne made of human flesh stitched crudely together. Sohāhn laughed and she clamped her hands over her ears. Overhead, the clouds grew thick and black, appearing more like oil than water.

'It is almost time.'

She awoke screaming. Within moments, her new lady-in-waiting was at her side, offering words of comfort. Exzalander gasped for breath and waved the woman away. It was an hour or so before dawn; the sky was beginning to lighten before the sun popped its head over the horizon. Exzalander ran her fingers through her matted hair, feeling the cold sweat that enveloped her entire body.

Getting out of bed, she was unable to stop herself from checking the floor for bodies. She plunged her hands into the bowl of the previous night's wash water, bathing her face, hoping to fully wake herself and chase away her nightmare.

Perhaps everything really has been too much for me, she thought. *Perhaps I am losing my mind.* She walked over to the mirror and felt her heart flip. For a moment, she did not recognise the reflection staring back at her.

'What is happening to me?' she whispered, watching the reflection with suspicion, in case it decided not to mirror her actions.

She tried to pretend that everything was all right to Katahl. If he noticed a change in her, then he did not say. Two more days and two more nights of hellish visions to rock the sanity of even the strongest willed individual, made the lady-in-waiting come to a decision.

'I'm going to fetch a healer, Your Highness,' she said. 'You can't go on like this. He'll be able to give you something to help you sleep properly.'

Exzalander shuddered. *Something that will prevent me escaping the horrors waiting behind closed eyes. No thank you.* 'Thank you, Beth, but I am quite well,' she said.

'My name's Kara, Your Highness,' said the girl quietly, her eyes filled with concern.

Exzalander looked up and seemed almost surprised not to see Beth there. Then she remembered.

'I am so sorry,' she said.

'Please do not apologise, Your Highness. Beth was with you for so many years and you are tired.'

I am tired; it is true, Exzalander thought.

'Will you let me fetch healer Salvek for you?'

The princess nodded. *What use is there in saying no?* she thought. *I will tell Salvek I am having bad dreams; he will think it understandable ... well it is. He will give me a sleeping draught and I will agree to take it and of course, not. Then, I will pretend everything is fine and hold out until Ardahl arrives.*

She lay back on the pillows, trying to clear her mind of morbid thoughts. After a time, a knock sounded at the door and Kara walked in.

'Healer Salvek to see you, Your Highness,' she said, curtseying. She beamed, obviously pleased she had managed to do her duty so well.

'Show him in,' Exzalander said.

'Your Highness.' Salvek bowed and came to sit by her side.

The questions began. He was not satisfied when she told him that she was having nightmares; he wanted to know details. She had no intention on telling a stranger anything, so she lied. His answering frown made it clear that he thought she was hiding something and such mistrust led to him staying to ensure she took the draught, leaving her silently cursing.

Satisfied he had done all that he could, he left the room. Kara did not return and Exzalander strained to hear what the hushed voices in the corridor were saying. The door opened without a knock and Exzalander frowned until she saw who it was.

'Katahl,' she said, 'you should not be here.'

He paced over to her, taking her hand in his own.

'Why did you not tell me about your dreams?'

'I did not want to worry you,' she said sheepishly.

'Do you not realise that I worry more when I do not know what is wrong with you?'

Her mouth twisted awkwardly. 'You knew there was something the matter then?'

He laughed quietly, squeezing her hand.

'Oh my love,' he said, 'if you had any notions of running off and joining the players then don't; you are not that good an actor. Best stick to being a princess.'

She pouted at his insult and he laughed again.

'Your dreams will improve with time,' he assured her.

'You are masquerading as a healer now, are you?' she asked sarcastically.

He raised an eyebrow at her and she stifled a yawn.

'I was hoping that Ardahl might fix me sooner rather than later,' she said, her eyes closing involuntarily.

'Majick? For bad dreams?'

'It is more than that ... I think ... I am losing my mind.'

She lay back, closing her eyes. Katahl frowned down at her sleeping form for a while, resisting the urge to shake her awake again to demand to know what she had meant. He bent down and kissed her lightly on the lips.

'Sleep soundly, my love,' he whispered.

She could hear the sea.

'No. No more bodies ... please,' she begged.

'Are you prepared? It is almost ...'

'Stop it!' she screamed, and the sound of the waves receded.

The sand was no longer beneath her feet and she seemed to float in warmth and light. A sense of peace cleansed all the fear and badness away.

'There is nothing to fear.'

Another voice from nowhere—female, so clear and beautiful that Exzalander wanted to cry with joy.

'Be strong, Exzalander.'

She wanted nothing more than to obey. She had never felt so much warmth; she welcomed it, embraced it, until all thoughts of death and mayhem were gone and she knew that when she awoke it would be a glorious day.

Thirty-Eight

Exzalander awoke feeling refreshed and eager to begin her day. Kara smiled as she helped the princess dress, commenting on how much better she was looking. When Exzalander skipped down to breakfast, she felt as though years had slipped from her in a single night. Katahl watched her from the opposite side of the table. All the questions he had for her seemed unimportant as she beamed at him. He longed for her parents to be elsewhere so that he might hold her in his arms. After breakfast, she gave Tuâth and Shénnin tight embraces and bid them good day.

'You are in a good mood,' her father remarked.

'Yes I am.' She grinned back at him. 'I cannot explain it; I just woke up this morning and realised that life is wonderful.'

'Katahl and I are going for a ride. We'll be back in time for dinner.' She waved and skipped from the room.

Katahl's eyes followed her with delighted disbelief. He gave a small shrug to the king and queen, before running after her.

Tölt was still upset with Exzalander and grumbled when she mounted him. It was only when she suggested to the stable master that she ride another horse that he decided to behave. The stable master gave a knowing smile as she rode the horse away.

'Where are we going?' Katahl asked.

'Whichever way the wind blows,' Exzalander replied.

She urged Tölt on and Katahl kicked his horse to catch up with her. He squinted at her and she laughed.

'What are you doing?' she asked.

'Trying to see through your disguise ... trying to tell if your acting skills have improved.'

'Oh I see,' she said, with a smile. 'Well, you need not worry, they are as bad as they apparently always were.'

'Truly? You are all right?'

She slowed Tölt down to a walk and held out her hand to Katahl.

'Yes,' she said. 'I suppose all I needed was proper rest. I feel good—amazing in fact.' And it was true; the horrors of her dreams had vanished in the brightness of day, and the sun seemed to warm through to her very soul, lifting her spirits and allowing her to remember the meaning of carefree. The imposing storm was but a memory and she did not give pause to consider it. The darkness was gone, her spirits lifted and all was well with the world. Why should she question it?

They rode as far as Cloud Peak and there held hands as they gazed down at the town of Yŏ catching a glimpse of the sea beyond. She did not think of Sohähn and the terrors she had endured. Staring out at the thin line of blue in the distance, she only saw her future and that future looked joyous to her.

It had been a magnificent day. The clear sky was dotted with dreamy clouds; the mild breeze refreshed the flora and fauna alike. From the palace gardens, came the sound of tinkering laughter as Exzalander freed herself from Katahl's embrace and ran swiftly away.

Tölt spluttered, as the stable master removed his bridle.

'You're in a better mood,' he said.

The horse nodded his head.

'Ah I see,' he laughed, 'you're speaking again now, are you?' Gazing over to the princess, he watched as she ran away from her betrothed.

Katahl stood and gazed as she danced about, the sunlight outlining her body through the shift in her dress. As he gazed at her, she smiled and threw her head back, spinning; her long red hair flowed like a shimmering stream at sunset, falling wildly across her back.

She dashed off once more, Katahl following. Reaching out, he tried to grab her long robe as it flowed behind her, but every time he neared, her speed would increase and she would dodge gracefully out of reach. Realising he hadn't a chance, he settled on the grass, exhausted. Exzalander continued until it became apparent that her fun was over. She knelt beside him and he gently touched her silk-like skin. Her eyes shone and she leaned forward, gazing intently at him. Instinctively, he moved his face toward hers, but suddenly she pulled away.

It was as though the peaceful illusion came crashing down in a single instant and she realised that she had been spared the pain of the past few hours, by being given the gift of blissful ignorance. Now the feeling of dread was more urgent than ever.

'Something is wrong!' she gasped, scarcely able to breathe.

Katahl sat up, smiled and prepared to embrace her, but she jumped to her feet and began to run in the direction of the castle.

Brëgwela, the great ancient building of her forefathers, loomed ahead. The castle was ablaze; black smoke encircled the turrets like carrion birds. Exzalander came to an abrupt halt, gazing on her home in horror. She blinked hard, waiting for the image to be another hallucination … hoping. Katahl caught up and stood at her side, catching his breath. His hand reached out for hers, clenching it firmly.

'Come' he said, 'let us go see if we can be of help.'

Realising it was no dream, Exzalander nodded and resumed sprint, resisting the urge to scream.

On reaching the courtyard, it became apparent that the cause of the fire was no accident. Dead bodies lay afoot, some with missing limbs which looked as though they had been simply torn off.

As fear seized Exzalander, she felt unable to turn away from the gruesome sight. It seemed more dream-like than her nightmares actually had.

'It is time.'

She remembered. It was suddenly so clear that she felt foolish for having forgotten. She knew that voice. Her mind drifted back to her childhood and she recalled hiding in her father's private study—a game of hide and find. Aware that the room was forbidden to all but the King, made it the perfect place for concealment; no-one would dare search for her there.

That was where she had found the book, where it had shown her visions from within its pages, and where the sword had caused her so much pain and that voice ... that voice.

'*Prepare yourself Exzalander, the pain is yet to come.*'

When her father had found her, he had cradled her so tenderly that she felt the fear pass, but he had warned her that day, warned her of a great evil and her duty.

'I thought that it was just a dream,' she murmured, as the memories flooded back, sharp and painfully clear. Confused and frightened, her mind raced, *What can I do? What is this evil? How can I confront it?*

'Exzalander, are you all right?'

The soothing and relatively calm voice of Katahl brought her wandering thoughts back to the present. She felt a strange tingling sensation inside her head and sensed a presence. Katahl felt it too. He grasped Exzalander's trembling hands and shuddered.

A painful cry sounded from above and the couple glanced upwards towards the noise. Suspended mid-air were the King and Queen, around whom the air seemed to quiver.

For a moment Exzalander froze, petrified by the sight. With as clear a voice as she could muster she shouted,

'LET THEM GO.'

There was a moment's silence before a deep laughter ensued, a terrible mocking sound, inhuman and hollow. Her father held her eyes and she saw only resignation there. She hated him at that instant, hated him and loved him; she wanted to scream her million regrets at him and wanted him to fight back, but he was held fast. Better to face his fate resigned than in terror as his wife. Queen Shénnin seemed unaware of her child, and sobbed for mercy.

Exzalander screamed for aid. 'Where are the guards? Where are the archers?

'Anyone?'

She watched helplessly as her parents were torn apart. She heard every tear and every scream, until finally their remains dropped to the ground, a mass of blood, bone and empty flesh. Tears brimmed in her terrified eyes, distorting the horrifying scene and she fancied that she could still hear the echoes of her parents' last moments resounding in her ears. She herself was unable to scream or cry out, her vocal cords as frozen as they had been as a child, when held captive by the mystical book of prophecy.

She blinked away her tears and tore her gaze away from her parents' remains. Her eyes searched for Katahl, her hand no longer in his. Luminous mist surrounded him, the same foreboding phenomenon that held her immobile.

Katahl cried out. His voice was fearful, but defiant as a disobedient child. 'What do you want with us?'

There came a metallic reply that chilled to the bone with its lack of emotion. 'We wish to teach you, Katahl; we will show you much. You Exzalander, we have no need of … yet. We therefore banish you from Maldahl. We will not meet again. Let the world know that one day you will return to reunite with Katahl and this will herald the coming of the new age—the age foretold to you. Maldahl will know divine order once more.'

As the words faded, Exzalander became aware of her own heartbeat thumping in her ears. The mist enveloped her; tangible it seemed, with a saline taste that made her retch. Consciousness was slipping away and she welcomed the darkness that consumed her—a small reprieve from the soul-wrenching pain of loss. She felt herself drifting—a mere spec through the vast immensity of time, passing through dimension after dimension in a dreamlike state close to death.

'Come to me; it is time. You belong with me now.'

She felt as though she was falling and she longed to plunge into the voice's maker and lose herself in His embrace. It was the screaming that forced her to open her eyes—that and the taste in her mouth. She was on her knees clutching at a familiar marble floor. The noise was terrible—a sound of deepest despair. She felt herself retch and cough; the sound stopped. It was then that she realised the screams were her own.

Memories of her parents' death hurtled into her and the screams started once more. Hands rested on her shoulders and she clung to them, her breath heaving. Forcing herself to lift her eyes, she expected to see Katahl.

Through the haze of her tears, she realised it was not the floor of the throne room of Brëgwela that she felt, but the strange marble palace from her dreams.

'You!' she sobbed, and looked into the face of the one with the perfect voice.

His skin was almost white and his leather jerkin was the same colour as the great forest that surrounded His fortress. Upon His head he wore a simple circlet of silver that bore a wolf insignia, the same as the mark at the top of his knee-high boots. About his neck was a silver torc, fashioned in the shape of stag's antlers. At first Exzalander thought that his eyes were black, like Katahl's, but as she lost herself in His gaze, she realised they were the deepest green.

Her tears stopped.

Everything stopped, as she stared transfixed by those eyes. It was like being born again … more than that, it was like staring into the beginning of all things and realising her own insignificance. She prostrated herself before Him and He immediately drew her up, adjusting His image to ease her feeling of helplessness in His presence.

'Arise Exzalander. We will achieve very little if you spend your time constantly cowering before me.'

As soon as He released her, the sorrow threatened to consume her once more.

'I must get back,' she said urgently. 'I must wake up.'

His eyes held no sympathy as He made his reply. 'You are not asleep, Exzalander. This is real; you are here and it is time for you to begin your education.'

The word education sent a shiver through her body as she remembered the words of the darkness. Katahl was to be educated too. She felt a stab of anger. *What did my father really know about this day?* she thought. *Why have I not been better prepared?* Guilt followed, for thinking ill of Tuâth. It was unbearable to think that he was gone.

'I demand to return home immediately,' she said. 'You have no right to keep me here.'

His returning smile sent a tingle across her skin.

'That's more like it! That is the fire that I wish to see from you. On your feet and let us return to your training.'

She backed away from Him, shaking her head. Without warning, she ran, fled His hall and away from Him. He did not pursue and she found herself dashing frantically through the empty palace, searching for escape. She screamed, but there came no reply; she banged on locked doors, but received no answer. Sinking to the floor, she scrunched into a ball and sobbed.

Anarkhane stared evenly at Taiohãhn, as He paced the Chamber of Light, which linked their two domains.

'I could order her to pull herself together,' He said, 'but then she just falls to her knees before me.'

The goddess swept her hand across the cool crystal wall, enjoying the way it responded to Her touch.

'She has lost both her parents, Taiohãhn. She needs time to grieve. Trust me in this; I understand humans better than you.'

Taiohãhn's jaw clenched at Her words.

'Perhaps I should take her with me first,' Anarkhane suggested.

'No! She needs to learn to weald my sword,' He said. 'It takes priority over everything else. It is the symbol of her place in the prophecy. She will learn to use it and she will learn her place.'

Anarkhane put her hand on His arm and His eyes glittered coldly at it. *I want this charade over*, He thought. *I want my godhood back.*

'If you terrify her, Taiohãhn, then she will never truly serve you. Remember, your father said that there must be a willing sacrifice. You brought her here ahead of time. She started to connect with the majick I instilled in her. She started to hear you, to see what was coming; you could have ruined everything with your impatience. If I had not blocked her eyes when I did, she would have been party to Mynogen's words.'

Taiohãhn held Her eyes defiantly, hating that She was right, but refusing to admit it.

'If I had not started training her, she may have been slave to the other human,' He said. 'I had to interfere. If I had not steered her toward Katahl when I did, she would never have loved him and she needs that connection if she is going to have enough desire to return.'

Anarkhane raised an eyebrow at him, remaining unconvinced.

'What do you suggest?' He asked.

She gave a small smile that sent a wave of desire through Him.

'Befriend her, Taiohähn; care for her. She must grow to trust you, to rely on you. She needs to devote herself to our cause and her place in the prophecy.'

He moved toward Her then, His eyes all desire, but She disappeared back to Her sky kingdom, leaving Him huffing in frustration.

Using His forelócian glæs, he gazed upon Exzalander's snivelling form.

Pathetic, He thought, *and yet ... there is strength there too. She demanded from me and that is a first. No Vampire Ælf would have dared and I have always considered them more worthy creatures than Anarkhane's progeny. Still, that's what makes humans so dangerous—too emotional, too unpredictable and their free will ... is it any wonder the Old Ones want to restore order? But I am the true order and if I have to demonstrate human feeling to achieve my aims, then so be it. Besides, I might finally find a human who is more devoted to me than to Anarkhane and I would take pleasure in seeing Her jealous. I might actually enjoy such devotion. That could make Anarkhane jealous too.*

Part Four

Thirty-Nine

Katahl awoke screaming. It was the fourth day since the Old Ones had arrived, the fourth day since Exzalander had been taken and his world had fallen apart.

A barrier had formed about the ruined castle, so that those few who remained alive following the initial assault, were trapped. Katahl had not been permitted to see anyone and would have died of thirst had it not been for Caitul, demanding that Katahl be served. The Old Ones allowed food and water to be left outside his chamber once a day, when they realised such sustenance was required to keep him alive. They found his refusal to feed himself interesting and asked him many questions, as if it was all an experiment to them. It was only when they threatened the lives of the remaining household, that a hole was punched through his grief, forcing him to be responsible.

Exzalander would not want this, he thought. *She will expect me to save all those that I can from the same fate as her parents*. It was too difficult to think about the horror of their fate, too terrible to contemplate how anyone could do such a thing to another. *These things, these beings are not human. They talk of dark and light as if it is all that matters. Life holds no concern for them, or pain or longing. It is simple—black and white and I have been chosen to be the darkness to Exzalander's light.*

He found that he was weeping again and longed to lose himself in his grief, but the Old Ones had other plans. His need for sleep having been met, it was time to continue his training once more.

Days turned into weeks, weeks into months. Reluctantly, Katahl's knowledge of majick grew. It was a miserable existence, kept isolated and alone, unaware of whom might still be living. It began to feel as though he alone was left and all Maldahl had perished. It was only the Old Ones threat that allowed him to continue; it was only their promise that he would be reunited with his love, which spurred him on.

On the thirteenth day of the fourth month since his imprisonment, Katahl had enough power to penetrate the barrier. As he stepped out into the corridor beyond his room, he expected resistance. He knew the Old Ones had seen what he had done and yet they made no move to prevent him.

'Milord!'

'Caitul?'

The First Knight stepped warily up to the dirty, skinny man before him, whose bushy black beard jutted out in all directions. If he had not known that Katahl had been confined to those quarters, then he would not have believed it to be the same man. He embraced his lord, trying to ignore the stench of his unwashed body.

'I never thought to see you again.'

'Nor I you, my friend,' Katahl rasped. His voice sounded strange, as if he had not made use of it in so long. 'How many survived?'

Caitul's face looked grave. 'Surprisingly few were actually killed, Milord. We were imprisoned and could offer no protection. All who tried were slaughtered. When I realised you were prisoner up here, I set watch as close as I could. I demanded that you were sent food ... Milord ...' his voice cracked slightly, as if he was asking a question to which he did not really want an answer. 'Were you alone in there?'

Katahl's eyes closed and a look of anguish twisted his features as he recalled Exzalander's expulsion.

'They sent her from me, Caitul. She is gone ... I did not truly believe in the prophecy. I was a fool.'

He collapsed into Caitul's arms, who lifted him up with ease. He seemed to slip in and out of consciousness as Caitul carried him to a new chamber and ordered terrified servants to attend him.

While Katahl was bathed, Caitul sat with him in silence. He wanted to ask about Exzalander—what had happened and where she was. If Katahl could break the outer barrier then he only needed to say the word and Caitul would go on any mission or errand to recover her.

'Did Ardahl arrive?' Katahl asked, as the towel was wrapped about him.

The First Knight could not help notice the brown water remaining in the tub.

'I know not, Milord,' he said. 'We've been prisoner since the day of the attack. Our food supplies are running desperately short. My brother put rationing in place weeks ago. If we don't break free soon, then I'm affeared we will all starve to death.'

Katahl looked out of the window, his shoulders seeming to stiffen. He did not want the responsibility; he wanted to be left alone to his grief.

'I will not allow that to happen,' he said. 'Leave me now. I wish to speak with our captors.'

Caitul bowed and took the dismissal as opportunity to go outside where he joined his fellow knights, notifying them of developments.

It was difficult to reason with seemingly all-powerful beings, ones who had no emotion or empathy of any kind. Katahl could not appeal to a better nature because such a thing did not exist. He laid bare the facts, fighting to keep his feelings in check. If they allowed the household to starve, then he would have no one to rule. If they continued to keep him confined to one room, he would be unfit to rule.

His control over his emotions made them more inclined to listen and they consented to his ordering a party to gather food. Katahl felt a cold thrill run through him as he realised that he might aid at least some of the household. His thoughts were a mistake; the Old Ones did not require words for understanding; they read his mind.

Searing pain spread throughout his limbs in punishment for his idiocy. He screamed as he felt the pulling on his body and he smiled savagely and ordered them to do it—tear him to pieces and let it be over. They released him and he crashed to the floor, his body trembling uncontrollably. He felt their approval at his feeling of pure hatred, which he directed back toward them.

'Good, now channel that feeling, Katahl. Direct it where it may be of some use.'

Katahl's head snapped up, his eyes wild as the pain in his limbs dispersed. An image of Sohāhn flashed in his mind and he wished at that moment that he could have been the one to have killed him. He wanted blood; his rage demanded it. The Old Ones fed the feeling until he was ready to slay the next person who entered the room, if they let him.

'We will allow food to be gathered,' they said in unison. 'If the people do not return, then they will be killed; make that clear to them. *You* Katahl, have taken your first steps this day. You, we allow to achieve your desire for revenge.'

Katahl grimaced, hating his mind being an open book for them. 'Sohāhn is already dead,' he spat. 'He cannot be killed twice.'

There followed the hollow laugh Katahl associated with the day that his love was taken. He remembered the fear and horror in her eyes, and forced back his grief, preferring the fire of hate to the slow drowning of tears.

'Your rival may be dead, Katahl, but those who aided him yet live.'

A savage smile spread across Katahl's features. 'The Mo-Rye,' he hissed.

'Yes, the ones who struck a bargain to enslave your mate—to ravage her into compliance. Are you willing to let them go unpunished?'

'No I am not. You will allow me to leave here; will you allow me to kill the Mo-Rye?'

'As of this morning, Katahl, our barriers can no longer hold you. You have earned your moment for revenge. Once you are done, you will return to us. Without you, we cannot assist your world in achieving divine balance once more. Without your willing presence here, your world will be destroyed. We cannot allow it to exist without guardianship.

'But you will come back, Katahl. You would not choose death when you long so for your princess to return to you. Now ready yourself. Stir your men into action; too long have they have been idle.'

Katahl felt their presence recede from his mind. He returned to his chamber, almost vomiting at the smell of filth within. Dressing swiftly, he left to gather the people of Tuâth to him. The threats of the Old Ones filled them with terror, but Katahl assured them of survival if they returned as they were bid.

Gathering soldiers for his campaign against the Mo-Rye was a more difficult task; Katahl's knights would stand with him as they had taken an oath to serve him, but his knights were just four men; the soldiers of Tuâth owed him no such allegiance and had since their imprisonment, taken orders from the Captain of the Guard.

Captain Theyl was wary when called into counsel with the lord and his knights. He threw a disdainful look to his brother as he took his seat. Theyl was no fool, however, and he listened to all Katahl had to say before making any judgement. Dahal shot a worried glance to Nimrïn as Katahl laid out his intention. Caitul stared down at the table, his hand kept moving back and forth to the hilt of his sword as though he was eager to use it. When Katahl finished telling them what he proposed to do, he looked at each of them in turn.

'Are you insane?' Theyl said, after a moment's silence. 'I thought that you brought me here to discuss rescuing the people, to plan an escape, not ride off on some fool quest to annihilate an entire race—a race who, I might add, are our allies. I'll have no part in this.'

The captain started to rise, but Katahl grabbed his arm. Theyl looked at him in alarm. No words were spoken, but Theyl took his seat once more and rubbed his arm, as if it pained him where Katahl had touched him.

'They ceased to be allies the moment they made a bargain with Sohãhn,' Katahl explained, 'the moment they plotted treason against this house.'

Theyl rolled his eyes and blew air out with a hiss of disbelief.

'It is true what he says, brother,' Caitul interrupted.

Theyl winced at his brother's words

'Even if it was true, the house of Tuâth and Shénnin has fallen,' he said. 'We're prisoners and we should be fighting for freedom. If they are to release us to ride to the Mo-Rye stronghold, then I say that we use the time given to us wisely. Don't fight the Mo-Rye; request their help. In fact, send emissaries to all peoples of Maldahl asking for aid. We've been training all hours every day; we'll stand with you against our captors, Lord Katahl.'

Katahl gave a wry smile and watched as the candle flickered in front of him. *If only it were that easy*, he thought.

'They will not be beaten by any strength of arms, Captain. They can kill with a thought and have no substance; no weapon can pierce them because there is nothing to pierce. They can pluck the very thoughts from our minds making impossible for your betrayal to come to fruition. We are slaves to their will and their will is to see the Mo-Rye fall.

'If nothing else, it will give the men a task, a purpose. Let them feel the wind on their faces and the thrill of battle and if they are to die, then let them die fighting an enemy that can be defeated. Let them die fighting, not with the dishonourable death your king and queen faced. Such an undignified end is not fitting for a warrior.'

Theyl's eyes flashed dangerously. 'Are you threatening us, Lord Katahl?' he asked slowly. 'Do we face such a death if we refuse to ride with you?'

'No, not I, but we are threatened and I must see that I can save all I can.'

'By having them follow you to battle?' Theyl asked.

'Yes, if needs be. We will do whatever we can to survive this occupation, until balance and power are restored.'

'But the people here will not follow you. You are not their sovereign.'

Katahl laid his hands palms down onto the table in front of him. They were strong hands—warrior's hands. He breathed slowly as he watched his fingers press into the wood.

'You will have to make them listen, Captain Theyl, for their own sake.'

'Milord!' gasped Aarnon. 'Your hands.'

Katahl lifted his hands from the table and understood what had shocked his knight. The wood was indented where they had been, and blackened, smoking handprints remained.

Katahl closed his eyes wearily. 'It is the power. I gain a little more by the day, but I find it difficult to control,' he sighed.

'Are you sure that we need the castle guard, Milord? If you're that powerful, we could take them alone,' offered Nimrïn boldly. 'Fried fish anyone?' His humour met with a cold reception though, making him instantly regret his words.

'I will talk with the men, Lord Katahl,' Theyl said fearfully. Rising, he walked swiftly from the room, without taking his leave.

'We need him to comply, Caitul,' said Katahl. 'There cannot be two rulers here. Perhaps I should address the people myself, make them see that as the sole heir's betrothed and the son of a king, I am the only lawful choice they have.'

'The people already know as much, Milord,' Aarnon said. 'The trouble is that you're our capture's choice too. I think it's *that* more than anything making them ill at ease, not your legitimacy to rule. Give them time, Milord; they've been through a lot.'

'We all have, Aarnon,' Katahl said. 'Leave me now, all except you, Caitul. There is a matter I wish to discuss with you.'

The knights bowed and left as they were bid. Caitul stared at his lord, his eyes full of expectation.

'I do not wish you to accompany me to the Mo-Rye stronghold,' he whispered. It was a foolish thing to do, he knew, for if the Old ones did decide to listen, then the quietest whisper would not prevent them.

'I do not understand, Milord.'

'I have another task for you, Caitul. One that I cannot entrust to anyone else.'

Caitul leaned forward on the edge of his seat. *He is going to send me to rescue Exzalander,* he thought.

'I need you to seek out Ardahl,' Katahl said. 'He must be informed what has happened. He knows the prophecy better than any. If there is a way to get Exzalander back, then he will find it. Will you do this for me, Caitul?'

The First Knight stiffened to attention. 'Yes Lord Katahl.' It was not quite the heroic mission that he had hoped for, but it was a start.

Forty

Exzalander awoke in an unfamiliar bed. She felt smooth sheets about her body and ran her hand across them. Her eyes refused to open at first, seeming painful and puffy. Blinking hard, she sat up, grief crashing into her once more, as memories of all that had occurred returned to haunt her. She wanted to crawl back under the sheets and pretend it wasn't real.

'You are awake, good,' Taiohãhn said, as He entered her room.

Instinctively, she drew the covers up around her. She could not remember how she had got there or how she had got into a nightgown.

'Get dressed,' Taiohãhn said formerly. 'We have work to do.'

She stared at Him and did not answer. He paced across the room and placed food on a marble bedside table, which seemed to grow up out of the floor as though the rock was a living entity. Looking at the food for a moment, she felt a groan from her empty stomach. It was followed by a wave of nausea, knotting her insides as her grief fought for attention.

'How did I get here?' she asked timidly.

He sat on the bed beside her and she shrank back from Him.

'I carried you; you have slept for days.'

Her eyes widened at the thought. 'I must go home ...'

She began to protest, but He placed a finger to her lips. His touch was like tiny sparks of electricity shooting up and down the length of her body. She wanted to slap Him away, but found that she could not move.

'You *are* home, Exzalander. You have much to learn and I will help you, but unless you try then you will never be able to return to Maldahl. I will train you; I will make you strong.'

'Strong enough to fight the things that killed my parents?' she asked desperately, trying to hold back her tears, but failing in the attempt.

He raised His hands again and wiped her cheeks, holding her face gently. Part of her felt guilty at how wonderful His touch made her feel; it was like she was betraying Katahl. Closing her eyes, she attempted to block out the view of the man before her. His lips brushed lightly against her brow and her body went rigid with fear and confusion.

'Open your eyes,' He said, 'know me.'

She obeyed and He saw the tears that threatened to fall. Her desire emanated from her, as did the sense of her pleading for Him not to seduce her. He drew back, remembering Anarkhane's words. Although He wanted to make the goddess jealous, He realised that above all else, He had to obtain Exzalander's trust. Too much depended on her for Him to jeopardise His very godhood in a petty game.

'Know me,' He breathed again.

It was as though blindness had been removed from her mind and she longed to fall down before Him.

'Taiohãhn,' she choked. Her voice felt a profanity compared to His. She felt utterly unworthy to even speak His name.

'Yes Exzalander, I am Taiohãhn and you have come to my kingdom as was foretold long ago.'

He released His hold on her once more and watched as she shrank back from Him, pinned up against the wall.

'I, I thought you were … gone, a myth even.'

Taiohãhn laid it out for her then, who she really was and what she was destined to do.

'You want me to defeat Katahl?' The fear and awe was gone and fire of fury flickered behind her eyes. 'I *will not*.'

'You have no choice, my warrior. The only way you might possibly save him is by being powerful enough to do so. To gain such strength, you must stay here with me. Let me teach you; let me guide you,' He coaxed, 'but if you continue to resist me, not only will Katahl fall, but all of Maldahl. Is that what you want?'

Her gaze shifted downwards, she saw His hands rested on the bed before her. His skin was like the smoothest alabaster and his fingers long and elegant. She sighed and felt keenly the burden of responsibility settle upon her shoulders and add itself to the weight of grief.

Of course I do not want Maldahl destroyed, she thought. *It is my duty to save it if I can. My people are counting on me … not to mention my parents … I cannot let their death stand for nothing.*

'I will save Maldahl, if I am able,' she said, 'however, I will not kill Katahl. He has done nothing to deserve such a fate and I intend to save him.'

Taiohãhn gave a slow smile at her words. He leaned over and picked a piece of bread off the plate he had prepared and held it toward her.

'Eat then. You will need your strength,' He coaxed.

She grimaced at the food before her and shook her head. 'I do not want it,' she said. 'The grief makes me nauseous. I do not think I can hold it down.'

Taiohãhn's jaw clenched slightly as He placed the food back onto the plate. 'Lie back,' He ordered.

'Why?' she asked, suspicion and the slightest show of fear on her features.

His face hardened at her resistance and His hand was a whirl of motion as He grabbed her ankles and pulled. She fell back onto the bed with a cry.

'You are not here to question me, Exzalander. You need to learn to trust and obey me.' He moved closer and could see that her body was trembling; memories of molestation emanated from her along with feelings of shame and fear. He contemplated her form for a moment. *She is very beautiful, for a human,* He thought. *Anarkhane has seen to that—Her finest work.*

His eyes ran along her long, lithe legs, to where her womanhood lay, barely covered by the nightgown. *Why should she feel shame at allowing herself pleasure? Why should she feel guilt? It is nothing but a foolish human custom to avoid such delights.* He felt it then, a stirring of desire within Him. But He was afraid; the girl had too much of Anarkhane in her. *I cannot allow such emotion to be directed toward a human; it is weakness, my own weakness not being able to obtain my love, turning to the next best thing.*

He reached out and placed His hand on her abdomen. She lay still but for the trembling of fear, whimpering softly at His touch, clearly expecting Him to take advantage. He could take her if He wished; she knew that. He smoothed his hands down the length of her stomach, feeling the sickness of her grief.

'Hush now,' He soothed. 'I am going to take the sickness away. There is nothing to fear.'

His words washed over her like a cosy blanket and tears of relief streamed from her eyes. He felt the relief but also a slight disappointment, until her conflicted emotions were overcome by her grief once more.

'I will not allow you to feel such fear of a man; when I'm through training you, you will never be a victim again.'

She sat up and touched her stomach; the queasiness was gone. 'Could you take away the pain?' she begged. 'Could you make me forget my grief completely?'

He touched her hair, stroking it out of her eyes. The tears that filled them were like morning dew on spring leaves— *beautiful.*

'I could, but you need that pain, Exzalander. I know that it does not feel like it at present, but it will drive you to succeed.'

She nodded in understanding, yet it did not stop the tears from falling without warning and she sobbed again. Taiohähn put His arms about her and she clung to Him. He let her have that moment, that comfort; it aided in allowing her trust for Him to grow, but He considered the danger of letting her have such comfort again and decided it was not worth the risk. Her scent and the warmth of her body were too much a distraction.

I cannot be father and teacher to her if she insists on needing me thus, He thought. He could feel the fire as it began to grow within Him, and He fought to extinguish the flames. *I must not take her; I must not lose control.*

She pulled away from Him and He stood, walking to the door, fighting to calm His urge.

'Thank you,' she said. 'I am ready to do as I must.'

'**Eat then; dress yourself,**' He replied. '**Let your mind guide you to the training room when you are ready.**' His head turned slightly back to her, but He dare not look, lest the sight of her make him change His mind.

'**Curse Anarkhane,**' He said to Himself, as He strode away. *What has She done? Was this Her plan all along? The girl even smells like Her. Well, I will not succumb. I had thought to play games, but am it seems, late to the board; Anarkhane's opening moves have already been made and I did not even see them. Why? Why would She want me to desire the girl? Does my love for Her really mean so little?*

He flung open the door and paced over to the nearest weapon rack. Picking up a spear, He threw it hard, channelling all His rage into the move. '**I will not play Anarkhane's game; I refuse to.**'

When Exzalander arrived at the training room, she gazed for a while at the spear protruding from the marble wall. Taiohãhn watched as she reached out to touch the fractured stone, marvelling at the strength of the throw. She was dressed in the loose silk trousers and shirt that He had left for her.

'**I was glad to see that you put what you already learned to use on Sohãhn.**'

Exzalander jumped, suddenly aware of His presence.

'I was glad to have been taught the skill,' she replied graciously.

'Your footwork was sloppy. Had he been a more skilled fighter then you would have been subdued easily. Now tell me, do you want to be prey to anyone again?'

Her nose wrinkled at His words and she pursed her lips tightly as she seethed. Her eyes were red and puffy from too much crying, but a grim determination had taken over the look of sorrow and self-pity.

'Well do you?' Taiohãhn asked a second time.

'No,' she said steadily.

'Good, then let us begin.'

Forty-One

$\mathcal{C}$aitul felt lighter as he passed through the barrier that had been his prison. He drew in the air and it felt cleaner and fresher than he had ever noticed before. He had half expected to see Ardahl outside the castle gates. In the town beyond, he felt a sense of unease settle upon him. Rítún was deserted; either the people were dead or had fled. It felt as though there was nobody left.

He glanced over to Katahl, whose forbidding features seemed to mirror his own dark thoughts. The sound of the horse's hooves seemed to clatter too loudly on the cobblestones. It was a solemn procession that took longer than it should. A hundred or so people left Brëgwela. Theyl directed many toward the outlying villages and farms. Their orders were to gather supplies. They had three days to do so, after which time, if they failed to return, then death would follow. They winced as he had issued the threat and the hungry, frightened faces that turned away, wrenched his gut.

'It is done Lord Katahl,' he said.

Katahl nodded grimly as the crowd of prisoners hunched away and he turned to Caitul.

'You know what you must do. Our journey's length will be about the same. Return quickly and meet us at the place you lit the signal fire.'

Caitul banged his fist against his chest in salute to his lord then sped his horse away south toward Ealdorbold. With every passing hour, he was certain he was being watched. The feeling of dread would not be extinguished. Even as the distance between himself and his captors lengthened, he became convinced that they knew what task he had been given. *Could they kill me at such a distance?* he wondered. *Probably. The question is, will they?* He hated the uncertainty of it all and found himself wishing he could be alongside Katahl, riding to avenge Exzalander's dishonour.

He had almost no provisions for his journey and was forced to stop at the town of Wílbec to rest and eat. The people saw his armour and were terrified. Word had reached them of the Old One's occupation. They recognised him as a knight of Starigorat and knew that he had ridden from Brëgwela.

At first they were reluctant to help him; even showing them the token of Tuâth, the highest honour that could be awarded, meaning he would receive aid and shelter from all within Tuâth's domain; even showing that he had the trust of the king, the people displayed disinclination. He took provisions and left. He could understand their fear and had not the time or will to apprise them of events at the castle. *No doubt they will hear all soon enough*, he thought, *but for now they must content themselves with rumours.*

In Ealdorbold, Ardahl poured over the ancient texts once again, hoping to find something to aid him in breaking the barrier around Brëgwela.

'Master, will you not take a little food?' Gailon asked.

Ardahl grunted a negative and leaned closer to the text he was reading, muttering to himself.

Gailon tutted. 'It will do Exzalander no good if you starve to death, Master Ardahl,' he said, hoping his cheeky tone might bring the wizard away from his brooding study. It didn't.

Gailon huffed and set a plate of bread and cold meats next to the old man, then walked away in search of sanity.

'*He* may be willing to wither away, but I certainly am not,' he said to himself, as he trudged along the corridors back to civilisation.

Life at the palace was strained. The entire Council, Ardahl and many other people of import, had arrived in time for

Exzalander's wedding, only to find the castle sealed tight by an impenetrable barrier.

The Council withdrew at once, suspecting that their lives might be threatened. Ardahl had stayed on, only to exhaust himself in trying to break the strongest majick he had ever known. He gave up eventually, not because of his apprentice's protests, but rather the belief that even if he were to break through, his efforts would prove fruitless.

He knew in his heart that the king and queen were dead and that Exzalander was too far away to be saved by any conventional means, such as soldiers storming the castle. If there was an answer to be found, then it lay in his ancient texts. So he devoted every waking hour to constant study, until exhaustion forced him to occasional bouts of fitful sleep.

Caitul entered the gate of Ealdorbold to an array of shouts from above. He braced himself for the wave of questions that would inevitably ensue. He did not, however, expect the bone-crushing embrace of his father as he dismounted his horse. Neither said a word and simply enjoyed the moment for what it was.

A servant approached, seeming out of breath. 'Knight Caitul,' he said. 'I am sent to bid you attend the Council at once.'

Caitul removed his helmet and ruffled his hair. His jaw clenched suddenly and he turned to Thomn.

'Father, my orders were very specific and they did not include answering to the Council. I must get to Ardahl and quickly. Will you help me?'

Thomn gave a sly smile and a nod. 'Of course,' he replied quietly. 'Knight Caitul will attend the Council shortly. You may leave now,' he barked.

The servant looked unsure for a moment, then nodded and left.

'Thank you father,' Caitul said. ' Now, how do I get to the tower?'

Thomn frowned, shaking his head. 'The only person here who knows the way, other than Ardahl of course, is young Gailon. All the others moved with the king when he went north.'

At the mention of the king, Thomn saw the shadow pass over Caitul's features and he found he could not ask why. He was too afraid of the answer and even more afraid that he would feel nothing if informed the king had met his end.

'Come, let's try the kitchens,' Thomn said, pulling his son out of plain view and toward the building. 'He can often be found hiding out there. That boy can eat!'

They avoided the main walkway and stuck to smaller, plainer corridors that were favoured by servants, until they reached the palace kitchens.

On seeing who it was that approached him, Gailon spilled soup down his front.

'Y,you're alive!' he stuttered. 'What happened? Is everyone all right?'

Caitul frowned at the apprentice.

'That news must reach Ardahl's ears before any others, Gailon,' he said.

Gailon glanced about him, wary of the eyes that watched their meeting. He beckoned Caitul to follow him, wiping his tunic as he paced away.

Thomn followed; there seemed little else to do. *Besides,* he thought, *Elsbeth will want to know all and will chew my ear off if she discovers that I had the chance to find out anything before the Council, yet passed up the opportunity.*

'Master Ardahl,' Gailon cried, as he dashed into the tower.

Ardahl did not glance up, but grunted his annoyance at his apprentice.

'I told you before, boy, no disturbances!'

Caitul placed his helmet down by the papers Ardahl was reading and the wizard's gaze slowly went from the helmet to armour, to Caitul's face.

'Tell me all,' he said urgently.

Caitul related every detail of the occupation from the arrival of the Old Ones, the deaths of the king and queen to the confinement and tutelage of Katahl. His face darkened as he spoke of what had happened to Exzalander, and he struggled to find the words to tell them she was gone. By the time that Caitul had finished speaking, he felt exhausted. His hard ride and the anguish of recent events caught up with him at last and he sagged forward.

Thomn and Gailon helped him over to Ardahl's bed, unfastening and removing his upper armour—rerebraces, pauldrons and cuirass. He made no move to prevent them, his eyes closing involuntarily.

'We must get her back, Ardahl,' he said. 'Katahl sent me to beg for your aid.'

As sleep took the knight at last, Thomn sat next to him, drawing up the blanket. Ardahl watched, his mouth set into a line. He continued to stare at Caitul, as if the answer might lie in the knight's face; the next moment, he dashed to the corner of the room and started rifling through old books, drawing Thomn's attention away from his sleeping son.

'Ah, here it is,' he said. Running over to his desk, he swept the contents onto the floor with a single movement.

Caitul did not even stir as his helmet clattered across the floor toward him. Ardahl too was oblivious to the noise and began to paw through an ancient tome with a growing sense of urgency.

'I should report to the Council,' Thomn interrupted. 'The last thing I want is for them to have an excuse to have my son arrested. If I tell them what I know, it may appease them. Can you show me the way, Gailon?'

'Of course.'

As he left the room, Thomn looked back at Ardahl, hunched over the text; he had not even noticed their departure. Turning back to Gailon, Thomn followed him along the corridor to the catacombs beyond.

Forty-Two

The order of Vivianne felt the arrival of the Old Ones, like a ripple of pure energy, which spread out across the whole of Maldahl. They watched and waited, unsure how long it would take for the prophecy to be fulfilled. As the weeks went by, they sensed Katahl's power become strong enough to pierce the barrier. As he left the confines of the castle, the wizards gained a clear picture of his intent.

Fahl snapped his head up from the meditative circle. 'We should warn them,' he said.

The wizards opened their eyes and looked concerned.

'Why?' Elgon asked.

Fahl got to his feet and stared west toward Brëgwela Castle. 'Because we can,' he offered.

Morion shook his head. 'We cannot get involved. Our purpose is to aid the princess on her return; all else is unimportant.'

'But he plans on annihilating them!'

'It is not our concern, Fahl.'

'You are wrong. If your conscience will not prompt you to action, then know this; a Mo-Rye warrior stands in the final battle; he stands defending Exzalander. It is written in the book of CODM.'

The order looked at each other nervously. None knew the prophecy better than Fahl and they were aware that he would not speak such a thing were it not true.

'But if that is the case,' said Iseren, 'then the prophecy runs the risk of being broken. One of the Mo-Rye must be saved.'

'We cannot risk being caught by Katahl,' Elgon said. 'He knows who we are. If he does not try to kill us for aiding his enemy, he will at least bring us to the attention of the dark power. We cannot afford for them to know of us. We must remain an unknown factor, lest we be destroyed before fulfilling our true purpose.'

It was then that Fahl repeated the relevant part of the prophecy so that all those present might interpret its meaning. It was suddenly so clear to them that a Mo-Rye is only identified as a warrior because of his armour. Saving one Mo-Rye was of no use, as it was unknown how long he would need to survive. It might be centuries before Exzalander returned, by which time, the sole surviving Mo-Rye, would be dead.

Save a handful then.

They still ran the risk of being seen by Katahl.

'So it is decided then?' asked Treoraí.

All nodded and Fahl among them.

'We do nothing. Once Katahl has left them, we must recover a warrior's armour and keep it safe until it is needed.'

They all clasped hands as an agreement was struck, but Fahl felt his faith tested that day. The CODM Prophecy should not have needed them to cheat in order to see it fulfilled. He shook off his doubts and sat to meditate once again, but he found that he could not concentrate; the vision of the slaughtered Mo-Rye haunted his thoughts. He saw every blow struck and felt the guilt of each death, knowing that he might have prevented them.

Nimrïn had been right; despite Katahl begging the aid of those who followed him to battle, his power was such that none could stand against him. Nimrïn struggled against a large Mo-Rye warrior; they were fierce fighters and worthy opponents. As he finally despatched his foe, he caught sight of his lord and felt that he had lost him.

Katahl laughed as he slew; his sword and knife were soon discarded, as he turned to the power that had been gifted him, sending sheets of flame toward the living quarters. He allowed their dying screams to wash over him as he recalled what Exzalander had related about Sohāhn's deal with them. Many parts of the stronghold were underwater, but still Katahl was not deterred as he turned the water to ice, freezing to death the cowards who refused to face his wrath.

Several of Katahl's spells rebounded, killing his own men; still he seemed not to care. His allies retreated back and even his knights stopped fighting to watch the ferocity in their lord's eyes as he slaughtered all before him.

At the last, the Mo-Rye leader stepped up and begged for mercy. Sinking to his knees in a mixture of seawater and blood, he placed his head to the floor and swore servitude to the great lord.

Katahl raised his hand and his sword answered his silent call. Frightened faces watched as the weapon flew from where it lay embedded in a fallen Mo-Rye, to Katahl's waiting hand, whereupon he raised it above the leader's neck.

'Milord!' Dahal cried. 'He's surrendering.'

But before Dahal could finish his protest, Katahl sank the blade deep into the spine of the Mo-Rye leader. Dahal blinked, unable to comprehend what he was seeing.

'Round them up and finish them,' Katahl hissed, a wild light in his eyes.

'Milord, only the females and children remain,' Aarnon said. 'We've killed them all.' His voice quivered as he stared at the carnage about him.

Without warning, Katahl paced over to where the females housed themselves. They screamed for mercy, but he showed none. He sent flame into every part of their home, until it cracked and crumbled into the sea below. Still Katahl sent flames forward until the ocean beyond hissed and boiled.

Nimrïn grabbed Katahl's arm.

'Enough!' he said

Katahl felt his power drained and fell forward. 'What have I done, Nimrïn?' he whispered, as if seeing for the first time, the devastation he had wrought.

A deathly quiet fell over the company as Nimrïn lowered Katahl's weakened form to the ground, where he lay amongst the fallen.

'I say we kill him now, while he's weak,' shouted one of the guards of Tuâth.

The knights acted in an instant, shielding their lord from the mass of angry men before them. Captain Theyl shouted for them to stand down, but they would not listen. They had seen how Katahl had killed his own without a care for anything other than his lust for revenge. He had caused more deaths amongst the company than the Mo-Rye had been able. As the angry mob advanced, Theyl was knocked to the ground and they trampled over him in effort to reach Katahl.

The knights fought off oncoming blows, but were outnumbered more than ten to one. As the knights began to tire, they sustained injuries, but fought on as they were honour-bound to do so. Without warning, the front attackers screamed and fell to the floor, writhing in agony. The next row of attackers did the same. The knights held up their swords defensively, but as the third row fell, the attacking guards backed away. Their betrayal was to be their doom, and even as they ran from the insanity of the fortress, they fell and died slow deaths.

Nimrïn lifted his visor as he surveyed the scene; nothing could be done to ease their passing, other than the sword. But he could not bring himself to wield his weapon in such a way, not even in mercy.

The bloodied form of Theyl groaned and Dahal ran to his aid.

'We must get him back. He's badly wounded.'

Aarnon knelt and hurled Katahl over his shoulder, removing him from the chaos of destruction. Nimrïn took hold of Theyl, whose breathing seemed to rasp. Dahal surveyed the devastation once more and then began to release the guards from their misery, dispatching them each in turn so that their torment might end, but with each life he took, he felt a little piece of his soul slip away.

At the meeting point, they waited for Caitul. Katahl was awake and used what power he had to keep Theyl alive. Nobody spoke; the shock of so much death lay heavily upon them and it seemed to Dahal that his hands would never be clean.

'How long should we wait?' Aarnon asked. 'Those things already know that we completed the task. They must have been watching all along.'

'We will wait as long as we must,' Katahl said. He was the only one of them who seemed unchanged by the slaughter. He tended to Theyl's wounds with humility and concentration showing none of his former insanity.

It was evening of that day when Caitul arrived. He had a different horse, having exhausted his former.

'Theyl!' he cried, as he dismounted and ran to his brother's side.

His brother coughed. 'It looks worse than it is,' he said.

Caitul glanced up to Katahl for confirmation and felt himself soothed by his lord's smile.

'He will live, Caitul; do not fear. But now you are back, we must return to Brëgwela at once.'

Caitul's brow creased as he looked about him. 'Are the others on their way back?'

Aarnon and Nimrïn exchanged looks, but did not speak. Dahal turned away, saddling his horse.

'What is it?' Caitul asked. 'What has happened?'

'They're all dead, brother,' Theyl answered, as nobody else seemed willing to speak.

'Come Caitul,' Katahl said sharply. 'We'll explain on the way, but we must get moving. I will not risk harm coming to any of you.'

However, Katahl did not explain as they rode; it was left to Caitul to fill the silence as he showed Katahl what Ardahl had made for him.

Katahl ran his hand over the smooth glass. 'What is it?' he asked.

'Ardahl called it a forelócian glaes. He knew that he would not be able to return with me and so created this so that you might speak to one another. He's searching for a way to leave our world in order to find Exzalander, and will inform you if he discovers anything that might be of use.'

Katahl placed the glass into his pack, with a smile. Aarnon frowned, unsure how his lord could make such a gesture after what he had done.

* * * * *

Time passed differently in the Underworld, and although Taiohăhn manipulated it as best He could to enable Exzalander longer to train, He could not muster enough power to synchronise the passage of time between His realm and Maldahl. As a result, when she trained hard for weeks in Taiohăhn's kingdom, months passed in the land of her birth.

Taiohăhn marvelled at her stamina, having to force her to take rest, as she would work without sleep if He let her. He knew why; it was not just her determination to succeed, but the thought of her nightmares that made her want to remain awake. Hearing her screams each time she slept, He resisted the urge to wake her and offer comfort. The nightmares focused her will and He needed that strength in her. He had seen how much power Katahl accumulated and began to have concerns that she would never be ready.

It was time He introduced her to the sword.

She stared eagerly at the weapon, it seeming to call to her and as she took it in her grasp, she felt the familiarity of the hilt. They were one–that bond had been formed long ago, now all that remained was for her to wield it. The blade sang as she swung it, ringing out Taiohãhn's name. She moved through her defences, marvelling at the perfect balance between hilt and blade.

Taiohãhn crouched down, mesmerised by her gracefulness, losing Himself in her beautiful and deadly dance. It was Anarkhane's presence that drew Him reluctantly away and He stepped out of the training room, taking Himself to the Chamber of Light where He knew the goddess awaited Him. Exzalander did not seem to notice.

The brightness of the place where the two kingdoms met never ceased to surprise Him; neither did Her beauty. He had not seen Her since Exzalander's arrival and He felt the familiar stir within Him.

'I have spent much time here of late,' She said, 'but you have not been to see me.'

Taiohãhn felt amusement grow at Her words. *Perhaps She is jealous after all*, He thought. 'I have been busy with my warrior,' He replied. 'She takes up much of my time.'

She pouted. 'Indeed? Rightly so I suppose.'

The game is back on, He realised.

'I have been watching Maldahl from your glæs,' She continued. 'Katahl intends to send his First Knight to retrieve our protégé.'

'Impossible!' Taiohãhn laughed. 'He may have the power, but not the means.'

She smiled sweetly, unintentionally revealing Her next move in the game.

'What have you done, Anarkhane?' He demanded.

She flounced across to the forelócian glaes and stared into it, ignoring His anger toward Her.

'The wizard had a dream, that is all,' She said innocently. 'I cannot influence Katahl directly, but he has obtained one of these,' She pointed to the forelócian glaes, 'so has contact with the wizard.'

'The knight cannot have her, Anarkhane. It'll be years before she's ready; you know that.'

Anarkhane placed a hand onto His chest and ran Her fingers along.

'She'll never have as long to prepare as Katahl. We only have to be seen to prepare her; she's to die anyhow.'

'No!' Taiohãhn hissed

He gripped Anarkhane's hand to stop Her teasing and She laughed, making every part of His being want to take Himself inside Her and punish Her at the same time.

'You're not falling in love with her, are you?' She mocked.

His eyes blazed and He pulled Her to Him, forcing a kiss upon Her. She fought him half-heartedly until His lips grew more urgent and She thrust Him away.

'Katahl will be the one to die,' He said. 'He'll offer his life for hers.'

The smile Anarkhane gave Him in return for His words was cold. 'If that is what you wish,' She said, 'but I hope you do not get too attached to your charge.'

He grabbed Her about the waist, furious at Her teasing.

'What did you do to her, Anarkhane? Why do I think of you when I am with her?'

The same tinkering laugh issued forth and Taiohãhn pushed Her away. She fell back, hitting her head on the crystal wall.

'I gave her part of me,' She hissed, 'that is what you sense and it's driving you mad. Just as you drove me mad when you took away that which I held most dear.'

He was on Her in moments, His hands about Her throat. If She was frightened, then She did not show it.

'You're a fool, Anarkhane. They'll be nothing left to restore if you continue making gifts of your immortality.'

Her eyes darted toward the door in alarm, and She disappeared.

Exzalander's voice sounded from outside. 'Lord Taiohãhn?' she called.

In an instant, He moved to prevent her entry. The brightness behind Him burst forth, filling her with familiar warmth.

'What is that place?' she asked.

He stood, blocking her view, His arms held out to each side of the doorway and she tried peaking around. His eyes blazed with the fury that He still felt and He fought to prevent Himself from striking her in consolation for being unable to punish Anarkhane.

Exzalander stopped staring at the light; it seemed suddenly swallowed up by Him as He shook with anger.

'Lord Taiohãhn,' she whispered. 'What has happened?'

As He gazed upon her, He knew that she should be terrified. She should be on her knees, but it was not fear, rather concern, He saw there. He had been worshipped for millennia; He had inspired and terrified, but never had anyone shown him such feelings. He grasped her about the shoulders and squeezed gently. She seemed to glow slightly, being so near to the tear in the veil to Anarkhane's kingdom. He drew the door closed with His mind, but she no longer noticed.

'Thank you,' He said at last.

'What for?'

He shook Himself and released her, His face stern once more.

'It is no matter. Come, I wish to see you wield the sword.'

She followed Him as He paced away, pausing to turn back to the hidden room and memorising the corridors leading back there.

Forty-three

Taiohãhn beamed as Exzalander ran up the wall and used it to springboard her into a somersault over Him.

'Very good,' He said.

She grinned back, basking in His praise.

'Could you do the same thing without any walls?' He challenged, as He thrust His practice sword forward.

She parried with ease and slashed at Him. The force of His block sent her staggering backward.

'Mind your footing! How many times do I …'

She sprang up and over Him, but landed awkwardly with a cry of pain. Taiohãhn sheathed His weapon and crouched beside her.

'Let me see,' He said in a fatherly tone.

'It's nothing,' she replied, gritting her teeth. Clearly in pain, she was determined not to show it. She avoided His gaze, having no desire to observe His commanding features as He chastised her.

'Your stubbornness will be the death of you, girl, either that or your temper. You need to learn to control your anger and to channel it. The blade will respond to your will more readily if you do.'

He held out His hand to her ankle; she winced until He sent healing warmth into and along the length of her leg.

'Better?'

She beamed up at Him and nodded.

'Can you teach me to do that?' she asked.

Taiohãhn frowned. 'I could, but Anarkhane is more of a healer than I. You would be better waiting until I send you to Her.'

Exzalander's eyes seemed panicked. 'You're sending me away?' she cried.

Taiohãhn stood and offering His hand, He pulled her to her feet.

'You cannot hope to win through sword skill alone; Anarkhane will teach you to use the majick gifted you at birth.'

'But can you not teach me that? Your majick is powerful.'

'I thought you were eager to be away from this place, my warrior,' Taiohãhn mused.

She had been, it was true and yet being there with Him had become to feel like home and the thought of being taken away from His presence, terrified her. She had spent countless sleepless hours pondering her feelings. She knew that it was foolish to desire Him and dare not tell Him of her feelings. She was His warrior and had a duty to perform; the fact that she awoke longing to be near Him again was irrelevant and the chance of anything coming of such an attraction, impossible.

She circled her foot and put weight upon it once more, realising that she had not answered His assertion. Was she eager to be away from Him? No, she would be happy to be at His side forever.

'I am not eager to have to acquaint myself with a new teacher,' she said.

Taiohãhn raised an eyebrow at her evasiveness and was met with a dazzling smile that left Him feeling warm. He shook His head and settled in fighting stance once again.

It was foolish to believe the Old Ones were not aware of Katahl's use of the forelócian glaes, so when Ardahl gave Katahl the means to pierce the veil between worlds, the Old Ones were ready. Calling Caitul to him, Katahl explained what must be done. Had it been anyone else, they might have argued, explaining that it would be prudent to wait; Exzalander would return eventually–that was what the prophecy said. However, Caitul, like his lord, was ruled by his heart in such a matter and more than anything, he desired the safe return of the princess.

As Katahl began to weave the protection spell about his First Knight, Caitul stood in silence, a look of unyielding resolve on his face.

'Are you ready?' Katahl asked.

'Yes.' Caitul nodded.

It was a complicated spell and although it required no ingredients, the chanting took many hours, all the while draining Katahl's significant power and the defences he had put up to keep control over that power, crumbled.

Exzalander knew that she should not have been there. If Taiohãhn had wanted her in the room, then he would not have locked it. *Still, Taiohãhn is not here,* she thought, *and I have known a variety of lock spells since I was a small child. One of them is bound to work and if not, I will get creative.* He had informed her that a human was lost in His forest. As the forest was vast, she figured He would be gone for quite a while.

All her lock spells spent, she tried to prise it open with Taiohãhn's sword. To her surprise, the gem in the pommel began to glow, causing her to drop it in surprise. Memories of the pain it could cause flooded her mind and she backed away, but her fear lessened as the glow increased, drawing her nearer as its power sang.

The door to the chamber clicked open. Part of her wanted to flee, to abandon the sword and her curiosity and hide in the safety of her room until Taiohãhn returned and she could beg His forgiveness. The song from the discarded weapon enthralled her fear away and before she realised what she was doing, she bent down to retrieve the blade.

Broken the stone may have been, but it was the largest of the pieces of the gem that had created life on her world and as it called to its counterparts, the power in her hand threatened to overwhelm her.

The door swung open, or she could have pushed it; she was unsure. All she was aware of was the brightness beyond, familiar warmth that reassured her as she stepped over the threshold. She had seen the light before, in a dream the night before her parent's death. It had saved her the few hours of fear. However, what she felt now was resentment.

Taiohãhn tried to warn me, prepare me, she thought. *All Anarkhane did was have me remain ignorant when I might have prevented such a disaster.* She gripped the sword tightly in her hand, fighting to suppress the surge of anger. The stone within glowed more brightly than ever, reacting to her mood.

Gazing about, she noticed how different the chamber was to the rest of Taiohãhn's kingdom. No marble existed there, but a mixture of opal and crystal, which seemed illuminated from within. She ran her hand over the cold of the crystal walls, but her eyes were drawn toward another glow of green. In the centre of the chamber upon a pedestal, sat another piece of the broken stone, glowing as it called out to the gem in the sword.

'It's beautiful, is it not?' came a voice from above.

'Anarkhane ... show yourself!' Exzalander demanded.

The goddess was not in the habit of complying with orders and it was well that Exzalander could not see Her at that moment, so as not to bear witness to Her anger.

'Do not issue your venom upon me, daughter. It is not I who keeps you from your home—your love.'

Exzalander spun about, sword drawn, but the goddess had not revealed Herself.

'Taiohãhn saved me,' Exzalander said. 'He helps me to prepare to throw down my enemy.'

'And yet your love is in danger. If he perishes, what use is all your training? Look.' She urged.

Exzalander saw the glow from the forelócian glaes and stepped up, hesitant. She was accosted immediately with the image of Katahl as he chanted the spell. Her heart ached as she watched him ... so thin, so pale, a shadow of his former self.

'Katahl,' she whispered, and reached out instinctively toward him.

'He needs you, daughter. While you remain here allowing Taiohãhn to seduce you, your love...'

'He has not,' Exzalander protested. 'He's training me!'

The laugh, which echoed about the chamber, chilled her to the bone.

'You think so highly of Him, do you not? And yet He knows Katahl's plight and lifts not a finger to prevent him from harm. See ...'

As Exzalander gazed into the forelócian glæs, she saw Taiohãhn as He rode through a forest that was not His own—where He had claimed He would be.

'It is Maldahl,' Anarkhane affirmed, as if answering an unspoken question. 'The Forest of Tûlg. He rides to meet is favourite creation—the Vampire Ælves, those whom your father sought to destroy so that he might protect you. Taiohãhn could easily have ridden to the aid of Katahl.'

The image of her betrothed returned and she took a gulp of air, realising she had been holding her breath. Caitul gazed intently down at Katahl. His features were grim and serious. He had not lost weight as Katahl had, but rather, seemed broader and weightier, as if he had been in hard training. He mouthed something to his lord, but Katahl was too deep in his chant to notice.

Exzalander forced herself to blink, believing she was not seeing the image correctly as it began to fade. When she opened her eyes again, she realised it was not the image that had faded, but Caitul out of it. She gasped and cried out.

'He is sent to find you, daughter, and now he is lost.' Anarkhane explained. 'He will drift forever in the void between worlds.'

'Please,' Exzalander begged. 'You have to help him. He is a good man, loyal and true. You cannot leave him to perish in the darkness.'

'You care for him it seems. Tell me, daughter, does your betrothed know of your feelings for his First Knight?'

Exzalander screamed in rage, but her anger was pointless. There was nobody to direct it at other than a disembodied voice.

'You are fickle, daughter. The First Knight, now Taiohãhn … perhaps you no longer care for what happens to Katahl …'

Exzalander collapsed to the floor, her grief overwhelming her at last. Anarkhane's voice was silent and all she heard was the sound of her own sobs, which seemed to echo around the walls of the Chamber of Light.

* * * * *

When Taiohãhn returned, He knew instantly something was amiss. He strode to the training room, but Exzalander was not there. Setting down the dragon dagger, He went in search of her. Her room was empty and she did not answer His call. Reaching out to her with His mind, He felt her pain and grief and His arms wrapped about her before He had even fully materialised by her side.

It took a moment for either to react—He to realise where she was, and her to feel anger at His presence. As He recognised her surroundings, He opened His mouth to question her, but she grasped her sword holding it to His throat.

'You were there,' she screeched. 'You could have sent me back at any time and yet you've been keeping me prisoner.'

He disarmed her in an instant, sending the sword clattering across the floor. Her fists pounded suddenly on His chest.

'Send me back!' she demanded, and pounded again.

His form was like rock and did not even move against her attack. Finally, He caught her wrists and held them away from Him.

'I have never said that I could not send you back, only that I would not. I have not lied to you, Exzalander.'

'You are lying to me now!' she screamed as she struggled in His grasp. 'You told me that you were in your forest, but I saw you on Maldahl. I *saw* you!'

Taiohãhn showed a flicker of emotion as He glanced up to His forelócian glæs and back to the struggling woman. She had seen Him; there was no use denying it.

'It is true, Exzalander; I did not tell you because I did not want to upset you. When the time is right, I will send you back, but I need to ensure that you are ready. You will return with the sword and the other gem and it will be your task to reunite all the lost pieces.'

'I do not care about your stone,' she spat. 'I care that Katahl needs me. I care that Caitul is drifting in the darkness—lost and alone. I care that my parents were murdered and are not avenged. I care that my people are suffering and I am not there to aid them, I …'

He could bear it no longer; the fury in her features and the effort of her struggle overwhelmed His senses. He pressed His lips against her own, desiring to feel the same passion directed toward Himself.

She froze, her limbs stiffening as she recalled Anarkhane's words. Mere hours before, she would have returned such a kiss with passionate longing, but Anarkhane had put doubt and, most of all, guilt into her mind. All the time that she had been falling in love with Taiohãhn, she had been forgetting about the man who had stood by her, supported and loved her. The guilt at her own betrayal was too much to bear; it was far easier to transfer her shame to anger and direct it back at Him. *Am I just a plaything to Him?* she wondered.

He let go of her wrists and grasped her shoulders in effort to draw her closer, but she shoved Him, the anger within burning.

'Do not touch me!' she hissed.

It was a blow; He had never meant to show her His desire, but even less so that she would reject Him. He had almost convinced Himself of her love and now she turned Him away. *She is human; nothing more,* He thought, *and she has the audacity to reject me.* For a moment He considered forcing her, but managed to restrain Himself.

'I am not your whore!' she cried, her eyes all fury and confusion.

'No, you are my warrior,' He said calmly, although He felt anything but, 'and it's time that you started acting like it.' He got to His feet and held out His hand toward her.

She glared up at Him and followed Him up, without taking His hand. He smiled grimly as He directed her from the room, thinking that her stubbornness made her all the more desirable.

As she walked away from the chamber, the memory of Anarkhane's presence receded and she could only recall the discovery as if had been her own. Anarkhane had covered Her tracks well. The goddess had ensured that Exzalander remained focused on Katahl.

It did not matter whether it was love or guilt that would make her lay down her life, as long as she willingly sacrificed herself.

It has to be her, considered the goddess. *Why would Katahl do so? Not now he has gained so much power. It is naive to believe that he will be willing to give up his life, his power, to save Exzalander. He can have any woman that he wants now. It will be I who will vanquish Katahl, and the people will love me for it. I cannot wait to see Taiohāhn's face when His warrior shows that she would rather die than love Him. Finally, I can be avenged for my undoing.*

Katahl was aware of Caitul's voice, but could not distinguish what words were spoken. He felt his friend leave their plane, but did not see it. Collapsing with exhaustion–his power drained, he closed his eyes, desiring nothing at that moment other than the blissful oblivion of sleep. However, the darkness that enveloped him had nothing to do with rest. It crept in slowly, testing him for any signs of consciousness, or fight. It seeped into every unprotected pore and by the time Katahl became conscious of the Old Ones invasion, it was too late. His scream ended abruptly as his body felt renewed vigour and he wondered why he had felt the need for such a cry.

Exzalander awoke from a nightmare where Katahl was lost and could not be found. She breathed heavily and wiped the perspiration from her brow. Her limbs felt leaden from the afternoon's training. Taiohāhn had worked her much harder than usual, probably to distract her from her anger and the kiss. *As if I could forget such a thing,* she thought. *He crossed a line and I will never forgive him.* Of course she made him believe that she had, and they bid each other goodnight in friendship.

The useful thing about being so headstrong and passionate was that everyone believed her emotions were always written on her face — there for anyone to read. It made it easy to conceal when she wished to, what she really felt. He believed, as many others, that she could not hide her emotions, that she was too transparent to be manipulative. *That is His failing, not mine,* she considered. When she wiped the sweat from her brow and came to her decision. She felt no guilt. *It is Taiohãhn's own fault for not having foreseen my intention*, she thought. *He is a god after all.*

In truth, she was not actually angry with Him, but rather herself. She was the one who discarded Katahl's love so easily. She was the one who allowed herself to fall for a god. The fact that such feelings might be reciprocated terrified her beyond the point of being able to think or act rationally.

She dressed herself in silence, securing her weapon belt about her waist, then without a backward glance, she crept silently through Taiohãhn's palace until she reached the Chamber of Light. As if in welcome, the door swung open at her approach. She stood in front of the great forelócian glæs, willing it to show her the way back home. The surface seemed to ripple as the image of Ealdorbold appeared. She thought hard again, trying to clarify her thoughts so that she might discover the gateway between their two worlds.

The surface rippled and she reached out cautiously, suspecting what it was trying to tell her. Taiohãhn's forelócian glæs was for more than just seeing; it allowed Him to step between worlds—a similar device to Ardahl's invention only much more powerful. She grabbed the shard of the Anarkhane stone from its place on the pedestal and walked back toward home, determination to do the right thing driving her on.

Taiohãhn had been brooding. He had considered watching his warrior sleep for a while; He enjoyed that pastime. Exzalander's slow, steady breathing always made Him feel peaceful. However, he considered that even after her difficult training, she was likely to be restless. *It would not do to be caught in her room—not tonight*, He thought. *She seemed to forgive me, but I am not about to risk all over so trivial an activity.*

He made His way toward the Chamber of Light, determined to discover how she had managed to enter at all.

The door was open on His arrival and He was just in time to see Exzalander step into the forelócian glǽs.

'No!' He yelled.

Changing the image as she stepped through, prevented her return to Maldahl. His sword came back at His bidding, but He lost the shard. It would not obey Him. Too long had it been out of His power. Exzalander did not obey Him either, choosing to escape rather than return to Him.

He sent a wave of fire before He lost her altogether. It was her will that defied Him and her will controlled her body. It was her body that He needed to train and so He sent His flame to separate body from soul and He flinched as her screams reached Him. Anarkhane heard them too. She saw the separation, knowing that Her plan had failed; unless Exzalander was whole and chose to sacrifice herself, they would never return to claim Maldahl. She tried to retrieve her, but the soul was slippery in Her grasp. Gritting her teeth, She exerted more force, causing the soul to tear. She watched with dismay as both the fractured soul and the piece of Her beautiful stone fell down into the darkness where She could not follow.

Resisting the urge to torture the fractured soul in Her hands, She encased it in Her light, both protecting and imprisoning. She knew that She should speak with Taiohãhn, but was aware what would meet her eyes the moment She set foot in His realm.

He'll no doubt be cradling the soulless body of His warrior in His arms, mourning the loss ... pathetic, She thought. *I have no intention of sitting idly by whilst my godhood is at risk.*

Reaching into the void, She sent Her light forth to call on Caitul. *Exzalander wanted him to be saved—well now her wish is granted.*

He drifted into Anarkhane's kingdom, believing himself to be dead as She spoke kind words to him. She needed Exzalander back; She needed the stone back. His quest was to retrieve her and She could help him do so—everyone happy. She smiled at Her own cleverness as She began to weave Her spell upon him.

Taiohãhn has a pack of dogs that lives in His forest, She thought. *They used to travel to Earth with Him to collect unworthy souls. Now, I have my own hound and the object I will use to introduce Exzalander's scent—the girl's soul. The princess could end up anywhere, in body or out. Caitul needs to recognise her no matter where she chooses to conceal herself.*

By the time Exzalander stepped into the forelócian glæs, Katahl had been long lost. Perhaps she had dreamed of echoes from the past, or what he had already begun to do. The Old Ones watched with interest as their protégé ordered Brëgwela's people to take arms; servants, lords, ladies, peasants, and farmers who had been unlucky enough to have chosen the day of the Old Ones arrival to sell their wares and so became trapped with the rest of the household. All were to form Katahl's new army now that Tuâth's guard were dead. Not only that, but all were ordered to swear an oath of loyalty to Katahl. Those who refused were imprisoned until he saw fit to address them personally.

Training began while Katahl watched on, ever weaving new majicks to improve their skill.

'I have brought Theyl, Milord, as I was bid to do,' Dahal said. His voice sounded more monotonous than was his wont. His face had paled over the past weeks, but if he was ailing for something then he failed to notice. He felt very little; ever since the incident with the Mo-Rye and since Caitul had departed, it was growing rapidly worse. It was a loss of sense of self. Some nights he would wake in a panic, gripping at his soul as it slipped away from him.

The others had the same sensations, yet none of them spoke of it. They all knew that Katahl had changed and their pledge to him was causing them to change too. Talking about it would not alter that fact.

'Ah Theyl, glad am I to see you,' Katahl said. 'Thank you Dahal; that will be all.'

Dahal bowed and left without a word. Returning to the yard, he assisted in training the new recruits, his master's purpose seeming his only one.

Katahl sat back in Tuâth's throne, looking very much at home. He no longer appeared unwell, but Theyl was unsure that he looked particularly human either. His face was more like an artistic representation of a man—slightly too beautiful—too perfect.

'Nimrïn has led me to understand that you have refused to take the oath. May I ask why?' Katahl spoke evenly, no flicker of emotion on his perfect features.

Theyl strived for the same level of control as he gave his answer, all too aware of the people who were being held in the dungeon and eager to avoid their fate. 'I have sworn allegiance to the House of Tuâth,' he said. 'I cannot have two masters.'

Katahl gave a small smile that displayed no warmth whatsoever. 'Tuâth is no more, Captain Theyl. You are free from your oath to him.'

'With respect, Lord Katahl, I am not. Exzalander is his heir and she is yet living.'

'Am I not to be her husband?'

Theyl nodded, trying not to dwell on such an event. He was trying to take each day as it came. Thinking too far ahead filled him with such fear that he was barely able to function. 'Indeed you are,' he acknowledged, 'and once you are wed to my mistress, then will you be of the house to which my loyalties are sworn.'

Katahl was silent; his hands gripped the arms of the dead king's throne as he contemplated the situation. His instincts told him to rid himself of the troublesome captain. However,

Theyl was Caitul's brother and Caitul was his friend. *Still, while Theyl is sworn to serve Tuâth's house, he will do everything that he can to prevent my plan from succeeding,* Katahl thought and gave a wry smile.

'I will look forward to such a time, Captain Theyl, but until then you are free to leave.'

Theyl frowned, as if to contemplate if Katahl was in jest.

'I am still willing to aid you,' he said. 'I want to do all that I can to prepare for Exzalander's return.'

'That is good to hear, Captain. I suggest that you return to Ealdorbold and apprise the Council of events. Tell them that I will meet with them soon.'

Theyl felt an icy thread of fear spread across his body as he realised what such an order meant, but he had to be sure. 'But are you not prisoner here, Lord Katahl?' he asked.

Katahl held Theyl's eyes, such a penetrating stare that Theyl was compelled to drop his gaze.

'I am no longer prisoner, Theyl. It is *I* who controls the barrier now and I have even strengthened it. It will prove good protection from all those who will take Exzalander's absence as a chance to seize power. I will not allow that to happen, Captain. I must ensure that my betrothed still has a kingdom to rule on her return.'

Theyl wanted to question Katahl's logic. He was sure that the races of Maldahl had no interest in the High King's crown, but Katahl's face was almost maniacal as he spoke and the captain had no doubt that the Old Ones had placed such notions into the young lord's mind. In the circumstances, he felt that he had no option other than to ride to Ealdorbold and inform the Council what was to come.

'I will take my leave, if that is your wish.'

'Safe journey, Theyl. Send the Council my regards.'

Theyl gave a stiff nod and turned on his heel, pacing from the room. His vision was blurred and he felt sick. Katahl had as good as admitted that he was to declare war on all the races of Maldahl. He broke into a run, wanting nothing more than to escape the madness.

Nimrïn watched from the tower, as Caitul's brother sped southward toward Ealdorbold. The forelócian glæs that Caitul had brought back from the palace had been set in a pedestal of rock, looking as though it had always been there.

Katahl approached his knight and stood beside him.

'Something troubles you, Nimrïn,' he said.

The knight continued to stare, long after Theyl was lost from sight. 'He will warn the Council; they will be ready for us.'

Katahl gave a thin smile and clapped a hand on the knight's shoulder.

'That he will,' he said. 'They'll piss themselves and submit. My love can decide their fate. I am going to visit the dungeon now. Is everything as I ordered?'

A shadow crossed Nimrïn's face, as he thought of the restraints on the table and surgical devices.

'Yes Milord,' he replied, 'but I thought that you intended to talk to the prisoners, not torture them into submission.'

Katahl felt a tug of regret pass quickly. He had always appreciated Nimrïn's forthright manner and his wit. He was stronger than the others and had not completely succumbed — so much was obvious by his questioning. Part of him did not want to lose Nimrïn, though he knew it was necessary; such humour had no place in preparation for Exzalander's return.

'I have no intention of torturing the people,' Katahl said. 'I am going to make them loyal subjects of the realm.'

Nimrïn considered his master's words and thought that was exactly why they were in prison to begin with, but he had not the strength to question Katahl further. He was tired; each moment that passed was a battle, a battle that he knew he could not win and yet he chose to fight it anyhow. *There is still a chance that Caitul will return and Exzalander will bring light to the darkness that has infested Katahl's soul,* Nimrïn thought. *The worst thing of all is how Katahl cannot see anything wrong in what he's doing. His actions, no matter how brutal, all proclaim to be for Exzalander's benefit.*

Theyl sped on toward the palace, determined to warn them about the Katahl's insanity. He rode hard, with barely a pause, as if death itself was on his horse's heels, indeed he believed that was the case, remaining convinced that he would be struck down at any moment as his comrades had been in the stronghold of the Mo-Rye.

They had been right; I can see that now, he thought. *I should have put an end to the madman while I had the chance. If I had tried though, I would most likely be as dead as my friends, and then there would be nobody to prepare the Council for what is to come.*

It was not until he reached Ealdorbold that he realised there was something wrong. The Council that came out to greet him was not the one he remembered. As he dismounted, he felt a wave of tiredness; having ridden many days without sleep and little rest, his body was worn out. Having been prisoner for so long, he was unaccustomed to such hard riding and he stumbled as his legs threatened to give way beneath him.

'Captain Theyl?'

The voice that spoke was familiar and yet Theyl struggled at first to recognise the face. Each in turn was surprised by opposite things, one by change and the other by a lack of it.

'But you haven't aged a day!' Counsellor Serin said. 'What has happened?'

Even as he stared at the much-aged Counsellor, Theyl remembered Katahl's words. He had strengthened the barrier around Brëgwela; so much so it appeared that time had passed much more slowly for the prisoners within it. At Ealdorbold, new Counsellors formed the younger ranks and the young were now the older. It was too much for Theyl; overwhelmed, he sank to the ground, his head in his hands, as if he could will the whole nightmare away.

If so much time has truly passed, will my family be yet living? he thought. *They could be dead and gone and I did not even have the chance to say goodbye.*

'Captain Theyl, you need food and rest,' Serin said. 'We have waited so many years for news, a few more hours will make little difference.'

'My father?' Theyl asked, as hands helped him to his feet.

Serin's face looked grey.

'Dead?' asked Theyl.

'We do not know, Captain. Please, you must rest. We can speak when you are well.'

'Well?' Theyl said incredulous. 'How can anyone be truly well in such dark times as these?'

The Counsellor's glanced at one another as Theyl was taken inside. Theyl's words unnerved them. The times had not seemed so dark to them. Without the control of the king and queen, they had prospered. In the years gone by, they formed new laws and new order. Nobody had bothered them and the people paid their taxes. Life was good. Katahl and the invaders had seen fit to stay behind the barrier and all were happy with that. Those who had lost people who had been trapped inside Tuâth's Castle, had long since moved on.

Time, it seemed, had not moved on for those behind the barrier. For them the crisis was still very real. Theyl had been seen and word would spread. The Counsellors rushed inside, making for their chamber with orders they were not to be disturbed. They did not, however, leave orders that Theyl should not receive visitors and that being so, an elderly woman was guided to him without question.

Realising taking a break would not matter, Theyl forced himself to drink and eat, trying to push away his shock. The door opened and he looked up as an old woman entered. She stood and stared, her eyes astonished by what she saw. Theyl took in her lined face and the look of shock in her blue eyes startled him.

'Mother?'

'Oh my son,' Elsbeth cried, running to embrace him.

Theyl stood and held her close. She was smaller than he recalled and seemed fragile in his arms.

'Your father was right,' she said. 'He believed you were still alive. He never gave up hope … Caitul, is he well also?'

Theyl held his mother at arm's length, trying to get used to her face in its aged state.

'Caitul has been sent to find the princess,' he said. 'The spell worked, as far as we can tell. We have to wait.'

Elsbeth smiled, accentuating the lines about her face. 'Then your father did not leave needlessly; that is something at least.'

Theyl felt his fingers tighten on his mother's arm and he forced himself to let go, for fear of hurting her. She sat and her son followed suit, taking her hand.

'He left many years ago,' Elsbeth explained. 'About a year after we saw Caitul, word came from Ardahl of his fear that should Exzalander return before passing through the kingdoms of the gods, then she would not be able to bring back the sword. Ardahl used a very powerful spell that sent your father to both warn and guard the princess, and a messenger who would send back news. Nothing has been heard of them since. Although I have no doubt in my heart that Thomn is still alive, I begin to think I will not see him again before I die.'

'Mother, don't say such things,' Theyl snapped.

Elsbeth waved her hand dismissively. 'He did it for the both of you, you know, and for his good name. He has never forgiven himself for killing those women that night, so many years ago. I think that he saw the quest as a chance to redeem himself.'

'Word may yet come,' Theyl said as if to convince himself. 'We must have faith, mother.'

'I do not see how, my son. After they were sent, Ardahl was consumed. The spell was too powerful for him. He is dead, Theyl; there are no wizards left. His apprentice, Gailon still has majick and yet is forbidden from using it. Anyone trying to reach Ardahl's Tower faces execution. Once Ardahl was gone … and your father, the Council wasted no time in taking advantage of the fact.

'I hate them Theyl; I always have. I sometimes wonder if things would have been quite different without them.'

Theyl's mouth thinned into a line at his mother's words.

'Like them or not,' he said grimly, 'they are all we have and trust me, you may appreciate their methods in the days to come. I have rested long enough. I need to apprise them of the situation. Go home, mother; I will come and see you when I am done.'

Elsbeth hesitated, as if there was something more that she wished to say but was trying to find the courage. She hugged him and he could feel the turmoil she had been forced to endure. He stiffened and fought to push back emotion, knowing it would not do to lose control.

The Council sat in a circle within their chamber; Theyl was seated in the centre as he told all; from the slaughter of the Mo-Rye and the death of the men of Tuâth's guard, to the use of the spell and its effect on Katahl, how he was raising an army to declare war on the rest of Maldahl, how his paranoia had driven him to such an action and how he planned on meeting with them soon and the implication of such a meeting.

'But surely he will not attack us,' cried the new High Counsellor, Cerastes. 'We are allies.'

'Katahl sees only foes and believes himself to be righteous in his cause. I fear that he will demand the throne and your army.'

The murmurs amongst the Council built to a crescendo of dismay and indignation, until High Counsellor Cerastes brought them to order once more.

'Send word to his father,' he said. 'If anyone can talk sense into the whelp, it will be Kryepast. We must prepare to parley. Send an emissary of peace to his door and ensure him that Exzalander's throne is not in jeopardy, that we are her humble servants and eagerly await her return; that should appease him.'

'But what of the other races of Maldahl?' Theyl questioned. 'Katahl is bent on destroying them all.'

'With respect, Captain Theyl, that is *their* concern, not ours. Let them defend themselves or negotiate peace as they may. We cannot afford to lose valuable soldiers in defending those who would not lift a finger to aid us, and we cannot be seen to ally ourselves with those whom Katahl considers an enemy. If indeed he is as powerful as you say, then he will need to be treated delicately. We cannot risk him misinterpreting our actions.'

Theyl looked horrified and his eyes sought the opinions from others present. Most nodded in agreement with High Counsellor Cerastes; those who did not bowed their heads, as if too fearful to make their opinion on the matter known.

'Counsellors, you could at least send warning,' Theyl pleaded. 'Tell them of Katahl's intentions. Let them not face him unprepared,'

'Thank you Theyl; that will be all,' Cerastes said. 'You may leave us to deliberate. Go and see your mother. I am sure that you will have much to say to one another.'

'I already know of my father,' Theyl said quietly, as he turned his back and made for the door.

'And your son?'

Theyl stopped and turned back to face them, his eyes all confusion.

'Speak with your mother, Theyl,' the High Counsellor said, with a note of finality.

Theyl looked horrified as he turned to leave again. Before the doors shut behind him, he broke into a run towards his mother's home.

Forty-Four

It soon became clear that Tuâth's household would not make good soldiers; they were merely for show. Katahl did not seem interested in their progress and spent increasing amounts of time in the dungeons where, despite the screams, he insisted he did not torture the people contained there.

Nimrïn watched from above, the clumsy undisciplined movement of the people down below, as they tried to match the skilful movements of Dahal and Aarnon. He had taken to climbing up to the battlements to see any sign of the world beyond. *Will the Council send aid?* he wondered. The world outside seemed so bright compared to the confines of the barrier and the light had begun to hurt his eyes. He had not had a drink in weeks and a woman in even longer. He considered it for a moment, thought about getting drunk. *But isn't that what Katahl did? Let down his defences so that apathy took him. No, I will not get drunk or lose myself in a woman. I will face the pain head on. But I make this promise … if I come out of this, then I will binge drink and take a horde of buxom wenches to my bed to make up for my abstinence.*

Tarak felt his cheeks burning when his Captain dismissed him saying he was needed at home. He had taken enough jibes about his wife's clingy nature and what was worse was how he knew that the jibes were justified. Elisa was clingy and since the baby had been born, things had only gotten worse. He slammed open the front door to his grandmother's house—not caring if she would shout at him. *I am soon to take over from Captain of the Guard,* he thought. *I have no intention of taking crap from the women of my house today.*

Instead of his grandmother though, he came face to face with a man—older than himself, about forty he reckoned and armed. In an instant, Tarak drew his sword and the stranger's reaction was instantaneous. They glared at one another, swords drawn, watching each other for a first move.

I was meant to have been on duty all day, Tarak thought. *There are only two reasons why a man would be in my home. One: he is robbing the place, or two: Elisa is seeing another man.* The second thought was too horrible to contemplate and made him grip tighter on his weapon.

'Who are you?' the man demanded. 'What do you mean, barging into my home in such a manner, boy?'

Boy? thought Tarak. *I'm hardly a boy, and what does he mean,* his *house?*

The door opened and both men heard a gasp but did not so much as glance toward the sound.

'Put down those swords this instant!' It was Elsbeth; she stepped between them, fury in her eyes. A baby began to cry and Theyl could bear it no longer, the words of the High Counsellor played back in his mind and he glanced toward the door.

A young woman stood, baby in her arms, her eyes wide in fear as she stared at the drawn swords.

Theyl lowered his blade, knowing that his mother must have known who the man was to risk stepping between them. The woman at the door rushed to the man and pawed at him.

'Oh my love, my husband,' she said, 'are you all right?'

The man's cheeks reddened, clearly embarrassed at his woman's display.

'Theyl, you wanted so badly to speak with the Council,' Elsbeth said, 'I did not have a chance to ...'

'Theyl?' Tarak interrupted, and his sword lowered at last. 'But ...'

Elsbeth smiled warmly. 'Theyl,' she continued, 'this is your son, Tarak, and this,' she said, as she stroked the baby's head, is your grandson, Theyl.'

Theyl took a few steps backward, too shocked to speak. His hand sought the back of one of the chairs and he lowered himself into it.

'I don't have a son, mother,' Theyl said, his voice wavering. 'However this man imposed himself upon you, he's lying.'

Tarak looked wounded at Theyl's words and his jaw tightened. Elisa shushed baby Theyl, and with one look from Elsbeth, she took her leave, retreating to the bedroom.

'Tarak, sit down,' Elsbeth ordered, 'and you Theyl, will listen to me. The reason you don't know about your son is because he was born after you were trapped at Brëgwela. Your father got an earful from me for not telling Caitul about him, I can tell you. Still, I'm not sure how your brother would have reacted considering who the mother was.'

She spoke as if Tarak was not in the room. Theyl glanced at him in time to see the man's jaw clench. It was clear that he had taken much grief about who his mother was over the years.

'Beth,' Theyl whispered, as if to himself.

'Well, it's a blessing that you're aware,' Elsbeth said. 'All these years I wondered if you'd know. Honestly Theyl, I thought I taught you better.'

'Mother, stop it … *now*. Stop talking about his mother that way … Beth … I cared for her. It was not just … I don't know what you've been told …'

Tarak winced; it was clear that he knew everything.

'Is she?'

'Dead of course,' butted in Elsbeth. 'As soon as she found out that she was expecting, they stayed her execution, but it was carried out the day after Tarak's birth. She told us it was yours, said that she took precautions when she seduced your brother.'

'Mother, that's enough! For Anarkhane's sake, can't you see your upsetting the lad? Leave us … please.'

Elsbeth gave him a look of defiance.

'I mean it. Go see to your great grandson. I wish to speak to my son alone.'

Elsbeth left as she was bid, her face fixed into a scowl. Theyl looked at Tarak, taking in his jaw line and long lashes

Definitely Caitul or me is the father, he thought, *that's something at least; either way, he's family.*

'Beth was a good woman,' he said. 'She made a mistake that is all ... I would have married her.'

His words were strained and uncomfortable, but seemed to work wonders on Tarak, who had never heard a kind word spoken about his mother. If it had not been for Thomn, he probably would never have been accepted into the guard.

Tarak gave a half smile, which reminded Theyl so much of his little brother. He thought it best not to mention it though. *I will accept Tarak, be him mine or no'*, he thought. *The poor lad has surely taken enough crap over the course of his life, best not to kick him in the teeth some more. Besides, Caitul would never accept him and best for the lad not to have to call the man who had his mother executed, father. It will certainly be an awkward family reunion, if it ever comes to that.*

It was only when the emissary arrived from Ealdorbold that Katahl truly realised how powerful his barrier was. It was clear from the messengers mind as he plundered it, that the Counsellors had been shocked by Theyl's youthful appearance. Such a detail was problematic; he had hoped to finish his experimentation before they rode to war, but he needed to send an immediate message to the people of Maldahl. It would not do let them get too complacent.

Lord Katahl gave his terms to the trembling messenger, promising that he would not destroy them, if they recognised his supreme authority and chose to turn a blind eye to his plans for the other peoples of Maldahl. He knew their greed and lust for power and knew that they would bite his hand off for the chance to retain their positions. They could prove useful puppets later on he deemed.

Still, the passage of time is a worry, he considered. *I wanted everything to be perfect for my love's return. I wonder if she may have aged wherever she is; it matters not if she has; de-aging is such a simple spell and I can fix her in an instant if needs be.*

As he sent the messenger back toward Ealdorbold, he summoned his knights to him.

'I ride south in the morning,' he said. 'Ensure the people are in uniform and ready to leave. We're going to pay a visit to your friends the Ptee Tsa.'

It was testament to how powerful Katahl's enchantment was, when Dahal did not show any reaction to the news. The knight had loved the Ptee Tsa, devoted many years of his life to his duties among them. He had vowed that once he retired from service as knight to Starigorat, that he would live among the winged race.

However, Katahl's loathing of them made the Ptee Tsa the primary target for his campaign. He rejoiced in the idea that he may never have to see the abominations again.

In the Underworld, Taiohãhn was unable to move at first. He held onto Exzalander's body as if He could will the soul back into it, but the soul was long gone, lost in the void. He had kept her from her home and averted immediate disaster, but the prophecy He had put into place was going awry. *I allowed myself to become too human,* He thought. *I should have been omnipresent, not respected her need for privacy like some whipped husband.*

Anarkhane had already started training what remained of Exzalander's consciousness. She taught her how to connect to Her kingdom of light and use the power there to knit flesh back together again.

Taiohãhn was reluctant to continue training. He knew it was necessary, but the sight of Exzalander's animated body, absent of all that made her the woman he knew, was disturbing to Him. He missed her. He longed to see her smile, hear her sighs of frustration as she failed to do something perfectly, to hear her voice, to see her eyes glittering back at Him.

Now that she was gone, He realised it was not just desire for her body that He felt; every fibre of His being longed for her because He loved her. After millennia of desire for Anarkhane, finally His feelings for the goddess waned, to be replaced by love for another—a human. A human with more passion, more humility than He could have received from Anarkhane.

He spent His time between longing and anger, questioning how much Exzalander must have despised Him to choose to leave in such a way.

It was He who had created the love she held for Katahl, having manipulated her feelings and steering her back to him, ensuring that Katahl would be the one who found her, who cared for her. Part of Him regretted the manipulation. He knew it was necessary, but He longed to release her from the prophecy—to see her free. That was how he knew He truly loved her.

Eventually, He set Exzalander's body to work, whilst He wrestled with His emotions, spending hour upon hour searching for any sign of her in the forelócian glæs, hoping to coax her back to Him.

There were many worlds that linked to the void, but only three He had any influence over. He figured she was more likely to be drawn to a world with humans, drawn to the most familiar rather than to try and enter a place where life was both strange and terrible.

Taiohãhn saw Katahl ride forth; he saw and knew that he meant to destroy many of Anarkhane's creations. *Good*, he thought. *Her humans have slaughtered many of my creatures; it is about time She lost hers as well. The humans will be safe for a time, but Mynogen has planted a seed in Katahl's mind. That seed will grow until he destroys all — Father's insurance against my failure. If Exzalander is not returned in time, then there will be no world to return to — only Katahl.*

It felt good to Katahl to be out of the confines of the Castle again. He failed to notice how terrified his company were; such observations were beyond his thought and caring. His mind was bent on singular purpose; to achieve his goal would assist in the return of his betrothed. That idea, the desire, seemed the only remnant of his human self, which remained.

Wanting to keep their presence unknown, they headed for the northern most tip of Freya Valley; it offered a good route to travel westward into Ánweald Forest, away from human settlements. Freya Valley was also the home of the Daleena, many of whom did not understand a word Katahl was saying when he demanded they bow down and take oaths of allegiance to him. Those who could not speak his tongue, looked on in eagerness, waiting for their elders' translation. Being a peaceful people for whom violence was unheard of, they offered little resistance as his army cut them down.

Katahl smiled as he stood by and watched Tuâth's former household kill all those before them in his name. He had not even had to lend a hand. He had not taken the chance to try out his experiment; it remained encased and was wheeled along behind the company.

Nobody questioned what he had brought up from the dungeon that day. They knew it was living, as they could hear the guttural sounds issuing forth on occasion. Every third day, it was somebody's task to feed raw meat to whatever it was. At the first feeding, great clawed hands reached through to snatch the food and the man had almost fainted with fear. He used to be a farmer and longed for the tilled fields of his home, but quickly pushed such feelings aside; Katahl was apt to pluck thoughts from a head and had already killed two members of the company for their disloyalty in desiring escape.

Following the annihilation of the Daleena, the Iyesmen were next on Katahl's mind. They were a warrior people and were to be the first real test. The Daleena had been an easy quarry, a way to introduce his troops to the shedding of blood.

They passed almost silently through outskirts of Ánweald Forest. Katahl wished that he were a little closer to the palace so that he might touch the minds of the Council and discover what they had planned. He smiled, considering how unimaginative they were. Whatever they had in store would harbour little surprise for him, he figured.

Despite the army's caution, word spread of their coming. The Iyesmen used many animals and birds as sources of information. Katahl had never taken such things seriously before, but when they came upon the Iyesmen fully armed and waiting, he decided it was time that he took no small creature for granted.

The Iyesmen were a proud race and they refused to recognise Katahl as their king. They fought bravely against swords and axes, showing their skill against such inexperienced troops, but as the crate was opened, they fled in all directions. Nimrïn felt a shiver down the length of his spine as he watched the onslaught. Like the Daleena, the Iyesmen had been their hosts on more than one occasion. They had shared food and stories, had laughed together. Now they were nothing more than cattle to be slaughtered.

As the creature emerged from its confinement, the full extent of Katahl's fall became clear. He had insisted that he had not tortured the prisoners; what he had actually done was much worse. The creature was not recognisable as human and yet Nimrïn knew that he was looking at one of the so-called 'loyal subjects', an experiment on Tuâth's people to create a monster to slay in Katahl's name, one who would spread fear and loathing throughout the people of Maldahl.

As the creature's claws ripped into the Iyesmen, leaving a bloody mess in its wake, Nimrïn finally let go of his humanity. It seemed easier to lose himself than have to face the horrors he was party to.

The majick Anarkhane wove about Caitul meant She could recall him at any time. He became increasingly frustrated that every time he thought he caught a scent of Exzalander, he felt the pulling back to the light and would have to begin again. The goddess was certainly not what he had imagined; She was obsessive and unstable, as if She feared for him to be out of Her sight for too long.

He was beginning to think that he would never find the princess. Time seemed to lose all meaning and he had witnessed that which no mortal man ever should, had experienced the impossible when he had felt his spirit detach itself to wander free from physical restraint.

Disconcerting as it was at first, he grew to appreciate it as a more effective way to search; his body would also act like an anchor if he needed it to and Anarkhane seemed a little less possessive if he showed he was willing to allow half of him to remain with Her. However, in order for Katahl's spell to work, he knew that he would have to physically touch Exzalander and his concern was that Anarkhane would never allow it.

He had to tell himself he would deal with that issue when he had to. First, he had to find her and that was no easy task. He had never imagined such darkness and the void seemed infinite. It was like searching a town for something smaller than an ant, and without the use of his eyes to guide him.

Occasionally he discovered a tear in the void and was obliged to enter the unknown in search of his quarry. The places he had entered were unpleasant and the minds he had occupied, unfathomable at first, forcing him to remain longer than desired in the hopes of discovering any hint of her—any trace of that which did not belong, but all he ever found was himself and so sought the darkness once again.

Taiohãhn set the forelócian glæs to search and it roved constantly, concentrating on the two worlds that were most familiar. He divided His time between training and watching. Exzalander's body, however, was not allowed rest. The only respite she received was healing majick that He administered every day or so, to keep her from collapsing with exhaustion.

Physically, she was perfect; her stamina greater, her reflexes and her skill with a sword could almost match His own. He introduced her to other weapons, so that she did not rely on one. Loath was He to give her the dragon dagger, but its power could not be denied. His creatures had been slaughtered for its making and yet He knew that the dragon, Tehtra, would serve as good protection for His warrior and once He had possession of the Creation Gem once more, He figured He could always remake the dragon race.

He huffed in frustration; ordinarily time meant so little to Him, but the past centuries had seemed so long, waiting to retrieve full power. He was annoyed, not understanding why He had to go to all the trouble when Mynogen, His father, could have granted him full godhood once more.

Perhaps such a thing is not in Mynogen's power for a second time, Taiohãhn thought. *It is the struggle and the sacrifice that are important now; these are part of majicks older than time itself, besides, this is my punishment for carelessness. Carelessness? No, foolishness. Foolishness for allowing myself to fall in love with my goddess, my creation.*

His thoughts strayed to His warrior; He missed her smile, her look of determination and her voice—even when it had been raised in anger. Anything was better than the cadaver before Him. Her absence had filled Him with so many regrets and so many doubts. He began to wish that He had never made the gem for Anarkhane.

Sometimes I regret ever making Her, he thought, *for what else could I have spawned from my darkness, other than the coldness that is Anarkhane. Her light offers warmth, but she, none. I doubt that She will fulfil Her promise to rule by my side. I seem now nothing more than a game to Her, one that She is ruthlessly determined to win at all costs. She is plotting even now, a way to rule without me—just as I am.*

Exzalander is blessed with Anarkhane's light; if she were gifted more, then mayhap she could replace Anarkhane altogether... He sighed and put His head in his hands. *Such notions are pointless,* He thought, *for without Exzalander returned and whole, I cannot restore my godhood, let alone grant Exzalander a place at my side.*

He watched as Exzalander's body punched the padded wall. Her moves were flawless and yet, without a soul, she lacked the imagination required to make her a truly great fighter. Blood trickled down her hand and yet she did not react. She would continue punching until He ordered her to stop. Her hands were no longer those of a princess—no longer soft and smooth. He had healed the lacerations and blisters but allowed them to callus. Soft hands were no use to a warrior.

Taiohãhn watched for a while, as the warrior's blood stained the wall, before ordering her to stop and face Him. She obeyed at once and He took her bloodied hands in His, setting to heal them. Her eyes stared ahead and He lifted her chin to gaze into the two empty windows, green as His forest, which He loved so. Grasping her by the shoulders, He pulled her closer and bent to whisper in her ear as if somehow her soul might hear, wherever it strayed.

'I *will* fix this. I will make you whole again.'

The warrior did not respond in any way and forgetting to set her to new task, Taiohãhn stormed from the room, leaving her a living statue, whilst He went to search for her once more.

As He opened the door to the door to the Chamber of Light, Taiohãhn was not expecting to see Anarkhane. She was standing at the forelócian glaes and did not even look up to acknowledge His arrival. He had not seen Her since before Exzalander made her escape attempt. He was not even sure if She knew.

'They send more to look for the girl,' Anarkhane said, without looking up. 'Am I to house everyone in my kingdom before she is returned to fulfil her duty?'

Taiohãhn felt the heat of anger as He considered Her words, and He paced over to His forelócian glaes. She had the good sense to make way for Him. He did not look directly at Her, having no desire to experience the familiar stirrings. She was right; two were coming, drifting blindly toward them.

'Who would do this? Surely not Katahl ...'

'It was the wizard from Ealdorbold.' Anarkhane affirmed. 'He is dead. He must have known that his spell would be his undoing, but considered it a worthwhile sacrifice. Foolish man; I could have put his death to better use. Still, I can set these two to work as I have the knight; they could prove useful.'

Taiohãhn's jaw clenched as He listened to Her speak. *She has been hiding much from me it seems*, He thought. She was obviously aware of Exzalander's absence and His suspicion rose at once. *How could She know? Unless She had a hand in what occurred.*

Considering the possibility, He trembled with fury, aware it was the only one that made any sense; how Exzalander had managed to get into the room, how she had known to use the forelócian glaes and why her mood changed so suddenly toward Him.

Anarkhane was so eager for Exzalander to be sent back and tried to bring it about, He thought. *Her plan has backfired though.*

Taiohãhn forced Himself to calm, determined not to show any display of emotion to Her. *She has seen too much of it already and I can no longer let Her use my emotion against me.*

Katahl was pleased with his creation—his Trolg. *A host of Trolgs are likely to make an unstoppable army,* he thought. *It is a pity that all attempts at creating females have been in vain.* All the women had perished and he ended up feeding their remains to the Trolg. Without females, they could not breed. *I will either have to attempt to cross them with human females or create my army one soldier at a time. It could take years; still ... it is not as though I am short on time.*

His army was silent as they rode through the Forest of Iyes, home to the Ptee Tsa and formerly, the Iyesmen. He was eager to see Auk's face as he condemned them all. He did not intend on offering them the chance to pledge their allegiance; he wanted them gone for good.

The sound of horses was unexpected; the winged race did not need such methods of transport. Katahl called the company to a halt, awaiting those who approached with a ready sword.

When King Kryepast came face to face with his son, he found himself conflicted. The ancient king had not seen him in decades and yet there he was, un-aged and yet so very different. At that moment he could not think of the dire news the messenger had brought; his only desire was to embrace his child after so long a parting.

Katahl saw the tears in the old king's eyes and found himself curious. He dismounted and went to meet the man he scarcely recognised. He tensed as Kryepast threw his arms about him and openly wept.

'Oh my boy ... my boy. So good it is to see you again.'

'Father,' Katahl acknowledged. He felt nothing but annoyance at the delay in achieving his goal. 'I have pressing matters to attend to. Once I am done here, you and I may talk.'

'Do not do this, my son,' Kryepast pleaded. He may have been old, but his eyes were bright and strong as any youth.

Katahl raised an eyebrow as the old king took a step back. *So he knows*, he thought. A slow smile touched his lips.

'You cannot prevent me, father, so I suggest that you do not try. Everything will be perfect for my Exzalander's return. I will not have those freaks littering up the forest. They should never have been allowed to exist to begin with.' His voice was cool and calm, betraying no hint of emotion.

Kryepast blanched at his son's speech. Assessing Katahl's demeanour, he knew that he would not dissuade him, unless ...

'There is no call for you to prepare for her coming,' he said. 'Her intention on return will not be to wed you, but destroy you. Look at what you've become; do you really think that she will join with you now? Why do you think I did not want this for you? I tried to warn you. She does not intend to marry you, Katahl; she means to kill you!'

'Say one more word, old man, and my knights will run you through,' Katahl snapped back, his body shaking.

'Your knights? Their oaths are made to my house, not you.'

Katahl's eyes widened as he realised with one word, his father could break the enchantment that bound his knights to him. The man was still talking, something about the CODM

Prophecy, about Taiohãhn, but Katahl struggled to hear what was being said as he considered what he must do.

'Only one of you will rule,' Kryepast continued. 'If Taiohãhn didn't intend for her to kill you then why is she named His warrior? If she was simply to return and be your queen, then she would have no need for fighting skill.'

All except for Katahl's knights jumped at Katahl's answering scream, as all that he had worked for came crashing down. He saw the truth in Kryepast's words and felt his last ounce of sanity snap as he impaled the king on his sword. Without warning, and before Kryepast's cries could form any words of condemnation, Katahl removed his father's head. He continued to hack at the body until his sword was blunted and the carcass a bloody mess, no longer discernable as human.

His company sobbed and cried with fear at their new master's madness, knowing that if he could do such a thing to his own father, then there was little hope for any of them. Katahl sank to his knees and his screams stopped abruptly as he assessed what he had done.

News of Exzalander's intention to kill him and the death of his father caused any sanity that remained to depart and never return. He muttered to the remains of the king as if he wished he had spoken before murdering him; those who were close enough heard his intention on introducing Exzalander to his Trolg—a gift for her betrayal.

The king's entourage fled, leaving only his most trusted knights to avenge him. The moment the sword was drawn, they had moved to intercept, only to be faced with Katahl's knights and they could do nothing as their king was hacked to pieces, except fight for their lives against fellow knights of Starigorat.

One of Katahl's company observed his collapse and took the knights' preoccupation as an opportunity to act, throwing himself at the young lord, hoping to take his life before any other atrocities could occur in his name.

If he thought Katahl overcome with grief and remorse, then he was wrong. Katahl blocked the oncoming blow, crushing the man's neck. He fell horror-stricken next to the bloody mess that had once been the king of Starigorat.

Katahl stood slowly. 'So perish all those who would oppose us,' he said. There was a wild light in his eyes and many who witnessed it, longed for such a swift ending as the dead man at his feet.

Only one knight of Kryepast was left with his life that day and he returned home to take news, and what dire news it was. The king of Starigorat was dead, mutilated by his own son's hands. He had been forced to kneel, watching hopelessly as Katahl pushed Kryepast's head onto a spear and ordered his standard bearer to carry it. Katahl had not even bothered to wipe his father's blood from his hands, wearing it proudly as he continued his rampage.

By the time that word reached Ealdorbold of the death of King Kryepast and the circumstances of his murder, Katahl was already heading back to the safety of Brëgwela.

On hearing the news, Theyl placed his head in his hands. Had it not been for Tarak, he would have ridden to warn Kryepast of the change in Katahl. He might have prevented the tragedy, but he did not and could not leave his family at such a time. All his life he had been ruled by duty and he made the decision that duty to his family had to take priority. It did not make him feel any less guilty though. He poured himself a drink and kept pouring until the alcohol numbed his senses.

Forty-Five

Exzalander drifted in the darkness, pained and disorientated. The little piece of her that remained, surrounding the shard of the gem of creation, spurring her on. Refusing to feel sorry for herself, she searched for a way from the darkness absolute; the darkness that had swallowed her but had been unable to consume her. She did not know how long she existed thus; time seemed to hold no meaning. There was no sleep, no rest, just the lonely expanse of the void and the driving need to find home once more.

The light came without warning and she did not consider that it could have been anywhere other than her desired destination. Skyscrapers and traffic went unnoticed, all thought bent on the solitary purpose—to find aid.

If I can get to Ardahl then he might restore me once more, she thought.

Ardahl, however, was beyond reaching. Having sent forth aid, he passed from life. Such majick was godly and no human could perform it safely, without divine assistance.

Exzalander fell as if she had substance, had mass. She sensed, rather than heard the screams. A woman below her was giving birth. It was not that fact which drew Exzalander's fractured soul, but some connection, a latent power connecting her to home. It was not until she settled in the body that she realised how weak the woman was. Darkness enveloped her once more, and yet there was warmth also— warmth and love. The feeling was short-lived, however, and cold crept in as life began to slip away.

She threw herself at the place where she felt the most strength, panicking as she felt life leaving the body about her. She had not intended on entering the child; the mother had been her target, but once she had settled, she could not escape. Memories were reaped and she felt herself slipping away. Ardahl, Katahl, her parents, Taiohãhn, and finally Exzalander … gone. The baby's brain unable to cope with her thoughts, conflicting with its own—light, food, sleep. As the baby was removed, free from its dead mother, the midwife gasped, a look of horror on her face.

Mr Vái was so grief-stricken at his wife's passing, that he was unsure what he was seeing; he could not trust his eyes at such a time. The newborn grasped a green jewel in its tiny hand. It could not have come from anywhere other than inside his wife and he wondered if it had been that which had killed her. The blood that smeared the stone was no different from the usual mess one expected to see after a birth and he could not tell if it had torn into her uterus or not.

As the midwife tried to prise the stone from the babe's grasp, the newborn shouted,

'Give that back!'

The voice that sounded made him wonder if he had gone mad, had lost himself forever in his grief, away from sanity and cruel reality.

The stone broke in two, leaving half with the midwife, where it began to glow in her hand. It was too much to bear. *First the woman I love dies and now this*, the father thought. *What madness is this? What have I helped bring into the world?*

The baby's scowl ceased and it began to cry, seeming nothing more than an ordinary baby. The midwife neglected her duty and sank to the floor, mesmerised by the gem in her hand.

Mr Vái felt numb as he cleaned the baby. He removed the stone from her grasp, placing it into his pocket. The umbilical cord was still attached and it was then that his fatherly instincts kicked in for the first time.

'Get on your feet and do your job,' he ordered the midwife.

She tore her gaze away from the gem; crazed she seemed.

'See to the baby. I want to say goodbye to my wife.'

His voice was stern enough to bring the woman back from her demented state and she took over as he cleaned the mess from his wife and covered her with a sheet. He did not say goodbye as he had intended. One look at those lifeless eyes convinced him that there was nothing to say farewell to. She was already gone, off on a new journey. He turned back to the child, pain stabbing at him once more. The midwife's hands were shaking as she tended to the screaming child.

Neither spoke for a long while. He knew that she would begin questioning before too long and he did not have any answers. He hadn't a clue what was going on. All he knew was, life was never going to be the same again.

Epilogue

Taiohãhn found her at last. He saw what transpired and smiled in quiet relief. She was safe. He considered calling Anarkhane and yet decided against it. He no longer trusted Her and the whereabouts of His warrior was important strategic information that He deemed best left to Himself. Anarkhane's actions had shown Her to wish for a speedy return of Exzalander before she was ready. *I can play Her game,* He thought. *I will ensure Exzalander remains safe and hidden until the time is right.*

The two new companions, a captain and a messenger, He led well into the depth of His forest, where they forgot all; such was the majick that existed there. He kept them well catered for and their presence a secret from the goddess.

He called upon Noch, the ruler of the Macara Shee, to send forth a volunteer to return to Earth.

The faerie king knew that whomever he sent would be unable to return—even if his Lord reunited the gem. It was a lot to ask, but he dare not disobey. He could not bring his clan before him and ask for volunteers, as Taiohãhn had emphasised the need for secrecy. So he watched and waited, deliberating carefully before making his decision. He chose an old faerie whose family ties were back on Earth, hoping it would give him enough incentive to obey without question.

Xantho knelt before his liege lord, and tried not to react as he was ordered to travel alone to the Forest of Tûlg, there to be offered safe passage into and through Taiohãhn's realm.

Xantho was no fool, and although his king had not given him a reason, he could guess well enough and he was sure to say his goodbyes before he began his journey.

Taiohãhn rode out on Ravenwing, to meet in the Forest of Forgetfulness, where he introduced Xantho to Thomn and the messenger, telling the faerie to mark them well.

'I have need for you to return to Earth. I will send these humans to you ere long, and you must conceal them. You may enlist the help of the Sídhe, the Moon Clans or your own kind, but choose only those loyal to me, only those you know who you can trust completely to keep the men's existence a secret. Can you do that?'

Xantho rubbed his nose and nodded. Taiohãhn took note of his yellow skin and wondered if he might be too conspicuous for the job.

'Do you not wish to know the reason for my asking such a thing of you?'

Xantho wrinkled his nose, as if considering whether or not to answer.

'I assume that it has something to do with the return of your warrior,' he said. 'I say that only because I cannot imagine any other matter occupying your mind at present, Milord.'

Taiohãhn's eyes were like steel. 'How very astute of you. I am glad King Noch has sent me someone with his wits about him. The princess is on Earth, trapped in the body of a babe. I want you to watch over her and keep her safe. She has one of the shards of the creation gem and it needs to be returned to Maldahl.

'These two will aid her in returning, but for now I need her to grow up. I will send these men later. It would be best if they could take roles of men who might come into contact with her … teachers perhaps … I'll leave it up to your discretion. You will be watching and you will know what is best. Their transition into life on Earth must be flawless. They must have complete memories. Am I clear in this? We cannot have them wondering around talking about other worlds. My hand in this must remain unknown.'

'I understand, Lord Taiohãhn.' Xantho knelt and touched his forehead to the ground.

'And make sure no human sees you like that. Long has it been since the humans were aware of your kind.'

Xantho smiled, considering what the sight of a tiny yellow man might do to a human's sanity. It was almost worth the risk of Taiohãhn's wrath to discover.

'I will do as you command,' he said, prostrating himself again.

Taiohãhn smiled. He had become fully committed to the game, setting in motion a series of moves in order to save His godhood.

Let Anarkhane compete if She wishes, He thought. *Let Her plot my downfall. My pieces are in place, my opening moves made; now all I have to do is wait.*

Natasha E Scholey

The End

Don't Miss

Broken Pieces

Book III of The CODM Prophecy

Coming Soon

Bibliography

Anwyl, E, *Celtic Religion in Pre-Christian Times*, (Archibald Constable & Co London, 1906)

Ashley, M, *The Giant Book of Myths and Legends* (Parragon Books, Bristol, 1995)

Bonwick, J, *Irish Druids and Old Irish Religion*, (Griffith, Farran, London, 1894)

Coffey G, *The Bronze Age in Ireland*, (Hodges, Figgis, & Co, Ltd, London, 1913)

Ebutt, M I, *Ancient Britain* (Chancellor Press, London, 1995)

Griffis, W E, *Welsh Fairy Tales*, (1921, reproduced to EBook by Project Gutemburg, 2005)

Hope Moncrieff, A R, *Classical Legends* (Chancellor Press, London, 1995)

Quiggin, E C, *Druids-A Short Introduction*, (Shamrock Eden Publishing, 2011)

Schreiber, Lady C (translator), *The Mabinogion* (first published 1849, Harper Collins London, 2000)

Seligmann, K, *The History of Magic*, (Quality paperback Book Club, New York, 1997)

Squire, C, *Celtic Myths and Legends* (Lomond Books, Bath) 2000

Thomas, K, *Religion and the Decline of Magic,* (Weidenfeld & Nicolson, London, 1971)

www.ingramcontent.com/pod-product-compliance
Lightning Source LLC
Chambersburg PA
CBHW020826030726
47496CB00001B/108